UNKNOWN SWITZERLAND.

UNKNOWN SWITZERLAND.

BY

VICTOR TISSOT.

TRANSLATED FROM THE TWELFTH EDITION,

BY MRS. WILSON.

NEW YORK:

A. D. F. RANDOLPH & CO.,

38, WEST TWENTY-THIRD STREET.

TABLE OF CONTENTS.

PART I.

FROM PARIS TO CHIAVENNA.

v

PART II.

THE ENGADINE.

CHAPTER I.

CHAPTER II.

CHAPTER III.

CHAPTER IV.

CHAPTER V.

CHAPTER VI.

PART IV.

THE VALAIS.

CHAPTER I.

CHAPTER II.

CHAPTER III.

CHAPTER IV.

CHAPTER V.

CHAPTER VI.

CONTENTS.

PART V.

IN THE GRUYÈRE.

CHAPTER I.

CHAPTER II.

CHAPTER III.

PART I.

FROM PARIS TO CHIAVENNA.

CHAPTER I.

UNKNOWN Switzerland! Is there such a region?
It is certainly neither here in Basle, where I have
just arrived, nor at Lucerne, where I expect to be in a few
hours.

That Switzerland, hiding away like a rare flower in
remote Alpine valleys, must be sought for far from the
common track followed by the holders of Cook's tickets, or
indicated in the best arranged circular tours.

We have already more than enough of descriptions of the
tourists' Switzerland, where foreigners are shown illuminated
waterfalls, glaciers, the access to which is guarded by turn-
stiles,—even sunrises and sunsets, all so exactly reduced to
rule, more or less exhibited according to the price paid,
that all might be the work of machinery.

That is the Switzerland of trade and money-making, of
speculation and bargaining; the Switzerland that deals in
long hotel-bills and busy clerks and dainty salads; that is
set in brooches and painted on cigar-cases, and made musical
in clocks and in the little carved boxes of the Oberland.

That Switzerland has lost all piquancy and impressiveness
and originality; there is no brightness left in it,—no poetry,

3

—no delicious surprise anywhere. Each troop of tourists follows in the footsteps of the last, like people passing through a crowded museum. They invariably dine either at noon or at six o'clock, in a dining-room with its invariable huge mirrors multiplying endlessly the waiters after the invariable pattern,—black dresscoat and white tie. The bill of fare never varies, and all the sauces are so exactly alike in taste, smell, and colour, that they must surely be made wholesale in some factory at Geneva or Berne.

In this shop-keeping Switzerland, decked for its summer show, the steamers have the dignified and cautious motion of a canal-boat; and the ascent of the mountains is performed by rail or tramway.

It is a very different Switzerland to which I am going, and to which I should like to take you, my reader, with me; for I am sure you would enjoy it. It is the charming Switzerland of mountain zigzag; the good old Switzerland of flower-bordered paths through shady woods; of cheerful roads, following no rule, and enlivened by the jingling of the *diligence* bells and the bold, merry blast of the postillion's horn;—sounds that draw all the prettiest damsels to the village windows.

In *this* Switzerland, instead of those hotels raised at enormous cost, where you must arrive in recognised English tourist style—knickerbockers and ribbed stockings, blue veil round your hat, binocular slung from your shoulder, and alpenstock in hand, amidst the bustle of a dozen obsequious hirelings,—unless you would be looked down on as a cobbler in his Sunday clothes; hotels where hospitality is dispensed at the rate of twenty to thirty francs for twenty-four hours; instead of such hotels there is the peaceful and patriarchal wayside inn, where you are entertained for four or five francs a day, with its kindly hostess and her smiling maidens, its overhanging eaves, its carved balconies with boxes of nasturtiums and pinks, its windows with little lozenge-shaped panes in leaden frames, its oak-panelled dining-room, of which the decorations are the old clock, the stone stove like a monument, and pictures illustrating the career of William Tell, or the not less authentic story of Genevieve of Brabant. This room is usually separated by a partition from the bar-parlour, which is occupied by pedlars, drivers, mountaineers, guides, chamois hunters, stone hunters, and plant hunters. There everything conventional, commercial, vulgar, or disturbing is utterly laid aside.

In the sacred solitude of those lonely valleys one feels as if he regained full possession of himself, and became once more the child of nature ; free as the marmot that whistles from the rocks or the eagle that sails among the clouds.

The joy of launching forth into the vast freedom of the mountains is like that of an escaped captive. And every danger braved, every toil sustained, is only a fresh intoxication and delight.

It is not on the dusty and beaten roads of the Oberland, in the midst of the flock of tourists browsing, every summer, like sheep, on the leaves of their Baedeker or their Conti that these strong and delicious sensations of solitude and freedom are to be experienced.

The Oberland is now nothing but a panorama,—an immense museum or show, got up and utilised by hotel-keepers of every nationality.

As Paris is twofold, so also is Switzerland. There is the foreigners' Switzerland and the natives' Switzerland. It is to some corners of the latter that I wish to introduce my readers.

As there must always be a starting-point, I shall begin by telling you how I set out, and what I saw by the way.

To-day, as you are aware, it is as easy to go from Paris to Switzerland, as from Paris to Pontoise. If the journey is a little longer, yet how conveniently and comfortably it is made. In the sumptuous sleeping saloons, with their luxuriously furnished couches, you seem to travel without the trouble of leaving your own bedroom.

It is only on awaking next morning that you discover how far you are from Paris. What a strange and delicious sensation it is, when the blue, dreamy light of dawn begins to steal through the lowered blinds, to step out of the close carriage in which you have spent the night, and to find yourself surrounded by mountains that *are* mountains, and great dense forests, and wide pastures with flocks and herds, and châlets that would stand on no chimney-piece or what-not. The grass of the meadows looks so green, so rich, so abundant, that while the eyes feast on it you experience not only a mental delight, but a physical exhilaration that renews your youth and stirs a whole world of memories.

We recall how, in days gone by, we strolled, not alone, through the meadows and woods, greeted by the early song of the birds, ere the gentle morning breeze had dried the dew from the flowers. Ah! how happy we were in the little arbour hidden under the apple-trees,—we two alone,— no others near. There is no place like the country for love ; there she runs barefoot and free.

It is such a joy to find one's self once more amidst those simple scenes; among trees and fields and woods and hills and vales and streams. There is such a sweet breath of spring about it all. And we begin to believe once more in an idyllic life,—in faithful shepherdesses, and bliss in a cottage.

We have already passed Delle, the first station on the Jura-Berne line. The train now traverses a pretty valley, through which clear, living streams are murmuring and leaping, winding and rushing; where mill-wheels are clattering merrily, and poplars stand in rows like soldiers formed in line, and red-roofed cottages lie half hidden among the tall herbage.

Suddenly, in the soft, rosy light of morning Porrentruy comes into view, with its white houses, its irregular roofs.

its gay, many-coloured gardens, its castle still wrapped
in slumber, with its old towers sharply defined against the
pale grey sky.

We stop for a few minutes at a very neat station, and when
we set off again the scene is entirely changed. Dark firs,
with great black drooping fringes, grow almost close down
to the line, and the drops of resin, hanging like amber neck-
laces to the branches, glitter like gold. In some places the
soil, rent into great fissures, has laid bare the rocks with
their bright red veins. Great blocks that have rolled down
into the valley lie at the edge of the way, and over these the
briers trail their ragged draperies like a pauper's shroud.
And in the midst of this sadness and misery, careless Nature
smiles gracefully through her flowers. Some of them are
very small, shining out like pale stars from the moss that
clothes the dead stones ; while others stand erect, proud and
haughty, on their tall, straight stems, or wave in wanton
clusters, or hang, like motionless butterflies, to the highest
branches of a blackthorn.

There is neither sound nor stir of life,—no song of bird or
sudden movement of timid, startled creature in this desolate
region. On the two opposite summits that overhang the
valley, the firs, standing out black against the blue sky, frown
down on us like the battlements of two rival fortresses
between which we pass. Then the valley suddenly widens
again, and we see in the distance a glittering church tower ;
in another minute the village itself, with its large wooden
houses, and from the open doors we hear the merry voices of
children, the cackling of fowls and the lowing of cattle,
mingled with the warm odour of the cow-houses.

A church bell is ringing. It is the hour for morning prayers.
A few old women, prayer-book in hand, are slowly making
their way to church with the help of their walking-sticks.

Now we are at Delémont, which is shrouded in a thin veil
of mist. The only thing visible is a grim-looking station ;
then all vanishes.

Next comes into view the little town of Grellingen, with its
dilapidated bridge, and its picturesque little houses scattered
along the side of the stream.   And now the valley opens out
still wider, and we begin to go down into the plain.   Here
are mowers knee deep in the hay, with sleeves rolled up from
their brown arms, and broad hats drawn down over their
eyes, making their scythes flash to and fro like lightning.
Silvery spires rise behind the trees in an aureola of sunshine, sharply cut on the green background of the hills; and
the sky is intense, heavenly blue, with only a few flecks of
pure fleecy cloud.

The train plunges with terrible jolting and clattering
through a smoky passage, and guttural voices shout "Basel!"
We have reached Basle at the morning hour when every
housekeeper in Helvetia is steeping in her coffee the allotted
number of obelisks of bread and butter.

On the way into the town we pass the monument that
commemorates the battle of St. Jaques.   It stands close to
the spot where a handful of Swiss held out for ten hours
against the overwhelming onset of the French Dauphin's
troops.

The Confederate Cantons were at war with the men of
Zurich, who supported the Emperor of Austria.   They had
laid siege to Zurich when news came that Charles VII. was
sending troops to relieve the city.   After the armistice
with England, France had been overrun by disbanded and
undisciplined troops, mercenaries of various nations, who
devoured and plundered wherever they came.   The king
fell on a happy expedient for ridding the country of their
presence.   He gathered them together under the leadership
of the Count of Armagnac, and giving the supreme command
of this army of adventurers, this promiscuous horde, to the
Dauphin, he sent them against the Swiss.

The Swiss leaders told off 600 men who remained encamped before Zurich, while the rest marched to meet the
enemy.   On the way they met two monks returning from

the Council at Basle. " Go back," said the monks; " in Heaven's name go back! You are marching to certain death. The Armagnacs are a hundred thousand, and you are not two thousand!"

This was a greatly exaggerated statement; but Hans Matter, the captain, made answer: " If it is so, if it is impossible that we should conquer, we will commit our souls to God, and our bodies to the Armagnacs!"

Near Prattelen they met and routed the advanced guard of the enemy, 8,000 strong.

The Confederates had received orders not to cross the Birs, but they were drawn on in pursuit. In their eagerness they plunged in, swam across, gained the top of the opposite bank, and at once found themselves confronted by the troops commanded by the Dauphin in person.

He received them with a fierce cannonade, which threw them into confusion. Five hundred of them took refuge on an exposed island in the river, where they were slain to the last man.

The remaining thousand entrenched themselves in the chapel and hospital of St. Jaques. Twice the Armagnacs rushed to the attack, and twice they were repulsed. The Swiss, invaded on their own soil, fought with heroic fury in defence of their houses, tearing the enemy's arrows from their wounds to send them back dripping with blood.

At last the Dauphin gave orders to set fire to the hospital and chapel, and the heroes perished fighting amid the flames to their last breath. Of the whole little army, ten men alone, who had been separated from their brethren in the passage of the river, remained alive.

When the field of battle lay under the pure moonlight like a lake of blood, the Chevalier Burkhard Mönch walked proudly over the crimsoned soil. Spurning with his foot the corpses of the brave Swiss, he turned to the noblemen who accompanied him, with the smiling remark, " Now I bathe in roses!"

A wounded soldier hears the words. With his last strength he grasps a stone, half raises himself from the ground, and hurls it at the insolent speaker with the words, " There ! there is one more rose for you ! "

The stone strikes Burkhard's forehead, and with a single cry he drops dead.

Armagnac urged the Dauphin to follow up his victory. " That," replied the Dauphin, " is more than I can afford. Another such victory as this, and I might return home alone, on foot, and staff in hand."

Eight thousand of the Dauphin's troops had fallen. He withdrew with the remains of his army into Alsace, and concluded a treaty of peace and alliance with the Confederates.

When the Paris-Lucerne express arrives at Basle, there is an hour or two that may be spent in seeing the city. That is long enough. The principal objects of curiosity in Basle are its ancient-looking buildings, giving it the aspect of an old German city ; its fortress gates, flanked by towers which in olden times were connected by rampart walls ; its long, winding streets, dark and narrow, with here a flight of many steps, and there a steep paved slope ; its dull little squares, adorned with playing fountains, and some of the houses with many-gabled roofs, and windows still made with round panes set in a slender trellis work of lead. The visitor should also notice the forged iron signs of the inns, hung from supports that look as light and delicate as lace work, and consisting of fantastic arabesques, conventional flowers, golden roses, heraldic birds, swans with expanded wings, wild men armed with clubs, or crowned lions bearing the sword and globe as emperors of the Holy Empire.

The large number of historical houses shows how important a position this town formerly occupied in the world.

The Emperor Rudolph of Hapsburg lodged at the Seidenhof; the conclave that elected Pope Felix II. was held in the house Zur Mücke ; Erasmus lived in the house Zur Luft ; peace between Prussia and France was signed, in 1795, in the house Burkhard; the members of the Convention who had been taken prisoners were exchanged for the Duchess of Angoulême in the house Hirsch.

The Town Hall occupies one side of a little square, in the middle of which a Gothic fountain sends up a pretty, bell-shaped jet of water. The Hall has a magnificent, delicately carved front, with a fine clock, a belfry pointed like an arrow, fresco paintings, and a herald-at-arms in splendid plumes, bearing the coat of arms of Basle. Its iron gate is like a great window blind, embroidered in open work. All over there are statues, doors of carved wood, and, in a prominent position, the escutcheon of Basle, held on one side by the Virgin and on the other by the emperor. A stone staircase, adorned with the statue of Munatius Plancus, the founder of the city, leads from the court to the vestibule on the first floor, where a Lutheran painter has depicted, according to his idea, some scenes of the last judgment. A devil in yellow trousers, with a cock's head and a duck's feet, is throwing nuns, monks, a pope, and a courtesan into the flames ; while another, as green as a frog, is bringing a lectern on his shoulders ; and above him, in all the glory of Paradise, and under the eye of a figure meant to represent the Eternal, rosy, chubby-cheeked angels sound the resurrection trumpet.

Religious disputes have always been carried on very keenly in Switzerland, and have everywhere left deep and permanent traces.

When you go up from the Town Hall to the Cathedral, you see how it has suffered in those times of strife,—how volleys of stones have defaced and mutilated the saints mutely praying under the arches of its three doorways. But you quickly lose sight of these marks of violence in looking at the building as a majestic whole, with its two graceful towers terminating in spires carved in wavy lines

like a delicate piece of goldsmith's work, and showing the
light through innumerable openings; and the grand outline of this huge red mass, thrown out from the deep
blue of the sky like a mountain of porphyry hewn out by
giants.

This cathedral of Basle is, like its sister temples on the
banks of the Rhine, a truly magnificent building. It was
begun in 1010, by the Emperor Henry II., and built after
the Byzantine school. Three centuries and a half later it
was rebuilt in Gothic style. Proudly holding its place as
the sentinel of an older time, on the bank of the river that
flows at its feet, it looks right across the plain broken up
into meadows, fields, and forests, to the great embattled
ramparts of the High Alps, pencilled faintly afar on a turquoise sky.

Close to the cathedral rise the graceful, tapering arches
of an old cloister, where many, once full of eager, busy life
now lie in their last long sleep. Under their cool shadow
there is a sense of restful solitude, of quiet well-being, as if
the soul had already laid aside its miserable garment of
flesh and of pain. In this quiet enclosure, pacing these
long, melancholy arcades, beside all those silent dead, we
feel as if we, like them, were delivered from all the troubles
and torments of life.

Those long aisles, paved with tombstones, were the
favourite walk of Erasmus. When he stayed his steps at
one of those deep Gothic windows looking towards the
town, with its streets rising one above another like the tiers
of a theatre, what looks of irony he must have cast at the
world,—its juggling tricks, its false appearances, its hypo-
crisies, its roguery and falsehood!

At such times he was meditating, with a cynical smile on
his face, on his " Praise of Folly," or composing his sceptical
and bitter " Colloquia " between The Soldier and the Carthusian, The Abbé and the Blue-stocking, The Liar and the
Man of Truth. All the characters with which the public

were familiar in the comedy of the period,—monks and soldiers, scholars and pilgrims, women and abbés,—he drew to the life in those dialogues, full of pungent wit, in which he makes them speak and act in a terribly realistic manner.

But now here we are on the terrace, in the cool, green shade of the great chestnut trees. The view that suddenly meets our eye is as charming as unexpected.

At our feet flows the Rhine, already broad enough to reflect a cathedral or a citadel; to the right, above the slopes that run down to the river, are seen fine trees, towers and pinnacles, weather-cocks and turret windows, mingling in delightful confusion amidst the uneven sea of old roofs; to the left, terraced gardens with white retaining walls, the end of a steep street, and the great stone bridge that partly replaces the old wooden one.

On the opposite side, Little Basle presents the regular lines of its modern houses, broken here and there by a factory with its tall red chimney; and beyond that, a vast plain, green as the Rhine, stretches away into the far distance, with little white points that are villages, and ribbons of silver that are brooks or rivers, or perhaps roads, with grey fringes, which are poplars, waving like plumes in the breeze.

On the dim horizon, half seen through a silvery haze, the mountains crowd one on another, rank after rank, like a whole procession of pilgrims kneeling before the white marble shrine of the eternal snows.

The two Basles have not always been good neighbours; for a long time they lived like brothers at war. The inhabitants of the left bank held themselves superior to those on the right; and there is a tradition that, in order to insult their rivals, they erected on the tower that guards the bridge a grotesque figure, which, at every quarter of an hour, thrust out its tongue towards Little Basle. But, though such a figure was really placed on the bridge, there seems to be no foundation for ascribing such a motive.

Until the close of the last century, it was the custom for all the clocks of Basle to strike an hour in advance. It was only in 1778 that the town authorities secretly agreed to set back the hands half a minute daily, and thus imperceptibly to reach correct time.

The origin of this custom dates as far back as the first Council that was held in Basle, during which it had been found necessary to put forward the clocks that the bishops and cardinals might rise in the morning ; for they were said to be " very lazy persons, never in a hurry to come to the meetings."

Basle is not a cheerful town. The bankers, who form a large part of its population, weave their webs in silence ; a solid and beautiful fabric of silver, which they do not hang out to shine and sparkle in the sun, but hide away in great iron coffers.

There is something angular and stiff about Basle,—something that belongs to its rigid orthodoxy and its Puritan worship. The most elegant houses have an austere aspect, which is owing, not only to their style of architecture, but to the people who live in them.

After leaving Paris only the day before,—Paris, so bright, so easily pleased, so wide awake, so full of life and stir, and yet so foolish and idle,—even the most unobservant person must be struck by the contrast. It seems like another world, cramped and restricted. Therefore we make no long stay at Basle.

And yet its Museum is really a wonder—a treasure beyond value. Whole days might be spent there in studying the works of Holbein and Dürer.

What a close relationship there is between those two men, so passionately devoted to truth ! Both worked at present- ing life, without giving any special regard to beauty. They painted reality ; and their work belongs to no age, for it will be eternally true.

The Museum of Basle is the museum of Holbein. The

beginning of it was the collection of Amerbach, a friend of Holbein's, who had acquired several of the master's paintings and about twenty-four of his drawings. These drawings, a unique and invaluable collection, make known to us an unedited Holbein, full of movement and imagination, and tempering the rudeness of style of the old German masters with the easy grace and haughty elegance of the Renaissance.

In several of these drawings we can trace the first idea, the earliest conception of certain pictures. We can see the thought springing up in the brain of the artist, and then the inspiration growing spontaneously in all its strength and freshness; we witness the creation of the work, and see it come forth from the first rough sketch, a living and mighty thing, without veil or ornament, like the goddess rising from the waves.

Some of these sketches are in crayon, some in sepia, some in colours, and others in pen and ink. Holbein's pen is as skilful as his brush. It has the same energy, the same flexibility, the same infallible correctness.

In portrait-painting Holbein is incomparable. His portraits are not pictures, they are living people. Those canvasses might be taken for magic mirrors, on which the image of the persons who looked into them had remained permanently stamped. The work of the brush is quite lost sight of.

In this museum is the famous portrait of Holbein's wife, an example of a vulgar type of beauty that the painter has made no attempt to qualify.

He presented his subjects just as they were in ordinary life, in their most natural surroundings and in every-day attire. Regardless of beauty, Holbein had one sole aim,—to be true to fact. His *Dead Christ* is itself a portrait,—that of a frightful drowned Jew. He painted with the sincerity and frankness that Cromwell demanded from Lely. "If you leave out a single one of my warts," said he, "I will not give you a penny!"

Although the greater number of Holbein's portraits in the Basle museum are only those of old and ordinary looking people, yet how they fix themselves on the memory !

There is nothing pleasing in the fat, prosaic faces of Froben the printer, Schneiger the goldsmith, Neyer the burgomaster, or Amerbach the lawyer; and yet, once seen, they are never forgotten, because Holbein in showing us the physical has shown us also the moral man; he has painted the *soul* of his subject.

There are two portraits of Erasmus, one in three-quarter length, on a blue background ; the other in profile, writing, with a black cap on his head, from under which stray a few locks of grey hair. In this second portrait the eyes have lost their lustre and seem to express a weariness of all things, a deep disgust at men and at life.

And what a marvellous collection is that gallery of portraits of Basle women ! It is not only a journal of fashions, a pictured history of costume, but a living procession of Swiss patrician ladies of the sixteenth century, richly dressed, laden with gold chains, and wearing large hats and feathers, while some have their foreheads hidden under the monastic wimple. There are others in gaily-ribboned caps, whose attitudes in holding up the superb folds of their draperies are full of nobleness.

Holbein came to Basle almost in his infancy. He was only nine years old when he left Bavaria for Switzerland. Basle was at that time an intellectual centre, and Holbein formed his views on the philosophical school of Erasmus. He afterwards went to England. Some of the English nobles having complained to Henry VIII. of the pride of his favourite, the king replied, " Out of seven peasants I could make as many lords, but out of twenty such as you I could not make one Holbein."

At the beginning of his career, Holbein had made a bargain with an apothecary of Basle to paint for him a fresco on the front of his house. But the young painter loved

merry company, and his days were much oftener spent in
the tavern than at his work.

The impatient apothecary was constantly coming to seek
him out and send him to finish his task. At last, to escape
from his importunity, Holbein painted a pair of legs hanging
down from the scaffolding, the upper part of which was
hidden under a canvas awning, and now the poor deceived
apothecary thought the painter was at work from morning
to night.

The hours of the journey between Basle and Lucerne pass
quickly, though the railway train is very leisurely. There
is in those Swiss landscapes a delicious freshness, a tender
softness and sweetness that produce a sense of comfort and
satisfaction like that of plunging, after some great fatigue,
into a perfumed bath.

And ever and anon the train stops before a pretty little
châlet, with its carved wooden balcony draped with the
large bronzed leaves of the hop or with other climbing
plants. An inscription in large black letters stands out
conspicuously on the front, and a round clock is hung outside like a bird-cage. In a garden shaded by young plum-
trees, and gay with roses, red and white, a Swiss girl with
flaxen hair and azure eyes, armed with an enormous kitchen
knife, is cutting off—like an innocent Judith, the head of a
cabbage, while a man in a laced hat marches about on the
steps.

This little châlet, that looks like a rural villa, is a railway station. The village or town is back there, behind the
trees.

In Switzerland there is a station every twenty minutes.
There would not be time, between one and the next, even to
assassinate a sub-prefect.

We cross a little valley, about as broad as the palm of the
hand, and here we are stopping again; but this time we are
right in the middle of a village, with triangular roofs, snuff-

2

box chimneys, and windows blooming with geraniums and pinks. A noisy flock of geese, gathered in front of the train, are trumpeting with their yellow bills, and strong, well-developed women, with sunburnt faces and large white sleeves, are standing framed liked pictures in the dark door-ways. In the middle of the open space we recognise the school-house, by the gymnastic appliances that surround it ; and beside it, we read on the front of another large building, " *Savings Bank.*" The Swiss are downright, practical, economical people. It was a banker of Basle who was something of a savings pilferer, who invented this savings bank. But we need not laugh. If each village has its school-house, it is because it had first its banking house.

In these Swiss villages the schools, as well as everything else, are under the charge of the Commune. It exercises an almost family and patriarchal authority. It nominates the pastor or parish priest, the schoolmaster, and the syndic or mayor ; it administers its own laws, and holds its meetings in its common Hall, the people's palace. In the Canton of Fribourg alone the syndic is appointed directly by the Government.

In Switzerland the liberty of the Communes was the beginning of the Republic, and the Republic has continued as the beginning of wisdom.

CHAPTER II.

A HEIGHT crowned with embattled ramparts that
bristle with loop-holed turrets; church towers mingling their graceful spires and peaceful crosses with those
warlike edifices; dazzling white villas, planted like tents
under curtains of verdure; tall houses with old red skylights on the roofs;—this is our first glimpse of the catholic
and warlike city of Lucerne.

We seem to be approaching some town of old feudal times
that has been left solitary and forgotten on the mountain
side, outside of the current of modern life.

But when we pass through the station we find ourselves
suddenly transported to the side of the lake, where whole
flotillas of large and small boats lie moored on the blue
waters of a large harbour. And along the banks of this
wonderful lake is a whole town of hotels, gay with many
coloured flags, their terraces and balconies rising tier above
tier, like the galleries of a grand theatre, whose scenery is
the mighty Alps.

Lucerne has the gaiety and the stir of one long international railway station. When the crowds of travellers
pour out of the carriages that are continually arriving, it is
like the escape of an entire human menagerie. There is the
lion-traveller, with his mane of long tangled locks, proudly

bearing his bundles of prey ; the ape-traveller, skipping and capering, making all kinds of grimaces, and practising his favourite attitudes ; the grave, ox-like traveller, with black, frizzled head, and hooked, semitic nose. And among the ladies, how many British storks and Prussian ostriches ; how many foolish little turkeys and gay parroquets !

In summer Lucerne is the Hyde Park of Switzerland. Its quays are thronged by people of every nation. There you meet pale women from the lands of snow, and dark women from the lands of the sun ; tall, six-foot English women, and lively, alert, trim Parisian women, with the light and graceful carriage of a bird on a bough.

At certain hours this promenade on the quays is like a charity fair or a rustic ball,—bright colours and airy draperies everywhere.

Nowhere can the least calm and repose be found but in the old town. There the gabled houses, with wooden galleries hanging over the waters of the Reuss, make a charming ancient picture, like a little bit of Venice set down amidst the verdant landscape of the valley.

I also discovered on the heights beyond the ramparts a pretty and peaceful convent of Capuchins, the way to which winds among wild plants, starry with flowers.

It is delicious to go right away, far from the town swarming and running over with Londoners, Germans, and Americans, and to find yourself among fragrant hedges, peopled by warblers whom it has not yet occurred to the hotel-keepers to teach to sing in English. This sweet path leads without fatigue to the convent of the good fathers.

In a garden flooded with sunshine and balmy with the fragrance of mignonette and vervain, where broad sunflowers erect their black discs fringed with gold, two brothers with fan-shaped beards, their brass-mounted spectacles astride on their flat noses, and arrayed in green gardening aprons, are plying enormous watering-pans ; while, in the green and cool half-twilight under the shadowy trees, big, rubicund brothers walk up and down, reading their red-edged breviaries in black leather bindings.

Happy monks! not a fraction of a pessimist among them! How well they understand life! A beautiful convent, beautiful nature, good wine and good cheer, neither disturbance nor care, neither wife nor children; and when they leave the world, heaven specially created for them, seraphim waiting for them with harps of gold, and angels with urns of rose-water to wash their feet!

Lucerne began as a nest of monks, hidden in an orchard like a nest of sparrows. The first house of the town was a monastery, erected by the side of the lake. The nest grew, became a village, then a town, then a city.

The monks of Murbach, to whom the monastery of St. Leger belonged, had got into debt; this sometimes does happen even to monks. They sold to King Rudolf all the property they possessed at Lucerne and in Unterwalden; and thus the town passed into the hands of the Hapsburgs.

When the first Cantons, after expelling the Austrian bailiffs, had declared their independence, Lucerne was still one of Austria's advanced posts. But its people were daily brought into contact with the shepherds of the Forest Cantons, who came into the town to supply themselves with provisions; and they were not long in beginning to ask themselves if there was any reason why they should not be, as well as their neighbours, absolutely free.

The position of the partisans of Austria soon became so precarious that they found it safe to leave the town.

The bailiff of Rothenbourg, under whose jurisdiction Lucerne was, seeing that the power was slipping from his hands, resolved on trying a bold stroke to reduce the rebellious city to obedience. On the 29th of June, 1362, soon after nightfall, a boy who had fallen asleep on the bank of the lake, was awakened by sounds of footsteps on the gravel. He saw five or six men gliding stealthily, like shadows, along the shore. There was something so sus-

picious-looking in their manner, that he at once concluded
they were about no good. He was a brave lad; so he
resolved to follow them, and warn the watch on the ramparts.

Just as the boy was going to rise, a new band of men
came towards his hiding-place. There were fifteen of them,
with a leader who wore a cockade of peacock feathers; two
strong arms protected by his coat of mail, appeared from
under the wide sleeves of his cloth tunic, and hanging by
a little iron chain from his leathern girdle was a battle axe
adorned with the Austrian eagle.

The night was not so dark as to hinder the lad, Pierre
Hohdorf, from recognising in this personage the bailiff of
Rothenbourg. He was talking with Jean de Malters, the
traitor who had deserted to the ranks of the adversary,
after being one of the warmest partisans of the Swiss party.
The bailiff was pointing to the towers and churches of
Lucerne, that showed in dark outline on the night sky.
" Our conscience," said he, " will have nothing with which
to reproach us. The men of Lucerne have been warned
often enough. I have done all I could to bring them back
to respect the rights that the Dukes of Austria have over
their town. Did they not pay good ready money for it—
the ungrateful town? But there is a contagious breath
of liberty blowing down from the mountains. The Swiss
party is growing more powerful every day, and their
insolence increases with their strength. If we do not crush
them to-day, they will crush us to-morrow."

Pierre Hohdorf worked with his father at his trade of
shoemaking, and from the many conversations he had
heard carried on in the shop, he had a thorough knowledge
of the bad feeling between the town and the representative
of Austria, and at once understood what danger threatened
Lucerne.

As soon as the band had passed on their way, he slipped
after them, keeping himself hidden behind blocks of stone.

Reaching a place where the houses were only separated from the lake by a narrow strip of sand and a few reeds, Pierre lost track of those whom he was following. Whither had they vanished? They must have stolen into the town by some secret entrance, known only to themselves.

The boy listened. Nothing was audible but the lapping of the waves.

Then, stretching up on tip-toe, he looked all around, his eyes searching into and exploring the darkness.

Suddenly, in the midst of the blackness, a feeble point of light appears a few yards before him. The boy throws himself down again on the sand, and seeing that the light remains stationary, he creeps towards it.

Now he knows where he is. He is opposite the Abbey of the Tailors, under which is a sort of natural grotto, forming a great vaulted cellar which is reached by a ladder descending from a trap-door in the floor of the stable.

The whole band are there. The tall form of the bailiff of Rothenbourg towers above the broad shouldered men-at-arms who surround him, and who are evidently only awaiting his signal to break into the town and massacre the inhabitants.

Jean de Malters is speaking with abrupt and violent gesticulation. He is giving his final directions.

Although Pierre has tracked them to earth, he still comes nearer. He has no fear; one sole thought fills his mind— the danger of the town, the peril that threatens his home. Ah! if he can only hear what Jean de Malters is saying!

He comes still nearer, stops,—listens—comes nearer still. Suddenly he hears steps behind him. He turns to flee, but a strong hand seizes him, holds him like a vice, and pushes him to the entrance of the cavern.

"A spy!" cries the man who holds him. The conspirators start, but are reassured at the sight of a child. Jean de Malters approaches Pierre with a wicked look, and roughly asks him,—

" Where do you come from ? "

" From the banks of the lake," replies Pierre calmly.

" What were you doing there ? "

" I was sleeping."

" You were sleeping ? And how came you to awake to follow us ? "

" You made a noise."

" You lie ! We made no noise. We cannot have wakened you. You are a spy. To your knees ! Say your prayers ! "

" I am not a spy," replies the child firmly.

But the iron hand that had seized him a moment before presses more heavily, and forces his knees to bend. He sinks to the ground.

Then Jean de Malters, bending towards the ear of the man who holds the child, gives him some orders in a low voice.

Pierre, pale and motionless, utters no word of prayer. His large blue eyes are fixed on the bailiff of Rothenbourg, at if beseeching him to have pity on his youth.

Jean de Malters again comes in front of the boy, and asks him a second time, in a yet more imperious tone, " Will you tell us who sent you ? "

And with a firm voice Pierre repeats, " Nobody sent me. I had bathed in the lake, and after dressing again, I fell asleep on the bank."

" You persist in your falsehoods ! Well, you shall die. I give you two minutes to consider and to speak."

The child thinks of his home, of his mother and his father whom he shall see no more ; and his breast heaves with a stifled sob.

But he remains silent ; and after a moment Jean de Malters makes a sign to the man whose grasp is still on Pierre's shoulder. The man draws a dagger from his belt.

But the bailiff of Rothenbourg, who until then had remained silent, stretched a protecting arm over the boy's head.

"No, no," said he ; "we must not begin with the murder of a child. A child's blood is innocent blood."

Then after closely questioning Pierre, he granted him his life, after making him swear by Christ and by his eternal salvation that he would not reveal "to a living soul" what he had seen and heard.

The moment he was free, Pierre ran, without once stopping to take breath, to the Abbey of the Butchers, where his father was accustomed to spend his evenings, and where the patriot party often met.

There were still lights in the windows of the common hall, and each time the door opened a sound of many eager voices was heard from within.

The child had stopped at the foot of the staircase, not sure of what he meant to do. He was trying to form some plan, puzzling his little head to find some device by which, without perjuring himself, he could reveal to his father what he had seen.

There was no time to lose. The Lucerners must be warned at once, or within a single hour every member of the Swiss party would be massacred.

Acting on a sudden inspiration, Pierre enters the hall, goes up to the enormous porcelain stove that stands in the middle of the room, and addressing it as if it had been a conscious being, capable of hearing and understanding him, he relates to it, without showing by sign or look that he is aware of living hearers, all that he has seen and heard, and what has befallen him on the banks of the lake.

At first the men who sat drinking round the table thought the boy was crazed. But there was such a tone of truth and of conviction in his way of speaking, that by degrees even the most noisy became silent, till at last the whole party had left the table and stood, a listening circle, round the child.

"If I am talking to you, O stove," he was saying, "it is because I have taken an oath not to repeat what I have seen and heard to 'a living soul.' Now *you* are an inanimate object; so in taking you for my confidant I do not perjure myself, and I save my people."

The chiefs of the Swiss party were expecting from day to day some outbreak by the partisans of Austria, and they were ready.

Men were despatched into the different quarters of the town to give the alarm quietly to the citizens; while a hundred tried patriots placed themselves in ambush in the streets adjoining the Abbey of the Tailors.

At eleven o'clock the town was secure against surprise, and guarded as in times of war, while the Austrian party, still concealed in their cavern on the lake side, had no suspicion that warning had been given.

The midnight hour struck. All was silent; it was like a city of the dead. Black clouds hung overhead like a pall, pierced only by a few glimmering stars.

Shortly after one o'clock the stable-door at the Abbey of the Tailors was cautiously opened, and a group of armed men came out and stole along close to the walls.

At the corner of the street they were surrounded, overpowered, and disarmed. At the sound of their cries all the rest in the abbey rush to the rescue, but concealed patriots are in wait for them in the angle of every door, and fall upon them from every direction.

The struggle was very fierce. Men slew each other without mercy, stabbing wildly in the dark without seeing or knowing their foe. The dry earth became soft with the blood that it drank.

The bailiff of Rothenbourg fled ignominiously with Jean de Malters, and Lucerne was thenceforward lost to Austria.

It was forbidden, on pain of death, to say, with the partisans of the Hapsburgs, that the oath taken by them to the Confederate Cantons was null, and that Lucerne was still subject to the Dukes of Austria;—for Lucerne was free!

A child had achieved her freedom!

CHAPTER III.

FROM the left bank of the Reuss, the view of Lucerne
is strikingly beautiful, with its bright quays covered
with splendid hotels amidst flowery terraces; its shady
promenade, so gay and animated; its clean, light squares;
its towers, raising into the sky their pepper-box roofs; its
bushy green hills, among which so many villas lie sheltered
like linnets' nests in thickets of roses. It gives one the
idea of a very large and very wealthy city; a kind of rural
Capua, which attracts and retains all who do not know what
to make of their life.

The opening of the St. Gothard railway has given a new
impulse to this cosmopolitan city, which has a great future
before it. Already it has supplanted Interlaken in the estima-
tion of the furbelowed, fashionable world,—the women who
come to Switzerland not to see but to be seen. Lucerne is
now the chief summer station of the twenty-two cantons. And
yet it does not possess many objects of interest. There is
the old bridge on the Reuss, with its ancient paintings; the
Church of St. Leger, with its lateral altars and its Campo
Santo, reminding us of Italian cemeteries; the museum at
the Town Hall, with its fine collection of stained glass; the
blood-stained standards from the Burgundian wars, and the

flag in which noble old Gundolfingen, after charging his fellow-citizens never to elect their magistrates for more than a year, wrapped himself as in a shroud of glory to die in the fight; finally, there is the Lion of Lucerne; and that is all.

The most wonderful thing of all is that you are allowed to see this Lion for nothing; for close beside it you are charged a franc for permission to cast an indifferent glance on some uninteresting excavations, which date, it is said, from the Glacial period. We do not care if they do.

The garden in which these latter "curiosities" are found is a distressingly dull place, with its pond of stagnant water in which some unfortunate ducks are imprisoned; its little wooden booths in which is sold "everything that your honours can fancy"; Havannah cigars at a penny, match-boxes, paper-cutters, little boxes with the Lion painted on the top and music inside, carved napkin-rings, and bears without number; dancing bears, bears wearing spectacles, performing military drill, carrying the federal banner or an umbrella, singing the "*Ranz des Vaches*," or enjoying a cup of Suchard chocolate. This continual fair going on close by is quite out of harmony with the feeling of reverence with which we regard the grand Lion dying so nobly, as the Swiss Guards died in Paris in 1792. Such a monument would stand more fittingly in the silent sanctuary of some beautiful forest.

But to return to the quay. The great quay of Lucerne is delightful; as good as the seashore at Dieppe or Trouville. Before you, limpid and blue, lies the lake, which from the character of its shores, at once stern and graceful, is the finest in Switzerland. In front rise the snow-clad peaks of Uri, to the left the Rigi, to the right the austere Pilatus, almost always wearing his high cap of clouds.

This beautiful walk on the quay, long and shady like the avenue of a gentleman's park, is the daily resort, towards four o'clock, of all the foreigners who are crowded in the hotels or packed in the boarding-houses. Here are Russian and Polish counts with long moustaches, and pins set with false brilliants; Englishmen with fishes' or horses' heads; Englishwomen with the figures of angels or of giraffes; Parisian women, daintily attired, sprightly and coquettish; American women, free in their bearing and eccentric in their dress, and their men as stiff as the smoke-pipes of steamboats; German women, with languishing voices, drooping and pale like willow branches, fair-haired and blue-eyed, talking in the same breath of Goethe and the price of sausages, of the moon and their glass of beer, of stars and black radishes. And here and there are a few little Swiss girls, fresh and rosy as wood strawberries, smiling darlings like Dresden shepherdesses, dreaming of scenes of platonic love in a great garden adorned with the statue of William Tell or General Dufour.

The quay is the great open-air drawing-room of this Alpine high-life which has its representatives from all nations, and which has selected Lucerne as one of its rendezvous, one of its summer halting-places.

There you meet at every step faces that you have seen before in Paris or London, in Vienna or in Berlin. There are dresses of tints as transparent as water-colours, fashions of an elegant modernism enough to ravish the eye of a *genre* painter. And what variety of types among all those holiday-making people who are walking and talking and jabbering and chattering, discussing and slandering, hating or loving, seeking out or avoiding each other, looking at others or exhibiting themselves! It does not take long to classify them.

Take first *the French.* Here is the married tourist—the most serious of all—already rather portly and half bald. You recognise him by his small figure, his short legs, by his wife walking like a sentinel at his side, and by his absorbing occupation as nurse-maid. He is continually in search of Paul or Jeanne, whom he is always in dread of seeing disappear over a precipice or into a torrent. Carries madame's waterproof and shawl, and the brats also when they are tired. Is always in a profuse perspiration, and casts envious looks at dogs without collars. Thinks nothing finer than the railways that go to the tops of mountains, and the tramways that carry him to the foot of the glaciers. Travels to be like everybody else, to write his name and designation in the hotel registers, and to enable his wife to say on her reception days next winter, " Ah, yes, the Rigi—that dear little baby railway; oh, delicious!"

Next comes the bachelor tourist, twenty-five or thirty; as alert and bold as the married tourist is prudent and slow. Treats the mountains with the familiarity of a superior towards an inferior; pats the Matterhorn on the shoulder, and takes the Jungfrau by the chin like a tavern barmaid. In close-fitting cloth suit, felt hat over his ear, knapsack on his back, gaitered, and armed with alpenstock, he goes every-where, fears nothing, climbs as far as the chamois does, and arrives in the evening, sunburnt and looking like a bandit, at some mountain hotel, where, after supper, he invites the ladies to waltz. Assumes with ease the airs of my lord, drinks hard, and finishes by marrying an heiress whom he has saved from an inundation or an avalanche.

The Tartarin (see Daudet.) A very common type. Travels in illusion and flannel, and changes his clothes four times a day for fear of catching cold. Discourses with the peasants in the plains to teach them how to sow wheat and to know turnips from potatoes; believes that the Swiss still shoot with cross-bows, and that the bears at Berne were caught in the Oberland. Greets everybody—chats familiarly with the hotel porter, whom he takes for the steward, or for a Swiss admiral, because of his gold-laced cap; makes jokes with the waiters and becomes confidential with the attendants in *cafés* and with street-porters; has seen everything, visited everything, ascended everything; relates stories that never happened; is infatuated with himself, thinks himself a better mountaineer than the men born on the mountains, and proclaims it aloud. The terror of *tables-d'hôtes*, the bugbear of all sensible people.

Next, the English. Finely and firmly built, accustomed from their early youth to violent exercise, they are invincible to fatigue; make thirty or forty miles a day without resting their iron limbs; the foremost and most intrepid climbers in the world, always rushing to a discovery or a conquest; fierce, tenacious spirits, full of passion under their apparent coldness; scaling mountains with a martial ardour and carrying inaccessible summits by assault. Seek out danger as an enjoyment and a luxury. Travel also as families, with a whole regiment of daughters dressed in the same material made on the same pattern; short dresses, Scotch petticoats, tight black stockings, hair cut short on the forehead, or hanging far down the back like a long mane, the neck imprisoned in a man's collar, a tight jacket of military cut—neither girl nor boy—just English. Carry telescopes, botanical boxes, fishing-rods, butterfly nets, and pick up all the little sparkling stones they see.

We also meet in Switzerland a type of Englishwoman who deserves special mention; the tall old maid, thin and wiry, as dry as the moral of an ill-written tract. She has been travelling since she was thirty, and is now approaching fifty; has crossed the Sahara alone on camel back; has been a prisoner for two months among Greek brigands; has ascended to the top of the Jungfrau with no guide but a little shepherd-boy. Travels with the sole object of accomplishing so many miles. Last year she had measured with the pair of compasses on which she walks, 7,500 miles; this year she has but one desire, one aim, one ambition—to go beyond that number.

This is the Englishwoman of our French caricatures, made up like a scarecrow, with a red-checked tartan shawl, her eyes covered up with great blue spectacles, a mouth from ear to ear, showing teeth like the keys of a piano, her

figure squeezed into a black gown like an umbrella case—
emptying her bottle of wine while she reads *The Times*.

All Englishwomen, we may add, think the crevasses
" *very lovely* " and the precipices " *charming* " !

Then the Germans. We meet almost as many of them
as of English now-a-days. They treat Switzerland rather
like an annexed province. Wear straw hats covered with
grey cloth, in the shape of a bombshell or a melon; are
always smoking something—pipe or cigar; very noisy in
public places, railway carriages, and decks of steamers. Are
perpetually discussing religious, social, or political questions; even on the Rigi, in presence of the rising sun, they
talk about the new law about alcohol; and knowing Switzerland better than the Swiss, are thoroughly skilled in the
science of travelling economically—eating and drinking
much and spending little. Merry fellows and good companions when they are neither nobles nor men of letters, nor
officers, nor corporals, nor lawyers, nor Prussians of Prussia,
nor have been covered with glory and laden with medals
in 1871.

One particular type is the *Jaegerite*, so called from the
name of Dr. Jaeger, who now counts more than fifty thousand disciples in Germany. The Jaegerite is entirely sworn
to wool, as the vegetarian is to vegetables. Apart from
woollen clothing there is no safety. The shirt is of wool,
the hat is of wool, the necktie is of wool; a knitted woollen
garment, something between an overall and a great-coat,
covers the back and the chest, and the shoes and stockings
are also of wool. The Jaegerite lets his hair grow long, and
performs as few ablutions as possible, lest he should catch
cold.

The Prussian woman steps along erect, stiff—her eye-
glass at her eye—like a corporal in woman's dress. These
daughters of soldiers have a soldierly carriage. No flexibility in the figure, no grace in the walk and bearing. They
are like figures screwed to a wooden stand, with an iron rod

running from head to heel. And what voices! they might be produced by iron machinery, they are so harsh and grating. Their pale eyes have the cold brightness of two steel buttons on a uniform.

Among the ladies, we must note also the little American girls of eighteen, who make the tour of Europe and of Switzerland in parties of two. But as they always travel in the compartments where there are gentlemen, they have the appearance of taking their amusement in parties of four.

These different species of tourists are capable of sub-division into endless varieties. There is the grave, con-scientious tourist, who goes to the mountain with the piety and fervour of a priest going to the altar; who is fulfilling a mission,—a sacred function. There is the fancy tourist, who dresses and fits himself out like a fashion plate; the drawing-room tourist, who only looks at Switzerland from the decks of steamboats, from the windows of the railway carriage, or from the balcony of his hotel; the listless or dreamy tourist, who spends his days on the banks of the streams, stretched at full length in the soft, cool grass. Or again, there is the easy, philosophic tourist; laughing over his bad dinner or his uncomfortable bed,—always content, even when he knows he is being scandalously overcharged; and the man of progress, wearing a helmet of elder-pith, dressed in waterproof and carrying appliances of all kinds, for doing his own cooking, for lighting up the glaciers at night, for taking instantaneous photographs of the chamois, for crossing the crevasses and climbing perpendicular rocks. But the funniest of all is the half-crazy *savant*, with his pockets filled with thermometers, with thermometers stuck in his hat, under his arms, in the band of his trowsers, and in his garters; he carries hydrometers, pedometers, instru-ments for measuring the height of the mountains and the depth of the rivers, plummets, hammers, microscopes, pincers, phials, and labelled note-books, in which he records

3

how many panes of glass there are in the windows of the
villages of the first zone, and if, in the second zone, the tails
of the pigs hang down or curl up.

Among all those varieties, the happiest is the cynical or
eccentric tourist, who laughs at Mrs. Grundy. Absolutely
at his ease, and scorning what may be thought of him, he
behaves among other people just as he does in his own
house; he lives and travels for himself alone, cares for
nobody, eats and sleeps with the shepherds, lets his beard
grow, returning to a state of nature; he defies all sorts of
weather and danger, carves out a kingdom for himself, and
wraps himself in a veritable royalty in the solitude of the
mountains.

It is one of the national characteristics of the English
thus to disregard the customs of society wherever they go;
and it is this want of politeness, this thorough egotism, this
offensive manner, that has caused them to be disliked by
almost all other travellers. (!)

On the quay of Lucerne, all these types, all these mas-
queraders without masks, pass along like a joyful procession
on Shrove Tuesday.

In another place, on a different stage, and amid different
stage-scenery, all those absurd costumes—those big men in
knickerbockers, those women in short dresses, those blue
veils, those bell-shaped and sugar-loaf hats, those alpenstocks spirally branded with the names of mountains—all
would be like the disguises of a comedy. But here it all
seems quite natural; nothing in those eccentricities shocks
you, nothing jars, unless perhaps the glaring colours of some
too British toilet, with waistbands of red ribbon; and standing out in puffs like a camel's hump.

It is amusing to watch some of the little scenes played
before you by these unconscious comedians. Here it is an
Englishman, as long as a fast-day and as lean as a verse of
Ponsard, leaning on the handle of his umbrella, with a
" guide" bound in red cloth in his hand, and his whole tribe

of juveniles ranged round him in order, like organ pipes, explaining to them the different points in the landscape— the Rigi, the Rothfluh, the Vitznauerstock, Toedi, Pilatus. There, a fashionable abbé, confidential counsellor of ladies, old and young, with smart step and spruce cassock, his blue eyes pricked like two periwinkles in his fat, dimpled, good-natured face; curled, pomaded, most carefully got up, chattering in the midst of a troop of charming penitents who have been confided to his care, and that of a portly "mother" in spectacles, with a moustache like a colonel American ladies, with porcelain complexions, in provoking and disconcerting dishabilles, pass, laughing loudly, with vulgar young fellows in scanty attire, with feet tortured into hideous deformity in boots pointed like a crescent.

Sitting on a bench are some grave, austere Germans, buried deep in the *Cologne Gazette*. They are not simply reading; they are studying, meditating; and nothing that is passing around them can distract their attention. They see neither the blue lake, nor the white mountains, nor the pretty women who, in a bright first instalment of holiday dresses, are passing before them. They are travelling inside their *Gazette*, like a Mainz sausage wrapped in double papers.

At the end of the avenue there is a vacant bench. I go and sit down on it, after buying the *Figaro*. We do not read the *Figaro* in the same way as the *Cologne Gazette*. We do not unfurl it like a flag, or entrench ourselves behind its thin paper as behind a fortress wall.

A young woman came and sat down near me. Suddenly, addressing me point-blank, she said,—

"Monsieur, excuse my addressing you, but the paper you are reading shows me that you speak French. For eight days I have not spoken a word of French; and I feel as if I were living in another planet, as if I were dead, and wandering like a troubled spirit in an unknown world. I should like so much to converse for a moment in that language, which I love as if it were my mother tongue, which in Russia we all love and speak. I come from St. Petersburg."

" So far, madam, and quite alone ? "

" Yes, sir, quite alone. Very naturally, for I *am* alone. And in the third class, too. If I had travelled second class, I should certainly have found some persons who spoke French. Oh, sir, what an infliction! Always German, nothing but German, German day and night! My ears are stunned with it, my nerves are shaken. At home we speak French. You cannot imagine the effect of this privation of the language you are accustomed to."

" Oh, yes, madam! Like yourself, I have experienced it, and that frequently."

And I told her how I had been, like herself, in countries far from home; and that if I had been told that there was a rag-picker twenty miles off, who could speak French, I would have rushed to embrace him.

The stranger who had come up to me so simply and without misgiving, was not pretty, but she had that great charm and attraction of the Slav women, a complexion of the pale yet warm tint of old ivory, lighted up by fine black eyes and rosy lips. We sat chatting together on the bench, like people who meet for an evening in the box of a theatre, or who are travelling together in a *diligence*. Her pure accent, her marked familiarity with the language, her manners, and the variety of her knowledge indicated an educated person of good family. Her father had a post under Government. She herself gave lessons, and took a journey every summer on her savings. She restricted herself to third class trains and hotels, that she might be able, by economising her resources, to go as far as possible.

While she was speaking to me of the enormous distance she had come, I was going over it also in my memory,—that same journey made so rapidly some years ago. I was seeing again those immense spaces we had traversed; the wild, boundless plains, dotted with black, gloomy forests, the villages, dull as burying-grounds, the stray railway-stations, like islets in the ocean of the steppes, the towns half seen in the red morning mist with their bulbous towers and golden domes glittering in the sun. What a journey for that young girl! Three days and nights in trains where filthy peasants are packed like cattle, smoking, spitting, drinking brandy ; unsavoury Jews and Germans, sending forth the sickening odour of sour beer and old damp rags!

We talked of the towns where I had been—St. Petersburg, Moscow, Kief; and an hour passed quickly, while before and around us the walkers continued to stream on, studying each other, observing, waiting for each other, passing each other in review, giving themselves up to the same little pieces of slander, the same nonsense, the same gossip and mischief as in the drawing-rooms of cosmopolitan Paris.

The sun was setting.

The lake was taking on the most delicate tints, steel-grey and rose shot with faint blue, as if many-coloured gems were rolling in the waves. The snow-fields of the High Alps were changed into rose-fields, and the sharp peaks of the rocks into ruby needles.

Then, while one gazed, the rose of the glaciers paled and faded ; the coloured light on the rocks changed and died away. Soon there remained only a glow in the sky—a few floating shreds of rosy cloud ; then, gradually those disappeared, lost in a veil of shadows. Like the light drapery drawn around an infant's cradle, a white mist spread slowly along the opposite shore of the lake, hiding the pretty smiling bays crowded with villas and hotels.

The barks that were hastening homewards with outspread, bending sails, were like great white sea-gulls skimming the water.

A steamer came into the harbour whistling and ringing its bell, with a quick splashing of paddles,—its red lights already burning, like the two eyes of a monster, the captain standing on the bridge, speaking-trumpet in hand; the passengers standing in crowds with their small luggage, armed with sticks and umbrellas, crushing and pushing each other, in swelling waves of shoulders, felt hats and straw hats; the feathers of the ladies rising above all; and forming, as it were, a great human billow at its height, ready to fall and break into a thousand little rills on the shore.

The promenade was growing empty. From all the hotels the sound of bells was summoning people to dinner. And already festoons of stars were shining out on the fronts of the hotels, and lighting up the high, open windows.

From the lake rose a cool breeze, which noiselessly waved the branches of the trees, as if to rock them to sleep. And above the heights that look down on the town, crowned with the broken lines of the old ramparts, the moon suddenly appears, pale as a victim; so softly melancholy that she might seem only to have come to light up with her modest radiance the antique towers and crumbling ruins.

The young Russian had left me. She was living with worthy townspeople, whose address she had found in the local advertisements. For twenty francs a week she had a room, board, light and service.

In Switzerland living is not dear except in the great hotels. Foreigners who call the Swiss "thieves" have probably never lunched or dined in the restaurants of the Bois de Boulogne or the Champs Elysées; and if they have been "robbed" in Switzerland, it has been their own fault. Even in the great hotels, a traveller who does not ask for a bottle of Chateau-Laffite at each of his meals, hardly spends more than twelve to fifteen francs a day. Besides those hotels that have cost thousands, and which are open only four months out of twelve, how many good, smaller hotels there are of the next class; old inns which, together with their wooden staircases, have retained their large dining-room with projecting beams—the glory of the olden time! No waiters in dress-coats there,—no insolent porter,—no landlord more difficult of access than a cabinet minister; but a kindly, stout hostess in white apron and cap, attended by a whole battalion of fair and rosy waitresses, who receive you chirping and smiling.

In these "hostelries," which bear very unassuming titles,—The Angel, The Hunters, The Falcon, The Rose, The Golden Sun, The Red Ox, etc., the price of a bedroom varies from a franc to a franc and a half; dinner two and a half, or with wine three francs; and in the evening a perfect supper for one and a half.

It is this kind of hotels that the people of the country frequent; and it is only by talking with them, questioning and observing them, that anything is to be learned in traveling in an unknown country.

In the evening, after eight o'clock, the scene of animation on the Schweizerhof quay is renewed.

When the evening is fine, the walking by the side of the lake goes on for a long time. The great mountains in the light of the moon show unfamiliar summits and assume fantastic forms; they might be a procession of phantoms along the horizon, some draped in snowy winding-sheets, others hidden under a great black mantle of forests. And nearer, almost opposite, Pilatus, mighty and grand, seems rising into the heavens to receive a crown of stars.

Modest little skiffs are seen leaving the shore, carrying away from the offing into the mystery of solitude and darkness two shadows, whose dark outlines are those of man and woman. And in the wake of the boat, as it skims the water like a great night bird, the stars are dancing like wild-fire on the point of every little wave.

In the chestnut avenue on the quay, too, couples are sauntering and talking in low voices; leaning confidentially towards each other, they disappear down the long vista into a quiet wood path.

From the hotels come sounds of dance music that give to the streets a festive air that quite harmonises with the gay dresses of the pretty worldlings who are walking up and down in the gilded saloons of the Hotel National and Hotel Suisse, waiting for the opening of the ball.

But at midnight all these delightful sounds are hushed. That is the virtuous and hygienic hour at which everybody goes to bed at Lucerne, even the most seasoned Parisians.

Alone, in its deep cradle of mountains, the lake stirs gently under the gaze of the moon.

CHAPTER IV.

IN order to cross the St. Gothard, people who are in a hurry take the railway to Fluelen; while walkers, leisurely tourists, lovers of nature, go by the lake in the steamer to the same point. It is the old classic voyage of beauty unsurpassed; for of all lakes in the world, the lake of the Four Cantons is the most sublime.

We leave Kussnacht at the head of its poetic bay:— Kussnacht, the name of which sounds like a kiss; and passing Hertenstein, lazily lying under the trees on its pretty peninsula, we stop for a few minutes at Weggis, where there is such a curious church, with its red tower with green shutters and gilded dial-plate. Between the graceful, green slopes of the left bank and the bare, rugged mountains and irregular rocks on the right, there is a contrast, the effect of which is magnificent. Is not all Alpine beauty the result of contrast?

As the steamer goes on, the scenery becomes wilder; great bare walls of the colour of iron rust are piled one upon another, and seem to forbid access to the Rigi in that direction.

41

Here we are at Vitznau, the station for the Rigi. In
1869 three engineers landed at this obscure village, and
scrambling along the rocky ledges, scaling the vertical
walls, they measured and surveyed the mountain from top
to bottom. A year later a locomotive went up by the way
they had gone, and the wonder was seen of a railway train
emulating the agility of the chamois, and carrying the public across precipices to a height of nearly 5,000 feet above
the level of the sea.

I admire man's work, but I regret the work of nature
thus spoiled and disfigured. The Rigi with its railways—
for greed of gain and competition have produced other lines
—the Rigi has now the effect on me of a false mountain—a
sham mountain, built by contractors and shareholders, a
mountain at a fair, that people ascend for sixpence.

All the mischief that engineers have done to Switzerland
will never be known.

Is there anywhere a point of view that attracts tourists,
a summit that climbers make fashionable;—at once the
mountain is rent and insulted ; it is stripped of its beautiful
forests, iron rails are screwed to its wounded and bleeding
sides, and you are carried up like a bundle of luggage! No
more roadside halts under the trees, no more flowers
gathered as trophies on the steep, uneven slopes, no more
merry arrival at the rustic inn hidden under the firs ; but
all along the way station-masters occurring as regularly as
telegraph posts, ticket collectors, stations railed in, and
hotels without style, without distinctive character, as stupid
as a barracks.

It was in the train that I left Lucerne to cross the St.
Gothard, and to seek, beyond the great wall, more distant
and less known alps.

Sometimes rising, sometimes descending, always going
through a fine country, well watered and intersected with
luxuriant meadows, pretty dimpled valleys with clear, laughing brooks, orchards shady with apple trees, we reach in

thirty minutes the little lonely station of Rothkreuz, on the edge of a melancholy lake overgrown with reeds with broad green leaves, sharp pointed and curved like sabres.

Further on, this covered wooden bridge that spans the Reuss is the bridge of Gislikon, near which the last act of the Sonderbund was played.

After the capitulation of Fribourg, General Dufour led his troops against those of the forest cantons, who had occupied the St. Gothard, beaten the radicals of Tessin, and now, drawn up on the other side of the river, were awaiting the federal army.

The attack was made on the 23rd November, at eight in the morning.

The carabineers of Unterwalden, and the *landsturm*, composed of old men, women, and children, resisted the first shock; but the fire of the artillery soon became so violent that the Catholics were obliged to fall back. Salis, who commanded them, had been wounded in charging the artillery of Soleure. At three o'clock the federal army, fifty thousand strong, completely surrounded the demoralised troops of the Sonderbund league. Next day Lucerne capitulated, and the Provisional Government decreed the expulsion of the Jesuits.

In order to avoid the recurrence of a division between the confederate cantons, the supreme authority of the Confederation was vested in the Federal Assembly, composed of the National Council and the Council of the States : the latter numbering forty-four deputies, being two for each canton ; the former consisting of deputies elected by the people in the proportion of one deputy for twenty thousand souls.

The executive authority was placed in the hands of a Federal Council of seven members, nominated for one year by the Federal Assembly, and presided over by the President of the Confederation ; and the city of Berne was chosen as the seat of the central Government.

Since 1847 the republican form of the Swiss Confederation has remained the same; but a revision of the Constitution, voted by the people, has extended the powers of the central Government and swept away some antiquated laws. For instance, until the time of this revision, the punishment of flogging was still publicly practised.

Now we disappear into a tunnel. On emerging at the other end, we find ourselves near a second lake, the pretty Lake of Zug, set like a fine pearl in a necklace of woods and gardens and fertile fields and hills, over which white houses are scattered like tents.

I know no lake the banks of which are more graceful, and which reflects in its clear waters so varied a vegetation—of chestnuts with thick light-green foliage, rounded like a dome and as it were lighted up from within; of bushy apple-trees, glowing red with fruit, and slender plum-trees, quite blue with plums.

Villages and hamlets, framed in orchards that surround them like great hedges, are scattered on the capes and promontories that rise above the shores covered with willows and osier-beds; there are wide marshes dotted with motionless pools, in the midst of which great silvery water lilies shine like the pale image of a dead star. A few islets, covered with exuberant vegetation, look like baskets of flowers floating on the lake.

But to see this little Lake of Zug in all its slighted charm, its unknown grace, the tour of it must be made on foot or in a boat.

The boatman will relate to you its legends, he will tell you that fairies, illusive and fleeting as the mist, dance by moonlight on its waters. He will repeat to you the story of the young girl who one day lost her way, and found herself unexpectedly on the bank of the lake which was blazing in the sunshine and glittering like a sheet of gold.

For a long time she remained there, gazing with wide open, astonished eyes; then a strange feeling passed over her, she was overwhelmed with irresistible lassitude, sat down, and fell asleep. And while she slept she saw a beautiful youth, with curling locks and eyes clear as crystal, rise from the lake and send her a loving greeting. When she awoke it was night. She returned quickly to the village. She was in a burning fever, and had to be put to bed at once. Then she said to her mother, "Oh, mother, this is my last night! I have seen the youth of the lake; he looked at me so strangely, and I heard him speak words of love. Mother, I am his betrothed!" At this moment a slight sound broke the silence of the night, and a fair head with curling locks and eyes clear as crystal was seen at the window. And in the distance, shown clearly by the light of the moon, a gay marriage party approached. The young girl smiled, made an effort to rise, and fell back dead.

The train slowly ascends the valley, creeps along the foot of the Rigi, and crosses the ruins of Goldau. To right and left stand blocks of rock in all kinds of strange forms, like warriors' cairns or broken monumental columns. We seem to be among the fragments of a mountain shattered by the fall of a planet.

It is a tragic spot. A whole village still lies buried under those enormous blocks.

But in this cemetery Nature has resumed her right of conquest; she smiles all over it in flowers, invading at random in rich and fanciful ways; crowning the forehead of the rugged rocks with long, trailing briers, spreading her mosses with their golden gleams, and planting the grasses that spring in white and red tufts from all the fissures, waving in the wind like light plumes, and dropping their little seeds like showers of pearls.

And there are perennial plants,—purple thistles, ferns, epilobiums, campanulas, orchids in splendid spikes, growing straight up in fragrant bunches; strong grasses crunching under the teeth of the goats; a whole youth of robust and invading verdure stretches like a green covering, undulates like the waves of a grassy lake, rolls and stretches out among those enormous fragments that look like reefs on a rocky shore.

In the train the conversation turned on the terrible catastrophe.

" At what time did it take place ? " asked a young married lady who sat near me.

A little " Guide to the St. Gothard," which I had bought at Lucerne, enabled me to reply that the fall of the Rossberg, which buried three villages, two churches, a hundred houses, and four hundred persons, began on the 2nd September, 1806, with a simple avalanche of mud. The Rigi, all the hills, the whole landscape, had disappeared, as if drowned in the fog ; it rained in torrents ; for a month an incessant deluge had been falling, that melted down and diluted the soil into liquid, penetrated to the heart of the rocks, and dug out a multitude of invisible canals, mining and disintegrating the bases of the mountain.

Slowly the stream of mud flowed down, swallowing up meadows, overthrowing trees and châlets, carrying down earth and stones like a torrent that overflows its banks. The ravens and crows were flying in terror from the neighbouring forests, from which were heard deep crackling sounds, as if a subterraneous current were breaking the roots of the fir trees ; suddenly the earth trembled, the solid land became alive and was seized with convulsions, a horrible crash was heard, and the great wall of rocks known as the *Gemeinde-Maercht* hung tottering for a moment, and fell. Enormous blocks, some of them still covered with trees, shot through the air as if sent from a projectile, or tossed about like grains of dust ; while others, as if charged with dynamite, burst into a thousand pieces, and shot into the air innumerable fragments that met and crashed together like thunder.

In a few minutes the prosperous villages of Goldau, Busingen, and Lowertz were annihilated. The sound of the fall was so loud that it was heard as far as Zurich, and at the top of the alps of Uri.

For some minutes a black cloud, streaked with lurid red, covered the whole region; and when it passed away, the rich valley was nothing but a heap of stones and mud,—a land of misery and death.

As in all such great catastrophes, there were some miraculous deliverances.

Messeer Blaezzi, who had gone to bring the curé of Arth to exorcise the mountain and drive out the evil spirits who were carrying on their infernal machinations, came back just in time to see his house swallowed up before his eyes. But his wife and child were safe. His wife, doubtful whether to flee or to stay, had said to herself that if her child was sleeping, she would wait quietly till it awoke; but it lay smiling in its cradle, with bright, open eyes. She took it in her arms, fled, and was saved.

Blaezzi had a brother, whose châlet was five hundred steps below his own. He ran there. The châlet had disappeared; not a trace left, nothing,—not so much as a blade of grass. But presently something catches his eye—the end of a mattress projecting from the stiffening mud. He draws near and discovers a baby, his brother's child, with its little hands crossed on its breast, breathing softly in a peaceful sleep in the midst of the frightful wreck.

We go along the side of the pretty little Lake of Lowertz, into which also fell enormous fragments of the Rossberg; great blocks of rock now covered with a verdant drapery of shrubs, and wearing young firs like plumes of victory.

On a little island, beside a farmhouse bright with the warm colour of its red tiles, are seen some weather-stained ruins; and close by is a chapel, whose white tower rises above the trees like the long neck of a stork. The ruins are those of a castle, in which, in the time of the Austrian rule, lived a wicked lord, the dread of all the country round.

One day, when taking a walk, he met one of the most

beautiful girls of a neighbouring village, and made his people carry her off. Soon after the revolted Swiss burned the castle and slew its master.

But, says the legend, his punishment continued after his death. Every time the storms howl, a woman's voice is heard uttering cries in the ruins, and the ghost of a young girl armed with a firebrand is seen pursuing a knight. She pursues him to the bitter end, rushing fiercely across the piled-up fragments, over the heaps of stones, over the broken walls, over the skeleton staircases hanging in the air like ladders; she follows him furiously, shaking her Eumenides torch, and he still flees before her until, no longer able to escape, he throws himself into the lake, which closes over him.

Those Swiss lakes blossom all over with legends. Here is another of them.

In former days, on the side of the Lake of Lowertz, a handsome white church was seated like a queen on a high rising ground. Every Sunday crowds flocked to it from far and near. And as the church stood alone, and there was no inn in the neighbourhood, everybody brought their own provisions and wine with them.

At first all went on in a becoming manner. After service the faithful sat down on the grass in the shade of the trees, and quietly took their refreshments. Then, when the bells rang for vespers, they returned to take their places piously in the church.

But gradually these good ways got out of use. Some men installed themselves on the steps of the church to drink and gamble, shouting as if they were in a tavern.

It was a scandal which the priest himself could not put a stop to.

One Sunday, when the playing and drinking company was more numerous than usual, and the drinking was carried to excess, the sky all at once grew dark, great black clouds gathered and hid the heavens, and the thunder burst forth.

The gamblers, absorbed in their stakes, went on with their play, and the drinkers, who had jugs of wine beside them, went on with their drinking.

Then the lake was seen boiling and swelling and rising, and still mounting higher, till it surrounded the little hill and made it into an island; and mounting still till it covered the lowest of the steps, at the top of which the players were sitting.

They went on with their game.

The lake still rose and rose; players and drinkers were engulfed, and finally the church itself utterly disappeared.

Ever since that time, when people are sailing over that place on Sunday, they hear distinctly, at the hours of morning and evening service, sweet silvery sounds coming up from the depths of the water. It is the passing bell of the submerged church, still sounding for the poor victims.

The two *Mythens*, raising their dark, rocky pyramids into the blue depths of the sky, where a few light white clouds are floating like flights of birds, announce our approach to Schwyz, the large and rich village of six thousand inhabitants, which has given its name and arms to the Swiss Confederation.

The iron road describes a long curve, and comes back across a little earthly Paradise of green meadows and fruit-trees, to the Lake of the Four Cantons, at Brunnen. There is something overflowing, something extraordinary, in the fertility of this whole region; the alluvial deposits left by the Muotta have made it into a real land of Canaan,—a mosaic of meadows and wheatfields, orchards and fine woods.

Brunnen, at the gate of the Axenstrasse,—that splendid road cut out like an open gallery on the face of the rocks above the lake,—is the port of Schwyz; and of all the picturesque and romantic bays on the Lake of the Four Cantons, it is the best known and the one oftenest reproduced in photography and painting.

4

The site is imposing, wild, with an austere, almost religious, grandeur. But for the incessant sound of the trains
and boats, setting off and arriving in constant succession,
one might feel withdrawn there as in the depths of a calm
retreat of liberty, solitude, and peace, in a soft nest of verdure and flowers hung by the side of the water.

Again the train is in motion. It disappears under the
mountain, then emerges to daylight and winds like a great
black lizard along the steep banks of the lake, following its
long undulations; the graceful bays, cut into bowers, the
creeks, the gulfs and fiords, in which the firs lie reflected in
delicate shadow.

The train is going too quickly; we feel inclined to call to
the driver, " Take time ! "

And again the train plunges into a tunnel, like a huge
black beast going back into his den; and each time it
emerges the landscape is different, either softer or more
stern. We pass by places where the lake is narrowed or
confined in a deep gorge, and looks like the Rhine or Danube.
We greet, in passing, the lonely plateau of Rütli, which a
national subscription has made safe from the profanations of
hotel-keepers.

From point to point, from one bridge to another, out of
one tunnel into another, we reach the end of the lake, at
Fluelen.

In former times, before the opening of the St. Gothard,
what a scene of animation this little port was! And that
Altorf road, how bustling and gay it was !

Cabriolets dragged all the way from the heart of Italy;
old episcopal coaches, fitted up with what was once violet
velvet, but is now moth-eaten and faded to pale blue; basket
carriages, surmounted with a red-fringed linen canopy; Irish
cars, wagonettes, phaetons, with nothing Olympian but the
name; hundreds of vehicles of every age and form and
country, were packed together at the landing-place, like a
huge exhibition of coach-building; and above them all

towered the federal *diligence*, painted canary yellow, loaded
with a mountain of luggage, and drawn by five white horses,
driven by a most imposing postillion. The tourists, for
whom the whole greedy band of drivers, porters, and guides
lay in wait as for their prey, were harassed, seized on, taken
possession of, pulled this way and that, half torn in pieces ;
and in the heat of the battle some lost their hats, some their
sticks, some their wives ; children were carried off and placed
as prisoners and hostages in the carriages.

It was a confusion of shouts and oaths in every language
—an indescribable tumult, that was only allayed when the
last of those vehicles got into motion, and set off with a
hollow rumbling of old iron, and fled, as if in a retreat, amid
the loud cracking of the drivers' whips.

Then what amusing scenes went on ! A stout lady, her
arms bent like the handles of a pitcher over two great parcels,
all out of breath with running, and as red as a lobster, is in
pursuit of her dog, her shawl trailing like a sheet behind
her. A gentleman already in a carriage, is shouting to the
driver to stop ; he has forgotten his wife. A mother-in-law
makes signals of distress to a coachman who is going off
with her daughter and son-in-law, leaving her behind. An
Englishwoman in curl papers, with a manual of conversation
in her hand, is saying to the coachman she has engaged :
" Attendez-vô. Jé veux avoir le times de prendre oune tasse
de thé avec de la rhoum dedans." And then there is also
Bompart, the famous Bompart of Tarascon, the friend of Tartarin, relating to the Swiss ladies of Lucerne the story of
William Tell, the shooting of the apple, the flight across the
lake, the tragic ambush of the mountain way. And amidst
the stirring, buzzing, noisy crowd, hotel porters are touting,
and little peasant girls in short petticoats and white stockings offer edelweiss, bunches of alpenrose, carved needle-
cases, rock crystals, and pen-holders with a bear turning a
somersault on the top.

We enter the valley of the Reuss, and follow the line of

the old St. Gothard road, poor forsaken thing, towards which the locomotive seems to send a mocking whistle as it goes.

Here is Altorf, recalling Karl Girardet's drawings; a church and a square tower stand out picturesquely from a background of mountains, woods, and orchards; and in a square stands a fountain surrounded by merry gossips, and near it a statue of William Tell. Lying luxuriously in the full sunshine, which pours down in golden radiance on its blooming gardens, its trees laden with fruit, its cool, fresh, grassy slopes, the capital of Canton Uri looks like a great water-colour painting.

In the church is preserved a Nativity attributed to Van-Dyck, and in the Town Hall are some old flags won on the bloody field of Morgarten.

The building above the town on the mountain side, solidly built like a fortress, is the oldest Capuchin monastery in Switzerland. These " sappers in God's militia," as a German poet, I think, calls them, were widely scattered formerly in the High Alps. They were sent forward to clear paganism and heresy out of the way, to erect bridges and open communications with the faith.

Popular legends have perpetuated the memory of several of those convents.

One summer day a Capuchin of Altorf was taking his siesta in the open air, under a bower of honeysuckle at the end of the garden, along which wound a cool path, gay with wild roses and garlands of convolvulus.

The sun was hot, the flies vicious, and the good monk's nose so purple !

Flies have no respect for the Church. They ran about on him, scratching him with their little feet finer than hairs, and tickling him with their gauzy wings.

The monk awoke with a start, and snatching his handkerchief from the depths of his sleeve, he drove off the troublesome insects ; then throwing himself back with a yawn, he was about to return to the slumber so inopportunely broken, when his eyes, which were just closing, opened wide.

Along the garden path, in the full sunshine, was coming a beautiful peasant girl, with fresh, rosy cheeks, and fair hair like an aureola.

The monk rose and went to meet her.

" Give me," said he, " the bouquet that you have in your belt, and permit me to touch your pretty hand with my lips."

" My bouquet," replied the girl, " is for my betrothed, and my hand belongs to him."

" But do you not know," replied the monk, " that I am the superior of the convent, and that you owe me obedience ? "

He was going to seize the bouquet, but suddenly the earth shook under his feet, a cloud of smoke enveloped him, and before he had time to call for help, his neck was caught in a running knot, and he found himself tied up, high and short, to the branch of a tree.

And while he remained dangling there, the girl fled back to the village and threw herself, trembling, into the arms of her betrothed.

From that time, says the chronicle, no monk of that convent ever greets the pretty peasants of the valley.

Now the country becomes more barren, the rocks stand bare like ramparts ; and in the midst of the wild solitude, a little meadow makes a green spot like a block of malachite rolled down from the mountain.

On this meadow the people of Uri hold, every year, on the first Sunday in May, their *Landsgemeine*, that is, their popular assembly, whose duty it is to nominate the magistrates, to approve the accounts of the Government, and to deliberate on proposed laws.

The crowd begins to arrive in the morning from all directions, the men with their woollen caps, and in their mouths a wooden pipe with a little chain and a horn shank ; the women with their head-dress of black lace erected in a crest, their massive silver combs spread out like filigree roses incrusted with stones, and planted in the chignon at the back of the head.

There is a compact crowd round the open-air shops of the sellers of wine, beer, warm sausages, and coffee. And people are continually arriving in long processions.

At last loud trumpet blasts awaken the echoes of the mountains, and along the road from Altorf a grand train, with military escort, and banners displayed, is seen approaching. First march two archers in the costume of the 15th century, carrying on their shoulders the Horn of Uri; then hussars, in cloaks of cantonal colours; and lastly the magistrates in carriages.

Each of them takes his place on the circular tiers of seats that surround the little platform reserved for the members of the Government. The Landamman seats himself behind a table covered with a green cloth, on which are laid the account books for the period of his administration. Near him, supported on two drums, is the flag of Uri.

The soldiers pile their arms, the Landamman rises and opens the assembly by invoking the blessing of Heaven, and then delivers what is really a speech from the throne, in which, before turning to local business, he makes a review of foreign policy, noting the most marked events in the East and in the West. Then a vote of approval of the public accounts is asked for, the new budget is arranged, and the new magistrates elected by a show of hands. Everybody has the right to speak and to discuss the doings of those to whom the power has been entrusted. Is there any more democratic manner of carrying on a government? It is a republican republic; a government of the people by the people. And with what order and calmness these popular meetings are carried on; held as they have been for four centuries, always in the same place, at the same time, on the same day, and never disturbed by any strife, or any occurrence but such as are incident to parliaments!

Farther on, the valley contracts, and is confined in a narrow gorge. The railway and the road both run near the Reuss, which flows along foaming and brawling, tearing itself on the rolling stones that form its bed.

On the right, opens, like a beautiful side-scene, a valley that looks almost desolate, but has a wonderful charm in its picturesque beauty; with waterfalls leaping, bounding, throwing themselves from rock to rock, and then forming little fairy alpine lakes, to the banks of which the eagle and the chamois come down to drink. A dazzling sun is shining in a bright blue sky, in which float a few clouds lighter than gauze. Fresh breezes come down from the mountains, and softly wave the silken heads of the ripe grasses, and stir the bells of the campanulas and the red spikes of the orchis.

And at the very end of the valley the icy head of the Bristenstock glitters like a diamond. In the evening, in the dusk, when the valley is already totally wrapt in shadow, this giant peak sparkles with light as if cascades of melted gold were trickling down its sides.

"What beautiful weather, madam!" said I to my neighbour, by way of resuming the conversation which had been suspended since leaving Altorf.

"Charming weather, sir. And it is this fine weather which has led you to cross the St. Gothard?"

"Yes, madam; and you also, doubtless?"

"Oh, as for me, sir, I am travelling because I am obliged to do so. My husband is waiting for me at the other side of the mountain, at Lugano. I have been to see a sister at Lucerne, and I am on my way to rejoin my husband, who delights in nothing but high alps and dangerous expeditions, and has chosen the Engadine this year as the scene of his exploits."

"A superb region, known especially by English and Germans, but almost unknown to French tourists. There is no inhabited country higher than that, except some parts of the Cordilleras."

"My husband means to explore the Bernina group."

It must be understood that the Piz Bernina is something like the Matterhorn of the Engadine.

I told my companion that I was going in that direction, and that I intended to stay for a week at Pontrésina.

She had been advised by her physician to try the waters of St. Moritz, so she meant to be there while her husband was wandering over the mountain. She was an Italian from Milan, and her sister had married a Swiss gentleman.

With that exaggerated, somewhat theatrical admiration that belongs to the southern races, she was continually going into ecstasies, with grand phrases and poetical exclamations at the beauty of the landscape, and gesticulating with her half bare arms, which were encircled with gold bracelets. Her dress was exquisite, in good taste, which is rare in Italian ladies, and revealed a fine and original mind. A felt hat, turned up at one side and held there by an owl's claw, covered her pretty head of dark red golden hair, and shaded her black eyes. She wore a man's collar, and a jacket turned back with brown satin with a red satin hood. A Tyrolese glove perfectly fitted her hand of Byzantine delicacy.

We had passed through the little village of Silenen, with its wooden houses thinly sown along the bank of the Reuss, looking as if they were crushed under the heavy stones that hold on their roofs. Then, passing above Amsteg, nestling in the gorge of the Maderan,—a wild and grandly picturesque valley,—we disappear into a tunnel. It is here that the dangerous region of the avalanches begins. During the winter and spring the frozen masses become loosened, slide down those bare slopes and roll over, dropping or bounding into the valley which they fill with their ruins. To be safe from this, the railway has been obliged to hide in the mountain,—to flee by a subterraneous path.

Here, then, begin the great works of art of the St. Gothard.

With what boldness all those bridges and viaducts have

been thrown across abysses the horrible depth of which the eye has not time to search ! And what thousands of people have been brought in from Italy and Germany to hollow out all these galleries, to dig into the very heart of the mountain, to pierce it and carve it in open work, like a colossal ivory ornament.

The train rushes into the heart of the earth, and there makes a thousand turns and circuits with the speed and agility of a mole.

The sensation in coming out again to the daylight is very strange. You have no longer any idea where you are, you can give yourself no account of the way you have come, you have completely lost your bearings, just as if you had lost your way. And you are quite bewildered with this plunge into night,—this drowning in darkness. The train goes down wild declivities, winds, turns, disappears, comes back, keeping always above the precipice. On all sides hang walls of rock of a sanguine red, moist with a greenish ooze. And far below, in the black, mysterious depths, the Reuss howls like a torrent of the lower regions.

We arrive at the Monk's Leap.

Legend relates that a monk, fleeing with a young girl whom he had carried off, was pursued by her two brothers ; and reaching this spot, he seized the girl in his arms and leapt across the gorge, twenty-two feet broad, with the Reuss roaring below.

The devil was supposed to have come to his aid. Or perhaps the monk was no other than Satan himself.

A church stands like a sentinel on a steep hill. It is the church of Wasen. By skilfully arranged windings, now crossing the Maienbach, now the Reuss, the train reaches the entrance of a new tunnel, which swallows it up ; in a few minutes it reappears, and winds, beneath the open sky, along the perpendicular sides of the mountain. The whole of this part of the way is enough to make one giddy. It is like the work of sorcerers or of new Titans.

And now the view widens out into blue distances, and long vistas of rocks rent into great fissures and lighted up with a sparkling mica of snow and ice. Nearer, on a high, arid platform, some little houses, crowded into a flock, cautiously approach the edge of a gulf, at the bottom of which a wild stream is foaming and struggling.

This is Geschenen, at the entrance of the great tunnel, the meeting place of the upper gorges of the Reuss, the valley of Urseren, of the Oberalp, and of the Furka.

Geschenen has now the calm tranquillity of old age.

But during the nine years that it took to bore the great tunnel, what juvenile activity there was here, what feverish eagerness in this village, crowded, inundated, overflowed by workmen from Italy, from Tessin, from Germany and France! One would have thought that out of that dark hole, dug out in the mountain, they were bringing nuggets of gold.

On all the roads nothing was to be seen but bands of workmen arriving, with miners' lamps hung to their old soldiers' knapsacks. Nobody could tell how they were all to be lodged. One double bed was occupied in succession by twenty-four men in twenty-four hours. Some of the workmen set up their establishments in barns; in all directions movable canteens sprung up, built all awry and hardly holding together, and in mean sheds, doubtful, bad-looking places, the German hastened to sell his adulterated brandy.

In front of the houses, Piedmontese in pantaloons of ribbed velvet, held in at the waist by a red flannel band, and shirt open over the bony, bronzed chest, lay stretched in the sunshine, playing at *mora*, shouting like street boys; while other Italians played bowls, and laughed beyond measure if, by accident, their ball, by a succession of bounds, disappeared in the Reuss.

In the evenings, in the little restaurants, national airs were played on accordions, calling up, as in a dream, before all these exiles condemned to the mines, beloved scenes of their fatherland, little paths bordered with orange and citron trees fragrant with blossom, pretty village-girls dancing in a ring under trees laden with fruit. They saw again the spire of their native village, their old parents in the cottage with its door standing open to the fowls and the goats, to the poor and to the sunshine; the bower of vines under which they exchanged the first kiss. And then an attack of home-sickness came upon them and gave them no peace; and one by one they dropped away, like cowards or deserters. One workman only is mentioned who stayed from the beginning to the end of the work, Pietro Chirio by name. To him was given the honour of striking the last blow of the pick-axe, of opening to the light the stone door of the great tunnel, of being the first to greet the sunlight, the blue heavens of Italy, on the other side of the pierced Alps.

The knowledge of being about to travel for more than $9\frac{1}{4}$ miles underground is for many travellers suggestive of reflections by no means pleasant. My neighbour, the young Milanese lady, made little nervous starts which she tried hard to conceal. And yet she had twice before made the passage; but it was too strong for her; she said it caused her a strange emotion, an indefinable discomfort, as if she were in a ship driven before the tempest.

The St. Gothard tunnel is about $1\frac{2}{3}$ mile longer than that of Mont Cenis, and more than 3 miles longer than that of Arlberg. While the train is passing with a dull rumbling sound under these gloomy vaults, let us explain how the great work of boring the Alps was accomplished.

The mechanical work of perforation was begun simultaneously on the north and south sides of the mountain, working towards the same point, so as to meet towards the middle of the boring.

The waters of the Reuss and the Tessin supplied the necessary motive power for working the screws attached to machinery for compressing the air. The borers applied to the rock the piston of a cylinder made to rotate with great rapidity by the pressure of air reduced to one-twentieth of its ordinary volume; then when they had made holes sufficiently deep, they withdrew the machines and charged the mines with dynamite. Immediately after the explosion, streams of wholesome air were liberated, which dissipated the smoke; then the *débris* was cleared away, and the borers returned to their place. The same work was thus carried on, day and night, for nine consecutive years.

On the Geschenen side all went well; but on the other side, on the Italian slope, unforeseen obstacles and difficulties had to be overcome. Instead of having to encounter the solid rock, they found themselves among a moving soil formed by the deposit of glaciers and broken by streams of water. Springs burst out, like the jet of a fountain, under the stroke of the pick, flooding and driving away the workmen. For twelve months they seemed to be in the midst of a lake. But nothing could damp the ardour of the contractor, Favre.

His troubles were greater still when the undertaking had almost been suspended for want of money, when the workmen struck in 1875, and when, two years later, the village of Arola was destroyed by fire. And how many times, again and again, the mason-work of the vaulted roof gave way and fell!

Certain "bad places," as they were called, cost more than nine hundred pounds per yard.

In the interior of the mountain the thermometer marked 86 degrees (Fahr.), but so long as the tunnel was still not completely bored, the workmen were sustained by a kind of fever, and made redoubled efforts. Discouragement and desertion did not appear among them till the goal was almost reached.

The great tunnel passed, we find ourselves fairly in Italy.

The mulberry trees, with silky white bark and delicate, transparent leaves; the chestnuts, with enormous trunks like cathedral columns; the vine, hanging to high trellises supported by granite pillars, its festoons as capricious as the feasts of those who partake too freely of its fruits; the white tufty heads of the maize tossing in the breeze; all that strong and luxuriant vegetation through which waves of moist warm air are passing; those flowers of rare beauty, of a grace and brilliancy that belong only to privileged zones;—all this indicates a more robust and fertile soil, and a more fervid sky, than those of the upper villages which we have just left.

Faido, the capital of the Leventina, lies luxuriously in the rich valley of the Ticino, which bears at its beginning the name of Val Bedretto, then that of Leventina, and finally that of the Riviera. The florid style of Italian architecture is seen in the stone houses with colonnades, in the church with its tall campanile, bearing a clock, the face of which, with its gilded pointers, is turned towards the village like a motionless, never-setting sun.

Quite near Faido the Fimmegna springs from a fissure in the rocks, spreads out its snowy sheet of water that floats above some sawmills, whose wheels it sets in motion, and falls in a noisy cascade into the troubled bed of the Ticino.

Everywhere strong, abundant vegetation, pretty, happy-looking houses under the trees and among the grass, terraces on which are clustered villages garlanded with vines. We are getting quite down into the bright, luxuriant regions of the Italian Alps.

The delight of people from the north may be imagined when they thus find themselves suddenly transported into a kind of promised land, into the midst of a sunny, blooming scene, with the freshness of an oasis, fragrant as a garden, under a soft blue sky in which light clouds rise and disappear like a distant flight of wild birds. And the enchantment goes on as we get farther from the great mass of the

St. Gothard and the pale summits of the glaciers; and the surprise is greater and more delicious each time we emerge from these corkscrew tunnels that seem to wind upon themselves like a top, the deep darkness of which brings out more magnificently the landscape, dazzling in light, that comes after.

And now we find ourselves in the lower basin of the valley, opposite the village of Giornico, the name of which is a glorious one in the history of the Swiss nation. From the time when the Duke of Burgundy had lost in a first battle his treasures, his army in a second, and his life in a third, the Swiss, says Zschokke, were no longer afraid of anybody. Now it came to pass that one day some subjects of the Duke of Milan cut down some wood in a forest of the Val Livino. Immediately some young men of Uri, stirred to revenge, crossed the St. Gothard and pillaged and maltreated the inhabitants of some Milanese villages.

Instead of punishing the aggressors, Canton Uri took them under her protection, declared war against the Milanese, and summoned the Confederates to their help.

In spite of the snows accumulated in the valleys and gorges of the St. Gothard, and the long, cold nights of December, ten thousand Swiss crossed the mountain and descended the Alps.

The soldiers of Uri had already taken Bellinzona by storm, without regard to the negotiations opened at Milan. This precipitation displeased the Confederates, who had come rather as mediators than as combatants. They withdrew, leaving only six hundred soldiers round Giornico for the defence of the Leventina.

The Duke of Milan considered it a favourable moment to call this handful of men to account.

He sent against them Count Borelli, commander of the Lombard forces, with an army of ten thousand soldiers.

The Swiss, warned of the approach of the enemy, had flooded the surrounding meadow with the waters of the Ticino, and withdrawn to the hill-side.

When the Italians arrived, they found themselves confronted by a great frozen plain, on which they were imprudent enough to venture. The Swiss, who had their mountain shoes roughened with strong frost nails, were only waiting for this; they rolled down on the enemy like an avalanche, and put them completely to rout. Fifteen hundred Lombards were cut to pieces in a few hours. The snow was red with blood as far as Bellinzona.

A cloth merchant of Lucerne, the intrepid Frischaus Theilig, was the hero of the day. With his long heavy sword he seemed to mow down the enemy's ranks; he passed on, leaving behind him a ridge of mangled corpses.

The Duke of Milan was compelled to purchase peace at the price of 25,000 florins and giving up the Leventina.

After crossing the Brenno, the train stops at Biasca, the capital of the Riviera. A fine waterfall pours from the top of a lofty precipice, floats for moment like a ribbon of silver, and then falls again in sparkling jets and silvery dust.

The descent continues along the course of the river, between two chains of mountains, in a gorge into which other valleys open.

A stop of a few minutes is made at Castione at the entrance to the valley of Mesocco, which leads to the Col of the Bernardino, in the Grisons Canton. Then the train proceeds, describing long circuits; we catch sight, through a far-off rosy haze, of the three turrets that rise in feudal style above Bellinzona, still proudly fortified behind her ancient ramparts.

Bellinzona is to the people of Milan the gate of the north, and to the men of the north it is one of the gates of the south. The Italians and the Swiss long disputed the possession of this strategic pass, this key to the St. Gothard and central Switzerland.

Leaving Bellinzona, we come to Monte Cenere, which we climb half-way up in zig-zags, and then pass through a tunnel less than a mile long.

On emerging from the second tunnel, beyond a wild and narrow gorge, there lies suddenly before us, as in a gorgeous fairyland or the landscape of a dream, the blue expanse of lake Lugano, with its setting of green meadows and purple mountains, with the many-coloured village spires, and the great white fronts of the hotels and villas. Oh, what a wonderful picture!

We feel as if we were going down into an enchanted garden that had been hidden by the great snowy walls of the Alps. The air is full of the perfume of roses and jessamine. The hedges are in flower, butterflies are dancing, insects are humming, birds are singing. Up above, in the mountain, is snow, ice, winter, and silence; here there is sunshine, life, joy, love,—all the living delights of spring and summer.

Golden harvests are shining on the plains, and the lake in the distance is like a piece of the sky brought down to earth.

Lugano is already Italy, not only because of the richness of the soil and the magnificence of the vegetation, but also as regards the language, the manners, and the picturesque costumes. In each valley the dress is different; in one place the women wear a short skirt, an apron held in by a girdle, and a bright coloured bodice; in another they wear a cap above which is a large shady hat; in the Val Maroblio they have a woollen dress not very different from that of the Capuchins.

The men have not the square figure, the slow, heavy walk of the people of Bâle and Lucerne; they are brisk, vigorous, easy; and the women have something of the wavy suppleness of vine branches twining among the trees.

These people have the happy, childlike joyousness, the frank goodnature, of those who live in the open air, who do not shut themselves up in their houses, but grow freely like the flowers under the strong, glowing sunshine.

At every street corner sellers are sitting behind baskets

of extraordinary vegetables and magnificent fruit; and under the arcades that run along the houses, big grocers in shirt sleeves come at intervals to their shop doors to take breath, like hippopotami coming out of the water for the same purpose. In this town, ultramontane in its piety, the bells of churches and covents are sounding all day long, and women are seen going to make their evening prayer together in the nearest chapel.

But if the fair sex in Lugano are diligent in frequenting the churches, they by no means scorn the cafés. After sunset the little tables that are all over the great square are surrounded by an entire population of men and women.

How gay and amusing those Italian cafés are! full of sound and colour, with their red and blue striped awnings, their advanced guard of little tables under the shade of the orange-trees, and their babbling, stirring, gesticulating company. The waiters, in black vest and leather slippers, a corner of their apron tucked up in their belt, run with the speed of kangaroos, carrying on metal plates syrups of every shade, ices, sweets in red, yellow, or green pyramids.

Between seven and nine o'clock the whole society of Lugano defiles before you. There are lawyers with their wives, doctors with their daughters, bankers, professors, merchants, public officials, with whom are sometimes mixed stout, comfortable, jovial-looking canons, wrapping themselves in the bitter smoke of a *regalia*, as in a cloud of incense.

When night has fallen and the stars shine out, travelling musicians and singers come and form groups in the square, and improvise a concert. Fresh, clear voices sing with enthusiasm in praise of Italy with her blue sky, the beautiful daughters of Naples with their burning eyes, and ring out to the sound of harps the united names of Garibaldi and Liberty.

After returning to my hotel I remained for a long time leaning on the balcony of my room, inhaling with delight

5

the perfume stolen by the night breezes from the orange-trees, watching the lake disappearing into the mysterious darkness, and near the shore boats lying at anchor, their sails furled, and their motionless masts with transverse bars making them into crosses. Towards midnight the moon rose, round and luminous, like an enormous glass ball lit up from within with electric light. The lake became covered with little glittering spangles, silvery points that were reflected again and again in the blue, transparent shadow. The surrounding mountains were sleeping in the silent night, while faint sounds were still audible from the town, and some lights were still burning in the hotel.

Below me, on a little terrace, two shadowy figures were walking up and down. They sat down on a bench, and then the lady threw off her hat and gently laid her head on her companion's shoulder. By the soft, clear light of the moon I recognised my travelling companion, the young Italian, who had joined her husband at Lugano.

CHAPTER V.

THE next day—it was a Sunday—I took the boat about ten o'clock, in order to reach Chiavenna the same evening.

However little one may be skilled in organising, calculating his time, and making a little itinerary by studying maps and time-tables beforehand, yet how many things he can see in the course of one day!

He has perhaps a few short fever-fits; but then what delight for the mind, what a feast for the eyes, is that succession of landscapes, pictures, and scenes that pass before you, occupy your attention unceasingly, and keep you wakeful and interested from morning to night.

The day begins splendidly. It is a joy to be alive! The sky is blue, the lake is blue, deep, changeless, metallic blue; and as the steamer carries us forward, Lugano, with its white houses on the vine-clad hills under the shadowing chestnuts, rapidly recedes from our sight.

The deck is crowded with families in holiday attire; women in gaudy dresses, and hats trimmed with ribbons or red feathers; men in complete suits of yellow nankeen, with green, blue, or red neck-ties, gold chains festooned across their vests, branches of coral mounted as pins, and large rings on their fingers.

As I walk up and down smoking a cigar, one of the passengers comes to meet me, and drawing a long *virginia* from a green leather case, says,—

" May I trouble you for a light, sir ? "

" With pleasure." And we enter into conversation.

" Have you come far ? "

" From Paris."

At the word the little man draws himself up, his eyes sparkle, he draws a few rapid whiffs of his cigar.

" I also," he exclaims, " have been in Paris! It was in the time of the Empire. I was in a hairdresser's shop, but I plotted much more than I dressed hair. Orsini and I were a pair of friends. I played a famous stroke for him on the night of the bombs, and I had no more than time to make my escape. I stayed a long time in hiding at Marseilles ; but at last I found an opportunity of embarking for Genoa, and returned to Lugano."

" To join Mazzini ? "

" Mazzini was in fact, at that time, directing the whole revolutionary movement in Europe, from that little Swiss town. He had emissaries whom he sent to carry his orders in all directions. It was at Lugano that he prepared the emancipation of Italy. Are you aware that he was in close communication with Cavour ? The imperial Government was well informed about it all. They incessantly demanded from the Federal Council the arrest, or at least the expulsion, of Mazzini. At last it was decided that, in order not to displease the emperor something must be done. Mazzini, warned the day before that he would be arrested in the night, concealed himself with some friends, and I was the person whom he left to represent him. In Paris I had done some work in the theatres. I disguised myself so skilfully that even Mazzini's maid-servant was deceived, and took me for her master. Towards eleven o'clock the police surround the house, the gendarmes come upstairs, exhibit their warrant, and I follow them to the municipal prison. There was so little expectation of seeing Mazzini arrested that they

were puzzled what to do with me. I carrried on the mys-
tification till the morning; and then it was telegraphed in
all directions that the dangerous conspirator had succeeded
in making his escape."

We had arrived at a little station at the foot of Monte
Caprino. There the whole holiday crowd got out, the hair-
dresser included, who was redolent of pomade, and who
advised me to conceal my cigars from the Italian custom-
house officers.

"They lately," said he, "made me pay duty on the cigar
that I had in my mouth, on the pretext that I had just newly
lighted it."

Monte Caprino, a real mountain of goats, as its name indicates, with steep, rocky paths, and coarse, yellow herbage,
and deep winding crevasses, through which the tempests
roar, rises between Monte Bré and Monte San Salvatore, at
the extremity of the bay of Lugano. The pretty little red
cottages with green blinds, which seem grouped into a
village on the terraces of the mountain, are summer pavilions,
country houses to which the inhabitants of Lugano repair
to devote to Bacchus the days which the Romish calendar
devotes to religion.

Monte Caprino, hollowed out into grottoes and excavations,
is a vast store-house, an immense wine-cellar, in which huge
barrels lie hidden in obscurity, like monsters in the time of
the cave-dwellers.

Nowhere are the wines of the Valtelline and of Upper Italy
better preserved, nowhere can *Asti* be obtained colder and
more sparkling. It is drunk from heavy earthenware cups,
as if there were a fear of glasses being carried away by a
gust of wind.

The tuning of musical instruments, and trying over of
airs on the accordion, are already preparing for the afternoon dances.

The steamer goes on towards the north. At our left is

Monte Bré, the summit of which is reached in two hours and a half, on foot, from Lugano, going round by the other side of the mountain. Here, at the foot of the mountain, is Grandia, with stone houses rising in pyramids in the midst of vineyards and hanging gardens.

Next comes San Mametto, surrounded by fields of silky tufted maize, which lie below a strange, martial-looking village, with walls built like the ramparts of a strong castle. The shores of the lake become more thinly peopled; but this absence of houses and villas makes their beauty none the less; on the contrary, it gives an added charm, by helping us to lose sight of money and speculation.

A little farther on, however, villages are seen perched high up on the hills that rise direct from the lake, and churches that look like great white birds sitting motionless with necks stretched upwards.

Leaving Osteno behind us, we enter a bay overhung by lofty mountains, and at the head of a peaceful, charming creek we reach Porlezza, with its many-coloured houses and its coquettish-looking new church, which stands beside the old one, like a brilliant lily beside a weather-beaten trunk.

From Porlezza to Menaggio we make the journey in carriages, across a bright, dusty plain, a dried up marsh, in the midst of which the little Lake of Piano lies glowing like a sapphire, enclosed in a golden frame of tall grasses.

At Crocce we are again in a fertile region, amidst laurels, orange, and mulberry trees; we feel thoroughly on Italian soil; the vines hang out their ruddy clusters like offerings to the god Sol, the maize sends up tall green spears, the enormous copper-coloured gourds are like strange fruits that have dropped from the moon, bringing with them its form and colour. And like a splendid background through a beautiful scene of verdure, is seen in the distance the Lake of Como, its grand blue line lying along below the hills and mountains that surround it, all of them covered with luxuriant vegetation and dotted over with houses, elegant villas and hotels like palaces. I am going to wait for the Colico boat at Cadenabbia, which is reached in thirty minutes by the road which winds along the lake side like a long, dusty ribbon. Cadenabbia is a hermitage of love, a happy and tranquil retreat, an asylum for modest pleasure or for calm repose; one of those corners of Paradise to which people go to hide their happiness or to plunge into a delicious Nirvana.

A few hotels,—Bellevue, Belle Ile, Britannia, a restaurant, a café, a score of one-storey houses, with two or three windows each, smiling under their festoons of vines; a shore of fine sand lapped by the blue waves; a whole flotilla of gaily-coloured boats; a terraced walk shaded by large trees, through which the light only comes caressing and soft as the twilight, or cool as the dawn; a historical villa, the saloons of which are museums, standing in a fairy garden that reaches down to the lake, with marble fountains and statues, avenues of magnolias and orange trees, sudden openings to splendid views;—such is Cadenabbia, a little hidden spot on these magnificent banks of the Lake of Como, less praised, less puffed, less visited than the banks of Lake Maggiore, and yet more profoundly peaceful, more powerfully attractive to loving or bleeding hearts.

And now that we have admired the treasures of the Villa Carlotta, let us take a boat to the eastern shore and spend an hour at Bellagio, on the point of the promontory that divides the lake into two arms.

With his long white beard spread out like a fan, Baptisto Gesarrio, my boatman, looks like an ancient mythological pilot.

And in this blue atmosphere, on this blue water, facing those blue mountains, softly wrapped in this celestial and elysian light, the soul becomes so light and ethereal, that it really seems to be freed from its material garment, released from the body that weighed it down and chained it to earth.

Slowly the little boat makes its way, raising little waves and silvery eddies which pursue and overtake each other, part and meet again, and finally join and are lost in each other.

Butterflies flutter around us, and hang quivering in the warm air, like pure white souls that have come to meet us—infantile, virginal souls.

Bellagio is not nearly so pleasant as Cadenabbia. We find there all the ugliness of civilization ; a nasty street, bearing the name of Victor Emmanuel ; ragged, filthy, brawling children, yawning gendarmes, and a villa which, in spite of its name, Villa Serbelloni, people have not been afraid to transform into a *hôtel-pension* for families ; and in the grounds of which you may not walk without buying a ticket, as if you were going to a concert in a tea-garden.

Some pictures by old painters remain hanging in the corridors of the ancient villa, and between these are pasted up advertisements of shipping companies, railway time-tables on yellow paper, addresses of photographers and confectioners, and hotel announcements.

The whole hotel is like an auction room ; it has the same gloom and funereal odour.

The park would counterbalance all those horrid things by its seductive parterres, the variety of its plants and perfumes, the beauty of its magnolias and palms, and the diversity of its splendid points of view, if at every turn of a path, in every walk, you did not meet some of those travelling Englishwomen of whom Heine speaks, a kind of plum-puddings, with eyes of grapes, and a throat of roast beef, festooned with bands of horse radish ! They camp everywhere, climb everywhere, seize upon everything, those indefatigable and imperturbable Englishwomen.

Other famous villas display their rich palatial façades on the palm-shaded terraces of Bellagio; but a shameless and thoroughly Italian greed of gain spoils the pleasure there might be in visiting them. To cross the threshold of

M. the Duke of Melzi's villa costs a franc and a half, and a supplement of another half franc to walk in the gardens. The charge is posted up as if on a booth at a fair. To see the proprietor it is no doubt half a crown, and little though it may please the English ladies, he must make a fine income!

I had told my boatman to wait for me in the arbour of a little common inn, at the side of the lake, and had ordered for myself and him a bottle of wine of the country.

When pay-time came, I asked the waiter, "How much?"

"Two francs."

"What! you rascal, two francs? My boatman has just been telling me that the *vino del paese* is sold at 60 centimes a bottle."

"Ah! but Signore,—the bottle had a cork."

"A cork! You dare to call that a bottle of corked wine. I saw you putting in that old cork as you were bringing the bottle!"

"Oh! but—signore—just as you please; the cork was there all the same; and whenever there is a cork, then it is corked wine, and two francs; and——I am not the master."

The boatmen who were present at the dialogue went into shouts of laughter; the lad himself laughed so frankly that, laughing myself, I paid the money, that thus I might have the laughers on my side.

The sun was now less powerful; the lake showed rosy lights, crossed and shot with trembling gleams of gold. Before us the terraced gardens of Cadenabbia, like one of the great decorative landscapes of the 18th century, sloped gently down towards the lake.

The steamer which had left Como about noon was not long in appearing at the little quay, where I was waiting for it.

We passed in succession the villas and hotels of Menaggio; Bellano, at the foot of Monte Grigna, and Rezzonico, still guarded by its old fortress of the 13th century, now a gigantic ruin, showing through the gaps in its broken walls the brilliant blue of the horizon.

The whole of this part of the journey is delicious and most enjoyable.

The Lake of Como has more both of grace and of dignity than Lake Maggiore. The surrounding mountains bathe their summits in the blue heavens and their bases in the blue waters. Among all the Italian lakes, it is the one I prefer.

At the inner end of its picturesquely formed, tranquil bays, into which the waves roll like soft caresses, how many pretty, unknown villages there are, in nooks full of shade and silence and peace! What a sweet siesta the soul might take there!

The English never travel on Sunday; the best seats in the steamer were vacant; in the second class, forward, were crowds of peasants in holiday clothes, merrily laughing, singing, talking loudly; glad to be alive and to be doing nothing; giving themselves up to the noisy effusiveness of the excitable races who grow up under a southern sun.

One old woman, alone, sat apart, keeping an unmoved grave and serious look. Still as a statue, she kept her eyes steadily fixed on a distant little promontory that was growing larger to our sight.

I was looking at her with curiosity as I walked up and down on the deck; for her countenance was not a common one; and I was also admiring the large earrings and the necklace she wore. The necklace, composed of coins bearing the stamp of Maria-Theresa, reminded me of those I had seen on the necks of the women of Bosnia and of the military boundaries. As for the earrings, they were miracles of old goldsmith work.

The old woman at last noticed that her ornaments were attracting my attention; she seemed gratified by it, and as I was passing, she said to me in Italian,—

" They are very old, sir; are not they ? "

"And very handsome,—especially the earrings." She unfastened one, and laid it in my hand.

"Just feel the weight of that! There is gold enough to make two napoleons. I have been offered a hundred francs for them, but I said, No. They belonged both to my mother and my grandmother. People do not sell family relics : at least," she added, in a deep, repressed voice that betrayed some anger, "unless they are obliged to do it."

While saying this she had lowered her eyes, but at once she raised them again, and turned them with redoubled watchfulness towards Dongo.

Becoming curious, as all travellers do, I said to the old woman,—

"Is some one expecting you over there?"

"Oh, no!" she replied quickly. "I hope not. What a misfortune if *he* were there! He would have been caught."

"The person in whom you are interested is making his escape, then?"

"Yes ; it is my husband."

"Your husband! Why, what has he done?"

"Nothing. He is a smuggler."

She was silent for a moment, then she resumed.

"You are not aware, then, sir, that smugglers are hunted like thieves?" and she began to exclaim loudly that the real thief was the Government, who every year increased taxes and imposts without reason; that everything is cheaper in Switzerland, and that those who have good legs are quite at liberty to go and buy their provisions beyond the frontier.

The words of the Italian strongly excited my curiosity ; I seemed to be on the scent of some stirring story; and sitting down beside the old woman, I begged her to tell me about her husband's adventure.

"Ah! sir," said she, "such a misfortune! Three days ago, on the Eve of the Assumption, my husband came back, as he always does, to be present at High Mass, for he is a good

Christian. As the night was dark, he brought with him the package of tobacco that he had gone to buy at Lugano, instead of leaving it in the mountain. Who informed on him, you ask? Who saw him? That we shall hear by-and-by. He met neither gendarmes nor custom-house officers, and his dog never once barked, though he scents those people a hundred yards off, and bears them a grudge for all the shots they have sent after him. Poor Turco! He will never say anything more, now! Such a faithful creature, and as fearless as a lion! Those brigands killed him for me." . . .

A tear rolled down the old woman's cheek. She wiped it away with the back of her hand, and then went on.

" My husband tossed his bundle into a corner in the kitchen, ate his polenta, and went to bed. When I joined him he was sleeping like a block; he had walked forty-five miles. About four o'clock I was awakened by the dog growling. The village seemed still buried in deep sleep, the fête-day sleep that is so quiet ; outside nothing was to be heard but some cocks beginning to answer each other.

" I rose very softly, took my shoes in my hand, and went down to the kitchen where we had left Turco. He was standing with his tail and his ears stiffened, and his muzzle stretched out towards the door, growling hoarsely, as if he smelt some one suspicious prowling round the house.

" My heart beat ; I had dreadful forebodings. There was a grey dim dawn beginning ; I could see nothing. And yet Turco still continued his low growling, and his hair was all bristling up.

" Suddenly he made a spring and rushed with all his strength at the window. I had the greatest difficulty in holding him back. And at the same moment I perceived two black shadows crouching down and slipping behind the garden hedge. I knew them for the custom-house men.

" ' Silence, Turco ! ' I cried again, giving him a threatening look, and I dragged him with me to the stair that leads from the kitchen to the bedroom. My husband was still sleeping like the blessed.

" 'Get up quickly, get up,' I said, and shook him, ' the custom-house men are round the house.'

" He was on the floor with one spring, and asked me if I had hidden the tobacco.

" I told him ' Not yet.'

" ' Be quick and go and hide it,' he said.

" I went down again to the kitchen with Turco, but it was no longer possible to hold him. He sprang about barking like a fury, and at last fairly broke loose. If you had seen how furiously he dashed himself against the door ; one would have thought he was mad.

" I put my eye to the key-hole and saw the two men coming forward as stealthily as possible, to avoid making any noise. I barricaded the door with the big oaken kitchen table, and softly put in the large bolt.

" ' If I have only time to hide the tobacco !' I thought. I took up the sack on my back and ran with it to the barn, where I hid it under a heap of straw.

" While I was doing this the men, who had heard the dog barking, and were afraid of my husband coming upon them,—for he is a bold fellow, not afraid to face half a dozen men,—were trying to break open the door, but they did not succeed.

" Then they began to speak. But Turco was barking so furiously that I could not make out what they were saying. As I made no answer, the idea seemed to strike them that perhaps there was nobody there, and they thought they might risk trying the window.

" Turco was standing in the middle of the kitchen, with open mouth and blazing eyes, waiting.

" As soon as he saw a way out, he made a rush and sprang through the window at the throat of the foremost exciseman. Man and dog rolled together on the ground, the one shouting, the other silent, biting furiously at his enemy and trying to choke him. The man was as white as a corpse, and his torn hands were trying in vain to push away the dog, whose muzzle was now red with blood. The other men came running with their revolvers in their hands, but they were afraid to fire, for fear of hitting their comrade as well as the dog.

"There was a terrible battle between the men and Turco. Ah! sir, if you had been there, you would have cried, Bravo, he did so splendidly. He had let go his first enemy, who lay stretched senseless on the ground, and had turned against the other excisemen. He bit them and tore their clothes, springing from one to another with the agility of a tiger and the fury of a demon. They fired at him several times without touching him ; he seemed as if he were bewitched.

"At last they drew their sabres, and as Turco did not retreat, but only redoubled his fierce attacks, he received several deadly strokes all at once.

"My man had come down to the kitchen.

"'Have you hidden the tobacco?' he asked me.

"I said I had.

"'That is right,' he said. 'Good-bye, I must be off before they come in. Be sure to go to morrow and tell Luigi Cervi what has happened, and warn our comrades. They will give you news of me.'

"He went out by the little barn door, and I went up to the garret to watch him from the skylight. He slipped along by a hedge and reached the vineyards, where he disappeared. Once in the vineyards, he was in the mountains.

"When I came back to the kitchen, the men were there, upsetting everything, rummaging into everything, breaking everything as if they were drunk. One of them, whose dress was torn and his knee bleeding, clutched me by the throat and thrust me against the wall, crying, 'Ah, it was you, you witch, who let loose the dog on us!'

"I thought he was going to strangle me. My breath was gone, my eyes were turning. His comrades interfered.

"'Where is your husband?' they asked me.

" ' He is not here,' I said.

" ' You are lying! Search the house!'

" So they went all over, into every corner,—to the cellar, the garret, the stable, and the barn.

" They had left the kitchen door open, so I went out to see what they had done to Turco. Alas! the poor dog was lying dead, a few steps from the window he had defended, his throat half cut through, and the bloody foam on his lips. It broke my heart to see him so. I cried as if I had lost a child.

" The excisemen had found nothing, and had come back.

" ' Your husband has made off,' they said; ' he is a scoundrel, but we shall get hold of him again. Tell us, you witch, where the bag is, the bag of tobacco that he brought last night? '

" ' I suppose he must have taken it away,' I replied; 'as you have not seen it anywhere.'

" Then they wished to frighten me by threats, and pretended to arrest me; but I said, ' I know the law. You can do nothing to me without proof. You have none. Go away.' So they were obliged to let me alone. So they went off cursing.

" ' Your husband shall pay for all this,' the oldest of them said to me, shaking his fist in my face.

" I went up again to my skylight and looked after them a long, long time, till they were quite out of sight. At night I buried our poor Turco at the foot of the garden, and planted some flowers on his grave. I was very sorrowful, and cried for a good part of the night, always saying to myself, ' If, after all, they should catch your goodman, what would become of you, and what would become of him? '

" Next morning, at break of day, I was again on the watch in the garret. The plain was empty and silent, everything was motionless on the mountain.

" When the steamer passed I took it to go to Lenno, to see Luigi Cervi. This Luigi is a very rich merchant, whose fortune has been made by smugglers. He seemed very much annoyed at what I told him, and only said, 'See that your husband does not let himself be caught;' then he dismissed me.

"Near his house I met some of my husband's companions, who had already heard the news, and who spoke kind words to me. I was obliged to sleep at Lenno, for the boat does not come back the same night. In ten minutes more I shall be back at Dongo. It is that point just before us. . . . Ah! my blood runs cold, and my eyes seem confused. You see nothing, sir, do you?"

I took my glass, but I did not dare tell the old woman that I saw, in the midst of a great concourse of people, some armed custom-house officers who seemed to be guarding a prisoner.

The boat was quickly getting nearer the shore, towards which it was sending broad sheets of blue water fringed with light foam.

The naked eye could now distinguish the houses of the village with their green vines, the Dominican convent at the opening of the valley, the inn with its red sign, the little shaky, wooden landing-place, supported on trestles, and the holiday crowd making a circle around two custom-house men, between whom was a man with his hands bound.

The old woman had risen to her feet; she stood looking with the fixed gaze of one in a dream; then all at once she grew pale as a sheet, uttered a name—her husband's name, doubtless—in a choked voice, and sank down again on the bench.

The steamer hove to, the ropes were thrown, everybody was taken up with watching the performance, and seeing what was going on on the land. No one but myself had noticed the old woman's agitation.

A great many people got out. As soon as the little gangway was clear, the two excisemen closed step behind their prisoner, and came on board.

The man whom they were taking to Gravedona, where the prisons are much more substantial than at Dongo, was a tall, pale-complexioned wretch, with black hair and eyes, a stiff, frizzled beard like horsehair, and a lean neck on which the muscles stood out like cords; the skin of his face seemed glued to the bones, and was worn into deep wrinkles—the face, in fact, of a famished creature. He was dressed in an olive-coloured vest, faded and worn with rain and sunshine; his corduroy trousers were covered with mud and torn in several places.

His appearance produced a lively feeling of curiosity among the passengers, who questioned each other, asking if he was known, or if any one knew why he was arrested.

The old woman, beside whom I had kept my place, quickly turned away her face and looked in another direction.

As there was room on the seat beside her, the men came and sat down there with their prisoner, whom they placed between them.

The boat had set off again, coasting along by very flat, marshy banks, covered with beds of long, silvery osiers, and intersected by brooks and canals forming the mouth of the Dongo.

The prisoner had pulled down his broad felt hat over his eyes, and seemed to be asleep.

One of his guards said to his comrade,—

"I am thirsty; are you, Pietro?"

Pietro, who was next the old woman, replied,—

"Am I, do you say? after all the dust we have swallowed!"

"Well," said the other, "go you and drink first, while I keep guard, and then I will go."

"I'll send you a glass."

"Very well; go then."

Pietro rose and went down to the cabin. Two minutes later a stout waitress, with turned-up sleeves, arrived with a large glass of red wine on a plate.

6

She presented it to the exciseman, who slipped his gun under the bench in order to have his hands free, and to drink at his ease.

As he was leisurely enjoying his wine in little sips, licking his moustache, and chatting with a girl who sat near him, the old woman, who had been arranging her plan from the time she left Dongo, quickly drew from her pocket an open knife, cut in a moment the ropes that bound her husband's hands, and pointing to the shore, only about two hundred yards off, exclaimed, "Felipo, in the name of Our Lady, fly!"

The smuggler cast a hurried glance around, gathered up his whole strength, and sprang, at a single bound, over the parapet into the lake.

His keeper saw the movement just an instant too late. For a moment he stared stupidly as if petrified, holding his glass in one hand and the plate in the other.

Then he regained his senses, threw down the encumbering articles, and bent quickly to pick up his gun. A well-aimed ball might still reach the fugitive.

But the old woman was on the watch. The moment the exciseman stooped, she gave him a push with her whole strength. He lost his balance and rolled on the deck. Then, to keep him down, she threw herself upon him and seized him by the throat.

"Pietro! Here! help! he-e-elp!" howled the exciseman.

Pietro could not hear him, and none of the passengers were inclined to take sides against a woman. Besides, everybody was engrossed with watching the fugitive who was swimming desperately, and whose chances of safety increased with every second.

At last Pietro arrived, summoned by some of the steamer servants. He rushed upon the old woman, released his comrade with the utmost difficulty, and while the latter held the brave woman, fired rapidly after the fugitive, who replied by an ironical bow. He had just set foot on the shore; he was safe!

The baffled exciseman's look of vexation was so absurd that we all began to laugh.

The old woman—her grey locks dishevelled, her cap hanging down her back, her large white sleeves torn to rags—was laughing also, as if seized with a mad fit of joy.

When she saw her husband disappear behind the great clumps of osiers on the low, deserted shore, she clapped her hands and danced; but the two excisemen put an end to her mirthful demonstrations, each taking her roughly by an arm, and speaking harsh words to her. They forced her to sit down, and having knotted together the fragments of the rope that had been used for her husband, they bound her wrists with it. Gentle as a lamb now, she made no opposition, saying to them, "Do as you please. . . . It is all one to me. . . . He is saved! He would have died in your abominable prisons with no air to breathe. . . . As you please; it is all one to me, all one to me!"

And she laughed and laughed, mocking at the two excisemen, who were binding her hands, swearing at her while they did so, and drawing the ropes so tight that the blood oozed through the skin.

PART II.

THE ENGADINE.

CHAPTER I.

THE next morning, on opening my window, I had above
me a sky of the most delicate blue, a canopy decked
with little crumpled clouds of pale coloured satin; below
was a garden with pavilions and arbours, perfumed with
beautiful flowers, with red roses fresh and living like lips.
In the basin of a fountain with blue reflections, the sun
bathed his golden locks.

I was in a large hotel, with whitewashed walls, with
green shutters,—Italian in style, but Swiss in their irre-
proachable neatness.

I descended a wide staircase painted in frescoes, and on
going out into the street, I found myself face to face with
an old dismantled castle, its walls in holes, and looking like
a poor nobleman sitting on the roadside. This ruined manor
belonged formerly to the noble and powerful family of the
Salis, who no longer possess anything but a black cat, a lean
gutter-cat, whose heraldic effigy serves as the sign-board of
a public house.

The public *diligence* waited in front of the hotel, harnessed
with five strong mountain horses, a great contrast to the

Italian hacks who had conveyed me so slowly the evening before.

On alighting at the end of the lake at Collico, I had hired an ancient carriage, which had brought me in a very so-so fashion as far as Chiavenna, where I had arrived towards midnight and slept.

One does not stay long at Chiavenna. It is simply a resting-place on the road from Collico to St. Moritz, or from Coire to Milan. At the moment of departure our host, the most polite of men, came to wish us "*bon voyage.*" For a landlord he was very handsome, rotund and rubicund, sleek and shining. His red hair stuck out from under a small cap of black cloth, and his great ears looked like little wings; he had great goggle eyes, brown of a hazel shade, a nose like an onion, a mouth like a cherry, a chin like a galosh, mutton-chop whiskers, and the scarlet face of a singer. Cravat and waistcoat were white, he wore a gold chain with charms, a navy-blue coat and checked trousers. What a bow he made us, his body bent almost double, his legs close together, his mouth pursed up, his hat in his hand! One would have thought he was saluting a whole dynasty of crowned heads. His portly person creaked in the effort. When the *diligence* turned the corner of the street he was still on his doorstep, bent forward in an attitude at once humble and dignified, with the same smile on his half-opened mouth.

The road follows the valley of Bregaglia, enclosed in gloomy mountains; some of them streaked with snow looked as if they were veined with marble; at their foot the vines run in festoons, and the tall maize shakes its silky filaments like fair hair.

A torrent, the Maira, which breaks away into a waterfall in the shadow of large trees of a southern vegetation, and rolls over its pebbly bed with a fretful murmur; a church perched on a rock like an enormous white bird; a castle clothed in ivy, looking like a skeleton in a coat of mail, green with age; pretty houses in the midst of rich lawns announce Santa Croce, built opposite to the place where the town of Plurs was crushed in 1618 by the fall of a mountain.

These catastrophes are frequent in the Alps. Some fine day the mountain suddenly begins to move and walk, and comes down into the valley as if it were tired of remaining always in the same spot.

We cross the stream which separates Italy from Switzerland; during the night, to prevent carriages from passing, they stretch a chain across the bridge.

The first thing that strikes the eye on entering Helvetian territory is a school, and the school is the true boundary line between the two countries. For the Swiss the school is also the true fortress.[1]

As one penetrates further into the mountain region, the vine and the mulberries gradually disappear. The chestnuts wave their long tresses till we reach Bondo, where the Alpine rose flourishes. During three months of the year, the inhabitants of Bondo, buried in their narrow valley, do not see the sun, but seem to live in a dark, cold world, which he has abandoned and no longer shines on.

Following the slopes of the mountain, and overlooked by the castle of Castelmur, with its lofty warlike tower, the road now climbs upwards in long white loops, diminishing gradually to fine threads; it then passes between enormous blocks of rock, furnished formerly, it is said, with a gate.

At Vicosoprano we halt for breakfast. From this place, as from Bondo, one may make the most interesting excursions into the lateral valleys, where the glaciers pile themselves, or bare rocks shiver under eternal snow.

The road becomes more and more difficult. The steaming horses are covered with sweat. The *diligence* climbs a

[1] There are in Switzerland more than 6,000 primary schools; the most remote villages among the mountains have their school and their teacher.

tortuous path bordered with pines, great beards of lichen hanging from their branches. Large rosy, umbelliferous plants and ladies' slippers of a turquoise blue, bring into the sterility of these gloomy solitudes a burst of life, an awaking to colour and brightness.

On every side one sees nothing but summits bare, falling, fantastic, shaken by storms and torn up by rains, peaks where bands of snow hang like rags of cloth, needles, clocktowers in rock, broken monoliths, lofty slabs of wall falling away into ruins. At last we find ourselves at the highest point in the valley, the lofty plateau of Maloja, encircled by jagged mountains which ramify in the strangest fashion.

While the horses take breath, and the conductor and postillion refresh themselves, we climb a small rock, from which we can overlook the valley.

Below us the road which we have just traversed stands out quite white against the blackness of the pines. The valley, with its attendant retinue of mountains, forests, and villages, descends into the blue distance in an infinite perspective; it rolls its waves of green trees into the mists of the distance, into the light haze of the Italian sky, where the eye bathes itself in delights. Down there is the land of promise, rich and fertile meadows, beautiful golden fields, the generous vine, the most luscious fruits, the sun, this beautiful sun to which the greater number of the inhabitants of the Engadine come, to warm themselves in winter, emigrating to carry on their various trades in the plains of the south.

Behind us the landscape wears a totally different aspect. Desolate, almost naked, exposed to the killing breath of the winds, the plateau of Maloja is surrounded by bare mountains, burnt up by the summer, consumed by the winter, in lines broken and indented, which twist and bristle with the reddish colour of an extinct volcano.

Maloja is the highest point of the valley of the Inn. It is 5,941 feet above the sea level at the place where the waters part on the one side towards the Adriatic, on the other towards the Black Sea.

In the seventeenth century travellers who entered the hidden hostelry of Maloja were by no means sure of getting out of it. There was a terrible innkeeper, who did not always employ his knife for the slaying of sheep. One day he assassinated during his sleep a German student, returning from the celebrated University of Pavia. The next day a companion of the victim arrived at the inn, and his dog discovered the body in a cellar.

Now-a-days, in the great inn, they do not even put a narcotic in your wine to keep you a little longer; you may pass the night there without bolting your door, and with the absolute assurance of finding your head in its place on your shoulders in the morning. Several equipages without escort are waiting in a row, whilst unarmed families, quietly grouped on the plateau, gaze at the landscape through glasses of ivory and gold, and children chase the butterflies, the great mountain butterflies, their wings streaked with red or shimmering blue, and looking like microscopic humming-birds.

Near the road, his head in the shade and his feet in the sun, a poor basket-maker works beside his cart, under a ragged umbrella fastened to a pole.

Round the inn are some miserable hovels. A little pig, extremely disrespectful, but pretty as a rosy cherub, shows his tail to passers-by. Two furious geese, with open beak and outspread wings, hiss noisily their anger against some English ladies in red dresses who are looking at them.[1]

The postillion takes his seat again, and we set out. There are the desolate shores of the lake of Sils, into which the torrent which descends from the glacier of Fedoz falls with a loud noise. From the 15th December to the 15th May a thick coating of ice covers this little Alpine lake. In 1799 the French crossed it with all their artillery.

---

[1] A large hotel and a casino have just been built at Maloja.

Sils in the sixteenth century was only a poor village of fishery people. The old village of Sils consists now of only a few houses, whilst the new Sils, a little higher up, sheltered on every side by wooded hills, in a commanding situation, possesses fine hotels and pretty white houses in the midst of gardens in bloom.

Sils-Maria is one of the summer stations most favourable for the first period of chest complaint. And what varied excursions, and what easy ascents in the neighbourhood, even as far as the magnificent glacier of Fex! From Piz della Margna one sees the Upper Engadine in its entire length, with its necklace of melancholy lakes, spotted with the black shadow of its larches; with its pyramids of snow; its glaciers, which make one dream of polar landscapes; its mountains, so irregular in form and so differing in colour, pointed like daggers, cut out like a saw, or broken like ruined domes. These landscapes of the Engadine resemble in no respect the ordinary landscapes of classical Switzerland. They have a rude and savage beauty, and a melancholy which at first sight does not please; but when one becomes familiarized with this strange nature, with the broken contours of its mountains, the stern severity of its peaks, the pale deserts of its glaciers, one finds in it a rugged poetry, and feels moved by strong emotions.

Twenty years ago this long valley—one of the highest in Europe—was solitary and undreamed of. With no roads of communication, it had remained shut off from the rest of the world. And even now, to those who think of Switzerland as composed only of the Oberland and the Lake of Lucerne, it is a country absolutely new and remote from the great routes, which will give them all the joy of discovery.

In spite of the tourists who now resort to it, the Engadine has preserved the originality of its manners, its language, and its nature.

In 1850 it still recalled the valleys of ancient Helvetia,

with their wild animals gone. Long ago the great fallow deer, with his gigantic antlers, awoke the echoes on the shores of its silent lakes; the wild goats wandered over its snowy rocks; the bear stood sentinel at the entrance to its profound gorges. They still have the chamois, the bear, the marmoset, and the eagle, but the stag and the wild goat are only memories of old hunters; and what is to be regretted is that the forests are disappearing also, for decay of the tree precedes that of man. When wood is wanting to the hearth, there will no longer be a hearth; and when the trees no longer protect the village from the avalanche, what becomes of the village?

Sils Maria, through which we pass without stopping, is the highest point of the valley (5,895 feet). A cherry tree, preserved in a garden as a rare tree, sometimes produces fruit.

Whilst in the other parts of Switzerland the limit of the glaciers and of the eternal snow is met with at 8,740 feet, in the Engadine these limits do not begin below 10,070 feet. The climate has here exceptional strength and power. In the Hartz mountains trees disappear entirely at a height of 3,525 feet; in the Tyrolese and Bavarian Alps at a height of from 5,840 to 6,070 feet; in the Upper Engadine, on the northern slopes of the mountains, one still finds, at an elevation of 7,465 feet, hardy clumps of larches, of stone-pine,[1] and of fir. A similar resistance of the vegetation is not to be met with in the Pyrenees or even on Caucasus. The arolle, this last heroic representative of plants with a tall stem, originally from Siberia, is found even at an altitude of 8,000 feet. At the foot of these trees the golden moss spreads a silken and shaded carpet mixed with little flowers like fine jewels. On the sunny slopes of Célérina, of Samaden, and Pontrésina, cultivation climbs to over 6,000 feet; fields of rye, of oats, and of flax variegate the

[1] The *Pinus cambra*, or Swiss stone-pine, is called the "*arolle*" in the valley of the Inn.

alpine pastures with their green stripes and their yellow squares; and in the kitchen gardens, where all sorts of vegetables grow, the brilliant flowers of the lower valleys also bloom. In summer an Italian sun darts his rays from the depths of a sky of azure. In the morning hours there is not a breath of wind. The atmosphere is motionless, of unsullied clearness and transparency, enlarging objects, bringing them nearer, producing the most singular optical illusions. And this limpid purity of the air, which envelopes you like a fluid, produces a silence so profound that the country seems empty, and you believe yourself alone among the silent hills.

The rocks, whose lofty black peaks stood in profile above Sils, have now disappeared behind us.

The road winds away across the gloomy marshes, where the great mirror-like pools lie sleeping, guarded by the reeds and rushes, with their crossed sabres and lances.

In the distance a spot of blue grows larger; and among the branches of the larches the roofs of the village are seen —coquettish little houses, which look as if they were rolling in the grass, like white sheep become giddy and foolish from the caresses of the returning sun.

It is Silvaplana, on the shore of its motionless lake, held by the mountains as if in a cup of emerald. Opposite, towards the south, rise the bold ridges of Piz Surlej and of Mount Arlas; to the east the red pyramids, veined with snow, of Piz Albana and of Piz Julier.

At Silvaplana the country changes. It becomes more verdant, more populous, more animated. One meets with tourists, the blue veil round the hat, knickerbockers and woollen stockings, alpenstock in hand. One hears the tinkling of the bells, the swearing of coachmen, the barking of dogs. Near the bridge, in the current of the stream, women, bronzed like Arabs, are washing linen, their red skirts turned up and a white handkerchief round their head.

Another beautiful lake stretches along by the road, its

great sheet of pale green water all spangled with light, its islands standing out in silhouette against the promontories, which run down into it, planted with pines, arolles, and larches.

Beyond Campfer, its houses surrounding a third little lake, we come suddenly on a scene of extraordinary animation. All the cosmopolitan society of St. Moritz is there, saunter-ing, walking, running, in mountain parties, on afternoon excursions. The favourite walk is the one to the pretty lake of Campfer, with its shady margin, its resting-places hidden among the branches, its châlet-restaurant, from the terrace of which one overlooks the whole valley; and it would be difficult to find near St. Moritz a more interesting spot.

We meet at every step parties of English ladies, looking like plantations of umbrellas with their covers on and sur-mounted by immense straw hats; then there are German ladies, massive as citadels, but not impregnable, asking nothing better than to surrender to the young exquisites, with the figures of cuirassiers, who accompany them; further on, lively Italian ladies parade themselves in dresses of the carnival, the colours outrageously striking, and daz-zling to the eyes; with up-turned skirts they cross the Inn on great mossy stones, leaping with the grace of birds, and smiling, to show into the bargain the whiteness of their teeth. All this crowd passing in procession before us is composed of men and women of every age and condition; some with the grave face of a waxen saint, others beaming with the satisfied smile of rich people; there are also inva-lids, who go along hobbling and limping, or who are drawn in little carriages.

Soon handsome façades pierced with hundreds of windows show themselves in the grand and severe setting of moun-tains and glaciers. It is St. Moritz-les-Bains.

Here every house is a hotel, and as every hotel is a little palace, we do not alight from the *diligence*; we go a little farther and a little higher, to St. Moritz-le-Village, which

has a much more beautiful situation. It is at the top of a
little hill, whose sides slope down to a pretty lake, fresh and
green as a lawn. The eye reaches beyond Sils, the whole
length of the valley, with its mountains like embattled ramparts, its lakes like a row of great pearls, and its glaciers
showing their piles of snowy white against the azure depths
of the horizon.

CHAPTER II.

THE next day I was awakened by the goat-bells at six o'clock.

I descended the little footpath which zigzags down into the valley.

The washerwomen were already at their *battoirs*, sing-ing, as they washed the dirty linen of Messieurs, the strangers, in the purifying waters of the lake. The shops and stalls, which bring the street of a fair into the midst of a village, were being opened one after another. A big, un-gainly Englishman, with a complexion like raw meat, a napkin fastened round his neck, and his face swimming in white lather, was being shaved by the hair-dresser at the corner, whilst some Germans were buying paper collars and cuffs.

No one was as yet in the park of the Curhaus, with its carpet of thin, flowerless turf. Only the fountain babbled in its stone basin, and a little mountain-bird, his tail edged with a fine red line, trims himself on a railing.

The Curhaus, the Hotel Victoria, and the Baths form a large square. The park is in the middle, with a pavilion for the music. At eight o'clock the musicians of the band ar-rive, in black coats, white ties, stove-pipe hats, solemn and

sad as attendants at a funeral. Among them there is one
very old, very small, very shrivelled up, with a red nose, a
white beard, and on his nose a pair of spectacles with a brass
rim ; when he blows into his clarionet his cheeks round
themselves out like two wrinkled apples, and he half closes
his eyes like a sucking calf.

At last the waltzes of Strauss and the polkas of Métra
attract some of the bathers, who advance slowly, stopping
to inhale luxuriously the morning air. The air of the
mountains, the poet tells us, intoxicates and sets people
dancing. It is balmy with the exquisite perfume of flowers,
it is laden with the resins of the pines, it has the shivering
freshness of the glaciers ; limpid as the water of springs, its
fluid streams over you in an invisible shower. The sensation
is delicious. It seems as if wings were sprouting for you as
well as for the birds.

Soon the paths, which wind discreetly round the fountain
and the pavilion for the band, become as populous as a street ;
couples promenade arm in arm. English ladies read *The
Times*, wrapped up in it as in a dressing-gown ; Germans in
caps smoke long pipes with porcelain bowls, decorated with
the head of the Emperor William.

What sacrilege to smoke in that divine air, in that air of
heaven and paradise ! Little boys with bare bronzed knees
play with little girls in short petticoats, dressed like a
fashion-plate, and with the air of dolls. The crowd increases,
and now those who are walking give themselves up to the
exercise necessary after every tumbler of water. There are
some who, in order to save themselves the trouble of returning to the spring after the prescribed interval, carry a bottle
of mineral water under their arm and a glass in their
pocket. In the alleys there is a comical coming and going ;
all the people have such a grave, solemn air, such an appearance of settled conviction, and every instant they stop,
consult their watch, or note in a memorandum book how
many steps they have taken.

A huge German curé, with the figure of a Goliath, a soft hat on his head, his long surtout knocking against his square-toed boots, walks slowly, smoking his cigar and reading in his breviary.

Apart, shunning the crowd and the noise, I notice an old man stiff and erect, with the profile of a medallion, an aquiline nose, his forehead furrowed with wrinkles, thin lips, his chin cut in prominent angles, a martial gait under his black surtout. It is Marshal von Moltke, one of the habitual guests at St. Moritz. His long figure, like a silhouette from the "Dance of Death," makes one think of those phantoms who wander by night over battle-fields. Towards ten o'clock a tramway car arrives, a veritable tramway car; on its low wheels like paws it rolls along, uttering its hoarse cry like a beast; and on every side, omnibuses, carriages, breaks, victorias, are coming in, bringing for water treatment the people living in the hotels and private houses, pouring out on the place the noise and excitement of a fashionable bathing-place at the hour of bathing.

In front of the Curhaus there is a strange assembly,—a motley crowd like that at an international exhibition. Red hats, bright dresses stand out in the crude colours of an English water-colour, and form as it were great bouquets of wild flowers, red and white; groups of men in berets and suits of flannel, recall the elegant idlers of Trouville and Dieppe. Seated on chairs drawn close to each other, ladies have gathered round them a little court, where news are retailed, or the scandals of the day before are recounted and commented on. They must surely be wonderfully amusing, these stories of the bathers male and female, to cause so much laughter! The custom of having Heptamerons in the open air has not been lost with the Queen of Navarre; it is still the great distraction of watering-places, where every one has leisure to study his neighbour for the purpose of speaking evil of him.

Inside the Curhaus there is also stir. Girls of a waxen

paleness, young women with hollow cheeks, limp as a washed-out rag, their narrow shoulders wrapped in a woollen shawl, eyes sunk and surrounded with a blue ring, the expression discouraged and dying, are grouped round a great Swiss in a black coat, who' holds the handle of the pump and distributes the iron water with truly Helvetic parsimony. The water-drinkers, bending with a graceful dove-like motion, empty in little sips their coloured tumblers, ornamented with their name and sometimes with a device. Some of them use a glass tube to preserve their teeth from the action of the iron, or they have their water heated at the bath. The empty glass is returned and put in its hole, and other drinkers, male and female, present themselves, a buzzing swarm, and the big Swiss in his black coat once more plies the pump handle with the grave, silent air of a man fulfilling a sacred office. There are many German ladies in large black Rembrandt hats surrounded by a long, melancholy plume, a velvet bodice like a hussar's, blue spectacles or eye-glass on the end of the nose, leaning with one hand on the stick of their umbrella, with the other carrying to their large, thick red lips their glass of fresh and sparkling water. There are English ladies, also, with lanky tresses, and in splendid condition of body ; and Italian ladies, recognisable by their beautiful madonna type, their passionate mouths made expressly for the caresses of Italian words; agitated Russian ladies, who chatter like blind magpies; Swiss ladies, who say nothing at all, and who one would think were automatons, like the personages on the clock at Berne. Behind these feminine groups shine the gold spectacles of two or three German physicians, their fair, fan-shaped beards, silky and perfumed, in surtouts with broad facings, a great display of shirt front, and two chains—one for the watch, and the other for the thermometer or pencil-case.

The baths are at the extremity of the building, at the end of a passage which prolongs itself like an interminable tunnel. Compared to other watering-places, nothing can be simpler or more primitive than their arrangements. The baths are in pine wood, and you are enclosed by means of a lid, so that you have an appearance of being shut in a coffin. The funereal impression once dissipated, however, you find yourself deliciously comfortable on this bier, and never did you feel younger or more living; enveloped in the pleasant tepid water, gently tickled by the bubbles of sparkling gas that run along your body, you seem to be swimming in a bath of champagne.

There is not a single mineral spring in Switzerland which was not already celebrated in ancient times or in the middle ages. In the seventh century St. Moritz was a well-known place of pilgrimage; the bad roads and the difficult footpaths made the journey so much the more meritorious, and pious pilgrims found here at the same time health of body and salvation for their soul.

In 1854 a financial company rented the spring for fifty years, and worked real miracles. There sprung up those splendid hotels, which, from the 15th June to the 15th September, lodge about ten thousand bathers. The Curhaus, which had originally twenty-seven rooms, has now three hundred.

One would not think that here one is at the same altitude as the top of the Rigi. The climate is that of wild regions, —nine months of winter, three months of summer. The finest glaciers in Switzerland are within a step, and one can on foot, and without fatigue, ascend the highest summits of the Alps, which offer here only softened angles and easy inclinations.

The Canton of Grisons, of which the Engadine forms a part, counts more than a hundred and sixty glaciers, and a hundred and seventy valleys of every size.

St. Moritz is in the centre of the valley of the Upper Engadine, which extends to the length of eighteen or nineteen leagues, and which scarcely possesses a thousand inhabitants. Almost all the men emigrate to work for strangers, like their brothers, the mountaineers of Savoy and Auvergne, and do not return till they have amassed a sufficient fortune to allow them to build a little white house, with gilded window frames, and to die quietly in the spot where they were born.

The countries are rare in which love of the native soil is so strongly developed as in Switzerland. Ask a Swiss what he loves above everything, he will answer, " My country." To return to his village in the midst of his beloved mountains is the constant dream of his life; and to realize it he will endure every privation, and bind himself to the hardest and most painful toils. One hope possesses him,—to see again the snows, the glaciers, the lakes, the rivers, the great oaks and the familiar pines of his country; to see again the friends of his childhood, and the old parents who walk with tottering footsteps, or the place which they occupy in the cemetery full of flowers, where they sleep the great sleep.

Historians tell us that the first inhabitants of the Upper Engadine were Etruscans and Latins chased from Italy by the Gauls and Carthaginians, and taking refuge in these hidden altitudes. Whatever may have been their origin, the language spoken in the country is the "Ladin," or " Romanche," a dialect of new Latin, composed of Etruscan, Celtic, and Roman.

Some years B.C. the Engadine was conquered by the Roman legions, and remained subject to Rome during five hundred years. The Roman soldiers introduced Christianity into these hidden valleys, constructed roads for communication, and planted the vine on the slopes of the Lower Engadine.

After the fall of the Empire, the inhabitants of the Engadine fell under the dominion of the Franks and Lombards, then of the Dukes of Swabia; but the blood never mingled—the type remained Italian: black hair, the quick eye, the mobile countenance, the expressive features, and the supple figure.

In Switzerland the central or federal power has not destroyed the autonomy of the cantons, which have preserved the privilege of keeping each its own particular constitution, and of choosing its own form of Government. The Great Council of the Grisons, elected directly by the people, can pass no law without first submitting it to the popular sanction. A State Commission of three members administers the affairs of the country, and nothing could be simpler or less complicated than this administration, in harmony with the customs, the manners, and the ancient usages of the inhabitants.

With the exception of two or three hamlets near Tarasp, the Engadine is entirely Protestant : the Reformation was introduced here in the simplest manner in the world. On a November evening in the year 1549, a traveller who had crossed the Col de Bernina on foot, was about to sup in the only inn in Pontrésina, where he had stopped intending to pass the night. The innkeeper, who was the "*amann*," that is to say, the mayor of the village, told the stranger that he had just arrived in time to be present at an interesting discussion. "We have no curé, and the commune is to meet this evening at the inn to come to some decision."

"Oh, you have no curé!" said the stranger with an interest which did not escape the innkeeper.

"We have not," he repeated ; and he added, "One would think you had one to propose to us."

"Why not?"

The stranger rose, and approaching the *amann*, said to him,—

"Would it astonish you much to hear that I am a priest, and even more, for I bear the title of bishop. I am Peter Paul Verginio, Bishop of Capo d'Istria, formerly Pope's nuncio in Germany,—the friend of Luther and the enemy of the Holy Inquisition. It is to escape its severity that I have come to seek refuge in your mountains. I lived for a time at Poschiavo, where I set up a printing establishment, then

I was pastor at Vicosoprano. If you will have me, I will
stay with you."

The *amann* replied that the decision did not rest with
him, but that he would consult those in his jurisdiction.

When they were all met in the inn, the *amann* made
known the proposal of Paul Verginio. There was at first
lively opposition; however, they consented to hear the
Roman prelate.

He showed himself so persuasive and so eloquent, he
spoke with such conviction of the reforms necessary in the
Catholic Church, that the audience were vanquished, and
they begged him to preach next day, a Sunday, in the
church.

Seven other communes immediately followed the example
of Pontrésina, and embraced the Reformation.

Paul Verginio remained in the Upper Engadine till 1553.
At that time he was called to Tübingen, where he founded
the first Bible Society in Germany, then he travelled in
Austria and Poland; after his death his disciple and friend,
Paleario, died on the block.

CHAPTER III.

IN the afternoon, after having dined at the *table d'hôte*
of the Hotel Victoria, an exact reproduction of those of
the Grand Hotel and the Continental Hotel, I ascended
again to the village of St. Moritz, happy to leave behind me
those caravanserais, and those great barracks which would
spoil the most beautiful landscape, and all those shops and
bazaars, exposing in their window panes the infirmities and
the wants of civilization, the miseries of our riches.

Boldly situated on the crest of the mountain, with its
mixture of wooden châlets and stone houses, the village of
St. Moritz has something original and proud which attracts
and pleases. It overlooks the valley, thrown at its feet,
with its white hotels, its beautiful lakes framed in meadows
and in larches, its mountains with their strange shapes, and
its glaciers with their long copes of silver sparkling in the
sun.

Sheltered from the north winds, too high (6,090 feet) to
be reached by the winds of the plain, and far enough from
the lake to be out of reach of its mist, St. Moritz-le-Village
is a station recommended for those who are suffering from
diseases of the chest.

I am told that I may in the evening reach Pontrésina, the
central point for Alpine excursions in the Upper Engadine

the rendezvous of the tourists and mountain-climbers of the two worlds, a station as celebrated as that of Chamounix or of Zermatt.

A young Italian of Poschiavo, who keeps a confectioner's shop on the ground floor of the Hotel Suisse, presents me with a stirrup cup; with her delicate hands she puts in my button-hole the little sweet-smelling flower which is used in making the drink of the country, the *alpina*. In exchange for her little flower a poet would have left his heart, saying to her things more tender than the *patés* she rolls, sweeter than all the sweet things spread out in the window of her shop.

I pass through the village, mounting by a narrow street where they shoe horses; the forge, in a sort of cellar, is illuminated by red lights, in the midst of which rises a great blacksmith like a cyclops. On one side, under a shed, is a crowd of carriages, halt and lame, tattooed with the labels of the hotels. Farther off, some peasant women have stopped before the window of a photographer; nothing can be prettier than their bending, eager attitudes, and their scarlet petticoats showing their ankles.

Quite on the height of the hill, overlooking the two valleys, stands an old tottering church with a leaning tower, a legendary ruin which the rains crumble and the swallows crown in their flight. One sees, as far as the eye can reach, white mountains and black mountains, lakes shining like great pieces of glass, and villages which resemble little heaps of pebbles on the edge of a river or a road.

I take, on the left, a path which descends pleasantly the steep slope into the valley, on a fresh and velvety turf, while the coaches and carriages disappear on the high road in clouds of dust.

Oh, the pleasure of travelling on foot! Of going, with knapsack on back and alpenstock in hand, by the shortest way that opens up, a way that seems to have adorned itself expressly for your pleasure with new flowers! To go on foot is to follow one's own caprice or fancy, to depend on no one, to be sole and only master—it is to be at once horse and carriage and postillion, to run as freely as the air and the wind. It is a delicious vagabondage, which fills the head with ideas, when the country is pretty, when the stones are not too hard, when the brooks chatter beside you as if to keep you company. If you only knew what charming stories there are in the babbled confidences of the little streams that pass the villages! Their bright waves are eyes which see everything, and mirrors in which everything is reflected.

And as evening draws on, what can be more charming than to travel on foot in a beautiful mountain country? One thinks then of those who are left behind; of the dear and loved ones who are far away, down on the dusty plains. We speak to them in thought, and dream of the happiness it would be to have them here, going with us arm in arm along the peaceful valley path, or on the solitary mountain road.

Mowers, some in the grey blouse of the Capuchins, others in sheep-skin or goat-skin, appear to hang on the sides of the rocks which imprison the valley. I see them with my glass, leaning over the precipice mowing a few tufts of grass where the goats themselves could not climb. The mower is a type by himself in this world of the Alps, so picturesque and so curious. Like the chamois hunter, and the hunter for plants, he is accustomed to all the perils of the mountains, he braves death ten times a day. The day before the commencement of the mowing, a day fixed by special decree, he bids farewell, perhaps for the last time, to his wife and children. His scythe on his shoulder, armed with his iron-shod stick, provided with his cramp-irons, a cloth or a net rolled up on his bag, he sets out at midnight, in order that the dawn may find him at his work. During the two months of hay harvest he only goes down to the village three or four times to renew his supply of food or linen.

In these steep solitudes, which appear accessible only to the eagle and the chamois, the life of man is so exposed, and accidents are so frequent, that the law forbids that there should be more than one mower in a family. A rolling stone, a snowstorm, an attack of giddiness, nothing more is wanted to make another victim. By this hard and perilous occupation, an Alpine mower makes from three to five francs a day, his food not included. And when the châlets are very distant, it is under some projecting rock that he seeks a bed and passes the night.

Once dried, this wild hay is carefully gathered into a cloth or a net, and carried lower down, where it is made into a stack, which they load with large stones. In winter, when everything is covered with snow, the mower climbs again the perpendicular sides of the mountain, carrying his little wooden sledge on his shoulders. He loads it with hay, seats himself on the front, and shoots down with the swiftness of an arrow. Often, the snow, softened by the warm wind which blows upon the heights, is detached in an avalanche behind him, and swallows him up before he reaches the valley.

This aromatic hay, composed of the nourishing flora of the High Alps, of delicate and succulent plants, of the white-flowered chrysanthemum, the silky alchemilla, the dwarf carline thistle, the red veronica, the golden potentilla, of the milfoil with its black calyx, and the clover with its great tufts, gives a delicious milk, and is greatly sought after for the fattening of cattle.

Leaving on the left the pretty little houses of Célérina, lying among the green pastures like a herd of white heifers, I arrive in twenty minutes at Samaden, the chief town of the Upper Engadine, a summer and winter station, with its fine hotels, before which are standing a crowd of carriages grouped round a great yellow *diligence*, like grandchildren round their grandmother.

In the centre of the valley, on the Valtelline road which

passes over the Col de Bernina, whose enormous domes of
snow are seen shining in the distance, Samaden is a handsome and large village, well built, and looking more like an
aristocratic town. Its houses have a well-to-do appearance,
with railings of wrought iron, green shutters, windows with
convex panes, the balconies sheltered by curtains and ornamented with flowers. Some very highly privileged ones
even display a little pockethandkerchief of garden in front.
Their vegetables are protected from the night frosts by
boards. Snow falls not unfrequently even in August.
What cultivation could resist such sudden surprises? They
have given up the attempt even to cultivate oats.

At Samaden you find the old house of the Engadine, of a
severe and strange style of architecture. They are real
strongholds, with the thick walls of a fortress, long narrow
windows like loopholes, a vaulted doorway, forming a dark,
narrow vestibule like a postern. The dwelling-house, the
granary, and the stable are all protected behind the same
walls, against the same enemy—the terrible winter ; which
begins its siege in the month of October, and does not raise
it till the month of June. A great earthenware stove
reaching to the ceiling warms the common room, where the
family live amidst the portraits of their ancestors, the black
frames thrown out in relief against the beautiful panelling
in larch or pine, with the shining ruddy tints of old mahogany. Behind the stove a stair leads to a sort of hiding-
place concealed by little curtains, a sort of great Breton
bed suspended like a cage, into which, during the very
severe cold, the husband and wife creep, and roll themselves
up and keep warm, like a couple of marmots. The kitchen,
with its enormous chimney framed in beams, to which are
suspended all sorts of appetising and delicious things,
smoked victuals, sausages, hams, sides of bacon, is black as
a cavern, which the hearth lights up at the hour of meals.

I make myself late by visiting several of these venerable
old houses, which they show me with charming goodnature,

" Alas ! " a good mother said to me, " we seldom meet all together. My husband is dead. I have four sons: the oldest is in Paris, the youngest in Lugano, the two others are guides in summer, and in winter waiters in Milan."

I ask, " But who, then, does the field work ? "

" The women and the Tyrolese."

" The Tyrolese ? "

" Yes. They come here in summer to mow our meadows ; it was they who were driving the hay cart with the ash-coloured oxen that you met on the way. The people of the Engadine make more by doing other things, by guiding or serving strangers. Every stranger who enters our valley is a source of profit to us. We give them food, drink, lodging, we guide them over our mountains, we sell them our flowers and our pebbles. It is an industry like any other, but it is not within reach of every one. It requires one to be intelligent, to have studied and travelled. Now, every inhabitant of the Engadine has seen something of his country, and knows how to speak several languages."

At last I go to take up again my knapsack, which I left in a little restaurant opposite the hotel of the Bernina. And here again I delay myself talking with the old men, who have returned to their country, that they may be buried among their people, in the hallowed soil of their native land. I drink some of the wine of the Valtelline, which my walk and the open air make me find exquisite, and I am greatly amused in watching the stir of the street, the coming and going of the tourists, the eternal Englishwomen with their blue veils and their blue spectacles, navigating even into the mountain on their boat-like feet; Germans with hats like a mortar or like a pumpkin, and their ladies enveloped in grey dust cloaks, which blow out with the wind and give them the appearance of a hippopotamus in flight.

In front of the hotel, a postillion in a short coat and trousers trimmed with leather, his horn slung round his shoulders, his glazed hat adorned with the federal cross, harnesses the five horses of the *diligence* which is about to start for Coire, across the Col du Julier. Waiters and servants arrive from every quarter with baskets, parcels, luggage ; the dogs bark, the street boys throw stones at them ; the official of the coach office, with bare head, quill behind his ear, and sleeves of lustre, buttoned at the wrist and fastened at the elbow, calls out from his memorandum the names of the travellers. And each mounts in turn, seating himself in the appointed place, the most fortunate in the *coupé*, or up beside the driver. The coachman climbs to his seat, takes the reins in hand, the horses shake their bells noisily, and a resounding crack of the whip gives the signal for departure. On the balcony of the hotels hand-kerchiefs are waved, to which other handkerchiefs respond, shaken like little white flags from behind the windows of the *diligence*. The great yellow-bodied coach disappears in a cloud of dust, and the waiters and servants return, shoving and laughing, and the spectators disperse.

In winter the postal service is not wholly suspended between the Upper Engadine and Coire, in spite of the snow. The Col du Julier is crossed in a sledge ; and an army of labourers goes in front of the procession to open up the way, or work tunnels under the snow. What would become of the invalids of Saint Moritz and Samaden, if all communication with the outside world were to be inter-rupted for months ?

But it is getting late, and if I am to gain my halting-place, I must set forth. Already some points in the valley are bathed in shadow, and the sun is going down towards the Italian plains.

From Samaden to Pontrésina the road runs in a bend of the valley, across velvet meadows and under dark forest domes, without meeting a single habitation. The villages of the Upper Engadine are entirely isolated, and separated one from the other. They form a little world apart, and seem to have no connection with each other. One leaves

Célérina and falls at once into solitude, or quits Moritz and finds no further trace of a human dwelling; at ten minutes from Samaden you are in the open desert. No cultivation, no industry. A great silence, broken only by the passage of the carriages of tourists, or of the federal *diligences.* In the Upper Engadine the house is afraid, it does not like to stand alone, it needs a neighbour, and only feels safe under the shadow of the two churches of the village—one for the living, the other for the dead. The pretty châlet embowered in leaves, the little cottage hidden among trees, the solitary, but sweet homelike dwelling concealed behind its sweet-smelling hedge, is unknown in the stern, grave country, with its sad grandeur shut in by the cold ramparts of its glaciers.

The road winds across great bare spaces between two streams which run slowly over their pebbly bed, giving a life-like motion to their tall grasses. Then it crosses a little wood where not a wing moves, not a song or note is to be heard. Even the familiar and inquisitive magpie has forsaken the valleys of the Upper Engadine.

But what a magnificent panorama I have before me! The Bernina, with its glittering breastplate and its great white helmet, seems to command a colossal army of silver-casqued glaciers, ready to descend and fall upon the valley.

The night was falling fine as dust, as a black sifted snow-shower, a snow made of shadow; and the melancholy of the landscape, the grand nocturnal solitude of these lofty, un-known regions, had a charm profound and disquieting. I do not know why I fancied myself no longer in Switzerland, but in some country near the pole, in Sweden or Norway. At the foot of these bare mountains I looked for wild fiords, lit up by the moon.

Nothing can express the profound sombreness of these landscapes at nightfall; the long desert road, grey from the reflections of the starry sky, unrolls in an interminable ribbon along the depth of the valley ; the treeless mountains, hollowed out like ancient craters, lift their overhanging precipices; lakes sleeping in the midst of the pastures, behind curtains of pines and larches, glitter like drops of quicksilver; and on the horizon the immense glaciers crowd together and overflow like sheets of foam on a frozen sea.

The road ascends. From the distance comes a dull noise, the roaring of a torrent. We cross a little cluster of trees, and on issuing from it the superb amphitheatre of glaciers shows itself anew, overlooked by one white point glittering like an opal. On the hill a thousand little lights show me that I am at last at Pontrésina. I thought I should never have arrived there; nowhere does night deceive more than in the mountains; in proportion as you advance towards a point, it seems to retreat from you.

Soon the black fantastic lines of the houses show through the darkness. I enter a narrow street, formed of great gloomy buildings, their fronts like a convent or a prison. The hamlet is transformed into a little town of hotels, very comfortable, very elegant, very dear, but very stupid and very vulgar, with their laced porter in an admiral's hat, and their whiskered waiters, who have the air of Anglican ministers. Oh! how I detest them, and flee them, those hotels where the painter, or the tourist who arrives on foot, knapsack on his back and staff in hand, his trousers tucked into his leggings, his flask slung over his shoulder, and his hat awry, is received with less courtesy than a lackey. They are always lodged under the roof, if they are allowed to lodge at all, for the greed of some landlords is without bounds. It requires the arrival of a numerous family in a private carriage, with fifty packages, to unwrinkle their stupid countenances, frozen into the insolent arrogance of the upstart.

Besides those hotels some of which are veritable palaces, and where the ladies are almost bound to change their dress three times a day, there is the hotel of the second and of the third class; and there is the old inn; the comfortable,

hospitable, patriarchal inn, with its gothic signboard hanging at the end of its iron pole : *A L'Etoile, Au Lion d'Or, A
la Grappe, Au Bouquetin*, etc. There, not only is excellent
accommodation to be found for "man and beast," but the
house has not six storeys, and there is not a body of attendants in black coats, solemn as mutes at a funeral, but pretty,
laughing servant maids, eager to run in your service, to take
your knapsack and stick, and to conduct you to the best
room,—the one with the round table and the green carpet
with black flowers, a mirror in an antique frame, a sofa in
blue rep, chairs and easy chairs with mouldings, and pictures
representing the Oath of Rütli, the Diet of Stanz, and the
passage of the allies into Switzerland in 1813.

This inn of the olden time still exists in the greater
number of localities visited by tourists. It is simply
necessary to have it pointed out by the people of the country.
It is the inn of the *Journey in Switzerland at 3 francs 50 a
day.* Now that money has lost half its value, a young man
who travels on foot and avoids *tables-d'hôte* at six francs (wine
not included), does not spend more than from six to seven
francs a day. And when he stays anywhere, he pays the
pension price ; that is to say, from five to six francs.

At the restaurant where I stopped at Samaden, I asked an
old man who was warming himself in the sun,—

" Could you tell me of a hotel in Pontrésina ? "

" At twenty francs a day ? "

" No."

" At fifteen francs ? "

" No."

" At seven francs ? "

" Yes."

" Well, go to the Steinbock (Wild Goat), and I believe you
will get off with six francs. It is a good little hotel, outside
the village, in a very favourable situation. But there is no
marble vestibule, no mirrors in gold frames,—it is very
simple, but very clean."

The streets of Pontrésina are almost as animated in the evening as the neighbourhood of Pére-Lachaise. I was obliged to knock at two or three doors for information as to the direction I should follow to find the hotel.

On leaving the village I was again on the open mountain. In the distance the road penetrated into the valley, rising always. The moon had risen. She stood out sharply cut in a cloudless sky, and stars sparkling everywhere in profusion; not like nails of gold, but sown broadcast like a flying dust, a dust of carbuncles and diamonds. To the right, in the depths of the amphitheatre of mountains, an immense glacier looked like a frozen cascade; and above, a perfectly white peak rose draped in snow, like some legendary king in his mantle of silver.

Bending under my knapsack, and dragging my feet, I arrive at last at the Hotel Steinbock, where I am received, in the kindest manner in the world, by the two mistresses of the establishment, two sisters of open, benevolent countenance and of sweet expression.

And the poor little traveller who arrives, his bag on his back and without bustle, who has sent neither letter nor telegram to announce his arrival, is the object of the kindest and most delicate attentions; his clothes are brushed, he gets water for his refreshment, and is then conducted to a table bountifully spread, in a dining-room fragrant with good cookery and bouquets of flowers.

CHAPTER IV.

THE Steinbock hotel was full. They were obliged to
lodge me in a neighbouring house, near an old church
the faithful guardian of a poor little cemetery where—

" Les morts dorment en paix dans la sein de la terre."

In the mountains one goes early to bed, and sleep is very
restorative. The next morning by five o'clock I had already
opened my window and taken a bath of fresh air, the
balmy, strengthening air of the mountains. It was one of
those clear sweet mornings of August, which in these high
altitudes recall the commencement of spring, the first smile of
the earth freed from its icy swaddling clothes. The herbs,
sparkling with dew, seemed moistened with a shower of
white pearls; the hedge flowers, in colours of blood and
milk, shed their strong odours, the pleasant odours of the
woods and the wild country. The rising sun scatters its
fine gold dust, and sends its changing reflections along the
pale transparent blue of the sky. Not a speck of mist.
On every side peaks spotted with snow, glaciers which look
like mountains sleeping under great white coverings. And
a silence deep, religious, like that in a church at the elevation of the host. Not the opening of a door, nor the bark
of a dog, the crowing of a cock, or the song of a bird. Not
a sound troubles the earth prostrated before the sun-god

shining in his glory and about to show himself up there seated on his throne of clouds.

I dressed slowly, going unceasingly from the toilet table to the open window, to drink in the morning air and gaze on the beautiful, tranquil country. About six I went down. At this moment a little group of tourists passed into the stony road which rises directly up to the mountain. They were about ten, the men in gaiters and grey coats, the ladies also in country costume,—a short skirt, a little military jacket, a felt hat with turned-up brim and ornamented with a black feather. They had a bold, valiant manner, an air of conquest that became them amazingly. A pretty girl, young, handsome, lithe, and graceful, not afraid of showing her strength and agility, going on in front with a conquering air, as if marching to the assault of the mountain, grasping her iron-shod staff as Joan of Arc her banner, was all that one could dream that was charming and attractive.

" Where are they going ? " I asked the proprietor of the house as he cleaned my boots.

" To the Piz Languard."

" Is it far ? "

" No ; four hours."

" Then I have time to go there before luncheon ? "

" Certainly ; the path is good and the weather is fine."

I hastily swallow a cup of milk, fill my bottle, and am on my way.

The ascent at once becomes hard. The Piz Languard is no trifling knoll, it is 10,715 feet. One soon gets above the valley, where the thin blue smoke, which flickers in the sun, shows that the village is waking up.

Then we cross a forest, climb a steep rocky pathway, covered with *débris*, rubbish, blocks of stone,—a habitual road for avalanches,—and over the sombre pine tops we see, to the left, far away below us, St. Moritz, on the shores of its lake, its houses looking like a flock of ducks sitting round a pool. Samaden can also be seen, with its steeple planted like a

mast. Then we come to a sort of plateau where pines and
larches clothe in dark draperies a châlet, kept by a dirty
shepherd, with long unkempt hair and beard, and arms and
legs black with dirt. It would require one to be chased by
a storm, or pursued by all the unchained demons of the
mountain, to resign one's self to enter it.

The path now ascends across rocks of red granite, between
which flowers the white *immortelle* of the Alps, the beautiful edelweiss, then rising gradually and crossing fields of
snow or carpets of rare flowers, its brings us under the
peak, twenty minutes from the summit. A little shepherd's
hut, where one finds something to eat and drink, cowers in
by the side of the rock. The painter Georgy passed several
weeks here. I can distinguish inside a rickety table, some
chairs, a bed, and an old trunk on which a spirit lamp is
burning.

Formerly it was necessary to creep along a crevasse, but
now-a-days the path leads to the summit without presenting
any danger.

Here we are at last, and we are not alone : the whole party
who preceded me is grouped on a space of about sixteen
yards square, the ladies seated on blocks of rock, using their
opera glasses, the men standing leaning on their sticks and
passing a telescope to each other while they consult a map.

Stopping to take breath, I gazed, wondering and astonished,
at the magnificent panorama below me and around me.
The Languard has been called the Rigi of the Engadine ; but
how much more original is the view from its summit—more
imposing, grander, more picturesque—than from the Rigi.

There one sees only things we know, variegated fields,
green forests, blue lakes, yellow plains, white mountains,
arrested on the horizon like a fleet of great sailing vessels ;
whereas here the landscape has something quite unexpected
and wildly beautiful. It seems as if one had mounted high
enough in the clouds to have got to another planet, a planet
only in process of making and still in its rudimentary stage.

As far as the eye can reach there stretches a region of snowy and icy mountains, crowded, thrown together, hurled against each other, which cross and intercross, and open up into valleys or descend in cascades, and spread out into lakes and seas of foam, rolling their stormy, frozen waves away into the unseen distance, into the mysterious mists of chaos.

On the ridge of this bare rock we looked like a flock of poor little birds, beaten down by a gust of wind. And the sensations one experiences are singular, something calm and sweet, and detached from human interests. A forgetfulness of everything below invades you; earth gradually disappears from your thoughts, you no longer see anything but a vanishing point on the side of St. Moritz, whose houses look like ants' eggs, and its lake like a drop of dew. Everywhere else solitude, the desert, nothing that recalls man. Immense fields of snow, succeeding to immense fields of ice, hollowed into furrows, torn with large fissures with aqua-marine and opal reflections; snowfields spotless as an altar-cloth; and farther away, in the background, all the incomparable enchantment of the great glaciers, the sunbeams glittering on their rivers of quicksilver, their blocks and their needles of crystal, their pyramids of mother-of-pearl, their porticos and cupolas of marble. A phantasmagoria which Georgy has transferred to canvas, while no one has been able to paint the panorama of the Rigi.

A little apart, enveloped in a great mantle, seated on a pile of shawls, a lady whose face seemed not unknown to me was talking with a gentleman who surrounded her with all sorts of care and attentions. I approached: it was the Italian lady of St. Gothard and Lugano.

We greeted one another; she presented me to her husband, with whom I exchanged a few words.

Pointing with a beautifully gloved hand to the Piz de Bernina, whose white skull-cap the sun had embroidered with gold, "Is it not," she said, "a gross imprudence to climb there merely for the pleasure of climbing? I have been making inquiries. It is a very difficult ascent—indeed a dangerous one. But my husband is obstinate, he persists in wishing to go." He smiled, and tried to calm these feminine fears by a caress, as one would a child, then spoke of something else.

I had laid myself down on a great flat stone behind a rock which sheltered me on one side from the wind. And there, leaning over the abyss, I overhung all these gorges and wild precipices lined with snow; I followed their contours, their mazes, their ridges; I saw the swellings and breakings-up of the glaciers, the upheavals of a world still in revolution, where only two small lakes shone like living eyes.

And what notable heights, what savage peaks, what proud summits, what inaccessible needles, what lovely rounded white mountains, what dazzling glaciers, throwing their silver waterspouts into the depths of the sky!

To the south, the Piz Carral and Piz Cambrena, with their torn flanks, on which the snow lies like fine lint; the vast wall formed by the Piz Palü, the Mount Pers rising cliff-like above the snows of Morteratsch; the Piz Zupo and Piz Casta-güzza, crenellated like the white marble ramparts of a magical, mysterious city, a heavenly Jerusalem, invisible to the eyes of mortals. And towering above this majestic amphitheatre, filling the space with its enormous mass, like a tower of Babel in crystal, touching the sky, the Bernina, with its four points in stages, rises in terraces and courses of mountains, which are joined by the silver pathways of many glaciers.

Farther off, that dark pile of rocks, that summit which seems to have been broken up by a volcanic shock, is the Piz Tschierva; to the right and left of its broken pyramid, Piz Roseg and Piz Caputschin, stretch in long columns of onyx with milky and bluish reflections. Then the Piz Corvatsch, spreading its icy walls in a large cone, pierced with holes by the sun's rays; between Piz Surlej and the Piz Rosatch, that pearl-grey cloud is Mount Rosa; and proudly beside it rises the king, the giant Mont Blanc, under his crown of sparkling diamonds.

To the west there is the same resplendent and fantastic piling up of lofty ridges, the same unequal line of peaks and points, reduced by distance to the size of great trees, showing in the dim distance like a clearing in a forest of giant pines covered with snow.

One can scarcely discern the pale top of Tœdi, whilst to its right the Piz Ot diminishes to a pointed steeple, the Piz Uertsch is rounded into dome and cupola, and the Cresta Mora raises its crest reddened by the sun. And at the end of the immense chain, as if in the recess of an alcove hung with draperies of lace and satin, the Sentis seems to sleep on a golden-fringed pillow of cloud.

To the north the Piz Kesch has the appearance of a fortress; the Piz Plazetta stands out in a triangle; the Weisshorn raises through the rosy mist its tower of ivory lit up by the sun like a lighthouse; the Piz Linard shoots into the air like a great stone arrow; the Fluchthorn one would take for a roof covered with silver; the Peaks Pisoc, Saint-Jean, Madlein, Christannes, are like the teeth of a gigantic jaw; and to the east the Mont Zébru, is lashed by the waves of the Cima dei tre Signori; then the Piz Foscagno, with its two mitre-shaped points. Farther off are Mont Cembrosca, the Corno di Campo, and a number of other summits getting lower and lower, till we reach the Col du Bernina, whose two lakes are like two beetles with shining scales, motionless in the grass.

The Piz Languard is so favourably situated, and its pyramid is so lofty, that it overtops all the surrounding mountains except Bernina. Twenty years ago it was only known to shepherds and chamois-hunters; now its fame is universal, although in Paris there are not a hundred Parisians who are acquainted with it. The descent was done in an hour. It was a pleasure party, a fête. I found myself mixed up, I knew not how, with the party who set out to return at the same time as myself. We were almost acquaintances; these tourists were Austrians from Vienna, the gay capital of Strauss waltzes.

Arriving at the top of a great declivity of frozen snow, the guide stopped, and addressing himself to the ladies, asked,—

" Should you like to amuse yourselves a little ? "

" We should not be Viennese if we refused. Yes, yes ; let us amuse ourselves. It is so delightful, the snow ! " And, impatient and curious, they quickly grouped themselves round the guide.

" Well, we will descend this beautiful snowy slope in three or four minutes without the smallest danger. It is only necessary that these ladies should have courage. This is how we proceed. Each of these gentlemen must seat himself, and take a lady behind him, holding her firmly by the ankles ; at my signal you must all let yourselves slide down. It is not a bit difficult, and we shall gain half an hour.

This manner of descending, much used in the Alps, was new to these ladies, and it seemed to them so droll and original, that they accepted it without difficulty. Each of us seated ourselves on our overcoat folded in four, the ladies on their shawls which were drawn over their knees, and at the word of command we set off, dragging with us in our glissade our companions, laughing and uttering little shrieks. Some awkward couples came to grief, but not seriously, and the adventure terminated without further incident. At the foot of the slope, the travellers, a little giddy from the headlong journey, rose powdered with snow, and shook themselves like water-dogs which had just crossed a river. Then—" Gais et content, le cœur à l'aise," more at ease than the rest of the body, for we were somewhat damp with snow, we regained the Hotel Steinbock just in time for luncheon.

CHAPTER V.

THE next day it snowed. The snowflakes descended lightly, like down. These sudden changes, these disagreeable returns of winter in the height of summer, are frequent in the neighbourhood of the glaciers.

The *salon* of the little hotel, where every one took refuge after breakfast, presented a curious spectacle Impatient, feverish, the men paced up and down, stopping every instant to glue their sad and disappointed faces to the window. In the fireplace a great fire blazed; and the ladies crowded round it, shivering in their thin dresses. Such of them as had a pretty foot did not fail to hold it out to the fire, of course to warm it! Seated in easy chairs, the young girls listlessly turned over the leaves of books in which they had no interest, or the albums of newspaper eulogiums spread out on the table, turning lingering looks every minute towards the window.

But the snow fell, fell constantly, with a slow continuous movement, as if produced by a machine. And it all fell noiselessly, like celestial roses, like lilies of purity dropping petal by petal.

The green meadow grass blossomed visibly, and the tufted branches of the trees also, as if a second spring had come. The effect was charming. But at the end of some hours the picture changed; everything was white, everything was padded with snow; the tree-tops bent under avalanches; it

123

was no longer spring, but winter, winter in its full severity,
its dead sun, its sadness, its gloomy silence, its air of
mourning and desolation. Nothing could any longer be
distinguished. The snow fell, fell, hiding the sky behind
a curtain of moving muslin, burying the earth in a shroud of
lace, running its silver fretwork over the black trunks
of the trees, putting in the hollow of each leaf the calyx of
a white ivory flower.

A young Russian who was my neighbour at table, and
with whom I had made acquaintance, said to me with an
irritated air,—

"Oh let us go out! I feel as if I were in the *salle
d'attente* of a railway station. The sun will not come; one
must make up one's mind. It will snow till night."

As we came down the outside stairs of the hotel, where
some guides waited, stamping their feet, with their hands
in their pockets, we asked one another where we were going.
There was hardly a choice. I proposed to go down to the
village and go to the café. Baedeker had just revealed to
me the existence of an establishment of this kind in Pontrésina.

There was no longer a trace of the road. The snow fell
so thick that it blotted out our footsteps.

We followed the telegraph posts, and ten minutes later
we were installed behind a little table, on which a German
waiter had placed two cigar-racks.

Lighting his cigar, the young Russian related to me at
length the history of his mission to the Grisons, and when
we left the café the night had fallen. And still it snowed,
and still in front of the hotel the stolid guides waited,
smoking their pipes and stamping their feet. We made a
sign to one of them, a great solid fellow, short and broad-
shouldered, with a brown beard and quick, piercing eyes;
we asked if he would be willing to guide us to the glacier
of the Diavolezza. He said, "The snow is going to stop,
we can make the excursion to-morrow; but I warn you

that it will be disagreeable, for the fresh snow is truly abominable for walking. And there are crevasses. But I know the glacier better than my pocket. Don't be afraid, I will answer for you."

CHAPTER VI.

THE young Russian and I had parted, saying,—
" To-morrow, at five o'clock."

Punctuality is the first duty between travelling companions. As five o'clock struck we were sitting opposite each
other in the dining-room of the Steinbock, and two pretty
servants in white caps, their hair still in disorder, fluttered
round us, serving us with coffee, milk, cream, honey, and
preserves, five excellent things, without which a first breakfast in Switzerland would be incomplete. A good solid
provision is necessary for all who take the road for the
whole day.

Before the hotel our guide awaited us, the brave Schmidt,
with his ice-axe on his shoulder, and a bundle of rope in
his hand. The carriage also was ready, an old *char-à-bancs*
patched up who knows how, and all splashed with mud. In
front sat the coachman, a little hunchback, with an immense
hat, smoking one of those long Italian cigars like a rat's
tail.

I said to Schmidt,—
" Well, is the weather good ? "

He looked at the sky, which was visible, quite blue, through openings in silvery clouds, he searched the horizon with his piercing eyes, ambushed in great bushy eyebrows, then in an assured tone he replied,—

" It is good weather."

We mounted our carriage. The little servants smilingly brought us provisions packed up in newspaper, and making them our adieux we set forth.

The morning was fresh, a north wind blowing. Around us everything was white, everything was covered with a compact brilliant snow, like satin : the peaks of the mountains were like sugar loaves, and one would have said that their slopes were forests of camellias in flower.

At the top of an ascent we met a capuchin, who came from Italy, in an uncovered carriage ; he was pale, with the paleness of yellow wax ; he was lean like an invalid ; chilly, shrivelled, he was squeezed in between two handsome, buxom girls, expansive in face and figure. The painters have often shown us Death triumphing over Life—here it was Life victorious over Death.

Schmidt told us that before being a guide he had been a hunter.

Whilst the hunchback sucked his long cigar, and tried to get his bony old horse to a trot, Schmidt told us of some of his hunting expeditions. He had killed more than a hundred and fifty marmots in the neighbourhood of the Roseg glacier. The hunting of them is no easy matter. One must be well acquainted with the country, know which of the holes are inhabited, and several days beforehand must lie hidden flat on the ground, watching through a glass all the habits of the little colony. A wall is then constructed at forty or fifty paces from the burrow, behind which the hunter begins his watch while it is still night. It is only in winter that the marmot is lazy, which is natural, as he sleeps then. In summer they rise with the dawn.

The first day, the old marmot who conducts the band—and

as among the chamois, it is always to the females that the
surveillance and command is given—the old marmot sees a
heap of stones that was not there the night before, suspects
a trap, and returns to prevent her family from coming out.
However, she gradually gets accustomed to this wall, behind
which nothing moves, and at last she ventures out. It is
very pretty to see her put her nose out of doors at the break
of day. First she shows nothing but her pointed muzzle,
her grey moustache over her long teeth of golden yellow.
She sniffs the air, she scents the wind. Then she pricks
her ear to catch the least sound. If everything is quiet, if
there is silence near and far away, she begins by putting
out two paws, then she stops again and proceeds to a minute
inspection of the place. Her eyes of a shining black, with
a round eyeball like a bead of jet, are so piercing that they
see at a great distance. Next she comes out of her hole.
But still she hesitates, rises on her hind paws, then returns.

The whole band then joins her, the young ones with the
gaiety and carelessness of children. They glide among the
rocks, cropping some of the flowers to which they are
partial, and then group themselves together on a large flat
stone exposed to the sun, at some paces from their burrow.
And there, while the old ones keep watch, the young ones
take their sport, leap, skip, frisk, comb themselves, scratch
and lick themselves; this is the moment for the hunter to
take exact aim, for every animal that is only wounded is lost.
If he has time to get back to his hole, good-bye to him! One
must not move. As soon as the sentinel perceives anything
suspicious, it gives the alarm, and its cry is repeated by all
the marmots round about.

The marmots live in couples or in families. They have
often like foxes two dwelling-places, one for summer and
one for winter. The subterranean gallery of their summer
residence measures sometimes thirty feet. At the extremity
there is a chamber large enough to contain fifteen of them.
This chamber is padded with hay.

I said to the old hunter,—

" They assure us that the marmot in transporting his provision of hay, lies down on his back, while another draws him by the paws, as a horse draws a waggon, and that this is the reason why he has so little hair on his back.

Schmidt fell a-laughing.

" Stories! stories! The marmots transport their hay quite simply in their teeth, and if their backs are rubbed bare, it is because the galleries they dig out are not high enough."

I asked our guide how long they slept.

" From six to eight months. And do you know why they do not need to eat? A doctor explained it to me. Because they scarcely breathe. As respiration is after a fashion suspended, alimentation is no longer necessary. The body becomes cold, and falls into a kind of torpor. The sleep of the marmot is an apparent death, a true lethargy."

" I have heard it said that in winter the marmots live on their own fat? "

" More stories! I have killed them in the month of April, and they were as fat as in autumn."

" The fat is used as a remedy? "

" In the mountains it is the universal remedy. With marmot's fat they cure every disease : colic, whooping-cough, aches. The flesh is smoked. It is given to women in child-bed to give them strength."

I asked Schmidt, " Have you ever taken marmots alive? "

" Oh, yes; often."

" And how did you hunt them."

" In the simplest fashion in the world. When I had discovered through my glass that the marmots of a certain burrow were sleeping in the sun, I climbed up the rocks quite near their hole. Then, with a bound, I leaped to the entrance of the burrow, blocked it with a stone, and whistled. The poor infatuated creatures answered with a piercing whistle, and, seeing their retreat cut off, they threw themselves into the first cranny they found. Then I chose

9

my marmot, pressed it against the rock with my stick to
keep it from biting, and taking it by the hind paws I slipped
it into a bag. The marmots are also hunted with dogs; but
it is almost as barbarous a proceeding as that of digging
out the burrows in winter, and taking the poor things during their sleep."

We had arrived at the houses of the Col de Bernina,
grouping their grey walls, the colour of old ruins, round
two wan lakes, one black and one white.

The sun had succeeded in piercing the clouds that hid it,
and one saw, as if through rents in a dense smoke, his great
sparkling, golden disc.

We left our carriage, and climbed a long slope covered
with fresh snow. We walked slowly, sometimes sinking to
our thighs. At the end of an hour we reached the lake of
the Diavolezza. The snow had transformed its shores into
a great white marble basin.

The shepherds of the Carpathians call these alpine lakes
the "eyes of the earth." And they have, in truth, an infinite sadness, a profound melancholy. Their glaucous
water looks at you as if with a dying eye, in which all the
hidden sorrows of the world are reflected.

The existence of these ephemeral lakes indicates the last
zone of the glaciers ; in proportion as these retire, the lakes
are drained off—dry up. In the last century more than a
hundred lakes have disappeared thus in the Tyrol.

We climbed a new hill, more steep and difficult. It was
eleven o'clock. The sun mounted with us, climbing also
strange chains of clouds, piled up here and there like
mountains of snow. We had the greatest difficulty in the
world in advancing. I was bathed in perspiration, and
more than once our guide was obliged to drag us out of the
soft snow into which we plunged up to our middle. The
sensation was strange. It felt as if we were drowning, or
disappearing in an abyss of wadding.

At last, after redoubled efforts, we reached the ridge from

which we could overlook, as if from the heights of a rampart, all the great glaciers grouped round the Bernina. As far as the eye can reach, all is white, all is frozen, nothing but snow, and then more snow, and then enormous sheets of ice, an immense extent of *névés*, of whiteness, continual whiteness, which unrolls itself with the calmness of an infinite steppe, or which rises, agitated, tormented, in grand volutes, like foaming waves of a sea.

The ice fills the valleys and gorges, leaps against the rocks rising in cliffs, surges in its too narrow basins, clashes its frozen, rigid waves against each other.

With his crown and his cuirass of ice, under his snowy burnous, the Bernina has the air of a legendary warrior, of the giant king of some eastern tale.

Round him the lower peaks shiver in their snowy robes; they seem to cower down among the whiteness of soft ermine, of a chilly down, benumbed under their veil of gauze and tulle. This infinite, boundless white which invades everything, earth and sky, and dazzles like some vision of the frozen zone—it is superb, and fills you with a strong emotion!

One asks, wondering, how, in a place so near the habitations of men, it has been able to snow so much purity and innocence.

And what calm, what repose, what silence! Not the note of a bird, or even the cry of a marmot or chamois! One would say we were on the threshhold of a dead world, or, rather, of a new world still in the making, which is born in the slowness and sleep of the ages. Such must our globe have been at the Glacial epoch. The vast solitude, frozen and savage, waits its spark of life, its spring, its sun of love which will waken it, and clothe it with forests and turf, and people it with men and animals.

At our feet the glaciers of Pers and of Morteratsch unroll their vast frozen deluge, which falls into the valley with the enormous force of a cataract.

An island of rocks, Isola Persa, the Lost Island, has escaped the general submersion ; it rises above this amazingly motionless sea, its head partly covered with snow, like an old man's hair.

This region, so long unknown, a mysterious sanctuary where Nature seems to be working out a new world, is surrounded and defended by an embattled wall with towers as if of ivory, domes of snow, sharp needles planted with the stiffness of lances, obelisks and pyramids of ice, and points of silver.

Before us is united all that family " of an ethereal magnificence," as Tschudi says, which form the Bernina group. The Piz Morteratsch, the Piz Tschierva, the Cresta Agüzza, the Piz Zupo, first ascended on the 9th July, 1863, the Piz Palü, the Piz Cambrena. And there, dominating all in his august and proud royalty, draped in his mantle of snow, the Piz Bernina !

This lofty white summit, wildly majestic, makes one of the royal family of the great peaks of the Swiss Alps : Mount Rosa, the Matterhorn, and the Finsteraarhorn. Eight glaciers unite at the foot of the first, seven at the foot of the second, five at the foot of the third. The Mer de Glace, which surrounds the Bernina, is more than sixteen leagues in circumference. Its tempestuous waves, with azure reflections like lava, pile themselves in the defiles, precipitate themselves into the gorges, or run by a rapid descent into the depths of the valleys ; sometimes they leap up between two points of rocks, dart into space, and remain suspended above the abyss till the day when their frozen sheet is broken up and hurled into its depths. The *débris* of this ice avalanche is frozen anew into a single mass, and forms another glacier, which develops like the first, the structure of which it exactly reproduces. Pursuing its march forward, it proceeds by successive falls, like an immense cascade, always subdividing, until it reaches the limits, where the ice dissolves into water.

The immobility of the glacier is only apparent. The glacier is living. It moves and advances without ceasing. When the day has been warm, and is followed by a cool night, a terrible cracking is often heard, a noise like the rolling of a subterranean thunder. It is the glacier which is walking, coming down on uneven ground. The same crash is produced when a crevasse opens up. And in proportion as the glacier develops the fissures enlarge. Some of them form into deep valleys, abysses, and unfathomable gulfs. If you fall into one of these crevasses, you hear everything that is said above you, but you cannot make yourself heard. Nothing can equal the beauty of the ice of these fissures. It has tints of extraordinary fineness and delicacy; it is of a pale and tender blue, an ideal blue, which fascinates the eyes; but if you detach a morsel to examine it in full light, its beautiful colour disappears, vanishes, and you have nothing in your hand but a pale, colourless block. Naturalists have not, so far, found any explanation of this phenomenon.

Winter is the season of repose for the glacier. In spring all its life and activity return. *Savants* are almost at one as to the causes which set it in motion. Schoelzer holds that its expansion arises from thaw; Professor Hugi is of the same opinion: the glacier, like an enormous sponge, filled with aqueous particles, expands and grows larger when it freezes. Of all the theories, that of Saussure, the oldest, is the most generally accepted. He attributes the forward movement of the glacier to gravitation; that is to say, to the pressure of the superior masses on the inferior.

The incessant transformation of the *névés* produces the glaciers. The *névés* are those fields of dazzling snow which extend above the zone of the glaciers.

The snow of the *névés* does not resemble that of the plains; it is harder, colder, one would say it was made of needles of pounded ice, of little crystallized stars. It falls not in flakes, but in a fine dust as of mica. The alternations from frost to thaw give to this snow the brilliance of metal or porcelain, a consistency approaching that of ice; and the little streams which penetrate and furrow the lower *névés*, change them at length into true glaciers.

Switzerland is the country of glaciers. Tschudi counted 608; and every here and there we come on isolated ones, less extensive, independent, and unconnected with any of the great snow-fields, and which are in their period of formation : such as the Blaue Schnee of Sentis, the Gletscherli, in the Bernese Oberland, and the great slough of avalanches at Binna, in Valais, one of which already shows beds of ice at its base. The glacier of Rothelch, on the Simplon, dates from 1732 ; the Galenhorn, in the valley of Saas, from 1811 ; the glacier of Rosenlaui is also of recent date.

The sun was now blazing in the midst of the sky, like an enormous fire kindled to warm that frozen world.

Our guide unrolled his rope and tied us to one another, and then we went down into the glacier. The firmer snow crackled under the iron of our shoes. We crossed abysses on bridges of ice which looked like bridges of glass; we cleared at a bound crevasses half full of water. From a distance the glaciers look smooth and quiet, like a bed of snow; seen near, they are furrowed and upturned in huge waves; marble-like blocks and columns of ice rise like the ruins of a Babylonian city; and they are traversed with long undulations, striped with fissures, cut in wide, deep rents, which are slowly modified, getting larger or smaller, according to the mobility of the ice, whose azure waves have their quiet and invisible risings and fallings.

At the end of an hour after having crossed the glacier of Pers, we arrived at the Roche-aux-Chamois.

The sun right above us floated in a sea of azure ; not a single foam cloud was visible. Its intense light blinded us; the snow and ice sent back its rays upon us like arrows of fire, which penetrated our skin in spite of veil and spectacles.

Schmidt swept with his cap the snow which covered the stones on which we were to seat ourselves for breakfast, then unpacked the provisions; slices of veal and ham, hard boiled eggs, wine of the Valtelline. His knapsack covered with a napkin served for our table. While we sat, we devoured the landscape, the twelve glaciers spreading round us their carpets of swansdown and ermine, sinking into crevasses of a magical transparency, and raising their blocks, shaped into needles, or into Gothic steeples with pierced arches. The architecture of the glacier is marvellous. Its decorations are the decorations of fairyland.

Quite near us marks of animals in the snow attracted our attention. Schmidt said to us,—

"Chamois have been here this morning; the traces are quite fresh. They must have seen us and made off; the chamois are as distrustful, you see, as the marmots, and as wary. At this season they keep on the glaciers by preference. They live on so little! A few herbs, a few mosses, such as grow on isolated rocks like this. I assure you it is very amusing to see a herd of twenty or thirty chamois cross at a headlong pace a vast field of snow, or a glacier, where they bound over the crevasses in play. One would say they were reindeers in a Lapland scene. It is only at night that they come down into the valleys. In the moonlight they come out of the moraines, and go to pasture on the grassy slopes or in the forests adjoining the glaciers. During the day they go up again into the snow, for which they have an extraordinary love, and in which they skip and play, amusing themselves like a band of scholars in play hours. They tease one another, butt with their horns in fun, run off, return, pretend new attacks and new flights with charming agility and frolicsomeness. While the young ones give themselves up to their sports, an old female, posted as sentinel at some yards distance, watches the valley and scents the air. At the slightest indication of danger, she utters a sharp cry ; the games cease instantly, and the whole anxious troop assembles round the guardian, then the whole herd sets off at a gallop and disappears in the twinkling of an eye.

"Hunting on the *névés* and the glaciers is very dangerous. When the snow is fresh it is with difficulty one can advance. The hunters use wooden snowshoes, like those of the Esquimaux.

"One of my comrades, in hunting on the Roseg, disappeared in the bottom of a crevasse. It was over thirty feet deep. Imagine two perfectly smooth sides ; two walls of crystal. To reascend was impossible. It was certain death, either from cold or hunger ; for it was known that when he went chamois-hunting he was often absent for several days. He could not therefore count on help being sent ; he must resign himself to death. One thing, however, astonished him ; it was to find so little water in the bottom of the crevasse. Could there be then an opening at the bottom of the funnel into which he had fallen ? He stooped, examined this grave in which he had been buried alive, discovered that the heat of the sun had caused the base of the glacier to melt. A canal of drainage had been formed. Laying himself flat, he slid into this dark passage, and after a thousand efforts he arrived at the end of the glacier in the moraine, safe and sound."

We had finished breakfast. We wanted something warm, a little coffee. Schmidt set up our spirit-lamp behind two great stones that protected it from the wind. And while we waited for the water to boil, he related to us the story of Colani, the legendary hunter of the Upper Engadine.

Colani, in forty years, killed two thousand seven hundred chamois. This strange man had carved out for himself a little kingdom in the mountain. He claimed to reign there alone, to be absolute master. When a stranger penetrated into his residence, within the domain of "his reserved hunting-ground," as he called the regions of the Bernina, he

treated him as a poacher, and chased him with a gun. What
legends were told of him too! They said he had a room
quite full of the spoils and the arms of the hunters he had
killed. He had an ill-will especially against the Tyrolese,
because they are very adroit and rarely miss their aim. In
the district they were persuaded that Colani had sold his
soul to the devil, and that he fired with enchanted balls.
We are assured that once, on the Blaci du Lai Alp, he had
laid eight chamois stone dead with a single ball; that
another time he placed one of his sons at a great distance,
and made him hold up a bone of a horse, which he broke in
two. Still another time, hidden behind a larch-tree, he had
knocked the pipe out of the mouth of a woodcutter.

Colani was feared and dreaded as a diabolical and
supernatural being; and indeed he took no pains to un-
deceive the public, for the superstitious terrors inspired by
his person served to keep away all the chamois-hunters
from his chamois, which he cared for and managed as a great
lord cares for the deer in his forests. Round the little
house which he had built for himself on the Col de Bernina,
and where he passed the summer and autumn, two hundred
chamois, almost tame, might be seen wandering about and
browsing. Every year he killed about fifty old males.
These chamois he regarded as his property. If he had succeeded in attracting them quite close to his dwelling, it was
because he had established "salt-licks," by bringing there
saline stones, which these animals liked to lick. He spread
salt also at certain places in the neighbourhood of the White
Lake, and the chamois, which came every morning, found,
close at hand, fresh water to quench their thirst.

His reputation as a diabolical man brought an Englishman
to him one day, who asked him to let him see the devil.
Colani said to him: "One had better not jest with the
wicked one; I advise you to renounce this idea, which does
not seem to me a good one."

The Englishman insisted: "No, no, no; let me see the

demon, and I will pay you. I am not afraid; an Englishman is never afraid!"

Colani, not knowing how to get rid of his importunities, told him to return towards midnight. He conducted him into a cellar where he had a little forge, which he lit. He made an enormous fire, and went several times round the brazier, reciting magical formula.

At last, advancing towards the Englishman, who awaited, breathless, the apparition of the devil, he said, presenting his purse,—

"The devil,—well, if you wish to see him, my lord, he is in there!"

The Englishman took it in good part, and was generous enough to dislodge the devil from Colani's purse.

When Dr. Lenz, accompanied by one of his friends, M. de Planta, proposed to Colani to guide them in a hunting expedition on the Bernina glaciers, every one predicted that ill would come of it. During four or five days Colani, who was sixty-six, took them about in the most dangerous places, fatiguing them as he chose, not allowing them to fire when herds of chamois passed before them. The second day he conducted Dr. Lenz to the extremity of a very narrow *arête*, on which he could only slide on his stomach. While the doctor watched some chamois, standing lower down in a cleft of the rocks, an enormous *lacmmergeier* hovered over his head, ready to swoop down on him. These birds, whose size surpasses that of the eagle, seek, by a sharp blow of their wing, to precipitate into the chasm any man or animal they can take unawares and defenceless. Colani, seeing the danger with which his companion was threatened, gave a cry, which saved Dr. Lenz from certain death.

The third day he set them on the pursuit of bears, who had devoured three sheep in the neighbourhood of the shepherd's hut where the hunters had slept; but the gorge into which the flesh-eaters had retired was absolutely inaccessible. They were obliged, therefore, to content themselves with chamois. Unfortunately the marmots gave the alarm by their repeated cries, and the chamois scampered off at a mad pace.

The fourth day M. de Planta renounced this ridiculous and insane hunting party. Dr. Lenz set out alone with Colani. A violent wind blew in their faces, blinding them with snow. At last, at the end of half an hour, the wind fell. Colani took his glass, and said to Dr. Lenz : " I see five chamois browsing. At nine o'clock they will lie down ; but to get within range of them we must scramble round that enormous wall of rock. The way is dangerous. I have only done it once in my life. Do your best to get safely out of it ! "

Colani slung his carabine over his shoulder and set himself first to the difficult passage. The rock was perpendicular. It was necessary to step on broken points and jutting-out corners, clinging on as best they could. Arrived at the end of the ledge, Colani cried out, " Attention ! " And raising himself by his vigorous wrists, he disappeared on the other side, his body suspended in the air as in an acrobatic exercise. Dr. Lenz in his turn cleared this *mauvais pas*. Colani, seeing this, exclaimed,—" I should never have believed that we would both find ourselves on this side. Now that we have got round them, the chamois must be ours."

Lenz fired first, over Colani's shoulder. He had sighted a large male lying in the midst of the rhododendrons on the edge of the precipice. It made a bound of six feet, staggered, and fell backwards into the abyss. Colani leant his carabine on a stone, fired at a young chamois which accompanied the large one, but missed. Dr. Lenz wished to go to the bottom of the precipice to seek the animal he had killed. Colani opposed this, saying with a sinister air and a strange look,—

" Those who fall into this gulf remain buried there for ever."

They climbed up again by a valley where great blocks of rock were rolled one on the top of another, like an avalanche of stones. Suddenly Colani, who was all the while searching the country with his glass, threw himself behind a big stone, and made a sign to Dr. Lenz to imitate him. The doctor asked him,—

" What is it ? "

Colani, his eye fixed on his glass, did not at first reply; then clenching his fists, and contracting his brows, he broke out in a great oath. Dr. Lenz then looked through his glass in the same direction; and saw very high on the rocks, a human form which was moving, a little black silhouette, advancing towards them. Beside himself, furious, still shaking his fist at the unknown, Colani continued to swear. . . . " I don't know the scoundrel. There, he is looking with his glass; but, thank Heaven, he has not seen us! He may go away, so I'm going to prevent it."

He shouldered his carabine. Dr. Lenz stopped him :

" Colani, what are you doing? I did not come with you to see you fire on men."

The silhouette disappeared. Colani made a bound.

" Follow me," he said to the doctor; " in ten minutes we must be up there."

The slope was steep, bristling with stones and pieces of rock; but putting forth all their efforts, they were soon at the top. They hid themselves behind a stone, and waited. The unknown advanced towards them, suspecting nothing. Colani having loaded his carabine, adjusted it anew. Dr. Lenz put his hand on his shoulder, and said with an air of command :

" Colani, I will not allow you to commit a crime before my eyes."

It was the first time the wild hunter had ever heard a voice so imperious; he turned to the doctor and replied :

" We are not going to dispute. Stay here. Wait for me."

And with the agility of a snake he glided behind the rocks, always holding his loaded gun, ready to fire.

Arrived within a few paces of the unknown, who was quietly looking through his glass with an air full of security, Colani suddenly started up, as if a dead man had leapt out of the ground. The two men looked at each other for an instant without saying a word, then Colani quietly placed his rifle against a rock, and invited the man to sit down beside him. He offered Colani a pinch of snuff. Colani took the hunter's gun and examined it attentively. Dr. Lenz expected to see the unknown spoiled of his hunting gear, and then thrown over the precipice. But Colani was talking to his neighbour in quite a quiet tone when Dr. Lenz joined them. The man, whom Colani would certainly have killed if he had been alone, was an old man of Bevers. Having learned that Colani had set out for Bernina, he had said to himself that he would be running no risk in his absence ; and that he might not be denounced by the shepherds, he had disguised himself, putting on a false beard.

Colani left a son, who is also a guide and hunter ; but his true successor is Jean Rudé, of Pontrésina, who kills, on an average, from thirty to forty chamois in the year.

CHAPTER VII.

BEAR HUNTERS.—KÜNG.—JEAN RUOLF.—NICOLAS LECHTALER.—
THE SNOW PARTRIDGE.—M. JANCKA.—FLORA AND FAUNA OF
THE GLACIERS.—HOW THE GLACIERS ARE FORMED.—CRE-
VASSES, "TABLES," "MOULINS."—THE LEGENDS OF THE
GLACIER.—MORAINES.—EVENING NEAR THE GLACIERS.

EVERY locality in the Engadine has its celebrated
hunters. At Bergün, it is the brothers Sutter, who
have brought down among the three of them more than 2,000
chamois. Samuel and Matthieu killed one day five chamois
in the space of a quarter of an hour.

The chamois hunter is also a hunter of bears; and it is
in the Canton of the Grisons that these animals, now rare in
Switzerland, are most frequently met with. In 1857, eight
were killed in the Upper Engadine. In 1858, they devoured
twenty-two sheep on the Alpe de Buffalora. In 1860, a hunter
in the neighbourhood of Zernetz killed eleven. They were
seen coming to browse on the crops up to the foot of the
road. The same year, on 11th August, a shepherd, who was
crossing the Col de Buffalora on horseback, met a she-bear
and two young ones. She rushed on the horse, who had time
to turn and defend himself by energetic kicks. In leaping to
the ground the shepherd lost his sheepskin coat, and the bear
in her rage threw herself on it. Whilst she tore it, the shepherd quickly remounted his horse and fled.[1] In 1864, a great
bear brought terror among the bathers of Schuls. And the
travellers who passed in the *diligence* the same week, on the

[1] Tschudi.

opposite bank of the Inn saw two little bears quietly sucking the mother.

In the Lower Engadine, furrowed with wild gorges, covered
with dark and impenetrable forests, bears are still more
numerous than in the Upper Engadine, where the mountains
are almost bare. Jacob Küng, of Zernetz, has left a name
famous among bear hunters.

One day he set out with a comrade to hunt chamois. As
he climbed the gorge of Arpiglia, Küng, with his piercing
eye, discovered among the rocks on the slope an enormous
bear. The hunters descended, in order to approach the
creature, and to fire on him as he lay. But during this
manœuvre, the bear climbed the ravine, so that they did not
find him in the place they expected. After some searching,
Küng perceived the animal at some distance above them.
Getting a little nearer, Küng cried,—

" It is the moment to fire."

His comrade said to him, " It is impossible to hit him."

" It is possible," replied Küng, who at the same moment
gave a shout. The bear lifted his head, the shot was fired,
and the ball hit him. He came down in bounds into the
depths of the ravine.

The two hunters tried to get rapidly up the slope, so as to
place themselves above the bear ; but while this was being
done, Küng found himself in presence of the wounded
animal, separated from him only by an enormous stone. In
his haste he had not been able to load his gun. But Küng
did not lose his head ; he turned coolly to his companion,
snatched his carabine from his hand, and sent a second bullet
into the bear, which rolled over uttering a plaintive cry.
However, he was not dead ; after an instant he rose, his
powerful paws tore up the earth and made it fly round him ;
he ground his teeth, and his roaring resounded far through
the valley and mountain. Küng, always bold, recharged his
gun and descended in pursuit. At a little distance he sent
a third bullet, which grazed without wounding him. The

bear made reprisals by hurling a block of rock at the hunter, who avoided it by stooping down; and without moving, rested from his breathless chase, Küng watched his time to aim, and lodged a bullet exactly in the right eye of the bear, who fell an inert mass, his paws forward, his muzzle on the ground.[1]

Küng had while quite young a passion for the chase. At nine years old he had already killed six chamois. At sixteen, alone in the mountain, he had destroyed a bear by rolling an enormous stone on it. During his fifty-three years of hunting he had killed 150 bears, more than 1,500 chamois, five stags, and nine eagles.

There are, Schmidt told us, in the valley of Münster, two very renowned hunters, of whom M. Tschudi, whom he accompanied there, makes mention in his book on the Alps. One of them, Jean Ruolf, killed several eagles, and he kills on an average thirty chamois each summer. One day, in following a track in the Val Tavetsch, he came to a torrent where he saw an enormous she-bear bathing. Laying himself down flat, he crept across the brushwood to a stone, behind which he lay in ambush. As soon as the animal presented her breast, he let fly his two shots. The bear gave a terrible cry, came out of the water, shaking herself and writhing, and then fled. Ruolf quickly reloaded his gun; the water of the torrent, all reddened, showed that the animal was wounded. He set off in pursuit, but could not get up to her. Coming out into a glade, he discovered three little bears licking themselves, stretched in the sun. He killed two of them; the third got off into a tree; Ruolf sent a bullet into his head, and he rolled down like a squirrel.

Another hunter of the valley of Münster, Nicolas Lechtaler, went one day to hunt for partridges. The snow partridge is very common in the Engadine; they call it the "white hen," because it resembles a little hen, and because in winter it is white, like the snow in which it likes to roll

1 "L'Echo des Alpes."

itself. The mountain partridge is so tame that it may be killed by throwing stones at it. It lives in the midst of the rocks and the ice, and during the heat of the summer it gets into the shade of the rhododendron bushes. When the storm surprises it, it does not move from the place, but cowers against the ground, and remains several days buried in the snow.

Nicolas Lechtaler had gone, as we said, partridge hunting; when above the Val Cavel, he found himself face to face with a she-bear, accompanied by three young ones. The meeting was unexpected. Nicolas stopped, hesitating a moment about what he should do. His gun was only loaded with coarse shot, sufficient for a bird,—but for a bear! Passion does not reason. Nicolas said to himself, that if he could not kill the mother, he might succeed, perhaps, in killing a little one. He shouldered his gun, fired. Thereupon one of the little bears began to turn head over heels. The old bear gave a cry of fury, then rising on her hind legs, she ran upon the hunter; but he threw himself on one side, and the enraged animal, instead of pursuing the man, approached her dying little one, smelt him, licked him, turned him over, and finally taking him in her teeth carried him off, followed by her two other young ones.

When Lechtaler relates this story, he adds, quite low, that when he got home he wept for spite at having missed such a fine shot!

Schmidt continued: "We have three species of bears, the great black bear, the great grey bear, and the little brown bear. The bear will not attack a man unless he is himself attacked. This good, loyal animal never lies in wait for you, never takes you as a traitor. I have personal experience that the bear will not touch a body which has no longer an appearance of life. Once, in a hunt, one of my neighbours, who accompanied me, wounded an old bear. The animal rushed on me. I was posted thirty paces lower. I fired, but agitation made me miss my aim. Then I threw myself

10

into the forest, and, I do not know how, I rolled to the bottom of a little ravine. The bear, furious, came on in pursuit of me. He ran with a heavy step, roaring, and making the dry branches crack. I had not time to get up. I made as if I were dead. Oh, what a moment it was! My eyes shut, holding my breath, I expected to be crushed like a fly. The bear approached his muzzle to my ear, smelt me, shook me with his heavy paw; then seeing I did not move, he sat down on his hind quarters and began to lick his wound, watching me closely, as if he mistrusted me. During this time my companion had reloaded his gun, and had come noiselessly and posted himself above the ravine. He sent a second bullet into the bear, which this time, hit full on the breast, uttered a hoarse roar, fell over on its side, its head forward, and expired without another moan. Its body had rolled against me, I felt the last shudder of agony. When I rose I was covered with blood. My companion believed that I was half eaten. We made a litter of pine branches to transport the animal, who measured six feet, and weighed more than four hundred pounds.

"Not later than last month Jancka, a schoolmaster of Upper Saxony, was hunting chamois on the Piz Zavragia. Towards midday he noticed on the snow traces of a large quadruped, and recognised them as tracks of a bear. He followed them; forty paces higher he perceived a grey mass under a rock; it was the bear. M. Jancka, not being able to fire from below, made a detour and climbed on an eminence which overlooked the rock under which the bear was lying. M. Jancka fired; the ball hit the animal and came out again near his head; at the moment when he tried to rise a second ball hit him full in the breast, and he rolled to the bottom of the moraine. M. Jancka covered the slain animal with snow, and came next day to seek him with two men of Saxony. It was a silvery bear weighing about two hundred pounds. He had devoured some sheep a few days before."

I said to Schmidt that I had read that when the Austrian,

Russian, and French armies crossed the Grisons, the bodies of the unfortunate soldiers who were left without burial became immediately the prey of the wolves, and I asked him if they were numerous. He said that wolves had become very rare, and that when notice of one was given, they organized such battues that it could hardly escape. The forests are no longer vast enough for the wolves to propagate, and as their rapine gives notice of them at once, they are obliged to live in the deepest recesses, to prey on the hares and the young of the hazel-hen, and for the most part to be contented with a rat, a lizard, a frog, or a snake.

Whilst our guide gave us all these details about the life of the alpine animals, we sipped with relish from our silver goblets exquisite Mocha prepared by ourselves from ice water.

The water of ice is as good as the glacier water is bad. How the chamois hunters obtain it is,—they set a block of ice in the sun to melt, and they collect the drops in a goblet. In running over the stone this water becomes charged with carbonic acid, and is excellent, whilst water drawn in like manner from the glacier inflames the throat and augments the thirst.

When conversation flagged, when we were silent that we might fathom the white desert of snow which lost itself in the distance round us, the silence was so deep, so absolute, the void so profound, that we said to ourselves, in the pride of our littleness compared to the infinite grandeur of nature, " We are the kings of this solitude."

The weather had become quite settled and fine. We did not need to fear being surprised by one of those violent atmospheric revolutions, so dangerous in the regions of eternal ice. We enjoyed tranquilly the sight of those superb glaciers reflecting the sun.

On the horizon, the snowy peaks, standing out in their whiteness, in a cloudless sky, made one think of great tents erected round a sea of azure.

Our guide enumerated for us the names of all these celebrated summits, as in a museum of sculpture the cicerone points out all the most illustrious figures. Each of these mountains has its biography, its history. This one takes life, —it is the barbarous, sanguinary, homicidal alp. This other, on the contrary, is humane, hospitable; it offers sure sheltering places to the guides and to strayed travellers. Differing in form, attitude, colour, each of them has its physiognomy and its character, "its soul," as Michelet says. And the play of light, the variations of atmosphere, make the mountain as mobile and as changing as the sea.

On the solitary, frozen rock on which we were, an ephemeral life vegetated; quite a little world of plants, of insects whose existence is never prolonged beyond two months. Wherever the sun can get at the naked rock from July to September, wherever a fissure is opened, there vegetation climbs and, clinging, establishes itself; there it flourishes and blooms amidst the *névés* and the glaciers. One sees charming colonies of little flowers which have emigrated from the valleys and have come to hide themselves in the cold deserts, where the brevity of their life seems to enhance the beauty of their colour. The better to resist the hoar frost they grow in thick tufts closely pressed against each other.

The torn flanks of these islands of rock are velvet with lichens and mosses, all vibrating with golden reflections, and in capricious patterns which recall the carpets of the East. Frail saxifrages, small arborescent plants, similar to those which are found in Spitzbergen and Lapland, hang suspended over ice gulfs. Even animals inhabit these formidable solitudes. Infusoria, spiders, plant-lice hide under the leaves, among the mosses; and sometimes a beautiful glittering butterfly, with wings of mother-of-pearl or of carmine, driven by a spirit of adventure, loses itself in these inimical regions. Its boldness and courage are rewarded. On the summit of the sterile rock it finds the sweet and melancholy flower which awaits it. These savage deserts, struck with cold and with the immobility of death, still keep love.

Lower down we meet with some "wells," vast reservoirs
which go down to the bottom of the glacier and permit us to
see its structure, to see its beautiful, polished, transparent
ice, which shades from pale blue to dark blue, and which
is like azure solidified. In certain glaciers there are wells
eight hundred feet deep.

This glacier ice, made of annual beds, disposed in vertical
bands of white and blue, does not resemble ordinary ice,
which is homogeneous throughout. It is granular, traversed
by a multitude of small canals, by a network of veins in
which a bluish water circulates, and which penetrates the
whole thickness of the ice. Tschudi tried exposing a piece
of this ice to a high temperature; the capillary fissures became more distinct, the granules disintegrated, and the ice
was reduced to small fragments.

What surprises there are in these infinite solitudes which
have the appearance only of sleep and death! Seen from a
distance, from the midst of the plains or the depths of the
valleys, the glaciers have the profound sadness of cemeteries.
But when we penetrate into this unknown world of eternal
ice and snow, we see Nature there also pursuing her divine
work, accomplishing her marvellous mysteries.

The glaciers have not only a special fauna and flora, but
one would say they even amuse themselves by taking on the
most whimsical forms, the strangest shapes, the most fantastic appearances. Here they will open up in azure grottos;
they round themselves in vaults of lapis-lazuli, in arcades of
turquoise; there they raise domes of mother-of-pearl, silver
cupolas, obelisks of opal, columns of onyx; they crystallize
into enormous roses, roses of white cornelian, which are
called "glacier roses."

Sometimes their crevasses, all lined with the purest,
smoothest snow, open up like great alcoves hung in clouds of
lace, with delicate ornaments thrown on them by the wind.
And behind these white draperies, which have all the
coquettish neatness of a woman's paraphernalia, you may

hear a sound as if of kisses; the rippling of a brook which falls drop by drop.

The crevasses modify and change every spring, when the winter's accumulation of snow melts under the action of the heat, and the frost of the nights incorporates it with the glacier. The guides, therefore, before conducting parties at the beginning of the season, sound the old crevasses, and study the new features of the glacier, its curves, its bridges of snow suspended in the air, its abysses covered with a frail surface, its fantastic architecture of staircases and terraces of ice.

Quite near the Isola Persa, surrounded by the frozen waves of the glacier like some reef in the Polar sea, we find some "tables," raised on high supports, on thin needles of ice. One does not know by what miracle of equilibrium these heavy tables of stone are upheld. They are blocks of granite, of slate, or of limestone which have fallen on the glacier, and protected from the sun the ice which they cover. Melting has gone on all round them, so that their supports of ice make them look like enormous mushrooms. When this support is in its turn fretted away, the enormous block —some of them are more than seventy feet in circumference —bends over and slides down; and a new table is formed at the place where it falls.

In the midst of our long crossing we also met with a great hill of sand, a sort of solid dome, built by deposits of earth and gravel. Under this bed of *débris* the ice does not melt, and remains at its primitive level, cut into *arêtes* and into cones, as it is under the stones of the "tables."

On summer days the glacier is furrowed with thousands of threads of water, an innumerable quantity of little rills which run and sparkle over its sides like streams of quicksilver, and which disappear suddenly in the *moulins*, at the bottom of which invisible canals join the extremity of the glacier.

At night all these brooklets are silent, and stop; the cold

congeals and imprisons them in a thin coating of ice, which evaporates again the next day.

The descent became more and more difficult; enormous *séracs* barred our passage and compelled us to take long detours; fissures multiplied; all the experience of our guide was necessary to conduct us across the labyrinth of yawning crevasses. Some of them were hidden like wolf-pits under the fresh snow; and it was in order that we might be held back in case of a fall that we were all three attached to the same rope.

After some hours' uninterrupted march, we came out at last from the interminable glacier of Morteratsch, which descends much lower into the valley than all the others.

It is terminated by a marvellous portico framing a vast nave of ice, with columns of sapphire, pillars of agate, stairs of marble. From the vaulted roof hang, like silver lamps, great stalactites with iridescent reflections. And a sifted, softened light, falling as if from invisible church windows, bathes with mystic clearness the depths of this icy sanctuary, whence springs, as if from some symbolic fountain, a torrent of white and boiling waves.

From the depths of these azure catacombs the shepherds at night, under the livid disc of the moon, see the souls of the poor sinners shut up in the glaciers issue forth, and their sighs mingle with the noise of the torrent rolling blocks of the moraine in its bed.

This glacier, so white, so pure under its veil of snow spangled with sunshine, so beautiful under the reflections of its ice, which resembles a mountain of blue crystal, so poetic in its structure, and its forms fashioned by the hand of the Divine Artist;—this glacier, in the eyes of the credulous mountaineers, is nothing but a place of grief and exile, a place of penance and punishment, a place of expiation and tears.

Dante describes it in his " Inferno," when he says :—

" Into that secret place he led me on.
     Here sighs, with lamentations and loud moans
Resounded through the air pierced by no star,
That e'en I wept at entering. Various tongues,
Horrible languages, outcries of woe,
Accents of anger, voices deep and hoarse,
With hands together smote, that swell'd the sounds,
Made up a tumult, that for ever whirls
Round through that air, with solid darkness stain'd
Like to the sand that in the whirlwind flies.
     I then, with error yet encompass'd, cried :
' O master ! what is this I hear ? What race
Are these who seem so overcome with woe ? '
     He thus to me : ' Tis miserable fate
Suffer the wretched souls of those who liv'd
Without or praise or blame, with that ill band
Of angels mix'd, who nor rebellious prov'd
Nor yet were true to God, but for themselves
Were only. From his bounds Heaven drove them forth
Not to impair His lustre, nor the depth
Of Hell receives them, lest th' accursed tribe
Should glory thence with exultation vain.'
     I then : ' Master ! what doth aggrieve them thus
That they lament so loud ? ' He straight replied :
' That will I tell thee briefly. These of death
No hope may entertain : and their blind life
So meanly passes, that all other lots
They envy. Fame of them the world hath none,
Nor suffers ; mercy and justice scorn them both.
Speak not to them, but look and pass them by.' " [1]

Prisoners in the frozen caves of the mountains, the poor
souls tremble and shiver with cold ; and those among them
who are permitted to clothe themselves again in their cast-
off body, walk shivering in their nakedness, in the midst of
these mute and desolate regions, a sort of limbo from which
they can only escape at the expiration of their punishment.
The shepherds who have had a glimpse of them in the clear
darkness of starry nights, speak of a blond woman, an
Eve, beautiful as Venus, who has no other clothing than her

---

[1] " The Inferno." Canto III. Cary's translation.

long golden hair; they tell also of another woman, wonderfully graceful and seductive, who is condemned to walk naked on the sharp edge of the crevasses. To those who have interrogated her, because she uttered plaintive cries, she has answered: "My true body is shut up in Milan, in a tomb of stone, and my husband weeps for the young wife torn from him. God has condemned me to expiate on this glacier my sloth and idleness. Go and pray to God, that He may abridge my punishment, and pardon me." One may see, too, wandering on these slippery snowfields, betrothed couples, to whom the cold gives the livid pallor of corpses. They try to warm one another in a close embrace; but their bodies are of ice, and when they wish to speak or to kiss each other, they cannot open their frozen lips.

It is never graceful and charming apparitions, nymphs and fairies, who light up the legends of Swiss glaciers with their bright and supernatural beauty. Those with whom they are peopled are gloomy, unhappy beings, trembling with fear, weighed down by some malediction or chastisement.

Look at those white forms which one would take for two phantoms, who run like a couple of mad people on the snow-bridges of unfathomable crevasses; they have nothing on but a chemise of white cotton. They run barefoot on the cutting ice, on the sharp *arêtes*. Remorse harasses and pursues them.

And this long cortège, who pass in black mantles, and who, during the whole of Lent, go ceaselessly up and down the glacier, it is the cortège of unjust and prevaricating judges.

On the Ember days, also, a long procession of torches is seen advancing towards the glacier, and then suddenly extinguished.

In every fissure, in every rent, are souls who weep, who sob, who wait for deliverance. Their number is so great that to contain them the glacier is obliged to grow larger, to extend itself, to descend into the valley. God sometimes permits these poor shivering souls to go and warm themselves at the hospitable hearths of the shepherds. Then they surround the lighted-up châlets like a great flight of birds, and with a plaintive voice they cry : " Open to us, we are cold ! " And there are so many, so many, that they cannot all get in, and they press invisibly against the doors and windows with a mysterious humming.

The path crosses a vast moraine, and leads to a little châlet auberge, rising boldly opposite the great river of ice which fills the bottom of the valley.

The name moraine is given to those piles of stones pebbles, blocks of rock, *débris* of all sorts, that the glacier brings down with it in its course, and which it gets rid of as soon as possible. " The glacier is always cleansing itself," say the mountaineers. Enormous blocks of granite have been seen to fall into crevasses, and to be rejected by some occult force in a very short time. If the glacier expands it breaks up and disperses its frontal moraine, it pushes it with its enormous body, throwing out and piling on the sides even the largest blocks of stone ; if on the contrary it contracts, part of this chaos of *débris*, left in its place, becomes covered by degrees with a carpet of turf.

When two glaciers descend by two opposite valleys, abutting on the same bed, and meet, their moraines mingle with one another, and are sometimes piled up till they attain a width of almost a thousand feet, and a height of about seventy.

The little watercourse which we follow, and which leads us direct to Pontrésina, descends as far as Samaden, where it goes to swell the course of the Inn.

From each lip of the glacier flows a stream or a river. The Rhone issues from the Rhone glacier, the Rhine from that of the Rheinwald. Cradles worthy of the destiny and future greatness of the two rivers are these immense waves of ice, under the vaults of which they have been formed, and where they have uttered their first cry.

The water which escapes from a glacier is either black like ink, or green like absinthe, or white like milk; it is always troubled and charged with mud or earth full of fertilising matter.

After a short halt at the châlet of the Morteratsch, we took the road again at a rapid pace. The night came with the suddenness with which it comes in the desert and in the mountains.

The sun, like a great burning wreck in the midst of a sea of fire, floated on the red line of the horizon. And its reflections, as of conflagration, were sent back from all the snowy summits which rose on both sides of the valley, already invaded by shadow, filled with the ashes of darkness brought by the fresh wind which had suddenly begun to blow. The high peaks were illuminated like lighthouses; others, more carved out, resembled Gothic belfries, illuminated from the interior by Bengal lights. Spangles of ice hung on to a rocky pyramid had the rich scintillations of an incrustation of jewels. And the immovable *névés*, those thebaids of snow suspended on the sides of the Bernina, were changed into celestial gardens, into parterres of brilliant, coloured flowers. On the heights everything was in gala dress, everything blazing, whilst the valley was already almost plunged in night.

Now the great sun went down. It sank from view in the bloody waves of the horizon. Suddenly it disappeared, but the snowy peaks remained lighted up, as well as the light clouds which floated here and there, like morsels of red stuff carried by the wind. To the right the Mont Pers stood out in a clear sky, with its spot of snow with purple reflections, like a bloom of rhododendrons; whilst further off the glaciers stretched their great terraces of rose-coloured marble as far as Piz Palü and Piz Argient, above which rose in the far distance the august splendour of Piz Bernina, a citadel of silver, the fairy palace of the invisible queen of the snows and the ice.

The colouring of the crests softened and became rose-coloured. The high points, the solitary peaks, burned still, with a fainter light, like that of an expiring torch. In the sky, glowing with vivid lights, the needles of rock appeared elongated, the ragged *arêtes* of the high cliffs overhanging the sea of glaciers assumed sharper outlines.

The clearness of the firmament was in its turn extinguished, the peaks and summits floated in a tint of dark blue, into which the snow once more brought its immaculate whiteness and purity.

As the sun sank, one no longer saw anything but a thin ray of light, which made one think of a brook of gold running in the middle of a field of roses. Timid stars came trembling to take their accustomed place, whilst on the horizon an invisible hand appeared to cast them like a gold dust, a divine sowing, a sowing of worlds, a dust of stars!

A soft vapour caressed the drowsy mountains with its long veils, and a shepherd's dog, black like a demon, ugly as a gargoyle, crouched on a projecting rock, and bayed the moon which rose pale and cold like the sister of the glaciers. Slowly she mounted the long icy ridge of Bernina, like an enormous ball of gold, propelled by an invisible mechanism. And when she had scaled the peaks, she suddenly detached herself from it, let herself fall into the immense celestial sea, and floated gently like a luminous buoy. Her misty rays shone faintly like a nightlight, and all those beautiful mountains, white like phantoms, seemed to have donned their night attire, through which showed the superb forms of their giant bodies.

And beyond those fantastic summits, far far away, on the uncertain line of the horizon, there were so many stars that one would have thought they were a great flight of gilded birds flying from the night.

CHAPTER VIII.

NEXT morning we slept late. We breakfasted at ten
o'clock ; then my chance companion, the young
Russian, set out for St. Moritz, where he expected to fulfil
as quickly as possible the difficult mission of which he had
spoken to me.

By noon my limbs were no longer conscious of the thirty
miles of the day before ; and I set off for the glacier of
Roseg, a short, five hours' excursion, going and returning.
The mountain paths are so pretty and charming, they
wander about so capriciously and fancifully, they run so
merrily over the moss in the woods, and beside the babbling
or murmuring brooks ; they climb so cheerfully up the slopes
and hillsides, and lead you through so much freshness and
perfume and varied scenery, that the pleasures of sight soon
make you oblivious of bodily fatigue.

The path at first goes easily along under the light, delicately transparent foliage of a fir wood, the slender trunks
forming a long colonnade by the side of a stream that chafes
and brawls in the confinement of a little wild and pitiless
gorge.

It is a delicious corner. The faint blue of the sky is seen

through the branches with their close, fine network of needles; and the light comes sifted through them, a softened light that makes one think of starry nights.

The torrent is crossed by an old stone bridge, under which hang in green festoons all kinds of grasses and creeping plants, over which the passing stream throws a spray of drops that roll off like pearls from a broken necklace.

Right before you, through an opening in the foliage, is seen the white, regal Piz Roseg, its enormous glaciers like ramparts of silver and marble fortifications, its embattled summit, on which the sun is gathering his sheaves of long golden arrows. Then the path follows the course of a moraine, for in former times the Roseg glacier came down to this point, and in twenty minutes you pass the *acla* or house of Colani. It was in this poor, lonely abode, planted like the hut of a savage among the rocks, that the famous hunter spent his winters.

A broken-down wall runs down the mountain; a little miniature Chinese wall, which marks the boundaries of the communal property between Pontrésina, Samaden, and Celerina.

The scenery becomes rugged and stern. The rocks are still covered with the snow that fell two days ago.

Beside this dazzling, magnificent snow, covering the chain of lofty peaks like an immaculate altar cloth, what a gloomy, dull look there is in the snow of the plains! One might think it was made of sugar or confectionery, that it was false like all the rest.

To know what snow really is,—to get quit of this feeling of artificial snow that we have when we see the stunted shrubs in our Parisian gardens wrapped, as it were, in silk paper like bits of Christmas trees,—it must be seen here in these far-off, high valleys of the Engadine, that lie for eight months dead under their shroud of snow, and often, even in the height of summer, have to shiver anew under some wintry flakes.

It is here that snow is truly beautiful! It shines in the sun with a dazzling whiteness; it sparkles with a thousand fires like diamond dust; it shows gleams like the plumage of a white dove, and it is as firm under the foot as a marble pavement. It is so fine-grained, so compact, that it clings like dust to every crevice and bend, to every projecting edge and point, and follows every outline of the mountain, the form of which it leaves as clearly defined as if it were a covering of thin gauze. It sports in the most charming decorations, carves alabaster facings and cornices on the cliffs, wreathes them in delicate lace, covers them with vast canopies of white satin, spangled with stars and fringed with silver.

And yet this dry, hard snow is extremely susceptible to the slightest shock, and may be set in motion by a very trifling disturbance of the air. The flight of a bird, the cracking of a whip, a tinkling of bells, even the conversation of persons going along sometimes suffices to shake and loosen it from the vertical face of the cliffs to which it is clinging; and it runs down like grains of sand, growing as it falls, by drawing down with it other beds of snow. It is like a torrent, a snowy waterfall, bursting out suddenly from the side of the mountain; it rushes down with a terrible noise, swollen with the snows that it carries down in its furious course; it breaks against the rocks, divides and joins again like an overflowing stream, and with a wild tempest blast resumes its desolating course, filling the echoes with the deafening thunder of battle. You think for a moment that a storm has begun, but looking at the sky you see it serenely blue, smiling, cloudless. The rush becomes more and more violent; it comes nearer, the ground trembles, the trees bend and break with a sharp crack; enormous stones and blocks of ice are carried away like gravel; and the mighty avalanche, with a crash like a train running off the rails over a precipice, drops to the foot of the mountain, destroying, crushing down everything

before it, and covering the ground with a bed of snow from
thirty to fifty feet deep.

When a stream of water wears a passage for itself under
this compact mass, it is sometimes hollowed out into an
arched way, and the snow becomes so solid that carriages
and horses can go through without danger, even in the
middle of summer. But often the water does not find a course
by which to flow away ; and then, when the snow begins to
melt, the water seeks into the fissures, loosens the mass
that chokes up the valley, and carries it down, rending its
banks as it goes, carrying away bridges, mills, and trees,
and overthrowing houses. The avalanche has become an
inundation.

The mountaineers make a distinction between summer
and winter avalanches. The former are solid avalanches,
formed of old snow that has almost acquired the consistency of ice. The warm breath of spring softens it, loosens
it from the rocks on which it hangs, and it slides down into
the valleys. These are called " melting avalanches." They
regularly follow certain tracks, and these are embanked like
the course of a river with wood or bundles of branches. It
is in order to protect the alpine roads from these avalanches
that those long open galleries have been built on the face of
the precipices.

The most dreaded and most terrible avalanches, those of
dry, powdery snow, occur only in winter, when sudden
squalls and hurricanes of snow throw the whole atmosphere
into chaos. They come down in sudden whirlwinds, with
the violence of a waterspout, and in a few minutes whole
villages are buried.

The large quantity of snow that fell last year (1887) has
been followed by the descent of innumerable avalanches in
the Alps. In the Valais, the village of Randa, in the Vis-
pach valley was completely destroyed. The inhabitants,
with the exception of two, made their escape. Forty
buildings were destroyed, and thirty cattle perished.

At Listen an avalanche carried away a new house, belonging to one of the best guides of the Valais. On the day of the catastrophe he was absent; on his return he looked for his dwelling in vain.

At Saas-Grund, the priest, perceiving by certain atmospheric signs that the village was threatened with an avalanche, rang an alarm and fled with all his parishioners to a neighbouring hamlet. At 9 o'clock at night a noise like thunder shook the valley; the avalanche had passed through the village, carrying away five buildings and filling the church with snow.

Here, in the Grisons, the whole village of Selva was buried under an avalanche. Nothing remained visible but the top of the church steeple, looking like a pole planted in the snow. Baron Munchausen might have tied his horse there without inventing any lie about it.

The Val Verzasca was covered for several months by an avalanche of nearly 1,000 feet in length and 50 in depth. All communication through the valley was stopped; it was impossible to organize help; and the alarm-bell was incessantly sounding over the immense white desolation like a knell for the dead.

In the narrow defile in which we now are, there are many remains of avalanches that neither the water of the torrent nor the heat of the sun has had power to melt. The bed of the river is strewn with displaced and broken rocks, and great stones bound together by the snow as if with cement; the surges dash against these rocky obstacles, foaming angrily, with the blind fury of a wild beast. And the moan of the powerless water flows on into the depth of the valley, and is lost far off in a hollow murmur.

Above the path, wrapped in an old worn-out woollen cloak, torn into saw teeth, with a broad-brimmed sugar-loaf hat; his thin, bronzed face in profile, and short hair, like one of Doré's silhouettes of Spanish mountaineers, a Bergamese shepherd stands out in relief, sharply outlined in

11

the full sunshine with the clearness of a statue. His large sheep, scattered around him, are bleating hoarsely among the snow which they are obliged to scrape away in order to find their food, the blades of grass that are growing here and there.

Every spring these Italian shepherds from the valleys of Brescia, Soriana, and Brembana leave the fertile Milanese, and come up the course of the Adda in long caravans, following the shores of the Lake of Como, and reach the Upper Engadine by the Maloja Pass.

In the rear of the procession come large handsome asses, as supple and strong as horses, richly caparisoned, with flaming red tassels and tinkling bells. These are laden with parcels, blankets, boxes, pots, all kinds of household provisions and utensils.

The shepherds of Bergel, more devout, load one of their donkeys with a holy image, a wonder-working madonna, which they set up with great pomp, in a niche over the door of their principal châlet at the Maroz Alp. The Capuchin who is summoned to install the Virgin and to bless the châlet and the flock, goes away with a great basket packed full of ewe cheeses.

While these nomade shepherds spend the short summer on the grassy alps of the Engadine, their wives and children, who have remained in the plain, are busy with the hay-making, the harvest, the vintage, and the gathering in of other fruits.

The occupation of shepherds is hereditary among those people; and they are almost all related to each other in some way.

Several of them join in renting and working an alp, and themselves take care of their numerous flocks; the principal partner alone, whom they call *direttore*, is exempt from this work, which is made specially toilsome by bad weather, when fogs or sudden blasts of snow make it necessary to go and gather the sheep among the precipices.

The solitary and perilous life that these men lead gives them something of a sombre, wild, mistrustful character. They are never heard singing or "*joedling*," like the Swiss mountaineers; if a few brief sentences pass their lips from time to time, that is all. In spite of their bandit appearance, they are upright and honest and extremely sober; living on nothing whatever but polenta and cheese. Bread, butcher's meat, and soup seem unknown to them. Their only drink is water or skimmed milk. And yet these men, living on this miserable fare, have constitutions of iron. They are accounted well-to-do, and even rich. A little hay spread on a plank serves them for a bed; their only covering is their white woollen cloak. Among them are seen old men of eighty bearing without difficulty the hardships and privations of this cenobite life.

When the flock is changed to a new pasture, the scene is one to delight a painter. In front marches majestically a tall, thin shepherd, sunburnt and dirty, in his ragged cloak, armed with his long, iron-pointed stick, on which, from time to time, he leans in a statuesque attitude, one of those grave and dignified poses that it comes so naturally to Italians to assume. Behind him the whole mountain is covered with a moving mass of grey fleeces. Other shepherds are plunged waist-deep in this living flood, where the white wool surges like foaming waves. Now and then a whistle is heard. It is by whistling those thousands of sheep are guided, the straying lambs called back, and the dogs sent out and checked.

The Bergamese dog, with long, woolly hair and strange, sinister appearance, is the most vigilant of guardians. When a stranger comes near the flock, the dog's eyes never leave him, and if he should try to take away a sheep, the dog would rush upon him, and hold him till the shepherd arrived. But the real thieves in those rocky solitudes, in those little islets of verdure that the flocks find out amidst the snows and glaciers, are the *lammergeiers*, the

vultures.of Camogask, the lynxes, the wolves, and the bears.
The bears sometimes devour as many as thirty sheep in a
single night.

If by some accident one of the animals is killed in the
mountains, it is not entirely lost; the bones are taken out,
it is salted, stretched by means of little rods, and dried on
shelves or on the roof of the châlet. Often, says Tschudi,
twenty or thirty skinned sheep are seen thus exposed to
the air. This meat, preserved by the glacier air from
decomposition, finds a ready sale in Italy, where it brings
a high price.

The number of Bergamese sheep brought yearly from
Piedmont to the high mountain pastures of the Engadine,
is estimated at 40,000.

For some time longer the torrent continues its struggle
with the great blocks that impede its way, around which it
boils and froths and murmurs; then the defile suddenly
widens, and the valley opens out into a deep basin, and
rounds into a vast amphitheatre, down upon which the
ever-increasing Roseg glacier lets fall its white draperies.
An immense cathedral of alabaster, with its spire lost in
the clouds, rises in the background; it is the Piz Morteratsch. And to the right, in the quivering sunlight and the
lambent air, the Piz Bernina unfolds its terrible splendour
on the glowing blue of the sky, filling the whole horizon
with its immensity of ice and snow.

We cross a bridge, and presently arrive at a little châlet
restaurant, where there is also accommodation for lodging.
A fair-haired waitress gravely serves me with beer, like an
automatic puppet; then she goes and sits down behind a
table on which lies a zither. This is the Tyrolese musical
instrument,—a square guitar, set on a stand. I beg the
fair waitress to sing me some Romansch songs, some of the
popular ballads of the Engadine. Still as grave as a puppet,
she runs her fingers over the strings of the instrument, and
in a sleepy voice sings:—

" Montagnas, ste bain !
Tu gad e valleda
Tu fraischa contreda,
    Tu En sussurant.
Da vus he algerdeutscha
S qur eir in mi absinza,
    Montagnas, ste bain !

    Vus pasters, ste bain !
Cur me mi udida,
Chanz un zuond gradida,
    Sun Alp od darcho
Con led mien cour acclama,
Mien cour chi saimper sama :
    Vus pasters, ste bain !

    Alp chera, ste bain !
Algrez inefabla
Odur agriabla,
    Chin cunter an gnit !
Que cheu la resentira,
Bain dutsch al cour fluiva :
    Alp chera, ste bain ! "

Of which the following may be taken as a reasonably faithful rendering :—

        " Ye mountains, adieu !
    Thou vale with green bowers,
    Fresh meadows and flowers,
        Where Inn murmurs through.
    Of you I shall think ever,
    When from you I must sever,
        Ye mountains, adieu !

        Ye shepherds, adieu !
    For me, if the singing
    Of sweet songs is ringing
        Again from the alp,
    My heart, with love still beating,
    With joy shall leap, repeating,
        Ye shepherds, adieu !

Alp cherished, adieu !
O joy past all telling !
O perfumes exhaling
    Wherever I go !
My heart, with love still glowing,
With joy is overflowing ;
    Alp cherished, adieu !

I suppose the Engadine has other songs more original
than this one, which I transcribe merely to give an idea of
the Romansch language spoken in the country,—a unique
language, used only in those remote valleys of the Swiss
Alps, adjoining Italy and the Tyrol.

I went on my way and reached the glacier.

The Roseg glacier is unrivalled in its magnificence, with
its great waves curved over in shining volutes, its transparent grottos penetrated by the sun, and looking as if
lighted up within; its long, vaulted fissures, in the depths
of which the water is heard falling drop by drop, with a
mournful sound like a sigh or a stifled sob.

There is something spectral and impressive in the sight
of those immense expanses of ice and snow. It suggests
the cataclysm of some planet or the fall of a meteor, the
ruins of which have lain buried there under the white dust
of ages, since the wild shock of primeval worlds. The eye
is bewildered in that infinite accumulation of blocks, of
those monstrous masses covered with hardened snow, that
rise and still rise like giant steps by which to scale the
heavens.

High on a rock, his great pointed wings motionless, stood
an eagle, proudly erect, as if lord of the vast white solitude;
his eyes of carbuncle keeping watch, his murderous beak
ready for some small, weak creature to appear.

In these cemeteries of snow eagles are rare. They are
only seen in spring, when the flocks of sheep arrive.

When I left the restaurant where I had again stopped on

the way back, the glacier had no longer its resplendent halo
of golden rays, its dazzling reflections of the sunset. While
it was becoming enveloped in a transparent veil of blue
haze, the summits and peaks above it, high enough still to
catch the sunshine, were glowing in rosy warmth, and
glittering like rubies. The Piz Morteratsch and the Piz
Bernina were on fire. And this snow conflagration was
something utterly marvellous and fairy-like. It lasted for a
quarter of an hour, and then gradually died away. And
then there were clouds crimsoned by the setting sun that
still touched the summits with softer, ruddy tints and
reflections. Purple and deep blue shadows filled the valley.
Twilight was falling, darkness was slowly creeping on and
hanging the rocks with its long black draperies.

I hastened on, and overtook a young man who was going
in the same direction as myself. In the mountains people
accost each other freely. We wished each other good-even-
ing, and entered into conversation. He told me he was
schoolmaster at Pontrésina, and that in order to augment his
meagre 'salary, he exercised, during the vacations, the functions of communal forester. He was also, like all his
brethren in office, a chamois hunter. In the Engadine, as in
all those mountain districts, the school year lasts for eight
months, during the most severe season. Little boys and
girls of seven, whose parents live away from the village,
often walk three miles, and sometimes even six, to come
to school. Education being obligatory, the parents are
punished for each absence by a fine, and even by imprisonment. But there are cases in which a stronger power
interferes. When the valleys are obstructed by avalanches,
stopping all communication, the school is almost empty, or
closed altogether.

The languages taught are Romansch, German, Italian, and
French.

The children take part very early in public life ; there is
no festival held without them, and in more than one instance

they are the sole actors. At Easter all the echoes resound with gay peals of bells. It is the children who ring, they ring all day long, hanging on to the ropes of the church bells; they are ringing for the resurrection of the dead, and the whole population flocks to the cemetery. But under the thick winding-sheet of snow that covers it, the great dead, the earth itself, remains motionless in its sepulchral sleep. On the first of May, the children try again to awaken it. They run round the villages and the hay-stacks, ringing big bells and little bells, and celebrating in songs the festival of spring and sunshine. But the earth is still dead. And yet, above her frozen tomb, a few impatient flowers,—the spring crocus and anemone, and the alpine soldanella, show their tender points piercing the snow, and open their delicate, perfect corollas.

It is not till the month of June, when the warm breath of the "föhn" (a moist south wind) comes to the help of the sun, that the snow melts as if by enchantment, and plants and flowers can almost be seen growing. In eight days all the valleys are green and flowery. The blue saffron, primroses, daisies and violets form fragrant flower-beds, in which insects nestle and butterflies flit like joyous spirits of spring and summer.

On the 15th of September, when the shepherds bring down their flocks from the mountains, it is the children who go to meet them with songs and waving flags. In the evening of this day, so longed for by mothers and sweethearts, the whole village rejoices; dancing goes on for a part of the night; it is everybody's festival, for they are meeting again after three months and a half of absence. The returning ones have little news to relate. Up there on the lonely alp life is always the same, following its monotonous course like a slow, tranquil stream, only troubled occasionally by rain or storms; while those who have stayed in the hamlets of the valley, beside the busy road, have so many new and interesting stories to tell!

On the occasion of the festival of the **Three Kings**, all the young men disguise themselves, and indulge in all the follies and absurdities of the Carnival. In the evening, a little prophetic book with questions and answers is consulted; then a list is made out of all the girls eligible for marriage; their names are written on pieces of paper and drawn out by lot. In this lottery each lad draws the name of a girl whom he will call for the rest of the year his treasure, his jewel, his beloved.

The girls, on their side, go at night to the village green, and each throws one of her shoes into the air; if it falls with the point turned towards the cemetery, it is a sure sign that the owner will die within the year; if it points in some other direction, it indicates that from that quarter will appear the future husband.

In former times a wedding was a grand occasion, an imposing performance, in which the whole village took part. In the house of the newly-married pair there was open table, and drinking, dancing, and feasting went on all night. But these pantagruel repasts are now no longer in fashion. Among the lower classes, the day fixed for the wedding is always Sunday. In the morning, before going to church, the guests meet at the bride's house to partake of wine, soup, and fritters. After the marriage ceremony, the party goes in procession to the bridegroom's house, but the door is shut. They knock; no one answers. At last the door is opened. One of the groomsmen appears on the threshold, and in an elaborate speech states the conditions on which the bride will be received. There is discussion and argument, a little comedy played, in which all the clever members of the company take part. Finally they come to an agreement; the party go in and sit down round a table piled with provisions. During the feast several orators hold forth. The priest delivers a long discourse; then, in the evening, there is dancing. At the stroke of midnight the guests form a ring round the wedded pair and take off their crowns; and then, after a few words of " encouragement," they are left alone.

The last solemnities, those of death and burial, have still, among these Latin populations, something violent and passionate in their character. For several Sundays after a funeral, the women, dressed in mourning, with a head-band across the forehead, meet in the cemetery around the grave, and in a mournful and harrowing concert renew their tears and lamentations.

It must not be forgotten, Michelet remarks on this, that this out-of-the-way, isolated country of the Grisons, turning its back to German Switzerland, was the refuge of the most ancient people of Italy, the Etruscans, and that its language, like its temperament, is Romano-Celtic.

In these mountains, where life is so hard, the religious sentiment is strongly developed. On Sunday the churches are full and the psalms are sung in Romansch. The prayer-books are also printed in that language; and at noon the head of the family, or the grandfather, takes the venerable old Bible and reads aloud for a long time, sometimes continuing even during their meal.

An old local law enjoined the people, on pain of a fine, to be present at the sermon. Ecclesiastics and doctors were not allowed to travel on Sunday in any kind of conveyance. And no inhabitant could cross the threshold of an hotel or an inn during divine service without exposing himself to a severe punishment.

The Engadine used also to have its *Landsgemeinde.* The election of the new Landamman was the occasion of great public rejoicings. The electors who came to his house to congratulate him, were free to eat and drink at will. At one o'clock the new Landamman and his secretaries, in official costume, rode on horseback through the streets, followed by a whole cavalcade in procession, and carriages full of women and children. They alighted in the great square, where the retiring Landamman, after delivering a speech, handed solemnly over to his successor the sword, staff, and mantle, the insignia of his office.

Wine flowed in rivers.

Now-a-days things are done more simply. The electors prosaically deposit their votes in the electoral urn, but not the less does the weak wine of the Valtelline turn their heads.

In former days, a lord of Bergün owed his life to this partiality of his fellow-countrymen for the juice of the grape. Being accused of treason, and condemned to death, he begged of his judges the favour of being allowed to take a last meal with them the night before his execution. The favour was granted. He caused the company to be served with wines so good that a jovial gaiety very soon reigned among them. Taking advantage of this favourable moment, the felon lord threw himself at the feet of those who had condemned him, reminded them of the services rendered to the country by his father, one of the founders of the Grison League, and obtained his pardon.

It is also related that a Grison, who was considered the hardest drinker in the canton, went one day to confession, expecting to obtain absolution without difficulty. But the priest refused. " I cannot pass over your drunkenness, my son; it is a shameful sin. You drink a dozen bottles of wine in the day; when you have given up drinking more than two, you may come back to me." Our hero, not being able to make up his mind to such a sacrifice, discussed the matter with the priest for a long time, letting down the number of his bottles one by one; finally he said he would limit himself to six bottles a day.

The confessor dismissed him, without absolution.

The Grison leaves the church, angry at having all his offers rejected. Suddenly he retraces his steps, a brilliant idea has struck him; he runs to the confessional, and kicks at the door, calling to the priest, " Will you do it for four ? "

The confessor could not help laughing at the persistence

of the peasant, but we are assured that he did not give way.

According to an ancient custom, now fallen into disuse, if it was found that an innocent person had been wrongfully condemned, he was not only rehabilitated publicly, but a young girl presented him with a rose, which was called " the rose of innocence," and he was taken back to his house in triumph.

The people of the Engadine were formerly very credulous, especially in regard to witchcraft. A poor potter turned this to his own profit by giving himself out as a sorcerer. He foretold future events, cured all kinds of maladies, secured people against enchantments, and discovered buried treasures. He had a special way of his own of curing diseases that he did not in the least understand. He declared the sick person to be possessed by the devil; and, in order to drive out the evil spirit, he took the victim, in a dark night, to a lonely spot beside a roaring torrent. There after muttering some incoherent words, he seized a stick and furiously beat and kicked his patient; then exclaiming, " There is the devil going out ! " he took a gun and fired into the air.

Then the supposed demoniac, fancying himself cured by this volley of green wood, and convinced that the devil was dead, would thank the sorcerer and pay him generously.

The women, rich in domestic virtues, economical, active, go to and fro in their large wooden houses like bees in a hive. In the absence of the men they do all the work; they mow the grass, cut the wood, look after the cattle, make the cheese, bake the bread, spin the wool. Among them infidelity is as rare as jealousy.

The women of the Engadine are sociable and very polite, and would be pretty if they were not quite so badly dressed. Their slender figures are spoiled by an ill-made, stiff, and heavy garment. They care nothing about their beauty, and do nothing to preserve their youthful looks, which disappear very early. They are even giving up their ancient costume, which gave them a stamp of originality—a gown of cardinal red, with a black bodice embroidered with gold or silver, and red sleeves. The young girls used to wear a long silver pin through the hair.

They are a strong, vigorous, intelligent race, with a truly surprising faculty of assimilation, and an aptitude for all kinds of work. Most of the men emigrate, going to Italy or France, where they make fortunes as pastrycooks or confectioners, or by keeping restaurants. From their violent tempers their communal assemblies used sometimes to be turned into real battle fields, with bloody encounters; so that an old proverb said, " Let not him who values his skin enter the Engadine."

Schiller, taking his idea from this proverb, makes Franz, the hero of his " Robbers," say : " In order to become a finished rascal, one must have a certain national bent ; he must live in a certain climate and breathe a certain rascally atmosphere; so I advise you to go into the Grisons, for that is, in these days, the Athens of pickpockets."

This made the Council of the Leagues so angry that they threatened the Duke of Wurtemberg to withhold the money they had promised to lend him, if the offending poet was not punished. Schiller was obliged to apologise to the Grison government, and received an order " never to write more ! "

No one knows how much pride and susceptibility there is in the soul of these little republics. Fifty years ago the curator of the Berne museum used to say to the visitors, pointing to the portrait of Voltaire, " That is the portrait of that famous M. de Voltaire, who dared to write against the republic and against God."

While we were chatting, our way was lighted up by the moon. Below us the torrent flowed foaming round great white stones that looked in the moonlight like the petrified

bones of some antediluvian creatures. On leaving this wild
hole, this rent in the mountain, we noticed on the opposite
slope a cluster of little pale spots, like drops of light fallen
from the stars, or a dew of liquid diamonds. They were the
houses of Pontrésina.

On reaching the village we were struck with the unusual
excitement that appeared. Groups were standing in the
streets, and people were talking at their doors and questioning each other. Some foreigners, wrapped in plaids, were
talking with the hotel porters. What had been going on?
It was nine o'clock, and at that hour everybody was accustomed to go to bed, in order to rise early.

"Some misfortune has happened," said the schoolmaster
to me.

He stopped a boy who was running past.

"What is the matter, Jean?"

The lad, greatly moved, replied that a party had been
overtaken by the snow on the Piz Bernina, and that, in
going along a ledge, they had fallen over the precipice. The
sad news had just come from St. Moritz.

We questioned some other persons. The news was, un-
happily, true. A tourist had set out the day before to make
the ascent of the Bernina, and he ought to have been back
at St. Moritz about two o'clock. As he did not arrive,
people grew uneasy, and men were sent off in search of him.
They found his two guides lying on a slope of ice, holding
on above the precipice. They had succeeded in stopping
themselves in their descent; but the traveller whom they
accompanied had been precipitated into the abyss.

While we were hearing these details, a tall, thin man had
drawn near. He was apparently about sixty, with shaven
face, prominent cheek bones, and piercing eyes. The teacher
noticed him.

"Ah!" he exclaimed, "here is Hans Grass." And turning
to me, he added, "Hans Grass is our best guide. He will
tell us what he thinks about this catastrophe."

The old mountaineer took his pipe from his mouth, and winking with his left eye, he replied,—

"What I think? I think it is always the same thing. They don't know how to make stairs. In those ascents everything depends on the stairs. With good stairs you could climb to heaven without falling;—but there it is! They won't take the trouble to cut the ice; they *will* go on too quickly,—as if the mountain could run away. And such people call themselves guides! With real guides there are never any accidents. This gentleman must just have taken the first that came,—apprentices, that did not know their trade, that did not know the glacier, who have no prudence, and who undertake ascents with tourists whom they are not sure about. For my part, I never make one of the great ascents until I have tested the people I am to guide, by two or three preparatory expeditions. Why, you must know with whom you are risking yourself. It is not like climbing on the roof of a house!"

Quite a crowd had gathered around us, all eager to hear the opinion of the old glacier climber.

Of what nationality was the unfortunate tourist who had perished in so tragic a manner? No one could tell me, though I questioned anxiously. But I could not shake off the thought that this must be the husband of the young Italian lady who, three days before, on the Piz Languard, had told me of her husband's purpose to ascend the Piz Bernina.

All night I was tormented and oppressed by this idea. I found it impossible to fall asleep. I turned and turned again, feverishly, in my bed. In vain I closed my eyes; I seemed to see always before me a blood-stained form, with closed eyes and pallid lips, and, kneeling beside it, a young wife with dishevelled hair, weeping and praying.

I heard every hour strike. Towards morning I heard the cocks answering each other as far as the village. When the early dawn began to steal into my little room, I heard the sounds of voices and footsteps coming up from the road. But my vision was still before me. And now I thought some men in black approached the corpse. They wrapped it in a great sheet, and carried it away, in spite of the cries and entreaties of the young wife.

To escape from this oppression I rose and threw my window wide open. The sky was radiant. The snowy peaks, lighted up by the first rays of the morning, were piercing the azure with their glittering points. A holy peace was coming down from above; and the earth, under that great morning benediction, seemed to be chanting a universal Hosanna! The plants were singing, the streams were singing, the bushes, the hedges, the trees, the woods,—everything was joining in the hymn of life and love.

PART III.

FROM THE INN TO THE RHONE.

CHAPTER I.

THREE days in the *diligence!* But a journey is short
when the sky is blue and the air fresh and filled with
the odours of firs and larches ; and when, all along the route,
chains of mountains unroll in a gorgeous panorama, cleaving
the clouds with their fantastic peaks, lifting their snowy
summits like aerial fortresses, draped with forests and
cascades, and their sides furrowed with torrents and rivu-
lets like inlaid threads of silver. And on the other side,
looking downwards to the valley, what delightful stretches
of country, what charming nooks! Here it is a lonely,
sapphire lake, richly framed in soft, silky grasses ; there it
is a châlet planted on the hillside, and herds of cattle all
about, lying in the pastures ; further on it is a village with
tall, smoking chimneys, and carved balconies filled with
flowers, and a river gathered by a sluice into a mirror that
reflects its picturesque roofs.

And then the changing of horses! The pleasure of
arriving and setting off again, the short halt while the
horses eat their oats, and the postillion and conductor,
sitting on the bench in front of the old inn, drink their
half-pint and chat with the merry waiting-maid. Baedeker
in hand, we quickly find out everything of interest ; the
town-house, covered over with notices, and heads of bears

and wolves fastened up as trophies over the door; the church, where the old lords of the place lie sleeping on their stone tombs, and where, in the 15th century windows, bloom like mystic roses the sweet faces of virgins and saints, with golden hair and purple robes.

We buy a piping hot roll from the pretty bakeress, and then run to join the *diligence* which is waiting for us with the politeness of a great lady of the olden time. And so it goes on from morning to night, and it is exceedingly amusing, especially if you have been happy enough to find a pleasant companion. And if this companion is an amiable unknown lady, then it is the *Sentimental Journey* over again!

"Tra-tra-tra!" The postillion is sounding his horn, which means that we are coming near a hamlet or a village. Quite gay in his hussar jacket, with little cut-out flaps, ornamented with hunting horns, his waistcoat with metal buttons, his flat, broad-brimmed hat, covered with waxed linen,—the handsome postillion sounds his horn to give notice to the village maidens that he is coming; and all in a commotion, they lean from their windows and send greetings with hand and eye to the smart driver who checks the speed of his team as he passes.

"Tra-tra-tra!" The note of triumph that he now sends sounding through the valley announces that we are entering Samaden.

Leaving Pontrésina at seven o'clock on a sharply cold morning, we accomplished in thirty minutes the distance between the two places.

From the top of the imperial of the *diligence*, where I was perched, I waved my last greetings to the icy avalanche of the Roseg which glittered in the distance.

Samaden, with its new houses with white fronts and green blinds, its church with gilded dome, its shops with many-coloured signs, its bazaars for tourists, with bundles of alpenstocks at the doors, its old houses with fortress walls

and irregular windows, round or square, grated like the
loop-holes of a prison, its coming and going of tourists and
English and German women in blue veils, its tramway that
carries to the foot of the glaciers all this idle and cosmopolitan crowd, who come to see the Alps as if they were
curiosities at a fair;—this Samaden has no longer anything
that appeals to the feelings. In a few years there will be
nothing to be found there but new buildings, and people
in official garb; and this will be the greatest triumph of
civilization!

A tourist who had got out of the St. Moritz *diligence*,
which had just passed, was giving details of the catastrophe
of the Bernina to an eager group of listeners. I joined
them. He was telling that the guides had brought back
the body about eleven o'clock the night before. They had
been obliged to put it in a sack in order to let it down the
perpendicular walls of the glacier. The man had not died
by a fall, but of congestion. When the corpse arrived at
the hotel on a little cart drawn by one horse, the mournful
procession lighted by a torch on the end of a mountaineer's
staff, a tragic scene followed. A young woman, with dis-
ordered hair, wild with grief, threw herself on the dead
body, clasped it in her arms, and covered the pale, cold face
with kisses.

The narrator continued,—

"As these accidents do harm to the country, and as an
hotel gets empty at once when it is known there is a dead
body in it, it was arranged that the widow should set out
immediately with the body of her husband, which will be
buried at Milan. At the moment when I was getting into
the coach, the procession was just moving off, accompanied
by the whole population; the coffin covered with flowers
and branches of larch and pine, on a carriage drawn by two
horses; and behind it, in a close carriage, the poor young
wife, a beautiful Italian of twenty years old!"

I had obtained my information. I knew now who the

victim was!   I mounted again to my imperial, and during all
the rest of the day my thoughts were with the dead man,
following the mourner going away so sadly in the midst of
the festive summer, under the blue sky and the joyous
sunshine.

Two equally used passes lead from Pontrésina to Coire;
that of the Julier in the Upper Engadine, and that of the
Albula in the Lower Engadine.   If I had gone by the Julier
I must have returned to St. Moritz, and retraced a part of
the way that I already knew.

The Albula, quite as picturesque, had for me the ad-
ditional charm of the unknown.   On leaving Samaden we
pass first through Bevers and Ponte, where we stop only
long enough to change couriers.   Then we set off again
with a noisy jingling of bells that frightens away the hens,
sets the dogs barking and the boys shouting, while the big
innkeepers, with bonnet set awry, brilliant nose and largely-
developed figure, stand framed in their doorways, and cast
a long, melancholy look after us.   Nobody will ever know
all the bitterness that is in the heart of an hotel-keeper who
sees travellers pass without stopping.

Leaving Ponte on the left, we rise by a gloomy defile
into the heart of the Albula.   The gorge grows narrower,
sometimes becoming only a small winding passage, through
which the road, imprisoned between perpendicular walls
with wild plants hanging like drapery from every fissure,
finds its way above a torrent that boils along its stony bed.

The *diligence* progresses at a snail's pace.   We are now
surrounded by the grand, solemn silence of the High Alps,
the profound quiet of the mountains, the slumber of rocks
and trees.   Like bronze warriors on granite pedestals,
larches and firs of stately and heroic form stand on the
ledges and projecting points.

We are rising, and still rising.   The air is keener.   The
trees are becoming fewer.   Soon vegetation ceases entirely.
We reach a little plateau on which are a few poor châlets,

in front of which some black pigs lie basking in the sun, in all the blessedness of well-fed and innocent beings.

We are now at the top of the pass. In front of us is piled the enormous rocky pyramid of the Albula, draped with snow, and surrounded by bold, fantastic peaks. In moulding these mountains, Nature has shown herself more fanciful than proud or hostile. Almost all those summits are accessible. The Grison Alps form a series of ramifications running in all directions, a bewildering confusion of lines and edges crossing and re-crossing each other, with no order, and presenting to the eye landscapes endlessly changing in aspect and colour. Side by side with gloomy, forbidding rocks and wild, lonely gorges, lie broad, rolling pastures, cheerful plateaus and pleasant little valleys, with something of the soft melancholy of the North in their colour. Or again, there are perhaps wide, magnificent valleys, broken up by lakes, populous with rich villages and hotels, and ending in a mysterious glacier. Many of these ravines and valleys—a hundred and fifty such may be counted—have been formed by the sudden increase and rush of the streams. It is by the Cols of the mountains that the inhabitants of the Grisons hold communication with each other. From the 13th to the 15th century, the Col of the Julier was the great pass, the principal route for the merchandise that Genoa and Venice sent through Switzerland to France and Germany.

But here we are at the Albula Hospice, a poor, dull house, erected, not by charity but by an inn-keeper. Some black-bearded Italian workmen, in little round hats, red-cravats and velveteen jacket and trousers, are sitting at a table in a low room, drinking white wine, while some curly-haired children, in crimson aprons, are playing with a big dog at the door.

The road goes down into a valley where stones, great and small, torn from the mountain by avalanches, have been violently scattered or piled into heaps as they fell. This

dreary region is called the Devil's Valley. Nothing could
be more dismal than this accumulation of rocks, bleached in
the snow and washed by the rain, lying scattered, crushed
and defaced like ruined buildings. The descent continues
by interminable windings to the bottom of the valley. To
right and left rise bare, lofty mountains, sending down
numberless streams from their rent and ruddy sides. In
this place the husband of the hostess at the Steinbock inn,
Pontrésina, lost his life by an avalanche.

Now we arrive at a grassy lake, dark and gloomy as a
mill-pond. A stranded boat lies rotting in the mud. A few
houses show their pointed roofs behind the hedges. This is
the hamlet of Palpuogna. By the roadside a woman is
hanging out linen on ropes tied to the telegraph poles. The
inn before which we stop to leave the mail-bags has strongly
barred windows, as if the neighbourhood were swarming
with robbers.

Again the valley closes in ; between the branches of a
clump of firs a group of snowy peaks is seen, like a vision
of winter palaces of ice. We cross a torrent whose dark
waters are carrying down many dead trees. Then suddenly
the gorge widens. Opposite us rises a hillside on which
are scattered the little red wooden houses of a village. The
wild stream beside which lies our road is sometimes lost in
measureless depths, or disappears into crevices and hidden
beds, and then emerges, shining, playful, into the full sunshine, shouting in glee and tossing its white, foamy mane.

And now we reach the open valley. Along the two sides
of the road are rows of splendidly ornamental firs, and from
their cones, hanging in purple clusters, distil drops of resin
like beads of amber. These protecting forests have not
always been strong enough to withstand the shock of the
avalanche ; in more places than one they are laid waste and
broken, mown down, as if they had received the fire of several
batteries of cannon.

Bergün ! This is a large village in a bright little valley

amidst soft outlines and rich masses of verdure, and fresh, pleasant scenery. One would say the mountain had suddenly burst into flower, and produced a beautiful garden. The eye is charmed with the delicate colour of the roses, the pale flowers of the haricots twining fondly round their long poles, the smooth-leaved cabbages filling and rounding like the bald skulls of academicians. Bergün has an old Roman church where people go to pray, and an old tower where people are put in prison. Bergün has also three hotels; the *diligence* stopping at the Hotel Piz d'Aela, obliges us to sit down at one of the most detestable *tables-d'hôte* in all Helvetia. An inhabitant of the locality replies to my grumblings, " Ah, that is because you did not know! If you had known, you would have gone to dine twenty yards lower down, at Landmann Cloeta's. A man like the landmann always gives you the worth of your money ! "

Ingenious as the Knight of La Mancha, who, however, was not a knight of labour, the illustrious innkeeper of the Piz d'Aela, in order to detain travellers in his tavern (printers are at liberty to spell it *cavern*), has pasted up over his door a manuscript placard, bearing the words, " BEAU FIXE."

The *diligence* is surrounded by all the street boys of the village. The postillion has returned to his place. " Tra-tra-tra! " he sounds his horn, and before starting waves his melancholy adieus to trouble the hearts of the kitchen-maids and waitresses of Bergün.

The road again plunges into a gorge, shut in by cliffs crowned with firs,—a grim defile through which the Albula pours its doleful plaint. This road, cut in the rock, dating from the 17th century, is like a smaller edition of the Via Mala. If the horses should fall, if the wheels should deviate by the width of a few lines, the travellers would be precipitated to a depth of more than 600 feet. To lean over the yawning abyss from the height of the imperial causes a far from comfortable sensation.

At the end of a long half-hour we emerge into a wooded

valley; rows of venerable firs, centuries old, stretch out their broad branches, dark and drooping, like the sleeves of a necromancer's robe, some of them wearing long flowing locks of tangled lichens. In the night, when the uncertain light of the moon comes vaguely through the forest, those enormous trees must assume frightfully fantastic forms.

Again the landscape changes. Seeds of various kinds, carried by the wind, have found a place for themselves on the stony mountain side, and have wrapped it in a wild and luxuriant vegetation. Presently we come to fruit trees instead of firs, and smiling in a ray of sunshine are some old houses with reddened beams and carved doors, and windows of little round panes; some of them having their stone fronts decorated with half-effaced frescos.

This is Filisur, a happy village without a history; a charming and privileged little place, that rejoices the heart after the dismal solitude of the Bergüner-Stein.

We now descend rapidly. And once more the valley narrows in, and its walls rise perpendicularly; there is only room for the road and the roaring torrent. Then at last the pass widens more and more; from the top of a cliff a waterfall is floating like a white streamer; and we see in front, lying in the meadow, Bad-Alveneu. We are on the right bank of the stream, below the old weather-worn castle of Belfort; we pass through Brienz, and a little farther on, at Lenz, we join the Julier road.

Before reaching the summit of the pass, that road traverses a gloomy plateau, a dreary solitude, a desert, where nothing is to be seen but stones and stunted pines, and a few mountain tarns like fathomless black holes.

On the Col the view opens and stretches out over mountains of simple forms, with a succession of rounded summits, or one enormous curved ridge, or towering, threatening peaks.

We come down upon Parpan, situated in a lovely corner; then we reach Churwalden, and, at last, Coire,

CHAPTER II.

SOME other traveller must describe Coire and its old
cathedral, tell of its Roman origin, and guide over its
hill-sides where the figs are ripening. As for me, I arrived
at night, and was obliged to rise almost with the sun, and
set out again as I had come.

Our to-day's stretch is as long as yesterday's: about
fourteen hours' travelling in the *diligence* to reach Andermatt, at the end of that fine valley of the Vorder-Rhein
which runs into the valleys of the Rhone, the Reuss, and
the Leventina, and which is the most important strategic
road in Switzerland.

Behind these successive ranges of mountains which protect
it like ramparts, and which hollow out defensive trenches
around it, this valley is like an impregnable fortress built
by the hand of Nature. Its granite walls shelter a vigorous
active, and martial population.

Originally a country of priests and nobles, under the rule
of ecclesiastical and temporal lords, the Grisons gained
freedom, first by alliances, then by their Leagues; and side
by side with free Helvetia arose a free Rhætia, a Grison

Confederation, which only at a later date, in 1803, joined
the Confederate Cantons.

Jealous of their immunities and their freedom, the three
Leagues were not slow in following up words by actions.

A certain Planta, who came one day to take possession of
a wealthy priory, with the consent of the pope, but against
the will of the Leagues, was seized on the spot, led before
the tribunal of Coire, and condemned to death.

The learned historian of Switzerland, M. A. Daguet, remarks that the traditional history of Rhætia during the first
half of the 15th century presents a striking analogy with that
of the Forest Cantons in the century before. The same kinds
of outrages on property, on modesty, on men's relf-respect,
led to the same acts of legitimate defence, the same entering
into solemnly sworn covenants, and at last into the formation of identical confederations for the maintenance of rights
and resistance to tyranny. And to all this must be added
the special features that distinguish this country, the most
original and the least known part of the Switzerland of to-day.
Perhaps, also, from the large number of the nobles and the
isolation of the valleys, the tyranny was more harsh and
cruel there than anywhere else. And at last, says the
popular historian of the Grisons, Henri Zschokke, when the
iniquity was full, there were found brave men who rose up
to defend their eternal rights and to reanimate the courage
of the oppressed mountaineers.

One of these men was Adam de Camogask. The lord of
Gardovall coveted this man's only daughter. " Tell your
master," replied Adam to the messengers of the noble count,
" that I will myself bring her to him to-morrow." And the
next day the father kept his word. He took his daughter,
decked as a bride, to the castle of Gardovall. But when the
count hastened forward to meet and embrace her, the father
drew his sword and plunged it in the tyrant's heart. The
same day the peasants burned down the castle.

Another hero of Grison tradition was Jean Caldar or

Chialdærer, of Fardun. One day, seeing his field trampled by the horses which his lord had ordered to be let loose among the wheat of his serfs, he killed them with a blow of his powerful fist. Laid in irons and tortured for this audacious act, he had to wait till his family could redeem him with tears and gold.

After he was restored to his home, he was one day sitting at table with his family, when the lord of Fardun came into the cabin. All greeted him with respect; but the tyrant cast scornful looks on them, and spat in the soup they were eating. Caldar's wrath blazed forth like lightning; he clutched the throat of the noble count, grasped him with his two hands as with a vice, and exclaiming, "Swallow the soup you have seasoned!" he plunged the tyrant's head into the scalding soup and suffocated him.

And in the meantime the peasants were burning and sacking the castle of Fardun.

Hot-blooded, passionately addicted to strife, this people wasted and devoured each other for two centuries, in civil wars. Three factions had been formed; that of the Salis, who were in favour of French rule; that of the Plantas, who were for Austria; and that of the Travers, who had declared themselves on the side of Venice.

Judged by the tribunal of the Plantas, the Salis were exiled; but in the following year it was the tribunal of the Salis that expelled the Plantas.

And to these civil dissensions were added wars of religion. These were specially bloody in this corner of Europe. History has called the massacre of the reformed Church of the Valtelline, "the Saint Bartholomew of the Grisons." A band commanded by Jaques Roboustelli, the ally of the Plantas, found their way during the night of the 19th July, 1620, into the town of Tirano, the capital of the valley; and at the sound of the tocsin, and the church bells tolling a knell, they fell on the Protestants, who were massacred, men, women, and children, and their bodies thrown into the

Adda. The head of the reformed pastor of Tirano was fixed on the point of a pike and set up in the pulpit of his church. The slaughter lasted fourteen days, and many of the houses were destroyed by fire.

The League of the House of God and the League of the Ten Jurisdictions commissioned Baptiste de Salis to go and avenge the murder of the Lutherans of Tirano; but an Austrian corps, summoned by Planta, barred his way and obliged him to withdraw.

A new party was then formed—a national party, entirely devoted to the country, which they felt it was time to save from dismemberment and ruin. George Jénatsch placed himself at the head of it, and having, one day, received secret information that Planta was advancing on the re-formed village of Grüsch, to set it on fire, he took with him twenty men, scaled the walls of the castle of Rietberg, and with one blow of an axe slew Pompeius Planta, who was hidden in a chimney. Then he descended on the meadows of Prada, near Vallendas, where the Catholic band were encamped. After a struggle of seven hours, they were driven to the other side of the mountain. Jénatsch and his men obliged the monks of the monastery at Disentis to open their cellars to them. They emptied the barrels, but offered no injury to the monks, beyond that of compelling them for a few days to drink water.

In a short time Jénatsch was master of the whole Valtelline. But the Austrians invaded the region and gave it up to fire and sword, Jénatsch making his escape into Germany. At last Richelieu despatched an army to dislodge Austria from the Valtelline. Jénatsch, Rodolph Salis, and all the Grison exiles returned with the French, who were commanded by the Marquis de Comines, at once general and ambassador. The Austrians are driven out, and Louis XIII. commits the care of the Valtelline to papal troops. The peace does not last long. In 1629 the Grisons are again occupied by the imperial troops. After their departure, the head of the French Protestants, Henri de Rohan, arrives at Coire as royal mbassador. He and Jénatsch together recover the Valtelline; but instead of leaving it to the Grisons, Louis XIII. wishes to keep it for himself. The leaders of the eight Leagues meet secretly at Coire, and swear to free their country from the foreigner. Jénatsch now enters into negotiations with Austria and Spain, becomes a Catholic to please his new allies, and on the 18th March, 1637, the whole country rises at his summons; the French, in their entrenched camp, are surrounded, and obliged to capitulate. At the sight of Jénatsch, the Duke de Rohan, pale with rage, draws one of his pistols and aims at his head, shouting, "That is how we say good-bye to a traitor!" but the pistol hangs fire.

But Jénatsch was destined, after all, to a tragic end. Lucretia, the daughter of Pompeius Planta, who had been killed at the castle of Rietberg, had sworn to avenge her father. She had been married long before to Baron Travers d'Ortenstein, and had not hitherto found an opportunity of accomplishing her purpose. But time did not weaken her resolution. She waited; knowing that the hour always comes for those who wait.

One winter evening she hears that Jénatsch is at a ball in an inn at Coire. She disguises herself as a man, goes to the inn, and asks, on some pretext, to see Jénatsch. Hardly has he stepped out to the stair head, when she falls on him and strikes him down with the very axe that had killed her father.

The women of the Grisons have souls like the women of ancient Rome. The history of their country is made famous by their heroic actions. In the time of the civil wars, two brothers, Augustin and Antoine Travers, were at the head of opposing bands. The fight began, and already many lay dead on both sides. Suddenly the wives and sisters of the combatants, led by Anne de Juvalta, threw themselves into the midst of the fray, and stopped the fratricidal contest.

Another time it was the women who drew on their husbands and brothers to fall on the Austrian camp and take it unawares; one of them, Salome Lienhard, herself killed seven of them with a club.

During the wars of Suabia, a band of Austrians had surprised the village of Schleins, while everybody was at church at the funeral of a neighbour. In the house of the dead man there was nobody but one woman, who had stayed to prepare the funeral refreshments. The enemy found their way to the kitchen, and asked her for whom she was making such great preparation.

"For the Grisons and the Confederates," said she; "who are to be here in an hour."

The Austrians at once fled!

The brave woman ran to the church to give the alarm, and the whole village set off in pursuit of the enemy, who were pretty roughly handled.

In another village, Pfeiff, which was also saved by the courage of the women hindering the enemy from entering the valley, the women retain the privilege of sitting on the right hand side in the parish church.

The country still bears traces and memorials, in many places, of those savage struggles and ferocious wars. Many ruins, old broken towers, now only empty walls; castles on the heights, with the blue sky showing through the vacant carvings of their windows,—mournful skeletons of proud feudal times. Here is an historical tree, under which the alliance of the Leagues was sworn; an alliance for freedom that was to last, "as long as the earth and the mountains." A little farther on is a deep forest in which some shepherds hid themselves to make clubs bristling with nails and iron spikes, with which they fell unawares on the Austrian troops, killing four hundred, and putting the rest to flight. Those weapons were called the clubs of despair.

So many centuries of battles have made the inhabitants of these regions a serious people. These beautiful villages that are all along the valley, with their large rich houses in the midst of little plantations of fruit trees, have all something thoughtful and sober-looking about them. And yet how cheerful they look when you come to them out of the gloomy, dark gorges of the Albula! Soft velvet meadows, fields of wheat and golden maize, walnut trees like the columns of leafy cathedrals, cherry trees covered with crimson pearls, apple trees laden with little amber balls, streamlets flowing silently in long silvery windings, a few waterfalls like smoke in the distance, a dark-blue lake framed in rosy under-growth, hedges of barberry still hung with their festoons of coral, spires glittering in the sun, houses faced with maple-wood in rich copper tints, cows going to drink at a fountain where pretty young girls, with bare arms, are washing white linen; now and then a glimpse of a snowy peak between the slopes of two mountains; and the Rhine, always the Rhine, already of a considerable size, with a stately motion, and loaded with solid, covered wooden bridges, such as they made in the olden time;—such is the Grison valley of the Vorder-Rhein.

There is more than enough to charm and delight the eyes, to refresh the mind and occupy the imagination, especially if all these scenes and pictures are viewed from the imperial of a *diligence,* through a splendid summer day. In the *coupé,* a great master in the art of travelling has said, your only view is the harness of the horses; in the interior, you see, through a loop-hole, trees defiling past like soldiers at a review; in the rotunda you are in a cloud of dust that dims the landscape and stifles the passenger. Every one having the use of eyes and ears ought to travel on the imperial. The highest places are the finest,—ask those who occupy them. If you fall you break your neck,—ask the same people about that. But it is a pleasure while you are there.

Air, and space,—that is what you have on the imperial; and you are caressed by all the fresh, sweet odours floating in the air, the scent of the pine forests and the new-mown

13

hay; and eye and thought wander freely at will like a pair
of truant schoolboys.

We had left Coire at five in the morning, and arrived
about one o'clock at Disentis. We had passed Felsberg,
where some Englishmen have discovered real veins of gold;
Ems, with its great arched gateways and its ruins; Reichnau,
with a castle where Louis Philippe was hidden, and taught
French under the name of Chabot; the little town of Flims,
with windows full of flowers; Ilanz, with houses ornamented
with old armorial bearings; Truns, where the Grison league
was founded; and Somvix, on a hillside of intense green,—
thick, solid green, dear to the painters of Basle and Berne.

In Romanic, Disentis is called Muster, that is, monastery.
Some Benedictines came one day and built a convent in this
wilderness, and the convent was the beginning of the town,
and peopled the country. The abbey belongs to the 7th
century. It is now a professional school. The abbés of
Disentis, as powerful on earth as in heaven, exercised the
right of administering justice according to their will, and
were sovereign masters of the country in common with the
feudal lords who had perched their nests of stone on the
mountain sides.

Between Disentis and Andermatt, as we rise into colder
and less fertile regions, the villages become fewer. At the
outlet of the Tavetsch valley we come to Sedrun, near the
Piz Pazzola; then the road passes through Ruèras and
reaches Tschamut near the source of the Vorder-Rhein,
which rises in Lake Toma, hidden in a fold of the Badus;
and after reaching the wild Col of the Oberalp, we descend
in an hour to Andermatt.

At Disentis three German tourists, dressed in yellow
coutil, with green cravats and folding brown linen hats,
had left us to go across the Lukmanier and join the St.
Gothard railway at Biasca, in the valley of the Ticino.
These Teutons, who looked like Dutch canaries, and if they
stood among the pastures must have resembled enormous

dandelions, had been succeeded by a one-eyed gendarme, a stout lady from the Hague, with cheeks like scarlet tulips, her maid, a girl of eighteen, thin, fragile, as white as a lily, and an apothecary from Canton Lucerne, with broad-brimmed Panama hat, gilt spectacles, and his portly person squeezed into a blue cloth overcoat. In one hand he carried a worsted-work bag, and in the other a stick with a crow's beak top and a solid iron point; his rosy face was jovial and frank.

The apothecary had sat down next to me on the imperial; and with an easy good-fellowship, quite republican and essentially Swiss, he began without preamble to take me into his confidence; telling me where he came from, where he was going, what he ate and drank, and who he was. Born under an auspicious star, he was one of the lucky men; everything succeeded with him; the remedies he prepared were infallible cures. And he was not only an apothecary but a public functionary, and held offices without number. The time that he did not use in making up pills and powders he spent at the tribunal, in sending poor wretches to prison, for he was a judge. He was moreover a deputy, a communal councillor, president of the parish council and of the council for the care of orphans and the poor, editor of a weekly paper, vice-president of the society for town improvements, secretary of the Mutual Aid Society and of the Carabineers' Society, member of the Musical Society, member of the Alpine Club, and of every historical and scientific society in Switzerland. He had written several pamphlets on the diseases of the fish in the lakes of Lucerne and Geneva. For one of his pamphlets he had received a first prize of twenty-five francs from the federal department. Do not laugh! This apothecary may one day be President of the Confederation. Every vaccinated Swiss, able to read and write, may attain to this presidency, which costs the ratepayers only fifteen thousand francs a year, which lasts only for one year, and provides the holder of the office neither with a house nor free travelling; which does not even give him the honour and gratification of seeing his own image on postage stamps and ten-centime nickel coins; and which formally prohibits him from wearing decorations, even those of a sister republic, or from receiving any present. The Emir of Bokhara once sent a rich silk robe to the President of the Confederation, and he, not daring even to keep it to have it made into a dressing-gown, placed it in the museum at Berne, where the people went to see it.

Our *diligence* was passing near a little lake like a clear, beautiful eye. In its smooth, shining water were reflected on one side tall reeds crossing each other like lances, and a few shrubs, the thin, dark shadows of which were like engravings on transparent stone; on the other side, bright green mountains with great forests in broken outlines.

The apothecary pointed out the mountains, saying to me with emphasis:—

"Switzerland, sir, is an enclosed country; an island of rocks and forests in the midst of the troubled waters of Europe; all the shipwrecked find refuge and protection here. Switzerland has never given up or betrayed a political refugee. More than once she has been threatened; but she feels strong in her patriotism. She, the old republican, make herself a gendarme for kings! Never! We have pretty lively political and religious disputes in our twenty-two cantons, so various in their appearance, their manners and customs, their language and their religion; but when the country is at stake, all discordant voices are hushed, opposing parties lay down their arms, every Swiss becomes faithful to our motto, 'One for all, and all for one!' Look into the bottom of the heart of our little nation; and what you will find there, and what has made it so great in history, is love of country. And it is this passionate patriotism that causes our jealous distrust of our neighbours, German, Italian, and French. The original spirit of the nation has been cherished and developed; our history goes on with the same end in view—the maintaining of the national independence. Our schools are, before everything, schools of patriotism. All our public holidays form a part of the national education. You should see our federal reviews! With what enthusiasm the French Swiss receive the Italian and German Swiss; what a strong atmosphere of brotherhood breathes in the speeches, what harmony reigns in those meetings where the whole country seems on foot and in arms around the federal banner! Then it is understood how one source of the strength of Switzerland is its organization; and that this organization has formed out of so many different elements a homogeneous whole,—a nation, and not a mere mixing of peoples. Ah! it is to us, I tell you, that your young republicans of France ought to come to the school of the Republic. They would learn to be real republicans, and not to prostrate themselves before any idol, or to devour each other!"

After a pause my companion began again.

"See how simple our system of government is! Switzerland forms to-day a federative republic of twenty-two cantons, each having its own local government. A permanent council of seven members, called the Federal Council, and residing at Berne, directs the general business; they are the executive power of the Confederation, while the legislative power is exercised by two councils: the National Council, elected by the people, and the Council of the States, composed of two deputies from each canton. No federal law can be promulgated without the sanction of both councils, deliberating and voting separately. When the two councils meet, they form the Federal Assembly, which nominates the President of the Confederation, the federal council, the federal tribunal, the federal chancellor, the commander-in-chief, the chief of the staff, etc. You will tell me that this federative system, which respects the independence, the laws, the manners and customs of each canton, is not altogether the ideal of a republic, nor a reign of equality for all ; for there are governments so reactionary, so wrapped up in the past, that they are opposed to all progress, to every kind of reform, and systematically crush liberal minorities.

"But in revising our Constitution we have already made a great step; we have unified the army, and we hope to unify education and the administration of justice. This new stage in our progress towards a more complete centralisation will be accomplished by the force of circumstances and by time ; it will be hastened by the abuses of fanatical governments, deaf to all proposals of reform, and whose laws are no longer in harmony with the modern mind."

The excellent apothecary also gave me very interesting details on the different political parties which divide Switzerland.

"In Switzerland," said he, "we have several parties. First, there is the old radical party, who follow the traditions of 1848. Then there is the socialist-democratic party, whose birthplace was Zurich and the Grisons. It was they who made the *Referendum*. Leaving aside politics and religion, they concern themselves solely with social and workmen questions. In the Chambers, however, they join the radical party.

"There are two conservative parties, who have come to an understanding with each other ; the one Protestant, the other Catholic. The organ of the first is the *Gazette de Lausanne ;* of the second, the *Bien Public* of Fribourg, and also the *Vaterland* of Lucerne. Finally, there is the ultramontane party, the *intransigeants*, who are supported in Canton Fribourg by *L'Ami du Peuple* and *La Liberté*, and in Tessin by *La Libertà*. It is these extreme *intransigeants* who are dreaming of creating a Catholic University at Fribourg."

We had now reached the top of the Oberalp, in the mass of the great St. Gothard, at the spot where landmarks are set up to point out the frontier of the Cantons Grisons and

Uri. On the roof of a châlet, between the large stones that
kept the wooden shingles firm, some goats were lying with
heads erect, their jaws working, and shaking their white
beards with an automatic motion. One could have said they
were chatting together, commenting on our arrival, or
telling each other stories to beguile their weariness. An
old, ragged shepherd, with thick, bushy beard, and the eyes
of a vulture under a battered, steeple-crowned felt hat, came
offering some crystals,—pale, rose-coloured amethysts,—
which he had procured, by having himself let down by a
rope, in a cavern in the face of the precipice.

This elevated plateau was known to the Romans, who
considered it the highest point of the Alps. It gives birth
to four great rivers—the Rhine, the Rhone, the Reuss, and
the Tessin—and separates the Rhætian from the Pennine
Alps. As we advance across it, a splendid panorama unfolds before us; an immense view of points and needles,
arêtes and peaks, around which trembles a rosy haze, a
light, floating, ethereal vapour. Some of the nearer mountains show a band of black firs; others, entirely white, stand
like immovable colossal images.

The road makes an abrupt descent, and by nine great
loops we drop down on Andermatt, just at the moment
when all the lights are being put out.

There are no lamps in the streets; we arrive by round-
about, subterranean ways at the door of the Hotel St.
Gothard. The *diligence* stops; the one-eyed gendarme gets
out first, but having been emptying half-pints at each inn
on the way, it is with difficulty that he can still stand; his
shako wavers on the top of his pointed cranium; he uses
his gun as a mountain staff, and goes away muttering
strangely; while the stout Dutch lady loudly calls for a
little bench that she may get down more conveniently.

Escorted by persons carrying lanterns, we solemnly make
our entry into the hotel. Waiters in black coats and white
ties conduct us into a vast empty dining-room, where, beside

pyramids of plates on the tables, we are served with a cold chicken, which the stout Dutch lady considers too lean.   In order to make the close of our day a little more cheerful, I set free some corks of Asti, a merry kind of music which the stout lady applauds by a smile.   Beside her sits her little maid, dreaming—no doubt about the gendarme, whose one eye must have had considerable difficulty in finding his way through the dark lanes of the village, blocked up with carts and heaps of refuse.

CHAPTER III.

THE next morning I had breakfast in the same dining-room, with three abbés out on a holiday, who were disposing of an omelet of twenty-four eggs, and drinking white wine very freely.

The apothecary had eaten ten rolls, emptied three cups of coffee, reduced a pound of butter to a half, and disposed of the quarter of a honeycomb; then he lighted his pipe.

The stout Dutch lady, who suffered from cramp, was dipping bits of sugar in a little glass of brandy, while her maid, pensively leaning by the window, seemed to be the victim of gendarme-fever. This fair and fragile lily dreaming of a pair of boots interested me, and set me to dreaming myself. I pondered on the power of Swiss gendarmes, even when they are one-eyed. If there is on earth a policeman's Paradise, it is assuredly the republic of the twenty-two cantons. The Swiss gendarme rarely arrests actual criminals, —that is occasionally a dangerous feat; but if you cross a meadow which is closed to the public, you may be sure of being arrested at once. If, armed with an air-gun, you frighten away a sparrow, oh! then you are still more sure to be arrested. You will not be detained, but you will be made to pay; the Swiss police being only an institution for increasing the budget of each canton by means of fines. There are fines for every hour of the day, for every position of the body, and for every circumstance of daily life; a fine if you sit too long at table in the inns at night; a fine if you dance in a country where—as in the Canton of Fribourg—dancing is not permitted without the sanction of the authorities; a fine—as in Canton Fribourg—if you fish or hunt on Sunday; a fine—as in Canton Fribourg—if you dare, without permission, to take in on a Sunday your hay that is in danger of being destroyed by the rain; a fine if you *do this*, a fine if you *say that*.

There are, indeed, so many fines in Switzerland, that it ought to be called, not the land of pines, but the land of fines. The fine is a State institution, and the gendarmes have a special commission to collect them, just as elsewhere there are officials to collect the taxes.

Elisée Reclus having one day taken a prohibited path, was condemned to pay a fine of ten francs; he refused to pay, and was sent to prison.

A doctor of Berne, an amateur artist, who collected views of old monuments, set off one Sunday to photograph the church of Romont, in Canton Fribourg. A policeman in laced hat apprehends him in the act, and takes him to the court-house for having been "working on Sunday." The prefect is absent; the doctor is then taken to the apothecary at the corner, who is sub-prefect; but as an apothecary cannot, with decency, condemn a doctor, he is let go, and takes to his heels as if fleeing from among the Iroquois.

A Swiss traveller, who was breakfasting beside me, had also had cause to complain of these mean and annoying ways of the local police. He had bought a house in one of the mountain villages, had helped to improve the locality, and had opened his purse on various occasions; it was known who he was, whence he came, what he was doing. Well, one fine evening a gendarme—not blind of an eye, or drunk

—presented himself at his house, shako on his head and sabre by his side, as if in search of a dangerous criminal, for the purpose of announcing to him that he was contravening the law, because he had not lodged his papers with the "syndic," that is, with the maire.

"I was not at home," said M. V——; "the gendarme nevertheless came into my house and spoke most rudely to my wife ; and next day I was summoned before the tribunal, and ordered to pay a fine of thirty francs.

"The gendarme had thrust himself into my domicile by night without any necessity, for it was known that I had begun no preparations for departure. I complained of these uncivilised proceedings, and perhaps you think the man was rebuked? Oh dear, no! he is still reigning, more powerful than ever, in the same little neighbourhood, which finally I left. He even went so far the other day as to get up a case against an American painter who was finishing a water-colour sketch on Sunday!"

My interlocutor broke into a great fit of laughter ; then he resumed, warming as he went on,—

"Almost everywhere the use of passports is abolished. It is only our ingenious Helvetic gendarmerie who think they secure the safety of the villages and the roads by requiring every native and every foreigner who stays more than ten days in one place to deposit his papers. Those who lodge in the inns are, however, excused from this formality.

"That is easily understood. If the traveller, the tourist, by whom Switzerland lives throughout the summer, whom she feeds with her produce in her hotels and carries on her railways,—if he, every time he arrived at a new hotel, were subjected to such superannuated annoyances, Switzerland would be emptied at once; nobody would come there any longer.

"In many places the hotel-keeper is a municipal councillor, syndic, member of the Great Council, or deputy to the

National Council. As long as you are in his house the police have some respect for you. You even hunt without a written permission; you fish without a licence; your real or supposed name is written in the hotel register; you are 'in order' in the eyes of the police. And then the Swiss gendarmes, who are always very thirsty, have the most profound respect for those honoured gentlemen, the inn-keepers, and do not wish to annoy them. But if you stop giving your money to the publican, if your eye has been caught by a little châlet or a cottage, and you move in with your furniture, oh! then remember you become a suspicious character, and must send your papers to the authorities; for if not the police will be at your heels, and police means fines and prison. Here in Switzerland liberty is no joke."

But now the horses were harnessed, and the *diligence* at the door. I left the persecuted gentleman opposite the three abbés, who were now attacking half a millstone of cheese with the appetite of masons, and again scrambled up to my seat beside my friend the apothecary, on the imperial, which I had engaged for the whole journey.

We had a new postillion. He was a little red-nosed man, with a bristling white beard; on the top of his wax-cloth hat he had stuck, like a plume, a large squirrel's tail, which drooped on his shoulder. He gave us some information about the five strong horses he was driving. They are of German breed, and have only one year of training. They are fed on oats and bread, and in winter the Confederation send them, in order to recruit, to board with peasants who put them to light work.

The road and the river unfold before us like two immense ribbons, white and green, laid alongside of each other. And every time we pass through a village, women, children, hens, ducks, and dogs are all astir. The innkeeper, in his shirt-sleeves, with his hands under his embroidered braces, appears immediately at his door, and goes on bowing like a Chinese image. Some old men drag themselves, with the help of their sticks, as far as the post-house, hoping perhaps for the return of a son who has been away to try his fortune, or of a daughter who is far away beyond the hills, at service in the town. And then there is the farrier, standing out black in the firelight of his forge beside the wide chimney, which the great bellows are filling with dancing, golden sparks.

The *diligence*—oh! what a delicious style of travelling it is! There are still in Switzerland many of those remote and little-known valleys into which the post-carriage takes you in its moving house, with the sound of jingling bells, the cracking of the driver's whip, and the notes of the horn waking up the echoes of the woods. What better way could there be of seeing a country, of studying its manners and customs and language, than those halts and relays that make you mix with the population and travel with them?

We soon leave behind us the village of Hospenthal, in the midst of stern scenery, with an old Lombard tower, weather-stained and decayed, and a bridge as old as the tower. Its inns are in patriarchal style, with carved balustrades to their galleries, and old windows, in the dark woodwork of which we see framed, like one of Holbein's portraits, a young girl with a rose in her dress.

In passing a morass, we put to flight a flock of wild ducks; then, before reaching Réalp, a miserable hamlet at the end of the Urseren valley, we crossed the Reuss, which foamed and roared among the rocks, and dashed against them with fury. It storms and rages against the obstacles in the way of its freedom and its youthful eagerness, and contracts into windings like the coils of an enormous green serpent.

At half-past ten o'clock we had reached the top of the Furka Pass (7,992 feet), whence the eye sweeps over an immense amphitheatre of mountains, rising height above height, or in sheer precipices, or cut into pinnacles and needles that pierce the clouds. A few of the slopes have here and there great dark patches of fir woods. At the extremity of the long succession of valleys are seen glaciers sleeping under their snowy covering, and great, proud alps, robed in their royal ermine, and their brows crowned with a tiara of silver. The slender needles of the Bielenstock were hidden by fleecy clouds; while the snowy crests of the Furkahorn and the Galenstock were sharply pencilled on the soft blue.

We pass under the Galenstock, through a tract of frightful barrenness. A curse seems to have fallen on this hard and hostile soil, this land widowed of all vegetation, where the bitter winds nip in the bud all the plants and grasses, and Nature shows her wild and cruel aspect. A few sickly thistles alone put forth their little purple stars of stunted, dusty flowers among the yellow-veined flints by the roadside. Through this dismal way, this passage bare as the entrance to a prison, we arrive at a cluster of poor châlets, and suddenly, as if by magic, we are in a new world, with another kind of country before us, a vast horizon of mountain chains crossing and crossing again, rising and meeting in great rolling waves that seem to cover all the rest of the land, and to go on rising and falling even to the ends of the earth.

The road descends by a rough and rapid slope along the side of the cliffs, above a cataract of ice, which comes down as an immense white sheet and fills the valley. This is the Rhone glacier.

The postillion puts his horses to their utmost speed, and we come so near the glacier that we see within a few yards of us its great motionless waves, broken up with crevasses, grottos, and caverns, showing pale blue and lilac lights. Quite at the bottom the glacier opens out like an enormous pearly shell, from which escapes a tiny streamlet—the Rhone!

The capricious and beautifully fantastic forms of the ice, its varied mimic architecture—domes and turrets and minarets,—its swelling waves, combine to make the Rhone glacier a real work of art; one might take it for a wonderful piece of monumental carving, hewn out and chiselled by giants.

The *diligence* stops at the Glacier Hotel, in the midst of a motley crowd of tourists; no longer tourists such as are described by Töpffer and Alexander Dumas; but tourists of the newest fashion, in jackets which are poems, the rhymes of which are pockets with other little pockets added to them; tourists in coloured stockings, looking like ballet dancers, wearing hats with white scarfs like chiefs of Asiatic armies, and flannel shirts embroidered with flowers or pearls, or silk shirts that make them look like women. A few, in linen trousers and cloth gaiters, with a long band of red flannel round the waist, have come on velocipedes. All kinds of carriages, from the simple and rustic cross-seated car to the big Italian carriage, with red velvet cushions and silver mountings—the real prelate's coach—are standing out in front, with their shafts in the air. What a continual coming and going there is in this valley, leading, as it does, by the Grimsel into the Haslithal and the Oberland; by the Furka to the Leventina and Lake Maggiore; by the St. Gothard to Andermatt and the Lake of Lucerne; or by the Vorder-Rhein valley to Coire, the Grisons, and the Engadine. This Rhone Glacier Hotel, which has the proportions of a barracks, was in the days of my youth only a modest little inn; but the transformation of taverns into hotels, though slower in the Valais than in the Bernese Oberland, has not been less general. In places where were seen, fifteen years ago, poor mountain inns, built by a few guides, now stand three-storeyed hotels, with gorgeous dining-rooms and green shutters! At Zermatt the brothers Seiler have built veritable palaces at the edge of the glaciers. Happily the originality of the region has not disappeared with the old inns. The Valais continues to share with the Engadine the character of being the most primitive canton in Switzerland ; the one that has retained almost wholly its former curious physiognomy, its local colour, its personal tone.

In these lateral valleys, which at a multitude of points run into the central valley, towards the great artery of the Rhone, there are still found old-fashioned costumes, manners and customs of olden times, the children of nature, of whom Rousseau speaks. There you find yourself in quite a different world from this everyday world of railways; this carefully got-up world, gloved and starched, with its gold-headed canes, its plaids and red parasols, its patent leather shoes, and its foppish airs. The mountaineer in rags, coming out of his larch forest, brings with him a breath of wild nature ; and the young girl, mounted on her mule, fresh and rosy as the rhododendrons, is as simple and natural as they.

This is a stern-looking region ; its rocks, burned by glowing sunshine, clothed in summer with the broad leaves of creeping plants ; a region of stones and woods and pastures, where one must always be climbing, and where the mule takes the place of the horse. It is a region of waterfalls and glaciers and torrents, broken up with deep ravines and gloomy gorges ; a region in which, hidden in the folds of the barren mountain, you come upon charming oases, villages hanging on the sides of the precipices, with their dark cottages crowding fondly round a little white church ; a region of copper and silver and gold, but also of honest, simple hearts—soldier-spirits at perpetual warfare with the earth—the ungrateful, rebellious earth, that must be conquered and subdued continually, beaten and rent, in order to force life—daily food—from its hard and pitiless bosom.

And at the extremity of all those beautiful valleys, those hidden gorges, which hold in their mysterious depths all the treasures of the mineral kingdom, a sleeping glacier lies in long sinuous folds, and vomits from its yawning saurian mouth, bristling with icicles, a brawling stream or a mighty

river. Under the scorching summer sun the glacier is heard
crawling like an enormous reptile, emitting a harsh cry and
crackling its mighty vertebræ. It might be taken for a
gigantic mollusc, a cetacean from the Pole, an incomplete
monster, that has lain abandoned there since the creation.

While the glaciers thus make the higher valleys into a land
of desolation and misery;—while beyond a height of 6,500 feet
nothing grows but low shrubs and stunted firs and mournful
larches; while all forms of vegetation are small and poor,
like the offspring of an exhausted and deteriorating race;
lower down, on the two slopes that look towards the Rhone,
and drink life from its flood, it is a garden, an orchard, a
rich vine country, smiling hillsides shaded with trees and
crowned with vines and flowers.

If you only knew how lovely the spring is in this plain,
where the dark shade of the pines is exchanged for the soft,
sunny glow, creamy and rosy, of the fruit trees newly in
blossom! In May, the almond trees, powdered as with hoar
frost, are like young noblemen making their first entrance to
the gay world. At sight of them the young cherry trees are
covered with shy blushes, like girls listening to words of love
for the first time. The idyll of the spring time is seen here
in all its youthfulness and grace; the very brambles rise up
and twine their long arms, laden with flowers, among the
new, fresh green of the hedges.

How has it never occurred to the mind of a Swiss artist to
paint scenery like this?—so white, so bright, so rhythmical,
full of a poetry so heart-filling, bathed in so fair and pure
a light? Why do they not leave their studios before the
summer and during the autumn? Under the various fruit
trees in their spring blossom they would surprise Nature in
her lovely spring dishabille, in her youthful morning, in her
fair, pure, virgin beauty.

In summer this valley of the Rhone, which has the
gorgeous magnificence of the Pyrenees and their changeless
blue sky, has its burning rocks draped with thickets of myrtle

14

and clumps of wormwood; on its terraces stand gnarled
fig trees, with roots protruding from the soil like crooked
claws; and beside them plants with bright, dazzling colours
and powerful perfume, which attract strange insects with
ebony horns and bronze corslet barred with gold; in warm
nights the stimulating scent of the cantharides mingles with
the breeze; and the vine, the generous vine, the vine which
expands and makes glad the heart of man, stands in tri-
umphal order, from Sierre to Martigny, and sends down,
alongside of the other river, a broad river of wine from
which all Switzerland may drink abundantly.

PART IV.

THE VALAIS.

CHAPTER I.

THE *table-d'hôte* dinner finished, the *diligence* sets off once more with sounding horn and the jingling bells of its five horses.

The road continues to descend into the valley, which narrows into a defile, and the Rhone, already a strong stream, seems to follow like a great growling dog. We cross the river by a bridge and plunge into a gorge, darkened by narrowing rocky walls; then, emerging from this passage, which man has opened for himself with mine and pickaxe, we enter on a bright, fertile valley, with beautiful pastures shaded by thick trees and dotted with pretty wooden houses of golden mahogany tints or dark old oak. It might be taken for an Italian landscape. Northern nature has not this grace and elegance; its foliage has not this airy delicacy, this richness and variety, its sky has not this tender glow which draws forth from the land which it cherishes—wine! How original and pretty it is, this first Valaisian village, which we discover under a canopy of verdure, on the bank of the already tumultuous Rhone, whose waves seem pointed with glittering mica! The houses of larch wood, browned by the sun, have the old little windows with leaden partitions, and long outside stairs like ladders for poultry. Some black pigs and white goats flee in terror before the *diligence* through the narrow, choked-up village

street, in which the houses are crushed together as if to keep
each other warm in winter, and to form a rampart against
winds and avalanches. A frightful image, larger than life-
size, flesh-coloured and blood-stained, the arms decked with
withered garlands of moss that look like thick ropes, shows
that we are in a Roman Catholic country.

At the door of a wine vault we notice a tall, lean curé, six
feet high, with keen eye and black bristling beard of a
week's growth, a purple straw hat on his head, and a gun on
his shoulder. He has a dreadful countenance. If we had
been in Spain, we should have thought that he was waiting
for the *diligence*. Where was he going, armed in this way?
To the most innocent of pleasures, the most healthful of
exercises: he is going chamois hunting.

The huntsman curé is a special type in the Upper Valais,
where the people are of an active, restless temperament,
and the mind, even the clerical mind, has an independence
and pride entirely its own.

From one elevation to another we descend at last on
Münster, which has a church decorated with Italian frescos;
then, as we proceed farther, thick pine forests hang their
dark curtains over the mountains, that shut in the road and
the river. We continue to descend. The road cut in the
rock has rent the mountain in two, and overhanging arches
seem to threaten us from above. And now we are again
among the firs, with the sunshine softly sifting through the
foliage, and falling in golden flecks on the tender green of
the mosses.

Lower down we pass through a larch wood, bright and
lighted up like a ball-room, with raspberry bushes in
blossom and flocks of singing birds. Then more bearded
firs, growing tall and straight like long arrows stuck in the
earth. And then again there is a change of scenery; there
is delicious greensward through which pretty clear brooks
flow with merry laughter; the valley is less wild, and the
fruit trees begin to show their delicate treasures; cherry

trees that one might take to be covered with roses, richly laden apple trees, green meadows, and white houses with slated roofs. Beside a fountain, pretty girls are chattering, and an enormous "wirth" (innkeeper), made up of two round balls, rolls towards the *diligence* as it stops. He has in his hand a set of portable steps, while his wife appears at the door of the establishment in a dirty kitchen apron and armed with a skimmer, evidently indicating that they are accustomed to skim the *diligence ;* but we make our escape from them by going up at once to the Eggischhorn.

From Fiesch to the Eggischhorn, the highest peak of this part of the Valaisian Alps (9,650 feet), does not take long ; it is accomplished in three hours, by a good road, on mule back, and almost all the way under the shade of fir woods.

I send on my valise to Sierre, and taking my stick and my knapsack, I announce my purpose of going to sleep at the Eggischhorn hotel, to see the sun rise next morning on the glaciers of the Oberland and of the Pennine Alps. The big wirth, when he hears what I say, bursts into a Homeric laugh, with his mouth open from ear to ear. Holding his fat sides with his two hands, and the tears running down his cheeks, he exclaims,—

"Sleep at the Eggischhorn! Ah! ha! ha! And where, may I ask, does the gentleman come from? Perhaps he does not know that every bed is bespoken for a month in advance ; that the waiters sleep on the tables, and the hotel-keeper and his family on the chairs. A place in the stable would be charged dear if there were room ; but there is not room. Unless, indeed, the gentleman is accustomed to sleep on the fir trees?"

"Exactly," I replied. "I learned to sleep on fir trees in order to escape innkeepers like you."

The big landlord had too much interest in detaining travellers in the valley for me not to distrust his words a little. I set out at all events, saying to myself that one does not die of spending a single night under the stars ;

and that, at the worst, I could sleep on a bundle of hay, or under some rugs at the end of a corridor.

The panorama from the Eggischhorn is one of the most famous views in the Valais, or in all Switzerland. This mountain is so happily situated, that from the Eggischhorn Hotel can be made the ascent of the Jungfrau (13,671 feet), of the Finsteraarhorn (14,026 feet), and of the Great Aletschhorn (13,773 feet), the second highest peak of the Bernese Alps.

From the Eggischhorn descents also can be made to Grindelwald by the cols of the Moench and the Jungfrau; to Lauterbrunnen by the col of the Ebnefluh; and into the valley of Loetsch by the Aletsch glacier.

Throughout the season Mr. Seiler's hotel is too small to accommodate the caravans of English and American tourists who pass this way.

I had set out without a guide. The road is not a complicated one, and is excellent for a pedestrian; but night surprised me before I was clear of the wood. The lazy moon was not yet visible. Was she lighting up another part of the valley, or had she been devoured by some aerial monster? It was hardly the moment for composing ballads; grey shadows wrapped me round like a veil, I could not see three steps before me. I walked on like a blind man, stopping, from time to time, to listen.

Far down below me, as if in the depths of an abyss, a little bell rang out with sweet, silvery tones like the voices of birds growing fainter in the distance. It was the angelus.

Those who have ever, in their lives, been lost in the woods or on the mountains at the time when everything becomes blurred and confused and dark; when everything is enveloped in a mantle of mysterious gloom, and is hidden, and disappears into darkness; when Nature, lulled by the sweet voice of the streams and waterfalls, is falling asleep; when the birds are nestled close together on the tops of the trees or under the bushes; while the owl, with his fiery eyes,

comes hooting out of his old hollow tree, and the fox steals
noiselessly along the hedges to the poultry-yard;—those persons will understand all the poetry there is in hearing, in
this quaking solitude, the voice of the little bell telling out
the angelus, rising from earth to heaven, humble and modest,
like a prayer of the poor.

When the bell at Fiesch had ceased ringing, I resumed
my walk with fresh vigour, and soon reached the pastures,
where the stars served me as guides to the hotel.

Without troubling myself about where I was to sleep, I
ordered a comforting beefsteak, with a bottle of genuine
Glacier wine. Around me, English and Americans of every
age and colour were warming themselves at the stove. They
were in all kinds of positions, legs stretched on chairs, feet
in slippers, some without collar or neck-tie, in an easy dishabille, almost as if prepared for the night; and they were
reading large newspapers that served them for screens, and
in which they could have wrapped themselves as in sheets.

When I had finished my repast, I called the head waiter.

"Have you kept for me," said I, "a chair for to-night? I
know there is nothing but chairs left. You need make no
excuses. I was warned of it."

"In fact," he replied, "we have to-day refused by express
thirty travellers or more; but if you will be so good as to
give me your name, sir——."

I wrote, as usual, my name and designation on the little
sheet that the waiter had laid down before me. He took it
away, and in five minutes came back, saying, "Mr. Seiler has
found a room for you; please to come with me."

I followed him to the end of a corridor; he showed me
into a very little room, really a cabin, where there was, on a
table, a telegraphic apparatus, and in a corner a little iron
bed—oh, so little! like the edge of a knife—a doll's bed!

The waiter pointed to it.

"There, sir; it is our telegraphist's bed!"

And he went out and closed the door.

CHAPTER II

I DID not sleep with a quiet conscience.

The girl whose room I had usurped was perhaps more
tired than I was ; and she had no doubt been condemned to
the chair with which I should have been perfectly content.
I was humiliated at seeing the stronger sex treated as the
weaker. But there is no remorse so violent that it does not
in time yield to sleep.

At three in the morning the door of my room opened
softly, a mysterious hand lighted my candle, and I woke up
with a start, thinking I was to be summoned to give up
what I had unjustly taken. But it was only a servant.

"Sir," said he, "it is time to rise if you wish to join the
party that is going to the Eggischhorn."

In ten minutes I was ready, and we set out. At the head
of the procession was the servant, a great fellow six feet
high, with colossal shoulders, laden with plaids and shawls.

We had sufficient light to follow the path, covered with
little white pebbles. A few very brilliant stars were sparkling overhead, and indefinite sounds indicated that dawn
was near.

We climbed for two hours among fallen rocks, blocks rent
and shattered by lightning ; then, suddenly, we found ourselves on the top of a great sugar-loaf shaped rock, and a cry

of admiration burst from our lips. At our feet lies the Aletsch glacier—the largest in Switzerland,—its gloomy immensity, its great white mass filling the whole valley, flowing like a double river with foam-fringed eddies congealed for ever. Along the sides it is ploughed into wide furrows, rent in crevasses, hollowed out in deep gulfs, or rough with green edges as sharp as glass. In the middle stands a rock like a stony head above a white collar of ice ; and to the right, like a stainless mirror, the little Merjelen lake shows its dark surface, in which blocks of ice are floating. An intermediate zone of mountains confines the meanderings of the ice river. Beyond its steep shores, its wild, rugged, rocky banks, are seen, crowd upon crowd, the grand peaks of the Valaisian and Bernese Alps. All those peaks piercing the sky, all those teeth that gnaw and rend it, all those summits, wearing under their hoary locks the august gravity of aged giants, bear famous names, and for long defied the boldest climbers. Here, first, in the east is the Fletschhorn, like a newly whitewashed house, and black rocks showing through the snow, like a range of windows ; a little farther off the Mischabel, with its three peaks carved like battlements ; then, standing alone, and lifting their lofty brows above all the others, the king and queen of the Valais, the Matterhorn and the Dent Blanche, nearly the same in form, and sublime in their majesty. Next comes the Great Combin, like an organ, and Mont Blanc, like a dazzling tiara. The Aletschhorn is bent back at the top like an elephant's tusk ; the Jungfrau lifts her pure, queenly head, with its spotless crown of eternal snows ; the Moench, in his long white robe, is like a Carthusian kneeling before a vision of the Virgin ; the Finsteraarhorn, the Rothhorn, and the Weisshorn stand up like icebergs. Farther off other peaks rise and still rise, farther than the eye can reach, mingling in little bright spots, like sails of far-off ships, or swans resting on a silvery sea, until they are lost in chaos and infinity.

In the growing light of the dawn that was spreading and

opening out gradually on the horizon like a great pearly fan, these snows and glaciers took on spectral colours that suggested magic or phantasmagoria.

All at once, opposite to us a great band of light shot across the sky; it might have been a fiery serpent, or the flash of a golden blade; and the horizon assumed a ruddy glow in this sudden burst of light. Purple gleams were reflected from the loftiest peaks, and the snowy heights became incarnadined, as if all those sleeping and frozen Titans were trembling and awaking at the approach of the fructifying power, the sun, which was at last visible. It was like an enormous glowing ball, hanging in space. Perceptibly it grew larger, and very soon it was so large and so bright that it was impossible to look at it steadily. Its rays shot forth on every side like blazing arrows, spreading fire, and lighting up peak and summit and point. The glaciers burned like altars, and in view of this immense illumination, this apotheosis of light, this solemn morning gladness, we felt as if we were present at the magnificent nuptials of the Earth and the Sun.

At this point you yield to silent rapture and reflection. You say to yourself that this is a marvellous fairy-land, a unique spectacle, such as no king, nor any one else, were he a hundred times richer than all the Rothschilds put together, could obtain at home; and that those who wish to see it must come here, must ascend the mountain, go away from earth and approach heaven.

Just at this moment a butterfly passed above our heads and fluttered towards the glaciers. It went upwards, still upwards, slowly, gently, into the free, sunny air; joyous, careless it rose, light as a lily petal borne on the breeze; then all at once it vanished like a snowflake melted in the sun. Those who believe in the journeyings of souls must see them flitting and hovering in this little white ethereal form of the butterfly of the snows.

An hour later we were back to the Jungfrau Hotel, to which, the summer before, the Valaisian and Bernese guides

brought back the unhappy victims of the catastrophe that
was so much talked about. At last the virgin mountain
had avenged herself for so many insults. There they lay on
the grass, side by side, all the six, frozen and stiff, before
the members of the Valaisian tribunal, summoned to prove
their identity, and the twenty-two guides who had gone in
search of them. And during this melancholy scene, the
clouds that covered the Jungfrau dispersed, and it seemed
as if the white mountain were contemplating her victims,
the six vigorous young men whose life she had taken.

I had met on the Eggischhorn a pleasant Parisian lawyer,
with whom I had quickly made acquaintance. I proposed
to him to go down again into the valley, to Brieg, crossing
the Aletsch glacier, and, on the way, to dine at Bellalp.

Promptly we set forth, hastening down by a delightful
path through fresh spring pastures, under a blue sky filled
with soft morning light; pearly drops of dew still hung
glittering on the blades of grass; there were delicate
shades, pale rainbow tints, on the mountains; and farther
away the frozen peaks seemed as if dashed against each
other in a silent tempest of great white waves.

We crossed the Aletsch glacier without difficulty, and
without a guide; the troops of mules that cross it almost
daily had marked out as it were a little road, a dirty track
in the midst of the snow.

After partaking of a very dear and a very bad dinner at
Bellalp, we indulged ourselves, by way of dessert, with the
view of this magnificent Aletsch glacier from the terrace of
the hotel.

From Bellalp to Naters we descend in three hours, through
woods and pastures, and from Naters to Brieg; a charming
walk when the sun is not too hot; for in the middle of the
day this valley of the Rhone burns like a little purgatory.
In Swiss railway carriages the traveller is happily not subjected to the system of cells; you can be there at your ease,
imbibe the air by wide and numerous windows, and walk

about as in a great rolling verandah. At night they are very uncomfortable; but in Switzerland the trains go only till midnight.

Here we are, then, at Brieg, a large, dusty town, with something both of Spanish and oriental about it. Its houses are adorned with turrets and minarets, its churches are surmounted with bulbous cupolas, and in its little side streets you come upon old dwellings that ravish the eye, Renaissance fronts with columns and pilasters, emblazoned doors and carved balconies. It has a handsome civic building, the large, stately gateway of which is surmounted by a delicious loggia; and there is also here the old, original mansion of the Stockalper family, with its vast arcaded court, its magnificent gardens, its sumptuous halls adorned with family portraits and furnished with antique treasures that would be the pride of a cathedral. But our train is just going to start; we have no time to wait; for we hope before night to go up to Vissoye in the Val d'Anniviers.

We make a short stop at Visp, at the entrance to the valleys of Saas and St. Niklaus; the first leads to the Fée glacier, to Monte Moro, and into the valley of Anzasca, which leads down, almost unknown, as far as Lake Maggiore; the second leads to Zermatt, to Monte Rosa, to the Matterhorn, to the enchanted world of glaciers and eternal snows in the heart of the Pennine Alps. It is to Zermatt, to the Riffel, to the Gornergrat that one must go to have any idea of the pathetic beauty of the Valais, the most beautiful and picturesque canton in Switzerland. Theophile Gautier has described Zermatt and the Matterhorn in a hundred pages, which are pictures by a master hand, that cannot be repeated. To see Zermatt after having seen the Rigi, is to see the ocean after seeing Windermere.

Beyond Visp, two other lateral valleys open almost opposite each other; that of Loetsch, which leads back to Thun, and that of Turtman, bounded by a splendid glacier, above which towers the rugged Weisshorn.

At the entrance of the wild valley of Loetsch, the sight of Gampel in the midst of maize fields, under its apple trees shaped into cupolas, awakens in me a whole world of memories. Gampel reminds me of my first grand Alpine tour made with one of my professors; each with our knapsack on our back, and travelling for a month in the mountains at an outlay of a hundred francs. Those were the good old times, the days of travelling at three francs a day, of sleeping in châlets among the hay, of taking a grassy bank for dining-room, of refreshing rest in the arbour of a monastery or a parsonage. In most of these valleys there was no hotel, not even an inn. People lodged at the house of the minister or the priest. I have found in an old note-book my impressions at that period, my holiday notes of a student, written twenty years ago; a few pages of which will show what the valley of Loetsch and the old Canton Valais were at that time.

CHAPTER III.

WE are at Kippel,[1] the largest village in the Loetsch
valley, at the foot of the glacier that we have crossed
in coming from Thun. It is surrounded by green meadows
which are carefully watered by numberless little drains.
But what a dull thing is a Valaisian village! The houses
are heaped together, black and tumbling down; the close,
narrow streets are muddy, poisonous, full of unwholesome
odours; the little windows are covered with curtains of dirt
that intercept the daylight; the balconies are hung with
ragged, wretched garments, put out to dry, and down quilts
with their red squares many times patched.

At Kippel, as in most of the very remote villages of the
Valais, inns are unknown; and strangers go to lodge with
the parish priest, whose house is close by the church. It
is easily recognised by its red-tiled roof and its whitewashed stone front, brightened with green shutters. It is
surrounded by a garden, the only one in the village.

We knock with our sticks at the open front door. An

---

[1] This sketch, made, as I have said, twenty years ago, is no longer a
true picture. Cleanliness has made some advance, even at Kippel, and
the windows which then were nailed down are now made to open.
Kippel even possesses an hotel, and many strangers are to be seen there.

old servant arrives. Recognising strangers, she at once
asks us in, without even asking what we want. The low
room into which she shows us is furnished with carved
cupboards, antique dressers, to which are hung "*channes*,"
that is, tin pots of various sizes; iron candlesticks, a slate;
at the foot of the bed an old trunk to keep clothes in, and
over the bed two crossed guns, a pistol, a sabre, and some
holy images. We take our seats behind a big larch-wood
table, and while the servant goes to bring us some wine we
try to open the window; but in vain; it is nailed down!
It is the custom of the country.

A firm, decided step is suddenly heard on the rough
boards of the corridor; a vigorous hand opens the door, and
a man about thirty, tall and strong, with black hair, comes
in; he is the parish priest of Kippel.

We rise, and beg him to have the goodness to take us in
for the night.

"We have already one foot in your house, sir, as you see,
and are doing honour to your hospitality even before you
have given us leave to do so."

"That is just how I mean it to be," he replied. "Whether
I am here or from home, my servant has orders to receive
all who come. What would be thought of me if I closed
my door when, just opposite, God keeps the door of His
abode always open? People would say I was a disciple
unworthy to enter the Master's house, and they would be
right. But pray sit down, gentlemen; and while Greth
prepares an omelet for you—for, alas! I have nothing but
eggs to offer you—I should like you to taste a wine of the
Upper Valais with which you are not acquainted; it is
called 'hell-wine.'"

"If it is good, you will make us wish to go there,
sir."

"It is a singular name! I believe it is given because
the vines which produce it grow only in very hot places."

Our host took a key from the table drawer, went away

15

for a moment, and came back with an old bottle that seemed full of ink; so black was it, that when half empty one would have said it was still quite full.

It is no penance to drink "hell-wine." I know people who would willingly be condemned to drink this wine all their lives.

We receive from our host some details as to the manners and the inhabitants of the valley. In summer they live scattered on the mountains; he is sometimes obliged, in going to see a sick person, to walk for five or six hours. In autumn great bands of men and women go away to the vintage on the plains, on the banks of the Rhone. It is only in winter that the hive is full. And then they do like the bees, they eat what they have gathered in summer. They toil only to live—to get food. There is no superfluity. Each has his own little dwelling, his field, his patch of vines, two goats, and a few cows; and as the communal property is very considerable, that is enough. There are neither rich nor poor. A primitive, patriarchal life. Those mountain folk have so few wants that there is not a single tavern or wine-shop in the valley. They never play for money, and the fashions have been the same for centuries; all the clothes are made in the village from the wool of their own flocks. In every châlet there is a weaver. The young girl at her marriage wears the same head-dress as her grandmother,—a tall black hat with a broad ribbon of gold,—preserved as a relic. The sons wear their fathers' holiday clothes.

A desert during the week, the village becomes populous again every Sunday. Everybody comes to mass at the parish church. Some families rise at one o'clock in the morning in order to arrive in time. On certain Sundays long pious processions wind round the church-yard, with their old massive silver crosses, their torn banners, their red church standards with golden letters; members of the different fraternities in the costume of penitents, their heads masked in the horrible hood of the robe that hides the body in the rigid whiteness of a winding-sheet; women and girls, veiled, carrying tapers and rosaries; and bells tolling. After vespers on great fête days, the masculine youth of the valley give dramatic representations, which attract great numbers of people; the piece performed is a pathetic drama, an episode in the history of the Valais, versified by a parish priest of the valley. (These performances still take place once a year, on St. Maurice's day, in September.) Then are seen hundreds of actors in the old dress of French and Neapolitan soldiers, a red and white uniform, with an enormous shako with threatening plumes, and gold epaulettes. This martial population distinguished themselves in foreign service. A king of France gave to the five communes of Loetsch a flag that they treasure most carefully, and display on festival days and other great occasions. When a son of the valley becomes a priest, and celebrates his first mass at Kippel, the whole population turn out under arms, in the full uniform of Swiss Guards and Neapolitan soldiers, to be present at the ceremony, and march through the village to the music of drum and trumpet, with colours flying. Three or four times in the year there is a dance in the open air, near the church; and it is the priest who, so to speak, opens the ball, by honouring it with his presence for an hour.

In winter, in the long evenings, while the women spin, the old men tell over again to the young people the chronicles of the valley, or the wonderful legends of the glaciers, such as, "The noble Milanese lady," "The dragon of Naters," or, "The strange chamois." One day a chamois passed near a hunter, who quickly raised his rifle to his shoulder and fired. But when the smoke had dispersed, the animal had vanished. The hunter knew that he had not missed his aim, he was sure he had hit the creature, but he searched for it in vain. Some years afterwards he was in Milan. As he passed along the street a young lady, leaning from the window of a handsome house, spoke to him, and asked him to come up where she was.

"Do you not recognise me?" said she. "I also have been in the Valais."

"No," replied the hunter, "I do not recognise you."

Then the girl told him that she had been changed into a chamois by a wicked sorceress, who had said to her, "You shall keep that form till three hunters have fired at you."

"You," she continued, "were the third hunter to fire at me, so you delivered me. I was able to return to Milan, where I became again what I was before."

After telling us this legend, the priest showed us his church, ornamented with such a profusion of red and gilded flowers that it might be taken for a church in Italy. Its three pictures were painted by a tailor, who makes no higher charge for painting a Burial of Christ than for making a great-coat; he is paid by the day; twenty-four centimes for twelve hours of work. There is said to be one real masterpiece by this artist,—a Crucifixion, in which the Holy Virgin is seen, in the first sketch, wearing a straw hat and a shawl, standing at the foot of the cross, with a willow basket on her arm, like a good housekeeper returning from market.

The priest also said to us, "In the depth of winter the women cannot be distinguished from the men in our church. As there is more than three feet of snow in the valley, they could not walk in their petticoats; so they all dress like men, and some of them smoke pipes, like the Bernese."

When we returned to the parsonage the table was spread. The omelet was greeted with a hurrah! It was excellent, shining, golden with butter; then a bit of old cheese, somewhat perforated by inhabitants, served on a board, gave us a specimen of the exquisite flavour of the Valaisian manufacture.

"By the way, sir," said I, "I am commissioned to tell you from the landlord at Kandersteg, that your last chamois was a splendid article, and he hopes you will soon send him another. Do you often go hunting?"

" Does that surprise you? A Valaisian priest is so many things at once : schoolmaster, engineer, architect, doctor, secretary to the commune, lawyer, judge, guide, innkeeper, and hunter! Hunting is not a passion with me; it is a habit of my youth. Born in this village, I have always been seen setting out for the mountains with my gun ; people would be as much astonished if I gave up hunting as they would be at Sion if they saw an armed priest walking in the streets."

Here end the notes made in 1868 ; but I can still see, as if it had been yesterday, the room into which the worthy priest showed us for the night ; the wide bed with its counterpane in red, blue, and yellow stripes, woven in the last century ; a real rustic monument of a bed, with an old trunk in front of it, over which we had to climb to gain our rest. In the middle of the room was a massive table, ornamented with curious iron-work, and all round were old wooden benches, polished by the friction of many generations. The too short wick of our lamp left us in darkness before we had finished undressing, and we were obliged to grope about, with much laughter, in search of our bed.

Next day we left Kippel at cock-crow, and at noon reached Gampel, at the end of the valley, in time to dine at a bright, pretty rustic inn, with white walls, and a trellised awning over the door and windows. The hens came close up to our feet to pick up the crumbs we threw to them ; and now and then tall, handsome girls passed along, with a basket of fruit on the head or a spade or a rake on the shoulder ;— fair, blue-eyed girls, the " beautiful girls of Gampel," as they are called in the Valais. In the distance, as the background of the picture, we saw the plain, burnt and yellow, flooded with sunshine, and intersected by the long silver line of the Rhone ; and farthest away of all, the gigantic mountain ridge, its sides all shaggy with herbage, cut up here and there by torrents, and showing deep tracks down which avalanches have torn their way, or where wood has been sent down from the forests. It was one of those animated and delicious landscapes that are met with at every turn in the Valais.

CHAPTER IV.

SIERRE is a pretty little town, of bright, smiling aspect,
lying in this plain of the Rhone, nowhere broader or
more fertile than here. It has an old tower which seems to
be guarding it like a duenna watching over a young girl.
The two little blue lakes near the town, the hills with
villages and vineyards climbing up their slopes, luxuriant
meadows, fields of wheat with heads drooping with their
golden wealth, fields of maize as tall as forest trees, orchards
where branches are bending with their fruit ; all these give
the place a southern character which is borne out by its
climate, the best and sweetest in the Valais. Almost no
winter : their only snow is in spring ; the rosy, perfumed
snow of the almond blossom !

At Sierre all the products of warm regions are found in
cultivation. Bearing the sun in its coat of arms, it is the
region of the victorious sun, enclosing its golden drops in
the vine clusters; it is the intoxicating country of Malvoi-
sie and Glacier wines ; it is the garden of luscious fruits,
of choice vegetables ; the favourite resort of invalids and
foreigners.

In the town itself, in its narrow winding streets, is a
jumble of old houses, some of which look as if they were

falling down before the wind that finds its way in at their
windows and battered doors. There is a kind of country-
house or farmhouse appearance. Droves of cows and carts
of manure mix with elegant equipages passing the doors
of hotels. But nothing vulgar; a strong originality, like
everything else in the Valais.

Near the station some mules are standing tied. I inquire
if among these animals there are any that are going back to
Vissoye to-night. A sturdy man, with his felt hat down over
his eyes, and his lip hidden under a moustache like a brush,
replies :—

" Yes, sir; I am going up again to the hotel. I came
down with the luggage of two Englishmen who have gone
by the train."

" Will you hire your mule to me ? "

" Willingly."

" At what o'clock shall we be at Vissoye ? "

" Towards midnight."

" All right ; and you ask ? "

" Ten francs."

" Agreed."

I get astride the mule, and we set off.

There is a charm in this rate of progress only in a country
which you already know and have passed through several
times. In that case it is all your vagabond youth, your
memories of long ago, that awake and rise around you on the
familiar road, singing like a flock of birds hidden in the
bushes. And it is delightful to walk thus in the past, to
live over again your life in the flowery paths of youth on
the mountains, to see again what you saw before, in colours
eternally young ; to find again the same flowers, fresh and
lovely, the same scents in the hedges, the same feelings in
the soul; you forget for the moment that years have made
you old, that age has bent you, and that you are no longer
as erect as the firs that surround you.

We follow the picturesque road that goes back to the

Rhone along the side of the Lake of Géronde, whose motionless and transparent waters reflect the ruined monastery,
framed in Italian vegetation, that rises on its banks. Then
we cross the river by a large wooden bridge, and reach
Chippis, with its sheltered houses at the foot of the mountain,
at the confluence of the Rhone and the foaming Navigenze.

The road ascends in many zigzags and windings; and
slowly and toilsomely we climb the mountain. And as every
effort has its reward, on the mountains even more than elsewhere, we see below us the whole valley spread out in its
rich magnificence, the meadows and fields divided like chess
boards by the numerous watercourses, and quenching their
burning thirst with the water which the Rhone distributes
to them. The houses beside the Lake of Géronde are like
greyheaded white birds sitting among the grass, and the
tower and the church are reduced to children's toys. And
above the vineyard slopes, chains of mountains show their
tapering summits; frozen snowy peaks, in a bewildering
mass, crowd one upon another, as if they also would look
down into the valley. All those heights are bathed in
purple lights; soft, vaporous, changing shades that neither
pen nor pencil can depict. They look as if draped with
transparent robes of moonlight, shot with sunshine. It
recalls the Pyrenees, the mountains of Spain, the East.

And as night draws on, the daylight becomes so soft that
it seems to be sifted through invisible gauzy curtains,
floating on the horizon. The green loses all its hardness,
and melts into harmonious and tender tones. There is an
exquisite enjoyment in travelling at this delicious hour,
when the mountains are fragrant with all the sweet evening
perfumes; and everything is so calm, so tranquil! A cool
breath flows down from the glacier; and this bath of suddenly renewed air, this pure air coming to you from the
immaculate heights, restores to you your morning vigour,
and removes all the weariness of the day. The sun disappears, still sending a vast, glorious radiance above the

horizon. The farther range of mountains alone remains lighted up, and still stands out in relief. The part opposite the sunset becomes rosy, and in going through a forest you see, between the branches, golden gleams and strange fires; you feel as if you were in a cathedral, with the moon shining through its Gothic windows.

The shadow that has been creeping up from the valley, gliding from bush to bush, now overtakes us; the grass-hoppers grow more active and noisy; the grass becomes full of little whisperings and stir; wood-pigeons dart like arrows above our heads, and crows in their heavy flight are cawing to each other an inquiry which way they shall take.

The road is a marvel of audacity. It goes through gorges and along precipices, at the foot of which the Navigenze is heard boiling and roaring. On the other side of the torrent is seen Vercorin, whose black houses, clustered close together, mark the outlet of the valley.

For six years, with no subsidy from the State, relying only on their own resources, the Anniviards laboured at this road, hewed out the rock, toiled, spent themselves that they might themselves open their mountains to the people of the plain. Every one came in his turn to fulfil his allotted days of labour. The old road, of which some traces are still visible, was a break-neck path,—a real path of death.

Now, every summer, crowds of tourists go up by the new road; but the Anniviard is as indifferent as his own rocks to this passing stream. He remains what he was before; retains his manners and customs and ways; he has stood out against the ignominy of the blouse, that garb of the modern slave, brought in by commercial travellers and railways; he has still his typical face, his marked individuality. And now that the picturesque is disappearing, and originality is losing its keen edge, and tradition is bit by bit falling into decay, what still makes the charm of those inner recesses of the Valais is the unforeseen—the novelty that awaits you there, the sight of a thousand things that you fancy you are the first to discover, because you had no suspicion of their being there. Each of those valleys is a little separate world; no two are alike, either in costume, language, or manners. In this one they speak German; in another there is a mixture of Romanic *patois* and Italian; in yet another a pithy French, with expressions belonging to the 17th century,—a French imported from France, where all the mountaineers served. There is hardly a family in which there is not piously preserved in a trunk or an old cupboard a French, Italian, or Spanish uniform, with broad, flaming red facings, which is put on for great solemnities, for Corpus Christi day and the parish festival.

It is very rarely that any one ventures into these valleys in the winter, when they are blocked up with snow. Hence these numberless contrasts and differences, that are explained by the climate and the configuration of the soil.

If the inhabitants of the Loetsch valley are of German origin, the Anniviards, it is said, must be a Hungarian race. It is asserted that they are descended from the Huns; and this is how it is accounted for. This valley, in ancient times, was nothing but a frightful desert, covered with wood. After the death of Attila, when his terrible hordes were beaten on every hand and fleeing in all directions, some broken remnants of them took refuge with their flocks in this gorge; and finding themselves in safety there, they settled, and cleared the land. This was the origin of the Anniviards. For long they remained isolated; their neighbours feared and despised them, because they repulsed all the missionaries who were sent to them.

Even now a great many of their names are Hungarian. One of the most considerable families of the district is called Ruaz, like Attila's brother; there is also a mountain that bears this name; and there are found among them certain customs identical with the practices of those other descendants of the Huns, the Magyars. At Grementz, just as in all the villages on the banks of the Theiss, everybody is invited, by the ringing of a bell, to come and partake of the funeral feast. The crosses in the cemeteries are like those of the Hungarian cemeteries. The Huns used to clothe themselves with the wool of their flocks; brown or white or black, according to the colour of their sheep. The Anniviards wear black clothes; the colour of the wool of their sheep. Finally, the general typical features are alike: black hair, black eyes, high cheek-bones, hooked nose, and thick moustache.

The nomade habits of this people seem also to point to an Asiatic descent. Whole villages migrate, sometimes to the plain, sometimes to the mountain. It often happens that the tourist comes upon a hamlet completely deserted; no longer a single inhabitant or a living creature. Through the dingy windows of every house may be seen the tables and chairs in the room, but the bed is empty; and in the deserted street the grass flourishes at its own sweet will.

These nomade habits are so deeply rooted that most families possess two houses in the same village,—one for summer, another for winter; while the richest families have sometimes as many as six houses, in which they spend two months in succession. This migration, this change of place, is to them a necessity, a pleasure, an enjoyment.

In the vintage season the whole valley goes down to Sierre, where the finest vineyards belong to the Anniviards. The parish priest of Vissoye himself migrates at the head of his flock, with the schoolmaster, the president, and all the authorities. The families follow one after the other, like a caravan in the desert. First comes the mule, heavily laden, led by the "chef," with the little children snugly packed in the panniers, like birds in their nests; then the wife, taking charge of the goats, the sheep, and the calves; and behind her the pigs trot grunting along, driven by a thin little girl with tangled hair, or a toothless old woman, armed with a thick stick.

The vineyards, which belong to the four communes into

which the valley is divided, are cultivated and the vintage gathered, in common. On the days of communal service, daybreak is sounded by fife and drum at four in the morning, in the various hamlets around Sierre, where the Anniviards have houses. At six the call is sounded; then there is the setting forth to the work, with music and flag leading the way. The priest and the authorities accompany the workers, and at the end of the procession a cart conveys the communal wine that is to be drunk during the day. The teacher, the judge, the magistrates are obliged to work, just the same as the others, reaping-knife or spade in hand. Every citizen who fails to obey the summons is liable to a fine of three francs. The meals are taken in common, under the tree on the top of which the flag has been fixed. During the mid-day meal, to which all are summoned by fife and drum, public business is discussed, and the policy of the Government is censured or approved.

The election of deputies is also set about and carried through during the vintage, in the communal cellars belonging to the Anniviards at Sierre. Not a few electors sell their votes beforehand for a bottle of wine.

The ascent had become no longer difficult. My mule was keeping along the edge of the precipice, at the foot of which we heard the torrent roaring. It is the habit of these animals, cautious as they are, to go always towards the chasm, right above the abyss. The mule was going at a pleasant, easy pace, that did not hinder my chatting with the driver. The young mountaineer told me ghost stories, legends of the Upper Valais: that of the wrestler of Graechen, who seized his adversary in his arms, and crushing him against his breast, flattened him like a cake; that of the goat of Naters, with long curved horns and flaming eyes, and his body covered, not with hair, but with icicles, that made a fearful jingling as he ran; and the only safety for those who met him was in a chapel or holy house where sacred relics were kept. He told me also the legend of the " wild man's hole at Zermatt."

On the Riffel, in a deep cavern with a very narrow entrance, there lived a strange countryman, who from living always in solitude had become a thorough savage, and fled whenever he saw a human being. People were obliged to lay down food for him at a place where he came for it. But by-and-by he tired of what was prepared for him, and took to living entirely on the raw flesh of sheep that he stole. More than one attempt was made to seize the thief; but he fled to the Riffelhorn by a path of his own, and repulsed the assailants with a shower of stones. At last one day a chamois hunter laid wait for him, and shot him as he was creeping out of his cave.

And the legend of the bear! A mountaineer of extra-ordinary physical strength, but rather weak mentally, was once overtaken by a tempest of snow; one of those wild storms that blind you and bury you on the spot if you cannot quickly find shelter in a châlet. Happily our man spied one at hand, and ran to it. Hardly has he got in when a deep growling reveals to him that he has a bear for company. He does not lose his coolness; he hurls an insult at the bear, and stands firmly awaiting him. The bear rises on his hind paws, but before he has time to make his rush, the mountaineer grasps him in his iron arms, pushing his head hard under his muzzle, so that the bear is obliged to keep it in the air, and makes him pirouette as a dancer does his partner. For a long time the bear and the man go on together, round and round, over rocks and above precipices, still tightly clasped together, until the last turn carries them over the brink of the chasm, and they fall to the bottom of the abyss. The bear, being the heavier of the two, fell undermost, breaking his own neck, and breaking the fall of the man, who was thus miraculously saved!

I asked my driver what he had paid for his mule.

" A hundred and fifty francs."

" What!" I exclaimed, " a hundred and fifty francs! A good mule—and yours is a good one—is worth as much as a thousand francs."

" You are right, sir. But I have only the fourth part of this one. He was valued at six hundred francs. Four of us joined to buy him; it is the custom among us for several to join for a mule; some have half a one, others only a third or a fourth. We have the right to so many hours of the mule in the week, for he is not always wanted."

" And what is the name of your mule ? "

" Saute-en-Barque."

He laughed, and went on: " There is a whole story about it. It is written in a book, up there at the hotel, so you can read it. This is not the very, real Saute-en-Barque himself, however; he is one of his sons. We bought him in the Val d'Hérens."

We had now reached a place where the road plunges into a dubious-looking gorge, utterly dark,—disappears, as it were, into a hole. This evil passage is called the " Pontis," because the old road was carried over bridges and scaffoldings hanging above the abyss. When the new road was made, it was found necessary to cut long winding galleries in the rocks, where, even in broad daylight, it is almost dark.

I asked my guide if I should dismount.

" No, no," said he; " Saute-en-Barque walks in this oven as if it were the village green. Don't be afraid; he knows the way; he has done it often enough."

Saute-en-Barque, without the slightest hesitation, plunged into the gloomy vault,—a veritable cave, in which a traveller might be stripped in a moment, if the whole region were not absolutely safe. This little journey in the dark, inside the mountain, through a subterranean gallery with no openings to the daylight, lasted several minutes.

When we issued from the last gallery, the full moon was shining at the end of the valley, lighting up its depths, and showing in a long white line the course of the Navigenze, rushing and bounding and tossing its flowing locks, with a hollow murmuring and complaining sound.

Resuming our interrupted dialogue, I asked my guide,—

" Are you a married man ? "

" Oh, yes ! A young wife is a useful servant."

" And how did your marriage take place ? "

" Oh, just as others do; I chose out of the heap. The girls, with us, stand all together on Sundays in front of the church, just like the market. I offered a flower to the one that pleased me best; she did not refuse it, and we were married after Easter, early in the morning, according to the usual custom. Only the witnesses. We don't use much ceremony in the mountains."

" What! not even a little refreshment together ? "

" Nothing. There's not an inn in the valley, not a tavern. There is nothing but three hotels that are closed in winter, and they have no drinking-room for the like of us. As soon as a fellow is married, he goes straight off with his wife to work in the fields. She has to learn that marriage is no holiday. It is only at baptisms that we drink a glass, a good glass with the godfather and godmother, and make *raclettes*." [1]

" And at burials ? "

" Oh! that is more fun; for then there is something to eat and drink for everybody. It was the same when they used to drink the health of the corpse."

" Of the corpse ? "

" Yes; oh, it's just a way of speaking. When the dead person was laid in front of the house or of the church in his coffin, and the relations and friends and acquaintances were gathered round, drink was poured out, and each held out his full glass, saying to the dead, ' *Au revoir !* ' "

Suddenly my companion, pointing with his stick to a large white house on the roadside, exclaimed joyously,—

" Here we are ! The hotel ! "

---

[1] Slices of toasted cheese.

I was acquainted with this hotel, which was formerly kept so well by M. Monnier, now a deputy, up to the neck in honours. I had spent a week there with an old friend, a companion of my childhood, and how many merry excursions we made during that never-to-be-forgotten week, how many escapades and escalades! And how good it was, after a day of walking or hunting, to come back in the evening to the hotel, our limbs aching with delicious fatigue, to sit down before the steaming tureen, and to drink full glasses of that glacier wine, yellow as gold and hot as fire. And while our English neighbours were snoring in dreamless sleep, we gave free rein to our chat; and they were mad fancies, poems with neither rhyme nor reason, that the excellent M. Monnier used to interrupt with a wink, to tell us confidentially some good story of town or country.

To-night all the shutters were closed. The hotel seemed to be uninhabited, deserted.

"We will soon awaken them!" said my muleteer, with a knowing look.

Saute-en-Barque had stopped at the foot of the steps, while his master knocked loudly and repeatedly. The sound re-echoed as if from a cellar.

A key grated in the lock, and a man in coloured shirt and embroidered slippers, carrying a small candlestick, received us, and took us into the dining-room.

I was as hungry as an ogre. Having obtained some slices of ham, I invited my guide to share my supper.

At midnight, just as he was leaving us, he said to me,—

"I was forgetting the book, the story of Saute-en-Barque." And seizing the candle that the porter was holding, he went into the salon, and saying, "Allow me," took from the stand a blue-covered pamphlet, which he gave me.

"There, sir," said he, "you will see there why Pierre Bonvin's mule was called Saute-en-Barque, a name which he has handed on to his descendants."

16

When I had got into bed, I opened the book,[1] and read as follows. It is a mule who speaks, said to be the father of the animal that brought me from Sierre to Vissoye :—

"I think I have not yet told you my name. I feel some shame in pronouncing its syllables, they are so strange. I am called Saute-en-Barque. It is a most fanciful appellation, for I have no resemblance in any way to a bark, and my quiet walk excludes all idea of leaping or capering. The unlucky circumstances to which I owe the name are these : Marguerite, the priest's old servant, came home one day from Sierre arrayed in a garment that she had never been seen to wear before, and of a kind totally unknown in the village. When the priest saw her, he made two steps backward, uttering an exclamation expressive both of surprise and displeasure.

"In order to understand the old man's astonishment, it must be understood that in certain remote valleys of the twentieth Swiss canton there exist traditions in regard to dress as authoritative as the old sumptuary laws. Men and women cannot dress according to their own fancy. They must conform to the old customs, which, taking the place of so many wise rules, baffle in that way the lovers of picturesque extravagance and eccentricity. These traditions, of which certain pastors willingly constitute themselves the guardians, have their use. They contribute to the keeping up of good habits; they prevent the development of luxury, and save families and the district itself from becoming impoverished. To them is owing the special stamp of originality in the different races in the Valais.

"Thus it is in vain that the fair sex in the commune of Evolena cast wistful looks through the seductive shop-windows at the many-coloured stuffs and alluring bonnets that fashion displays there. There is an embargo on all those

---

[1] "Saute-en-Barque," a Valaisian novel, by M. Ch. de Bons, one of the most eminent men of the Valais, whose death is regretted by all who knew him.

productions of Parisian fingers and workshops. Beyond the woollen gown, made so narrow that it becomes difficult to step across the brooks, beyond the red stomacher laid like an escutcheon on the chest, and the white cap concealing the hair, there is, in the valley of the Borgne, no progress to be hoped for. Along the flowery slopes of the Vieze it is the same; rustic beauty is neither understood nor tolerated except when arrayed in the black gown, the red apron, and shoes of an extraordinary cut.

"How did I learn all these particulars? By a severe charge made by the priest against his young assistant, who had one day allowed some hint to escape him that, when *he* had the full charge of the parish, he might keep pace a little with the age. From all this the surprise of the worthy priest may be understood when he saw his old housekeeper dressed in a saute-en-barque.

"'What is the meaning of this masquerade, Guiton?' exclaimed the excellent ecclesiastic, looking very severe. 'Where have you fished up this garment of perdition?'

"'My foster-sister, the president's wife at Lovina, made me a present of it. I went to visit her on the way to Sierre. Was I to vex her by refusing it? And besides, what is the good of hurting the feelings of the people of the plain?'

"'And what is the thing called?'

"'A saute-en-barque.'

"'A saute—en—barque!' repeated the priest, not able to believe his ears.

"The name certainly doubled the enormity of the gift.

"'Yes; but if you are so displeased at the present, I'll go and take it off. I can make it into waistcoats for the churchwarden's children. I don't want to cause a scandal in the parish.'

"'That is right, Guiton! You can understand that if I had tolerated this novelty, I should soon have been no longer master of our people. A saute-en-barque! How can people misuse terms in such a way?'

"It will be seen by these exclamations that the old man, thoroughly equipped as to theology and that class of knowledge, was as simple as a child, and had never in his life looked into a catalogue of the ridiculous and unintelligible names invented by fashion.

"The old servant did as she had promised. But if the garment was consigned to obscurity, the name survived, and I bear the penalty of it.

"The fact was, the priest did not know what to call me. His assistant mischievously suggested to him the most high-sounding historical names, but did not succeed in making him choose one of them. According to him, there was no way of avoiding Pegasus, or Bucephalus, or Hippogriff. In the meantime Marguerite's visit to the plain had occurred, and the little scene that I have related.

"The priest, going on beating his brains to find the unfindable name, at last exclaimed,—

"'It is decided! He shall be called "Saute-en-Barque." That will please Marguerite by reminding her of her obedience to me, and her generosity towards the church-warden's children.'

"And this is how great things are sometimes the result of a trifling circumstance."

Having finished the interesting narrative of Saute-en-Barque (who became an artillery mule, and conveyed to the roughest heights those pretty mountain cannon that are like golden cigar-cases), I blew out my candle, and was soon sleeping that sound sleep of the tourist that is quite as good as the sleep of the just.

CHAPTER V.

EARLY in the morning I opened my shutters. Leaning
out at the window, half-dressed, I drank deep draughts
of the exquisite air, fresh and fragrant, coming down from
the mountain and laden with the breath of flowers. The
Val d'Anniviers is really a botanical garden. In it are
found the plants of the Pyrenees, of the Andes, of the
Himalayas; and on the edge of the glacier, the trembling,
fragile growth of polar regions. Above Vissoye begin
great rose-coloured beds of rhododendrons, pastures starry
with gentians, red and blue. There, too, are azaleas of
vivid carmine, and golden arnicas with their stately bearing, making one think of rays of sunshine turned into
flowers. The delicately cut edelweiss is seen against the
cliffs, and in every direction orchids diffuse a strong odour
of vanilla.

Almost over against my window, on the opposite slope of
the valley, I recognise Painsec; an amusing jumble of dis-
tressed roofs, a village running away like a waterfall, so
oddly, that its little houses, the colour of burnt bread-crust,

seem to be turning a somersault on the hillside. The Valais is full of those acrobatic villages, which remain hanging over vacancy by some miracle of attraction or equilibrium.

To the left, on a little hillock, stands the chapel of Vissoye, with its tin steeple, its grey-white leaden roof, and its plastered walls. Below, a group of strange-looking barns are insecurely planted on their rickety props, their roofs of fir planks held on with great stones; and beside the parish church, with its square tower, a great cross rises high over the village, stretching out its arms as if to send its benediction to the utmost bounds of the valley.

This scene is not new to me : there is no change in it since I saw it for the first time ten years ago. All the houses are still where they were ; and no others have been added to them. The old feudal ruin is still there, lying dead in the midst of the village; and in the depth of the valley the Navigenze still flows murmuring on, sending up its cry of a wild thing escaped from the cavern of the glaciers.

The very room in which I am is familiar to me ; it is the one I shared for a week with my friend Flamans. I recognise even the blue pattern of its paper, its little mirror, blackened by the flies, its chest of drawers in white wood. How many memories awake at the sight of those objects ! On that old sofa, infirm and lame, covered with scarlet rep, we threw ourselves every evening ; wearied, utterly worn out with our mad walks, our extravagant excursions, always carrying our guns, like bandits. And I see myself again perched on the top of that chimney, the Becs de Bosson, like a man who has managed to climb up on a roof, but does not know how he is to get down again. Monnier was my deliverer. He came up for me, leapt first, to show me where I must leap, and hid from me, with his broad shoulders, the yawning gulf that seemed to be waiting for its prey.

And our ascent of the Bella Tola ! We had been hunting all the morning ; then in the afternoon we found ourselves in a horrible wilderness of stones, a fallen avalanche of enormous blocks. Once involved in this labyrinth, it was impossible to go back. There was nothing for it but to go resolutely forward till the top of the mountain was gained. After three toilsome hours, we found ourselves, before we knew it, on the Bella Tola, a lofty peak rising like a belvidere in the centre of a splendid panorama of mountains and glaciers.

Some white partridges—birds of the snow—were flying round us. We were cruel enough to kill two of them.

Going down to Saint Luc, we were hospitably received at the parsonage. There were only three rooms, opening into each other. The priest slept in the first; in the second, which had only a red checked curtain by way of a door, was the servant, who was at the same time cook and schoolmistress; in the third, my friend and I, in the same bed. And next day we all set out together, the priest at the head of the procession on his mule, his hat pulled down over his nose, his elbows making triangles, reading his breviary; and behind him, Rose, the servant, holding on to the tail of the animal, to help her in climbing;—her cheeks as fresh as her name, her teeth shining like snow. She was in the costume of Saviezanne,—a straw hat turned up at the sides, black sleeves, short, plaited skirt, and white woollen stockings. What a picture this group of travellers made on the path winding up through the pastures dotted with flowers! And to hear us laughing with Rose, while the priest was gravely muttering his Latin orisons!

Our fancy indulged in various flights. There were numberless expeditions, in every direction,—to the end of the valley, to the glacier of Zinal, where the hotel is like a cold cloister, lost amid solitude and silence. Once, returning from hunting ptarmigan, in an almost virgin forest above Painsec, we met a marmot hunter, who had been more successful than ourselves. We bought from him the creature he had killed; a large male, with yellow

teeth and grey whiskers; and brought it triumphantly to
the cook at the hotel. The next day the animal was
brought to table boiled. The head had been removed; and
with its fore paws like little arms, its white body, neat and
plump, and its long hind legs, the marmot was very like
a baby! An English lady began to feel ill; a lady from
Lausanne had an attack of nerves; a grave professor from
Canton Berne sent for M. Monnier, and asked him if he
took his guests for anthropophagi; a captain of the federal
army threatened to write to the newspapers, that it might
be known everywhere that in this reactionary and Catholic
canton people were in the habit of eating babies. There
were only two guests, Americans, who were able to partake
of the dish. We had been counting on an epicure's feast,
an extraordinary dish, a most dainty discovery. Alas!
the marmot is nothing but an abomination. Our palates
remember him still.

The skin of the creature was sent to Sion and stuffed.
But the poor, inoffensive marmot was subjected to more
tribulations after his death than in his lifetime. The police
took possession of him, imprisoned him in a cupboard, and
refused to give him up until I had given a clear account of
the strange article.

And then we used to go in the evenings and sit in front
of the wooden houses, beside the " ancients," white-haired,
tottering old men, whose small eyes at first looked askance
at us, somewhat distrustfully. But they soon came round,
and told us whole volumes of curious stories. They
described to us the customs of their day, when young people
wore, as they did, short trousers with wide suspenders;
they made us familiar with their life and manners. And
now, at the end of ten years, I assert that those customs
have in no way changed.

Each village is still placed under the oversight of two
chiefs, who see to the maintaining of good order and
morality, and also to the keeping of the roads and the wells.

These chiefs, who have more authority than Members of Council, are elected for life by the people.

Every Sunday, after evening prayer, they preside at the meeting of the "men of the oath," that is, electors, citizens, who meet to discuss freely the local interests and the business of the commune. These village chiefs have great influence ; when the Council has any law or measure to submit to the public vote, it is necessary in the first place to come to an understanding with the chiefs.

The highest authority is that of the judge or president, whose functions are those of a town *maire.* The judge is elected once in four years, and is chosen each time from a different commune, whose electors meet on the second Sunday in December, and vote by secret ballot.

On the 17th of January, after public worship, the retiring judge solemnly hands in his demission and gives a summary of his administration to his electors, assembled at the side door of the church ; then he delivers to his successor the parish seal. The new president then makes his request for the goodwill and support of the old magistrates. All the population of the valley are present at this transference of powers. The new judge is expected to treat his electors to a luncheon of bread and cheese. The vice-judge, or substitute, gives sixty francs to the commune, and the bailiff or attorney gives a half-luncheon,—that is to say, cheese without bread. The first time the president assumes his state robe and takes his seat in the choir, he gives the two old magistrates a dinner or a full luncheon, composed of bread, cheese, and wine. The old magistrates retain a seat of honour in the church to the end of their lives, and at the feasts in the communal house they sit at the great table.

At the greater festivals, the judge, the deputies, and the civil and military officers wear a long black cloak, while the bailiff of the commune has a scarlet robe emblazoned with the arms of the valley in silver.

All the administrative functions are gratuitous. Only

the judge or president of the commune, and his secretary, are exempted from the usual allotment of public work.

There is no communal tax. All expenses are covered by the income from the communal property—vineyards and forests. The Anniviards are so happy at being able to live without taxes, and so much afraid of having any, that every time the State compels some extraordinary outlay, they at once create a reserve fund by having a supplementary amount of cutting done in the forests, and by resorting to personal assessments. When the salaries of the school-masters were raised, mere peasants were seen subscribing sums of two hundred or even three hundred francs.

The Anniviards, like the Hungarians, to whom they are said to be related, are great talkers. The time to hear them is on the eve of the elections; then they launch out in speeches and harangues; but their arguments never, as among their neighbours of Evolena, degenerate into blows. The electors almost always approve the choice made by the " ancients," the old men, whose opinions and counsels are always listened to with respect.

The old men have the precedence in all their meetings, and are consulted on all important occasions, especially about the election of the new magistrates.

These people are so jealous of their liberties and their privileges, that they claim to be consulted about everything, even about the election of their parish priests, who come from Sion. The priest of Vissoye said to me one day : " Such as you see me, I was nominated by the chapter at Sion; but for two years there was a strong feeling against me, because the people had not deliberated on my election. I had received a nomination elsewhere, and was preparing to go away, when all the bells in the valley were rung, a meeting of the commune was assembled in front of the church of Vissoye, and of the chapels in the other villages, and the people were asked if the present priest was to be retained,—yes or no. They were unanimous to keep me; then a deputation was sent begging me to remain, and from that time all bad feeling entirely disappeared."

Rogation Sunday is the day on which the accounts of the commune are given in. At five in the morning all the citizens meet at the communal house, and every one has the right to make remarks. Four years ago a lawsuit was begun against the president of Vissoye because a deficit of two francs and a half was found in his cash-box. He was afterwards able to explain it; he had forgotten to take credit for a paid bill.

The Rogation processions last for three days, and the villages of the three communes, Saint Jean, Ayer, and Grimentz, are visited. After mass the president makes a speech to those who are present, and invites them to drink wine of the commune, old "glacier," that has been ten or fifteen years in the cask. When everybody has been drinking plentifully for half an hour, the cellar doors are closed again; and then comes the partition of the interest on the communal property. These revenues are paid either in money (fifteen to twenty-five francs a head) or in kind—in loaves, for which each household sends its mule on the communal baking days.

There is yet another council, the Council of Morals, composed of the lay prior of the brotherhood of the Holy Sacrament, the sub-prior of the brotherhood of the Rosary, four councillors, and the parish priest. If the delinquent refuses to make honourable amends and to submit to the punishment to which he is sentenced, he is excluded from all the fraternities. Forty years ago thieves were obliged to remain on their knees during high mass, before a side altar, with a taper in one hand and the stolen article in the other. The Council of Morals still judges in cases of defamation, contempt of authority, and irreverence towards the Church.

The power of the family is very extensive and patriarchal. If a member of a family is guilty of a delinquency or a crime, they meet as a tribunal, judge the culprit, and save him from the shame of a prison by furnishing him with the needful money to make his escape and emigrate to America.

There is also in the valley of Anniviers an old and admirable custom, the " care of the poor children;" which consists in lodging, feeding, clothing, and educating poor children picked up in the plain and other localities of the canton. These children, on attaining their majority, receive from their adopted parents a little bit of land sufficient to feed two cows, and a house which is theirs for life. One of these children is found in almost every family, for their own are not numerous. The people generally marry late, after the death of the father or mother ; and in order to keep up the family traditions and not diminish the patrimony too much, only one in a family marries. The brothers and sisters take counsel together as to which of them is to devote himself. The one who is marked out for the sacrifice quits the parental dwelling on his marriage day.

Betrothals are made by exchanging a flower, a piece of money, a handkerchief, a book ; but if the marriage does not take place, it is expected that everything shall be returned. The bride brings neither dowry nor trousseau. Rich parents give the young couple a house and a few corners of land ; usually the farthest away, the worst, and the most difficult to cultivate.

The wedding is not a holiday nor an occasion of merrymaking. The pair present themselves at church at daybreak to receive the nuptial benediction; they are in working clothes, the man not even shaved ; and after drinking a glass of wine with the witnesses, husband and wife take up their implements and set off to their field. The neighbour women go and peep at them, and from their manner of working together, they draw their prognostics as to the happiness of the new couple.

It is during the first year of marriage that they put aside as a special reserve in the cellar, a cask of wine which they call " burial wine," and which is only used when a death occurs in the family, or a baptism, or when they receive a visit from the doctor, the president, a councillor, or the priest.

An old man said to me, "We are all our lives saving up for our death."

Funerals take place at Vissoye in the parochial cemetery. The burial service is held in front of the church. If the dead person belongs to a distant village, the body is carried on a ladder, firmly tied, and covered with a cloth; or if it is to be brought down from some lonely hamlet in one of the mountain gorges, it is put on the back of a mule. I have never met one of those melancholy convoys, but it is easy to imagine it: the corpse in the saddle, held up by means of a forked stick, and swaying from side to side like a parcel at every movement of the animal. At difficult places the sons, the relatives, even the women are obliged to hold up the corpse lest it should fall. The scene is lighted up by a livid moon or pale stars, like nightlights; for in summer they always carry the dead down to the valley by night.

What I did see one day was a corpse in a wine-cellar into which a peasant had taken me to give me a glass of wine.

The dead person, in all his clothes, was lying on a plank, —his eyes closed, his hat down over his forehead, like a drunken person asleep.

" A man !" I exclaimed.

" Don't mind it," replied the peasant; " it is just a neighbour that has died. They asked leave to put him in here because the cellar is cool. They will not be able to bury him till Sunday; and to-day is only Thursday."

" Why cannot he be buried before Sunday ? " I asked.

" Because that would put all the work out of order; and on Sunday nobody works, everybody goes to church at Vissoye."

This sight caused me to find the wine of the Valais, for the first time, not quite so good as usual.

Until not very long ago it was always the relations of the dead person who dug the grave.

There is always an orator who makes a speech in the name of the departed. He asks pardon, in his name, for all the offences and faults he may have committed against any one, and invites the company to drink his health. When it is one of the "ancients" who speaks, he almost invariably adds, in his peroration : "The dear departed has left the wherewith to do him honour ; follow his example, he was a merry fellow, and liked to take a glass. And now it will be the greatest pleasure to him to see you drinking to his happiness ! "

As soon as the passing bell has announced the death of an adult, two members of the communal council go to his house and inquire about the state of his affairs, who are his heirs, and if he has left a will. If the children are orphans or minors, they are committed to the care of a well-to-do family in the valley, who bring them up gratuitously ; and in this way the children's patrimony remains intact, its proceeds being carefully invested until their majority.

All questions of inheritance are settled by the " men of the oath," whose decisions are accepted beforehand, as judgments from which there is no appeal.

The funeral collation is made at the communal house.

In this primitive valley rich and poor are dressed alike, in the same coarse stuff, woven by themselves. The women do not wear the tall Valaisian hat, covered with gold lace and ribbon, but a straw hat with broad brim. Their costume is so sombre that a *savant* from Neuchâtel thought they were all in mourning.

The whole family eat together from one large wooden bowl. In former days this bowl was just a hollow dug out of the table itself, round which they gathered at mealtimes. I have been assured that these tables are still to be seen, with the holes closed up.

There is never more than a single room for the whole family, the kitchen serving as dining-room, and the wine-cellar as drawing-room or reception-room. Such is the simplicity of the common room, that there is rarely seen in it any object bought with money.

There is only one thing in the world that the Anniviard loves—that is, land. His one passion, the object on which all his energy goes out, is to enlarge the field he already possesses, and to take from the people of the plain the vineyard or the meadow that his soul covets. The one desire of these persistent mountaineers is to increase their property; the greater part of the vine-lands of Sierre belongs to them, and they possess "*mayens*" (châlets with pastures) down to just above Sion.

They know neither song nor dance; they have no passion but that of possession.

In all this long valley there is not to be seen a single beggar; or, if any are met with, they are foreigners. If one of their own people is threatened with indigence, the Anniviards promptly unite to help him.

An old author relates that such was the confidence felt in the good faith of this people, that the revenues due to the bishop were not entered in any book. He says: "It is on a slip of wood an inch wide, and of various length, that the mark of the debtor is placed on one side, and the form of the debt on the other; and on this each receipt is marked by a notch with a knife."

In looking over the travellers' book of the Hotel d'Anniviers, I found the following little note which my friend and I had written before leaving on the 19th September, 1877 :—

"After a stay of more than a week at the Hotel d'Anniviers, we cannot leave Vissoye without expressing our hearty gratitude to our hosts, MM. Tabin and Monnier, for all the kind care and delicate attentions we have received from them. Thanks to their information, we have been able to make a series of most interesting excursions: to the waterfalls of Grougé, by Mission, returning by Saint Jean; to Illgraben, by Saint Luc and Chandolin; to the Becs de Bosson, return-

ing by the Pas de Lonaz. Ascent of the Bella Tola by the
north side. Visit to the Pierre des Sauvages and to the
Druidical stones of Grimentz. An expedition to Zinal and
the alp of the Allée Verte, an amphitheatre around which
crowd the giants of the Pennine chain. Excursion to the
mountain of Trecuit, by Vercorin. Excursionists and tourists
may thus make Vissoye a centre of walks and ascents as
varied as picturesque."

I would fain have done them all over again, those expeditions of our youthful days. I would gladly have climbed,
one after another, those wandering paths of the past, where
the flowers of memory bloom beside the wild flowers of the
mountain; but my time was limited, and my wife and son
were waiting for me on the other side of the valley, in the
parsonage at Evolena.

I went, however, and took a walk to the village. Nothing
was changed. The same calm, quiet aspect, only a few more
graves in the cemetery. The same great tragic image was
still there against the wall, and at its feet the same flowers—
scarlet poppies.

I go up to the terrace of the old church, and look back on
all the way I came up the day before: the valley, dim with
blue shadows; the Navigenze, with its silvery foam rolling
down between two great fringes of larch and fir; and, on the
other side of the Rhone, the little houses of Sierre nestled
among the vineyards. Then, above, the mountains running
in long ridges, or rising in peaks, or curved almost spirally,
some of them showing, here and there, patches of snow.

In the church, which is of the Jesuit style, florid and
rococo, the seats are marked out by rows of little bouquets
laid at regular intervals along the benches; sometimes by a
single flower, a daisy or a marigold; or by an old, worn
prayer-book, yellow and greasy. I open one at random;
this is the inscription it bears on the fly-leaf: " I belong to
me, and I am called Marguerite Gavias, of Dayien village.
If I happen to lose it, I beg the person who finds it to bring

it back to me. I will faithfully pay for their trouble. As witness the truth of this; Marguerite Gavias."

Two large clothes-presses contain the banners, the ancient banners of the church and of war ; the latter rent in battle, the former dropping apart with the decay of ages. Religion and love of their country are one and the same idea with these mountain populations, and their flags are kept in the church.

The Israelites used to offer to God the firstfruits of their land ; the Anniviards still offer to their priest the first milk of their flocks. The day after the arrival of the animals at their summer pasture, all the milk of that day is made into cheese, and those cheeses are solemnly conveyed to the church of Vissoye on the fourth Sunday of August. After service, the shepherds, carrying their cheeses, and ranged in file according to the size of their pile, advance towards the choir to kiss the relics and deposit their offerings. The judge, in his black cloak, assisted by his bailiff, in red, verifies the weight of each article. The head men of the pastures are then received at the parsonage, where dinner is given them, at which a third of the firstfruits is eaten. The repast is a meagre one, composed of cheeses of three different years. Three speeches are made, one by the priest, another by the most important " chef " of the mountain, and the third by the judge,

CHAPTER VI.

I SAID adieu to Vissoye with some sadness of heart; and as I saw its steeple diminish behind me, and its houses and trees disappearing, it seemed to me that the weight of years grew heavier on my shoulders.

I was ascending, however, by a delicious road, bordered with richly variegated hedges, their long branches vibrating with the stir and the music of birds. And the scenery around me was bright and charmingly original, with little fields of rye about the size of handkerchiefs, marked out in straight lines, and here and there verdant nooks of such soft grace and rural beauty as to make one inclined to buy a crook and turn shepherd.

Before arriving at Grimentz, the roofs of which were sharply thrown out in dark shadow on the sky, I came upon an old woman crouching on a bank where she was making a heap of nettles. Her skin was sunburnt, her cheeks hollow, with a thousand wrinkles, and little folds like a leather purse; her hair was growing white, and many teeth were wanting between her faded lips.

At sight of me she stops her work; and as the sun is already strong, and I also stop to wipe my forehead, she says to me in that pretty singing tone of the Valais, and in that clipped and shortened French of Anniviers and Evolena:—

"Poor you. Very warm; where come from?"

"From Vissoye."

"Not far. Where going?"

"To Evolena, by the Col de Torrent."

"Oh, poor you, very far! Need courage."

"You are cutting nettles?"

"Yes, for the cows; in winter it's very good. I dry." And with her sickle she pointed out to me, heaped up on the balcony of an old châlet, a great store of herbs of all kinds, and branches of trees browning in the sun. Then laughing her toothless laugh and holding out her hands, red with the burning of the nettles, she added,—

"I not sleep; hands sting too much at night."

"You must rub them with oil."

"Oh! I believe you; too dear!"

"How many cows have you?"

"Five, and worse of goats and sheep. My husband gone for them to-day to the mountain—will see him on passing at the châlets of Torrent."

"Where do you live?"

"There, at the châlet, with the man and a servant. Children married, no more at home."

"Have you a school at Grimentz?"

"Yes, school in winter; winter long, very long. With us everybody to read and write. Where are you from?"

"Not from hereabouts."

"Where come from?"

"From France."

"Poor you! a long way. They are very religious people over there; have a cousin in France, but no more tidings of her now. You know her?"

"No. And are people very religious here too?"

"Yes, yes," she replied, scratching the top of her nose

with the end of her sickle; "but priest master at church,
not outside. How many cows you have?"

"!!! — —"

"Poor you!"

I bade good-day to the old woman and pursued my way,
while she called after me,—

"Go on, good-day, adieu!"

She waved her glittering sickle; then her tall bony figure,
draped in her black robe like a clerical gown, stood motionless on the top of the slope, strongly relieved in the full
light, like a bronze statue on a grassy hillock.

Grimentz is one of the typical Valaisian villages, with its
comical confusion of houses scorning straight lines, and looking as if they were playing hide-and-seek behind the old
barns, with roofs up here and down there, in irregular lines,
like bulging sails in some strange little sea-port; its dark
house-fronts with little window openings, above which
stalks of maize with their golden cones are hung in festoons;
its little lanes that run away nobody knows where, in the
most picturesque confusion, ploughed up with ruts, broken
into stagnant pools and choked up with dunghills; its storehouses built on piles, the floor raised on broad circular
stones, like millstones, to keep the mice from getting up.

H. Flamans said to me one day: "In the Valais, the
thing that is sometimes most difficult to find in a mountain
village is—houses. In that jumble of barns and haylofts
and storehouses, human dwellings are only distinguished
externally by two or three openings with glass in them,
smaller than the window of a monk's cell." And in this
same Valais, with which he is well acquainted, in those
remote hamlets where there is neither innkeeper nor priest,
my friend Flamans more than once came very near having
to sleep in the open air. One evening he had arrived about
nine o'clock, with a companion, a botanist, at Useigne, in
the Val d'Hérens, and was despairing of finding a house
in that village of barns and haylofts, when two men who

passed relieved them from their perplexity. Leading them
to the opening of a little dark lane, they pointed to a light,
saying, "They will give you lodging over there, at Marie
Bourdin's."

The two tourists made their way as best they could to
the old house, and groped cautiously in the dark up a kind
of staircase. At the first door they came to, Flamans
knocked; a young man opened, and the two strangers were
shown into a room where a large fire was blazing on a
hearth. The young man told them it was impossible to
lodge them, because there was a sick person in the house.
They consented, however, to let them spend the night
among the hay.

They sat down by the fire, and soon overheard an animated conversation going on in the adjoining room.

Then a woman appeared in the door-way, studied them
with a compassionate eye; then turning away, she threw
back these words,—

"Oh, we'll soon find you a room, yes. . . ."

"Believe me," said Flamans to his friend, "and let us go
to the hayloft; it is simpler and safer."

The friend makes no response; he is in a brown study
and goes on poking the fire without stopping. Wine is
brought to them in a large pewter pot. They find it
delicious; but it is their whole supper. The young man
comes back with two woollen quilts under his arm.

"I'm going to take you to bed," says he; "must come
with me."

They prepare to follow.

"But must pay!"

"We expected to pay to-morrow morning," replies
Flamans; "but it's all the same. How much do we owe?"

"Seventy-five centimes for the three pints, and fifty for
the room. If you like the hay better, it costs nothing."

The guide led them to the upper part of the village and
knocked at a door. No answer. He redoubled his efforts

made a din as if he would break the door. A light footstep was heard inside, then all was silence again.

The man then clambered up on a roof and knocked at the window. At this moment the travellers detected some sounds of whispering and laughing. The guide came back to them.

"Well," said the two friends, "can we get in?"

"Ah! here they are!" and the laughing began again.

"Do they take us, perhaps, for suitors?" said Flamans.

"Exactly; that is just it. She would not answer. I had to say that you were gentlemen."

At last the door is opened. They are taken into a room where there are three beds; one already occupied by a man with a long black beard. A woman shows them the third bed, one of those little creaking things on castors. This was where they were to sleep.

Flaman's friend, not accustomed to these primitive manners, was struck dumb; he looked up and down, to this side and to that, with a scared expression, and then turning to Flamans, he whispered,—

"I think we had better go somewhere else, and not disturb these worthy people."

Behold our two tourists, then, for the third time, in quest of a resting-place. It was pitch dark. Their guide walked first; and all three joining hands, they came down a long passage, dragging after them an avalanche of stones, logs of wood, and other objects less hard to the touch.

By dint of clambering with both hands and feet, they find themselves at last standing in front of a little square building. The guide opens a door, helps them to scramble up on a heap of hay, and is about to lock the door of the kennel.

The timid botanist protests vigorously; he will not be kept a prisoner; he demands the key. The Valaisian, on his side, giving back to the two foreigners trust for trust, is uneasy about his quilts. Tempers grow hot on both sides; and as Flamans said to me afterwards, "I saw that in another moment our man would call out for help; I interposed to make peace, which was concluded on the following conditions: the Valaisian shall keep his key; we shall keep our quilts; but the door shall remain half-open!"

The Valaisian had then no longer any doubts as to the honesty of the travellers. The agreement was faithfully kept on both sides. The night passed quietly; only at break of day the sleepers were aroused by the morning greeting of a cock, whose presence in their apartment they had not noticed.

There is great excitement in the principal street of Grimentz, and pretty picturesque scenes. Mules, tied at the doors, are being saddled; girls, women, men, all who are preparing to set out are in holiday garb. To-morrow the flocks and herds leave the high mountain châlet; and each family sends representatives to the alp of Zatelet-Praz, at the lower end of the Val de Moiry, for their share of the butter and cheese which have been made there during the summer.

At the common fountain, round the great black trough, hewn out of an enormous larch, the washerwomen are already busily beating their linen, while their tongues carry on an equally brisk business. And at the public oven, that opens its wide red mouth under an awning in the middle of the village, there is a no less busy scene. M. the Councillor Deloye (Daniel) and his wife are baking their bread,—beautiful light-coloured cakes, with crisp crust, that will keep for six months, with a pleasant smell of rye. M. the Councillor invites me to taste his bread, which he accompanies with a cup of "glacier,"—certainly the best I ever drank. It had been fifteen years in the cellar.

This exquisite wine is made from a quite common grape, called *rèze*. It is first allowed to ferment in the cellars at Sierre, and then taken to the mountain villages, and not, as M. Desor says, to the glacier of Zinal. At the end of ten years it undergoes a second fermentation, which gives it a particular flavour, the "glacier" bouquet. At Grimentz there is glacier wine drunk of fifty or sixty years old. The person who gives you a glass of this will say : " It was left to me by my father-in-law, who inherited it from his father." This wine is not in bottles, it is kept in the cask.

Leaving Grimentz, the road wanders leisurely through rich meadows ; it passes a ruined building, erected formerly by an English company for the working of mines of nickel, now given up ; then it plunges into a wild gorge, through which the Navigenze, coming down from the Moiry glacier, pours with a long sobbing sigh ; then it rises and rises from rock to rock, sometimes cut into steps for the cattle, until it reaches the place where the valley divides, at the opening of one of those dales that the poets used to put in their romances, and that the Genevan watchmakers still paint on their musical boxes. These dales, these "lovely dales of Helvetia," are indeed full of harmonies ; the bells of the flocks sound there day and night, and this concert of sheep-bells and cow-bells suddenly heard in solitude, and repeated by the echoes like a distant and mysterious choir, is one of the features of Alpine life that most powerfully impress the feelings and take hold of the imagination.

And what a joy it is, after a five or six hours' walk, to hear the tinkling of the little bells bringing the good news of a mountain dwelling, and the hope of a reviving halt in the châlet before the fire on which the great pot of cheese is boiling !

I had not yet come in sight of the châlets of the Alp de Torrent, but those musical sounds assured me they were near. And my enchanted ears were as keen as my appetite. I already perceived the pleasant smell of the *raclettes* (welsh-rabbit), and felt as it were the white intoxication of the mountain milk.

At last, after a final climb, I come out on a plateau. A conglomeration of blocks of grey stone is before me ; this is the châlet, the *remuentz*, as the Valaisians call it ; that is, the place to which they *remue* or move the cattle. The stones are simply piled up one above another, with the light showing through the interstices. The door is in very open work, with a chain to fasten it. The roof of slates, held on by great stones, comes down till it meets the slope against which it rests, and a great wall of huge blocks, a sort of rampart, defends it from the avalanches that threaten every spring to carry it away.

What a difference between these huts and the comfortable and even elegant châlets of Canton Fribourg and German Switzerland! The Valaisian châlet is still just what it was in the times when the shepherds built themselves a shelter with stones gathered in the mountains. Nothing can be imagined poorer, simpler, or more primitive.

Let us go in. The earthen floor is damp, and dirty with all kinds of litter; not a chair nor a table; over a fire of large logs hangs a pot full of yellowish milk; there is a large churn fixed to a beam; and at the back is the bed of the " master," an ox-skin spread on the ground, with a cover of which it would be impossible to tell the colour. In the Valaisian châlet there is no hay, that good hay in which one sleeps in the Fribourg châlet. The shepherds spend the night lying on sacks or sheepskins, before a blazing fire, with their feet turned to the hot embers. Through the holes in the roof they see the stars shining, and when it rains, streamlets trickle down their backs. I have more than once had occasion to put up my umbrella in a Valaisian châlet.

I have never, however, been obliged to sleep in the cheese pot, like the tourist who had neither sheepskin nor shawl to spread on the damp ground.

Close against this larger edifice of bare stones is a smaller erection, which is used as cellar and storehouse. In it are arranged, side by side, the little Valaisian cheeses, about the diameter of the wheel of a child's cart.

Above the cheeses, on a shelf that is reached by a ladder, the butter is kept, in large lumps, strongly salted. There are hundreds and hundreds of these, piled up to the roof, yellowish white in colour. This butter loses none of its excellence by being kept, and it is very sure to be pure from all adulteration. The churn in which it is made is a large barrel fixed to an axle in the middle of a stream coming down from the mountain, which sets it in motion. This is the butter-mill.

Some shepherds sitting on thick logs, are grouped round the fire, watching quarters of cheese that are exposed to the heat of the red cinders. When the cheese is sufficiently melted, one of them takes a long knife, scrapes off the melted layer and lays it on a slice of bread. This is what is called a *raclette*. And it is very good, accompanied with wine. They invited me to sit down among them, saying, " It is a festival to day ; to-morrow we divide the cheeses among us, and all the animals will go down."

The partition of the cheese is made according to the amount of milk produced by each cow, which has been measured on the fourth or the seventh day after coming up to the alp, in the presence of all the partners, and under the oversight of the chief men.

These shepherds, in their worn old garments, patched in twenty places and shining with grease, with linen and skin like colliers, are the happiest men in the world ; content with their lot, loving their free and nomade mountain life, with its long lazy times of rest and its moments of perilous activity, when they have to go, in the midst of darkness and tempest, to gather together the flock scattered among the precipices. There are no simpler, honester, braver hearts. H. Flamans, who has long been in the habit of going among them, says of them :—

" I have met with them in many an excursion ; I have always found them full of good feeling. No desire for anything more, no regret. How could they have such feelings in the midst of the natural splendours that surround them ! They looked with great curiosity at my

Lefaucheux gun, the tinned meats that I had with me, and the map, on which I showed them, marked with a black spot, the châlet that sheltered them; the blue line of their mountain torrent, and the figures indicating the height of the various peaks. It was the first time any one had shown them such things, and their surprise, their wonder, caused me exceeding pleasure. With what dignity the worthy people, as if their self-respect were wounded, refused my money when I wished to pay for my entertainment; for among them there are some things that are never sold, and hospitality is one of them.

"The simple abruptness of the greetings in the mountains is not without its charm. How far away one feels from the obsequious manners of the city, from profuse and insincere compliments, from bows repeated again and again, with hat in hand and smiling lips! Here you are welcomed in a rough voice, while the speaker applies his stick to the back of a troublesome cow. The shepherds or cowherds in one place are usually from ten to fifteen in number, and obey one chief, a *master*, elected annually by the joint proprietors of the alp. These elections, which are made by a majority of votes, are often of more importance in a Valaisian village than a political ballot.

"The master has no familiar intercourse with the shepherds below him. And they, on their side, show no meanness or servile flattery in their demeanour towards him; only a grave submission, necessary for the general good.

"Ah! what a beautiful sight it is to see the master coming down from the heights with his drove! Two hundred cows follow him leisurely, scattering among the clumps of juniper and rhododendron, and filling the mountain-side with life and stir. Small, as all cows of Valaisian breed are, lively in their motions, rather given to fighting; down they come, merrily jingling their bells, and, when they see you, stretch out their pink muzzles and lick their lips, as if asking for a handful of salt.

" The *queen* of the herd, a very large, handsome cow, red-brown spotted with white, takes her place on the top of a hillock, where she stands motionless and majestic, gazing vacantly at the horizon. Proud of her superior strength, she seems, with the calmness of a settled conviction, to be defying her companions, and to be seeking, impatient for combat, some antagonist worthy to measure strength with her.

" In the Valaisian alps each herd has its queen. The choice of the queen depends on her strength and her beauty. When the herd is in motion, she generally takes the head of the column. When two droves meet, it almost always happens that the two queens defy each other to single combat. The mountaineers themselves promote these curious struggles, and are very proud of the victory of their own queen.

" The master goes on observing the herd with that eye of which La Fontaine speaks, which loves to make sure and to take account of everything. From time to time he plunges his hands full of salt right and left into the open and eager mouths.

" No one is in a hurry. ' Tiauh! tiauh! ' shout the shepherds, who are scattered in all directions, busily separating the quarrelling groups. ' Aïe, then, the *motcila* (a black cow with a white star on her forehead), here the *zalandra*, the *griotta*, the *cuazou!* ' (names given from the colour of the animal). There are a thousand strange, wild cries taken up and multiplied by the echoes. Slowly the cows gather to a kind of plateau behind the châlet where they are accustomed to be milked. The tumult and the noise of bells become more and more deafening.

" Half an hour passes. The master is going through the lowing crowd, and receives more than one stroke from a flourishing tail. The herd is really gay and cheerful. It is in order not to disturb this happy mood, which foretells an abundant supply of milk, that the shepherds carefully refrain from harassing their cattle, and direct their course slowly and imperceptibly towards the foot of the hill.

"Suddenly a ripple of silvery, quivering sounds is borne to us on the air, followed by a cracking of whips and barking of dogs. Hundreds of sheep are coming down from the heights, and are passing along under an immense declivity. They can be distinguished in the distance by their white fleece against the almost perpendicular wall of rocks, at the foot of which a few heifers are looking at their own images in the clear waters of a little lake.

"After a prayer the milkers go through the herd, each seeking out the animals that are in his charge. The milking process finished, the cows paw the ground, lowing, and longing for liberty. They strike their horns together as if preparing to fight, and snuff up the wind; or perhaps lie at their ease chewing the cud. In the direction of the châlet they present an embattled front; and the shepherds, armed with long sticks, have difficulty in keeping back their eager ranks.

"At a signal from the master they come forward, and the whole herd get in motion, shaking and clanging their bells. Near the watering-place the grass grows thick and strong, full of sap and pure from any taint. There they stop for their evening portion. The bags of salt are emptied, the thick turf is browsed in a moment.

"'Tiauh! tiauh!' the shepherds begin again in chorus, and the cows, led by their queen, always grave and thoughtful, return to the high pastures where they are to spend the night.

"Before taking off their heavily-ironed shoes for the night, the shepherds offer a final prayer; the master recites or reads a passage from the Gospels, and then leads in some litanies, to which his subordinates respond vigorously with 'Have mercy upon us!' The alps form a natural setting for supplications. A continual menace of desolation and ruin reigns there.

" And next day, at early morning, the same round of toil
begins once more."

The master of the Torrent châlet had a large wooden bowl
of milk served up for me ; he himself prepared for me some
raclettes of cheese, and drew from the box under the slates
the hard loaf,—so hard sometimes that it must be cut with a
hatchet.

In the Alps of the Upper Valais, bread and the different
forms of milk are the whole food of the shepherds ; they are
not—like those huge Fribourg shepherds, with their jolly
faces like fat monks—acquainted with coffee, farinaceous
foods, sweetened rice, and the little glass of brandy, and
often a slice of salt meat besides. They are as sober and
lean as anchorites ; tall, pale, with something emphatically
masculine, as well as rough and hard, in their vigorous
and original appearance.

But it is time for me to set out again. The valley is full
of cattle ; and as one rises higher, the sight of those hundreds of cows, variously coloured, going and coming, lying
at the side of the stream or under sheds covered with rotten
planks,—their only shelter, even in foul weather and storm,
—this alpine picture in every varying tone of colour, with
the endless walls of the great eternal glaciers far in the
background, is both original and impressive.

The ascent of the Col de Torrent is pretty long. A strong
wind had suddenly sprung up, driving before it great armies
of clouds that were gathering on the horizon in ominous-
looking masses ; so I felt it needful to quicken my pace.

The view opened out before me as I got higher ; I could
see the Moiry glacier at the end of the valley, carving out
for itself bays and gulfs in the mountain, unfolding its great
white surface, united by a frozen isthmus to that icy sea
around which the Weisshorn, the Rothhorn, the great
Cornier, the Dent-Blanche, and the Matterhorn tower like
immense snow-clad reefs. And right below me the three

hundred cows peacefully grazing on the pastures of the alp of Zatelet-Praz, look like Nuremberg toys, little wooden cows no larger than frogs.

The sky has become streaked with long white lines, and light clouds still flit across the blue, like great flights of cranes with silvery wings. There is a close, suffocating heat. The ground is scorching. Not a sound, not a cry is heard. Even the bells of the cattle have ceased to sound. And the châlets down there at the foot of the mountain look only like little dead heaps of stones.

Changing shadows were now passing across the mountain, the sky had become of a leaden grey, oppressive to my frame and doleful to my eyes ; the great Cornier was no longer visible, nor even the Bouquetin, which was hidden by murky clouds. Then the rain began, a mountain rain, small, close, sharp and stinging like needles, that lashed my face as with strokes of a whip. My big woollen wrap was soon soaked through. The sodden earth was getting greasy, so that I made slower progress. And all round I could see nothing but that grey curtain of rain that closed me in and hid everything, even the road. Streams were forming in all directions, seeming to issue from the ground like springs, and growing before my eyes,—moving along like live creatures, like great serpents crawling or springing with strange rustling of their scales.

I passed along the side of the Lake of Zozanne without seeing it, and arrived right opposite a deserted châlet, half in ruins. Happily there was some wood left, and I lighted a large fire to dry myself. The wind that rushed through the holes in the walls gave strength to the flames, lengthened them out and twisted them in long spirals. In this broken-down hovel, letting in water everywhere, and beaten by the doleful-sounding deluge, I seemed to myself like an abandoned ship, alone in the midst of a raging sea.

Presently the rain grew more dense, congealed, and in-stead of drops of dark water, white snowy flakes began to

fall. It grew lighter, and I set off at a rapid pace, anxious,
by a special effort, to reach the top of the pass before the
snow should have completely hidden all trace of the path.
I went with the ardour of a soldier hastening to the assault.
The way had been exactly explained to me; I had been
told, " At the top of the pass you will see the wall behind
which Ballet and Roux waited in ambush to kill M. Grenzel,
the unfortunate Hanoverian tourist." In half an hour I
reached the wall indicated, and then all I had to do was to
get down to the Val d'Hérens. Evolena lay just below me.

The snow was still falling, slowly and steadily, whirling
silently in the blast like dead leaves on a pond. All round
me was pure, immaculate white; the mountain was clad in
ermine and pearls, and the sky was so low and thick that it
looked as if it were pressing down on the immense sheet of
snow. In less than an hour I was crossing the Cotter alp, and
I found myself in the midst of the *mayens* of Lassiores, in
a green, inhabited region! The snow had not come down
so far. A cup of milk mixed with rum revives me; I go
down almost at full speed across the pastures of Villa and
La Sage, cutting right across the long turnings and capricious
zigzags of the mule paths, and arrive by nightfall at Evolena.

CHAPTER VII.

MY family was lodging with the parish priest, who took
in some boarders. There is a hotel, of course, and
it is said to be excellent; but then in the hotel there is the
table-d'hôte, and I know of no more terrible infliction on a
vagrant tourist, accustomed to wander in his own free
and easy style among the mountains, than the being obliged
to sit down at a fixed hour in a black dress-coat, and always
newly shaved, at a long table where he knows nobody,
between an Englishwoman reading the *Times* or meditating
on her Bible, and a German, an American, or a Dutchman.
And those waiters, in white ties and black coats, with
English manners, as rigid as clergymen, stiff as figures in
cardboard, serving up to you the same soup and the same
sauce that you had at Berne, at Geneva, at Lucerne, at
Interlaken, at Lugano! After dinner, which lasts for an
eternity, people engage timidly in conversation, which never
turns on anything beyond the food, the wine, and the
weather. To hear all those English and Americans of the
table-d'hôte, one would say they travel only to eat and
drink; that the gorgeous scenes they behold in those mountains, on the shores of the lakes, and at the foot of the
glaciers,—those sunrises, glorious as the creation of a world,
—those sunsets, tragic as the death of a planet;—that all

this handiwork of the Divine Artist, who has here surpassed
Himself, awakens no response in them, stirs no fibre of their
being, plants not the germ of a thought in the arid brain of
those dealers in salt pork and manufacturers of cotton
nightcaps. For it must be said, since the invention of
Cook's tickets, since Mont Blanc has been brought within
reach of everybody's purse and everybody's legs, the quality
of the tourists from beyond the Channel and beyond the
ocean has terribly come down. The intelligent class, and
the high, aristocratic classes, have turned in another direction, from their horror of the common herd; for fear of
meeting their bootmaker's wife in the drawing-rooms of the
Schweizerhof, or being seated at the *table-d'hôte* side by
side with the pork butcher from their street corner. The
flower of English society goes now to the fiords of Norway,
to that country of splendid fishing and shooting; the only
country for holiday trips that is not yet swarming with
festive Sunday crowds, and where hordes of travellers with
little pink and blue tickets are not yet pouring in.

Here at Evolena, however, we cannot complain. We see,
it is true, a few melancholy-looking people coming out of
the hotel now and then; but it is easy to escape from them
in those pretty roads that run away in all directions like
truant schoolboys. A lovers-path goes down towards the
Borgne, crosses the wild torrent by a wooden bridge, and
wanders away with a playful freedom through the cool
greensward, along pretty woods of light green larches. On
the opposite side a mule track climbs up the mountain, and
leads to a promontory from which one can overlook the
whole valley, and the village nestling in a soft meadow in
the midst of a little smiling glade surrounded by rugged
mountains and frozen peaks.

If Evolena has not the amusing originality of Grimentz
and Hérémence, there is yet something very characteristic
in its tall houses of red pine, with their windows almost
touching each other, the roofs covered with thin slabs of

schist, overlaid with broad patches of golden mosses; and the great projecting beam, called *sablière*, on which are painted, amidst ornaments and flowers, the initials J. M. J. (Jesus, Mary, Joseph), as well as the name of the person for whom the house was made, and that of the master carpenter who built it.

Some of these houses are adorned with hanging galleries, reminding one of the East; others are entirely of stone, the front painted pink, and decorated in Italian fashion, with garlands of flowers and symbolical vases pouring out wine and milk.

The old buildings have an outside stair leading to the second, or even to a third storey. These houses are sometimes the property of several owners; for the peasant who, in the Valais, possesses the third part of a mule and the fourth of a cow, has often only the half of a house. These partnerships give rise to a great many lawsuits, and as the Evolenards are considered the most quarrelsome and litigious people of the Valais, they are quite a prize for the Sion lawyers. There are many deserted houses to be seen, crumbling to dust. They are those of co-proprietors, who have ruined themselves with law expenses, and who, rather than make an amicable arrangement, have preferred to abandon their property. Sometimes, after two or three years of fruitless litigation, they come and beg the priest to settle the dispute.

These Valaisian houses are very curious places to visit. Go in without fear, you will be received with a smiling " Good-day "; you are the guest, the stranger, you have the right to hospitality. If they were richer, how heartily they would serve you with a cup of " the old," but everything is growing so dear, and so little is earned !

The first part of the house that you enter is a dark, smoky kitchen, paved with cracked stones that rock under the foot. You rarely see—as in the Fribourg peasants' houses—hams, festoons of sausages, and flitches of bacon hanging over the fireplace in the vast chimney, where the swallows build their nests. In each family, however, a few sheep and one or two pigs are killed; but the dried legs of mutton find too good a market at Sion to be kept at home. They only eat a little meat on Sundays and festival days. For the remainder of the week they live on black bread, cheese, potatoes, and skimmed milk. Coffee is almost unknown. People in easy circumstances use it only as a medicine. The population are not the less healthy on this account, nor are their lives shorter. "When a man has caught a real pleurisy," said Beytrison to me, "they give him a good soup of salt meat; that is excellent for stitches in the side." There is not a single doctor in the valley; a fact which, no doubt, accounts for the longevity of the people.

From the kitchen you pass into the lower room, badly lighted, with thick beams crossing the ceiling, on which some rustic carpenter's chisel has cut rhyming sentences such as these:—

> " My God, my strength, whom I will trust,
>   A buckler unto me;
> The horn of my salvation,
>   And my high tower is He.
> Assuredly He shall thee save,
>   And give deliverance,
> From subtle fowler's snare, and from
>   The noisome pestilence.
> His feathers shall thee hide; thy trust
>   Under His wings shall be;
> His faithfulness shall be a shield
>   And buckler unto thee."

This is the family room. The beds are covered in with great canopies, and ornamented inside, like altars, with sacred images, crucifixes, and statuettes of the Virgin. In front of these very high beds, which are hidden within their curtains like a sanctuary, stands a more or less elaborately carved chest that serves as a wardrobe.

The whole family lives in this room, and often the household of the married son as well. And sometimes there are only three beds for ten or a dozen occupants.

Never any garden round the houses, as in the Lower Valais and the other parts of Switzerland. The only vegetables cultivated are cabbages and beans. The latter are dried on long horizontal poles, set up very high; for the sun reaches them late, and is quickly past.

The ordinary costume of the women consists of three articles; an under garment of coarse linen, a jacket or bodice, with or without sleeves, and a petticoat. In winter, or when it rains, they wrap themselves in a kind of coat of white wool bound with red braid. The use of an umbrella seems unknown throughout the valley. When at work they tie their skirt round their ankles after the fashion of ample oriental trousers.

The old costume was very rich. The gowns were in strong colours, black, blue, deep red; with showy trimming, and gold and silver embroidery on the sleeves; the hat was like a travelling cap with the peak turned to the back, and all the women wore the *pétra*, a sort of leathern cuirass cut in the shape of a heart, and covered with silk embroidery; kept in its place by cords or little brass chains. And the men were in knee-breeches and shoes with silver buckles, three-cornered hats and hair plaited in a pigtail, in which ribbons were interwoven, and a bit of lead tied into the end to keep it in its place. On festival and wedding-days they powdered their hair with flour, and put on smart garters, and even doublets, after the fashion of William Tell.

But now there are only three old men in Evolena who wear knee-breeches; the oldest of them was born in 1799.

But on the other hand, among the children, the costume of the villeins, the common people of the middle ages, remains unchanged. They are all dressed in a long gown of coarse woollen cloth, like a Capuchin's tunic; round the waist a leather belt, by which they are held when learning to walk; and on the head a ribbed cap of different colours.

And if you only knew how rosy and fresh and pretty they are, with their open, blooming faces, their soft azure eyes and their fair hair, looking like angels dropped from heaven!

Some of them wear little bells fastened to their belts. I thought these were put on to amuse the little ones; but this is the explanation a mother gave me :—

" When we are in the fields, and the children wander away, thanks to those bells we can always hear and find them; and besides, the sound of the bells drives away the serpents."

In those rocky valleys there are many serpents, especially vipers; but fatal accidents are extremely rare.

Each family manufactures its own cloth. There are a few tailors, who go round to the people's houses and make the clothes. Every girl of fifteen can not only read and write, but spin, weave, and sew.

The lads go to school up to the age of conscription, that is, twenty. But after their fifteenth year they are only bound to be present for a hundred and twenty hours in the year.

The communes themselves pay the teachers from a special fund for the purpose, and the instruction is absolutely gratuitous. The minimum salary of a schoolmaster is three hundred and fifty francs. And as there are communes that try to beat down the teacher's price, a cantonal law punishes with a fine the man who accepts a sum less than this.

The president, the councillors, and the secretary receive no salary, and cannot decline to be elected. The president of Evolena keeps a hotel. Here, as in Anniviers, there are no taxes; only, as money must be had, there is a toll of twopence on every cow that comes into the commune or leaves it.

The communal council holds its sittings on Sundays after vespers, most frequently in the open air, in front of the church. All the citizens are free to take part in the deliberations, and as the Evolenards have great powers of eloquence and facility of speech, the orators are seen, one after another, mounting a colossal stump that serves as a tribune, and delivering the most animated harangues.

They are hot blooded, almost Italian in temperament, and so it happens that knives sometimes play a conspicuous part in elections and communal assemblies. In 1855 the people had formed two parties on the subject of *alpages*, which one party demanded should be made common property, while the others claimed to have their old form of separate lots retained. The stronger party, in order to intimidate the others, made knives with very short blades, easy to conceal, and on coming out of church, attacked their opponents. Some lads had been posted with loaded carabines at the windows of neighbouring houses, with orders to fire if they saw their fathers and brothers obliged to give way. The knife party was victorious. From that time there has been no more bloodshed at Evolena.

This vigorous people love amusement, noisy holidays, dancing, carnival masquerades, long evenings of drinking and singing. They have not the stern gravity of the Anniviards; and so the valley of Hérens is called the "Devil's Valley," while that of Anniviers has been called the "Holy Valley."

In the olden times grand military parades were held annually. The chiefs arrayed themselves in knee-breeches of skins dyed blue, with a scarlet coat. The honour of carrying the flag was put up to auction, as well as the rank of captain of the troop. Payment was made in kind, and the soldiers received two measures of wine. The performance took place in the priest's orchard. There was shooting at a target; and when all the heads were heated with wine, they finished up by a general *mêlée*—a real battle. The last of these "parades" was held in 1839. They were suppressed by the predecessor of the present parish priest.

A wedding day is not, as in the Val d'Anniviers, a dull

working day. It is a festival in which friends, neighbours, and acquaintances all take part. In former days the girls who accompanied the bride to the altar wore crowns of artificial flowers, while the bridegroom and his men wore black coats. After the first repast the guests went out and threw into the air handfuls of apples, which they caught in their hats; and those who caught the most were sure to be the happiest during the year. Then they promenaded through the village, and danced on the village-green to the music of a violin.

In the Val d'Hérens, the only dowry of the girls is their wedding-dress.

The funeral ceremonies are less elaborate than among the Anniviards. There is no long and solemn meal. "On funeral days," said an old man to me, "we drink three glasses of wine; not one more." Thirty years ago, it was still the nearest relatives who carried the coffin and dug the grave. Little children followed the procession, dressed as angels, all in white, with crowns on their heads. Then came the *white penitents*, dressed in their death shirt or the robe of the brotherhood; the girls wore a white veil, the women a square of white linen on their heads. The white penitents now accompany only a deceased member of their own fraternity to his last resting-place.

Mourning is worn for three months. On the first Sunday of each month, and during Ember Week, each of the relatives presents to the priest a tallow candle and a penny. White is the mourning colour. Persons whom you meet with a broad white band on their dress have lost a member of their family.

When a death occurs in one of the remote mountain villages, the body is firmly bound to a plank, and carried on men's shoulders to Evolena.

But what a melancholy place the cemetery of this village is, compared with the one at Vissoye, where the well-kept little graves are like boats decked with flowers and anchored to a cross. Here—not even a tuft of wild pansies, a few sprays of pinks or white daisies, to brighten the mournful place with their cheerful colours. It is a field of rank weeds, in which the graves are smothered, like barks that have gone down, entangled in the reeds, before reaching the haven.

Some Valaisian friends had said to me, " Be sure to go and see old Beytrison, the poet of the Val d'Hérens." After having hunted through various little lanes, I at last discovered his house. He was sitting at the door, playing with his grandchildren. He is an old man with a fine, powerful head, the head of a rustic Dante, with strongly hooked nose, and remarkably deep and keen eyes. I sat down beside him, and as I was putting him through a whole catechism on manners and usages and old customs, his daughter-in-law, with the charmingly unceremonious manner of those mountain people, said laughingly to me : " Do you write almanacs, then ; when you want to know all those old stories ? "

Beytrison told me his own history also.

" My father," said he, " was a miller. As I was meant to have an ecclesiastical career, I was sent when I was four- teen to the college at Sion. I was set to study rhetoric, but I was so much behind that I made myself ill with hard work. Then the doctor made me stop my studies, and sent me back to Evolena. While wandering among the moun- tains, I became acquainted with a pretty peasant girl who became my wife. Then I was appointed secretary to the council, registrar of the tribunal, and bookkeeper of the commune. I have also been a teacher. In those days, each pupil was obliged to bring a load of wood to the school, and the master had only eighty francs a year. In my leisure moments I compose songs in our *patois*, which are sung in the châlets, and in winter when people are working together in the evenings. Our *patois* is very sonorous, very har-

monious : it is a mixture of Celtic, Latin, and Italian words.
For a whole summer I gave lessons in the *patois* to a learned
man from German Switzerland, who has written a grammar
of the language. I have also acted as guide; but now my
legs cannot manage that; we must leave that to younger
men."

I asked him to tell me some of his songs.

" With pleasure," said he. " But as they are all in the
patois, I will translate them into French for you. My songs
are suggested by circumstances. The other day at Haudères,
an old miser took me to see his cellar and his storehouse.
What an amount of things he had there, gathered up for
his heirs! In the storehouse there was certainly forty
napoleons' worth of suet and bacon, and another forty
napoleons' worth of dried mutton hams; some of them from
the time of his great-grandfather, two hundred years ago !
And the cellar,—it was stored with wine, and with cheeses
that were crumbling into dust ; and there were great lumps
of lard weighing at least sixty pounds. He never touches his
provisions. I made the following song about him, which is
now sung everywhere, before his very face:—

SONG.

" I pray you hear what I shall say
About a miser rich and grey.
He dares not taste his cheese so good,
Nor wine stored up in casks of wood ;
He lets all go to rot and waste,
His needful food he fears to taste ;
He counts his silver and his gold,
And loads of hay his barns scarce hold.

You ask for cash ? There's none until
Two wealthy sureties sign your bill,
And there is good hypothec too.
If beggars ask for bread, look you,
He growls, ' Go seek the mouldy bread.'
With this God's poor ones still are fed

To cheer their hearts. His oxen, too,—
He feeds them up with skim-milk blue.

Oh! poor, rich man! There comes a day
Your gains, your thefts shall flee away;
Whate'er in store or barn you keep,
And all your wine in cellars deep,
And all your silver and your gold.
Of all the riches you now hold
There shall be left you only this,—
Regret for using it amiss."

The *patois* of Evolena drops in silvery notes, like Provençal poetry. Philologists might perhaps find a field of interesting research in that direction. Has the learned professor of Roman languages, Mons. Gillieron, thought of it?

At Evolena, as in every other village of the valleys, there are various local superstitions. Those who mow in the dog-days, Beytrison told me, find the sign of the dog-star marked on their bodies. When the wind howls among the mountains, they say it is the wild huntsman passing. Many persons have also seen in the evening a red ox flying like a bat, or have met on their way a small dog barking terribly. At Savièze, after the angelus, numbers of headless riders are seen passing, mounted on mules.

It is believed that certain prayers, accompanied by special ceremonies and cabalistic signs, will cure all diseases of cattle; and there is a special belief in the evil eye, in bad luck, in the cast of the dice.

A bell rings,—the bell for evening prayer. As Beytrison is sacristan as well as poet, we are obliged to part.

In passing the village shop, I went in to buy some matches, and witnessed a primitive scene that reminded me of Hungary. Women were arriving with butter, cheese, and eggs, and simply exchanging those products for other goods; eggs for flour, butter for sugar, cheese for rice.

In crossing the cemetery, I noticed close to the door, a few yards from the parsonage, a little grave almost out of sight, but marked by a marble tablet, on which was cut, in half-effaced gilt letters, a foreign name,—a German name. " Here lies Guenzel . . ." Guenzel! That is the name of the Hanoverian tourist who was murdered by the notorious Ballet. It was a trial that set the whole Valais in commotion. A unique, unprecedented trial, an isolated, exceptional fact, of a kind unheard-of among those honest mountaineers, where one is safer than on the boulevards of Paris. Guenzel must have been born under an adverse star, and pursued by an evil fate.

Ballet had just bought a vineyard, and was not able to pay for it. He had said to himself, " I will make an Englishman pay for it ! " Guenzel was taken for an Englishman. It is a costly matter to be taken for an Englishman—even by a hotel keeper, though he only demands your purse, not your life. It was this mistake that led to Guenzel's death ; for Ballet had no grudge against any but the English ; having seen, when guiding them over the mountains, their leather pocket-books bulging out with bank notes, and the long purses with silver rings, and the gold shining through the meshes of the silk, as in a miraculous net. I had often heard of this famous trial, but did not know the details of it. Who could give me them better than Beytrison ? I went back and waited for him at the church door. When the service was finished he gave me this account :—

" Ballet was a violent man, of extraordinary strength and ability. The bailiffs were at his heels ; and money he must have, come what might, within twenty-four hours, if he would keep his vineyard. ' Well, then,' he said to himself, ' the first Englishman who comes past, I will do for him.' So he went with one of his comrades to lie in wait at the Col de Torrent. They had built, during the night, a little stone wall, as they do for marmot hunting ; and they lay behind this to watch without being seen. Ballet had heard the day before, when he went to Vissoye, that an Englishman was to pass over the Col. In the afternoon a foreigner comes in sight, with a guide. Then says Ballet to his comrade, 'The guide for you, the Englishman for me!' And the travellers pass close by the little wall, without a suspicion of what is about to befall them. They are beginning to go down the other side when a shot is heard, and Peter, the guide, drops with a ball through his arm. Ballet fires immediately after, but his hand is trembling, and Guenzel is only wounded. He throws up his arms and staggers, bleeding and calling for help. Ballet runs after him, intercepts his way, and with the gun close to his victim's breast, shoots him through the heart. Then he rushes on the guide to make an end of him; but Peter throws himself on his knees, beseeching him to have pity on his wife and children, and swearing not to say a word. Ballet, although a hard man, allows himself to be moved, even so far as to take his handkerchief and bind up the wounded arm; then, after searching Guenzel's pockets, he gives five francs more to Peter, who returns to Vissoye without breathing a word of the matter.

" The corpse might have lain a long time up there, if the people of the Torrent châlet had not sent a little boy to ask the priest to come and give the last sacrament to a dying man.

"The priest asked the boy who this dying man was,— what was his name. The boy said he was a stranger, and that he was lying in such a way, stretched in his blood beside the path. At once the priest, suspecting something, made me go up with him, seeing that, at that time, I was vice-president of the tribunal. So I took with me five armed men, and off we set. Guenzel had fallen with his head down-wards. I made a note before witnesses of the position of the fingers, left the five men to guard the corpse, and came down to give notice to the tribunal. They did not go up till next day. The fingers had not been moved. I picked up on the Col a horn full of powder, and the two sheepskins on which Ballet and his accomplice had been lying. The body was brought down to Evolena to hold the 'tapsie' [autopsy?], and it was put in the room of a guide who was absent. But back comes the poor fellow during the night, and finding his room locked, he gets in by the window and gets snugly to bed. Towards two o'clock he awakes, and by the bright moonlight sees stretched on his table a ghastly corpse, only half hidden under a bloody covering.

"Seized with terror, he makes but one spring from his bed to the window, and escapes in his shirt, roaring for help. Some of the neighbours open their door to him and explain everything.

"I carried Peter's stick and Guenzel's waistcoat to the registry; the waistcoat had a round hole burned where the ball had entered. It was plain that he had been shot at close quarters. However, as he had no scapulary nor medal, it was not known whether he was a Protestant or a Catholic, and they were afraid to bury an unbeliever in consecrated ground. The priest sent to the bishop for advice, and was told to bury Guenzel in the corner of the cemetery. So he was laid there, near the gate.

"Our president, M. Gaudin, believed that it was men of Evolena who had done the deed. He visited all the châlets, and on the door of one of them he found these words written with charcoal, 'Gone where you know.' This châlet belonged to Ballet. His writing was identified, and it was proved that he was the man who had been lying at the Col de Torrent.

"But don't imagine that he was to be caught in that way! Ah! he was a fellow who could make the policemen run! For two months, sir, our tall policemen were after him, and they have certainly good long legs. He escaped from châlet to châlet, from mountain to mountain, from glacier to glacier. He was a real demon, this Ballet; in fact, I wonder where he slept and what he ate. But at last they did get hold of him; but it was a difficult business.

"Soon afterwards a messenger came from the town of

Hanover. He showed me a photograph of Guenzel, and said, 'Do you recognise him?' 'Yes,' I said, 'only he does not look so well.' He had just been married when his portrait was taken.

"The messenger had the body disinterred in order to identify it. The hair was cut off for his widow.

"Ballet was condemned to perpetual imprisonment. But one day he sends for his judges to come to his prison, and says to them, 'You think that because I am chained like a galley slave, I cannot get away? Well, see here!' And he gives himself a shake,—so,—and down fall his chains in fragments. Then he gives a great kick at the wall, and makes a big hole in it.

"The judges, seeing that there were no prisons in Sion substantial enough for so strong a rascal, had him taken to the great prison at Lausanne, where he died."

CHAPTER VIII

A HOLIDAY MORNING IN A VALAISIAN VILLAGE.—THE MULES.—
THE YOUNG GIRLS.—THE PROCESSION.—THE PENITENTS.—
THE NURSERY.—THE CLOSE OF THE SERVICE.

NEXT morning at eight o'clock all the bells are clanging and pealing their loudest; it is high festival, —the festival of Saint Maurice, the patron saint of the Valais. We are looking out at the little windows of the parsonage over the splendid landscape of the high mountain, and the grand sweep of scenery over which towers the immense white pyramid of the Dent-Blanche; looking, too, at the picturesque groups and delightful rustic scenes that pass before our ravished eyes.

What a delicious picture a Sunday or a festival morning makes in a Valaisian mountain village! Those who have seen the beautiful paintings by my friend Ritz, know something about it. From all directions mules are arriving, bringing family parties; the man going first, the mother and daughters behind, and the children, their fair heads covered with parti-coloured caps,—in cloth or leather pockets hung on the sides of the animal. Sometimes the man, a tall, lean St. Joseph, all sunburnt, as the real St. Joseph must have been, walks in front with a stick, leading by the bridle the animal that carries his wife with a little Jesus in her arms.

The street is full of people, big and little, in holiday garb. The old men wear coats in French style, with gilt buttons; all the women have white or black aprons, tied round the waist with a coloured ribbon, or with little straps attached that cross on the back. They have all clean stockings,—the beautiful, dazzlingly white, woollen stocking that makes the foot stand out above the low-cut shoe,—the coquettish Louis XV. shoe, with a bow in front. And all wear little red embroidered kerchiefs, which hang down in a point between the shoulders. The hat is of black felt, the crown trimmed with a little band of different shades. Red and gold colour predominate in the hat-strings. The hat is set on slightly sideways, over one ear, with a saucy air that suits the young heads very well. The married women wear under their hat a little white cap with embroidered borders. The old women walk with long sticks. They wear on the front of their bodice a plastron of embroidered leather. Some of these have armorial bearings worked into them with gold thread, which glitters in the sun like church decorations.

The men, tall, thin, bony and very dark, thick-headed dragoons of fellows, go about carrying a bundle of white linen under their arms. This is their death-shirt,—the white penitent's shirt which on great festival days they must wear in their processions.

The mules continue to arrive in long picturesque files and amusing parties; while the gendarme marches up and down in white gloves, his chest imposingly padded under his sky-blue holiday uniform. With the eye of a conqueror he surveys from his majestic six feet height the pretty peasant girls who are hurrying up the cemetery steps and going into the church, carrying mass-books, with gilt edges glittering, as if they had picked up nuggets of gold by the way.

In front of all the barns and châlets, mules are standing tied; and the women who have come from a distance and have been on the way since three in the morning, proceed to make their toilet in the open air; they spit in their hands and smooth their hair, shake the dust from their dress, unfold the holiday apron and put it on.

The bells ring out a final summons. All the groups that are standing about turn toward the church with the slow step

19

of the mountain people, and we see coming down the outside stairs of the old houses bands of young girls with their smart, shining shoes and flowing dresses, and the coquettish hat tipped over the ear. Those fresh faces, with their rosy cheeks and bright smiles, coming out of tottering hovels and dark holes make one think of Spring issuing forth in joyous procession at the end of the winter from a dark, leafless forest into the sunlit meadows.

The service begins. The organ rolls out its great waves of harmony over the bowed heads of the faithful. Strong, resonant voices are heard,—the voices of the men singing. The village is deserted. Nothing is stirring but the mules eating their bunches of hay, and a few swallows that fly round and round the square church tower, uttering their shrill cries ; and at the end of the valley stands the Dent-Blanche, dazzling in its whiteness, like a great marble tabernacle or a silver altar reaching to heaven, and giving, far beyond any church with its narrow walls, an idea of the power and greatness of the creating God.

But now the bells are ringing again, sending forth deafening peals that sound to the extremity of the valley.

From the church porch appears a silver cross, mounted on a long pole ; then come men waving glittering, gold-spangled banners. They advance with a proud, defiant air, like Spanish monks unfurling standards of war. This begins the procession. Slowly it winds through the cemetery, through the streets and lanes of the village, which is all at once filled with its gay, fanciful mixture of colours, with the deafening sound of its bells, and the imposing music of its chants, as if hundreds of performers and choristers had appeared together on the stage of an immense theatre. Behind the two banners, which are hung with bells, like Chinese hats, and wave like great red flames, walk the young girls, the fair maidens under their virgin veils, with eyes piously cast down; the women with the forehead covered with a symbolical white cloth, the ends of it flapping like wings. Some of them carry their hat in their hand, others keep it on and put the napkin on the top. This cloth, which symbolises a shroud, is neither more nor less than a table napkin. The women have all a bouquet in the front of their dress, except the very old, wrinkled women, who wear the plastron of embroidered leather, shaped like a heart. Oh! there are some of them very old, dried up, parchment-looking, as if cut with an axe out of a boxwood root, and with faces like the Fates. With shaking head, and broken, trembling voice, they mutter litanies, swinging long chaplets of shining copper that jingle down to their knees. As they go they take a piece of bread, blessed by the priest, out of the little basket held out to them by a big fellow of the village, a substantial man with red face, shining and well-shaven cheeks, and the look of an innkeeper devoted to fat cookery; a tuft of hair set up on the top of his head and falling down like a rat's tail. As several walk abreast, the one who has first taken the bread passes it to the rest, and they cease their prayers for a moment to eat and talk. Some little children, sucking their thumbs, trot along with them, holding to their mothers' hands.

Lastly come the men, dressed as white penitents, in the funereal shirt that almost wholly covers them, and imprisons them like a white monkish frock. They are like people who have fled from their beds in night attire. The sun beats on their sinewy necks, and lights up their ruddy brown skin, as rough as the bark of the fir trees. There is one of them with a bald head, and a face so thin and emaciated,—every bone and sinew standing out in relief under the sunburned skin,— that he might be taken for a bronze statue; one of those old Florentine bronzes personifying Asceticism and Hunger.

Then there are the choristers surrounding the canopy under which the priest carries the holy sacrament; surpliced choristers with large books in their hands, ruled and dotted with black notes; opening mouths wide enough to swallow the mountains, and marching on stiffly with head erect and chest expanded; while a little choir boy in red, with close-cropped hair, rings a little bell; and men, also in white, carry wax tapers, protected by little rolls of grey paper from being extinguished by the air and the motion.

The procession passes down the street, disappears, then appears again; the little bells ringing at every step, the banners waving, and the plumes of the canopy and the gay embroideries and gilded decorations, all blending against the blue sky in the clear sunshine of the mountains, in a soft confusion of bright colours. Even the white penitents, confined in their rigid garb, produce, in the ascending and lengthened perspective of the street, an effect not at all sad or melancholy; they might be taken for a procession of pale shades winding through an immense living fresco,—a fresco laid on in vivid colours, red, white, and gold, in full light and sunshine.

As soon as the procession has come back we go down and take our places in the back seats. The church is a very simple one; the only pictures are those of the stations on the way to the cross. Over the high altar, of which the decorations are very good, hovers an immense symbolical Holy Spirit. The men sit in front, occupying the place of honour, while the women are relegated to the back or the side seats. The late comers stay outside, near the door. Around where we sit, it is really a nursery, so many of the women have their babies with them; while numbers of little ones, a stage farther advanced, are playing beside them, nibbling at bits of bread and munching apples, utterly unimpressed by the eloquence of the good priest. There is among them a little blue-eyed, curly-haired rogue who greatly amuses us. He is cramming bread into the mouth of his little sister, who is lying in his mother's arms; and as the bread does not go down, he tries to help it with the handle of a knife. Others of the children are gnawing at the coins of the chaplets, or giving each other little taps, as frolicsome and mischievous as kittens, and uttering little shouts with which nobody is in the least disturbed.

In the Valais there is something open and smiling in the Catholic religion; it has a picturesque and artistic side, both attractive and seductive. The worship is felt to be performed without hypocrisy and without constraint; it is a brotherly community, and not a trembling flock driven by the perpetual threatening of hell and the police, of the judge and the syndic.

From time to time a sudden ringing of bells bursts forth, produced by the sacristan setting in motion a disk set round with bells, hanging beside the altar. Then every one bends his head and smites on his breast in a solemn *meâ culpâ*. The offertory begins. The women, with their white napkins on their heads in token of mourning, come up to the choir, each carrying a lighted candle. The priest holds out a relic for them to kiss, and the sacristan blows out the candle and takes possession of it.

This terminates the service.

In going out, many of the men take off their white robe, fold it up, and carry it under their arm, while others still go about the village in their penitential costume. We see one of them who gets astride his mule still muffled up in this way, and sets off at a gallop in the funniest fashion, —like an Arab in his bournous or a phantom horseman.

In the cemetery the young girls in their gay, coloured aprons and coquettish hats are standing about in exquisitely pretty groups. All at once they join hands and run off laughing merrily.

CHAPTER IX.

A DINNER AT THE PARSONAGE OF EVOLENA.—HOW I WAS GUILTY, UNCONSCIOUSLY, OF A GRAVE IMPRUDENCE.—THE GUIDES GASPOZ AND BOVIER.—DEPARTURE OF MY SON FOR THE DENT BLANCHE.

DURING dinner, at which we had the company of M. the Vicar of La Sage,—a little lonely hamlet in the mountains,—the conversation turned on walks and excursions. The priest of Evolena relates to us that while he was a priest down in the plains, some peasants came one day to ask him to go and bless the Dent du Midi, which for a long time had been " no longer very firm." He sets forth, his sprinkler for holy water in one hand, his prayer-book in the other, with an escort of the villagers, men and women, in their Sunday clothes. But the ascent soon becomes so difficult that he is obliged to give up the attempt to go any higher. However, he blesses the mountain ; but as he did not reach the top, the peasants are convinced that the blessing has been ineffectual, and that ere long the Dent will come crashing down into the valley and fill it up.

From the Dent du Midi the conversation turns to the Dent Blanche, and all at once the priest says to me pointblank,—

" Do you wish to go to the Dent Blanche ? "

" Is it difficult ? "

" Difficult! I could go up on my mule with my eyes shut. Besides, with the guides that I can offer you, you could scale the heavens. They climb like bears, and are as strong as

304

elephants. It would be an opportunity for you to make an interesting expedition. One of those guides is my servant, and the other is a friend of his, a man of long experience, who has been to all the most difficult peaks in the Valais, except the Dent Blanche. But they have been studying for years, and they have resolved on trying the ascent to-night. They would be pleased to have a tourist with them; it would be an advantage to them, a certificate in their book— you understand—and along with that, a little article in the papers ——."

Still tired with the forced march of the previous day, I did not feel drawn to so long an excursion, even though, according to what M. the Curé had said, it were without danger.

My son André, who is mad upon mountaineering, looked inquiringly at me, not venturing to ask permission of me for what I would certainly have refused; but the priest returned to the charge so often and so skilfully, that I consented to see the two guides and hear what they had to say about their projected excursion.

They were both in the kitchen; the maid brought them in.

They were two strong, solidly-built fellows, with square shoulders,—formed, in fact, like bears. And added to that, were frank, goodnatured faces, and honest, loyal eyes that inspired confidence at once.

One of them said to me, " But if you do not wish to come, the young gentleman, your son, seems strong enough to go with us."

" Oh, yes, father ; let me go !" now exclaimed André.

We went on discussing for a long time. I had the way explained to me, having no idea of it; I was not even aware of the catastrophe that had happened on the Dent Blanche some years ago ; and overcome by my son's urgency, and trusting to the strength of his legs and to his skill as an experienced gymnast, I at last consented to entrust him to the two guides.

These men are not ignorant upstarts. The Valaisian authorities only grant licences to guides after severe examinations. They are obliged to take courses of study; they are taught topography, and how to read a map and find their way by it; to use the compass and the other instruments that are indispensable in journeys of exploration. They are also taught how to bind up wounds, so as to be able to do what is necessary at once in case of accidents.

My son and his guides set out at two o'clock. We accompanied them as far as the next village; and there we took from them a solemn promise that if the weather should be bad, or if the young traveller became too tired, they would return without persisting in getting to the top. And, finally, we agreed to meet, next day, at three o'clock, at the little hotel at Ferpècle.

The evening was beautiful; the stars shone brilliantly in the deep, quiet sky. We looked at them from our open windows, and thought of the absent one. And new stars were continually shining out, large glowing orbs, and little glittering diamond points. The moon was like a magic mirror hung on a wall of sapphire inlaid with gold. At the end of the valley, the Dent was seen towering above the neighbouring peaks, standing in the midst of that immense frozen desert, like an inaccessible pyramid. And we wondered, with anxious hearts, how a boy of fourteen could ever reach that summit—so high, so white, so near the stars!

Next day we set out for Ferpècle, with minds somewhat feverish and anxious. But the weather was fine, which reassured us.

In passing through La Sage, we stopped for a few minutes at the house of the excellent and worthy vicar, who lives there like a hermit or an exile, in the company of his sister and a pretty black cat with white paws. What a praiseworthy life that of those good mountain priests is! During those three years that this vicar of La Sage has been there, in his poor wooden châlet, furnished with one table, three chairs, and a bench, he has not once gone down to the plain. The winter begins in October, and does not end till May. He teaches fifty children, who come to school until they are fifteen. Never any recreation or amusement. A real trappist life. A forced fast.

"In summer," he said to us, "I never eat butcher-meat ; by the time it comes up from Sion, it has begun to spoil."

The State, the chapter or diocese of Sion, give nothing to the priest who ministers to this buried parish ; the benefice attached to the little alpine parsonage is two francs seventy-five centimes from each household. And on that he must manage to live.

We go through the village. The newly whitewashed church standing in the midst of the brown chocolate coloured houses, confusedly packed together, might be taken for an ornament in sugar. M. the Vicar points out to us a châlet inhabited by a famous chamois hunter, named Folonnier. I go in. In a large room, a woman and a girl are sitting on a bench dining from a pot full of polenta that stands on a tree stump before them.

"Where is Folonnier?" I ask ; and they reply, "On the mountain."

Seeing a gun hanging on the wall, I ask if Folonnier has killed many chamois.

"More than three hundred," they reply.

We go down through meadows in which some men wearing policemen's caps are at work. Clouds of grasshoppers are flying about us. Here is Forclaz, with its tiny chapel and its schist roofs, streaked with moss, that gives them a beautiful grey-green tint. Farther on some women are plying sickles, reaping a poor harvest of wheat. It is now the middle of September, and harvest rarely begins before that time.

As we get farther down, the Dent Blanche grows larger ; shining in the sun as if overlaid with silver. At half-past two we arrive at the hotel of Ferpècle,—a charming little hotel-châlet, exquisitely clean, kept by a model family, quite French in their politeness and kindness. I asked the proprietor : " Did you see a boy and two guides pass this way yesterday evening ? "

" Yes."

" That was my son."

" And where was he going ? "

" To the Dent Blanche."

" To the——" He stopped and looked at me. Then after a moment's hesitation, he said,—

" You are joking, sir ? "

" No, I am not. Why ? "

" Because you would not have said that, if you knew what the Dent Blanche is."

" Is it a very difficult ascent, then ? "

" Difficult ! Say dangerous, perilous. . . . I myself, an old hunter and a guide in former days, have never been able to accomplish it."

Then he gave me some details about this summit that I had not known before, and had not found even in Baedeker, which caused me a few very bad minutes.

When I became aware of the danger to which I had so rashly exposed my son; and when I saw that the hour agreed on for his return was past, when four o'clock came and we vainly searched with our glasses the snowy slopes and icy ridges of the gloomy Dent, fear took possession of me. My excited imagination showed me the child hanging over the abyss, clinging to some point of rock, and longing for help that did not come. I was reasoning no longer ; for I had only to think of the bravery of his guides, of their thorough experience of the mountain, and of their heroic mountaineer devotedness, and all those fears would have been dissipated. But in such moments we no longer reflect.

I had already gathered the few shepherds who were about the hotel, and had said to them : " I will give you whatever you please ; but you are coming with me to the Dent

Blanche ; we will go up until we meet them or find some traces of them."

The master of the hotel prepared everything needful for the relief expedition : provisions, meat, bread, brandy, wine, ropes, and lanterns ; and our little caravan was just setting out, when a boy came running, out of breath, and shouting at the top of his voice,—

" They are coming ! . . . I have just seen them with the glass ; they are coming down the glacier just now ! "

What a moment ! In my delight I caught the child in my arms. Then I said to him :—

" Then it is you who must come with me now to meet them. Here, take this bag ; it is the provisions. They must be hungry and thirsty. Come, let us be off ! "

Urged on by an irresistible impulse, I walked on foremost, utterly free from the oppressing dread that had weighed me down a moment before. My feet were winged, and my heart flew like a bird. Behind me the little goatherd ran with great strides, only able with the greatest difficulty to keep up with me.

Ten minutes before we reached the châlet of Bricola we saw three dark figures standing out clearly against the sky, three dark shadows waving their hats above their heads ; it was my son and the two guides.

This journey of a night and a day over snow and ice, this scaling of one of the highest peaks of the Alps, had changed the little fellow of fourteen into a young man.

The two guides were spent with fatigue. The face of Bovier especially, who had been in command of the expedition, showed a profound moral lassitude, the effect of the continuous mental effort it had been necessary for him to make in this audacious assault of a summit that he was scaling for the first time, and with such a responsibility !

" I knew," said he to me, " that those little Parisians are monkeys that can climb anywhere. And as to climbing, your son climbs well. He does not need to be urged on, he must

be held back. . . . A steady head too, . . . not
afraid of the precipices. . . . He walked well. . . .
I should like always to guide clubbists like him. . . ."

André himself said nothing; and to all my questions
replied only in monosyllables.

At dinner, however, in the pretty little dining-room of
the Ferpècle hotel, where the excellent Madame Crétaz had
provided so well for the guides and us, my son gave us his
impressions; but I prefer to allow him to record them
himself. Here is the account he wrote next morning, while
I had gone up again to Bricola. I reproduce his prose just
as it stands, without making any literary alteration.

CHAPTER X.

THE Dent Blanche is the sixth of the Swiss summits in
order of height; it was ascended for the first time in
1863, by Messrs. Kennedy and Wigram; and afterwards, in
1865, by the famous Mr. Whymper, who said of it: "This
ascent of 14,318 feet is the most laborious one I have ever
made; there is not a single step of it that can be called
easy." This mountain has remained just as it was in 1865;
no chains or ropes have been fixed to make the dangerous
places easier, as has been done on the Matterhorn and so
many other peaks. Notwithstanding its height and the
difficulties it presents, it is very little known, its name is
hardly to be found on the map, while its neighbour and
brother, the Matterhorn, has an immense renown. This is
because the Dent Blanche is hidden in the depths of a valley
little frequented by tourists, and the few climbers who have
grappled with it have most of them set out from Zermatt.

In 1882 it was the scene of a terrible catastrophe. A
party, led by the guides Lochmatter, made a frightful slip,
and were hurled over a precipice; the head of one of the
guides was severed from the body,—of the other nothing was
found but his cravat.

It was time for us to set out; it was one o'clock. We had just time to dress and to prepare the provisions.

I clothed myself very warmly, while the curé's servant was drawing the wine and preparing the bread and cheese; and when the shoemaker had put more nails in my shoes, we set off.

. . . It is half-past two; the sky is overcast; now and then the clouds break, showing a great piece of blue, which quickly disappears. But we are not too anxious, for the barometer is going up.

The two guides, Antoine Bovier and Maurice Gaspoz, two strong mountaineers, with tanned, swarthy complexion and eagle eyes, are armed with strong ice-axes. Each of them carries on his back a bag and an enormous tin bottle; and Gaspoz has besides, coiled round his shoulder, a long and strong rope, with which we are to be tied together when we reach the glacier.

In an hour we arrive at Haudères, a large village situated at the confluence of the Borgne from Ferpècle, and the Borgne from Arolla. Between the houses, we take the road to the left, which leads to the hotel of Ferpècle. The footpath runs winding up the side of a rapid slope, broken up with rocks and rubbish, at the bottom of which the Borgne flows along, roaring and foaming while it clears a way for itself among the enormous blocks that obstruct its course. Hedges of barberry border the road, which begins to grow steeper. We pass through green meadows, and among clumps of pine and larch, with dull, green foliage; we jump across little brooks, not a yard broad, murmuring among the grass, towards a châlet built of pine wood, and reddened by the weather. But the sun has now pierced through the clouds and is darting his rays on our backs; we are bathed in perspiration, and we wait for a moment under the shade of a hedge, after leaving on our left the little village of Sepey.

I look round; the view has already become much wider.

and the clouds, driven by the wind, are rapidly leaving the peaks which they covered. The Dent Blanche alone still keeps its moving crown. Behind us rises the imposing mass of the Etoile, with its rocky walls, all starry with snow; to the right, the two points of Veisivi, one of them lighted up by the sun, so that every projection and hollow is clearly distinguished; the other plunged in shadow, and the snow, resting on all the rough and broken places, showing brightly on the dark rock. The *arête* by which the two summits are joined is so delicately cut that you could think you were looking at stone soldiers, under arms, ranged in single file.

Opposite us stretches the glacier of Ferpècle, a mighty river of ice, in the midst of which rises, like an island, Mont Miné, the top of which is like the gaping mouth of a serpent.

A little higher up, near the peak of the same name, is the Col d'Hèrens, leading to Zermatt, and the cliff Mota-Rota, so black and grim, in the midst of all the whiteness, that it might be taken for the opening of a cavern. To the left rise several other lofty summits, continuing the chain of the Dent Blanche.

Having recovered our breath, we resume our march. In a few minutes we meet four mountaineers, striding along as if they wore seven-league boots. They are laden with large sacks, and carry iron-shod sticks, and are gravely smoking pipes which are hardly visible in their shaggy beards. They exchange a brief and deep-toned " Good-day " with us, and disappear round the corner of the path, going on with the same long, slow, elastic step, kicking away the stones with their heavy shoes, that seem as if soled with iron. Bovier tells me they are smugglers on their way to Arolla; thence they will cross the Col du Colon, and, when they reach Italy, will unload the tobacco they are carrying on their shoulders.

I chat with my guides. Antoine Bovier, the elder of the two, has been four times on the Matterhorn, and three times on Monte Rosa; he has scaled the Breithorn, the Weissmies, and I do not know how many other peaks. As for Gaspoz, he has attacked every summit in the neighbourhood. These two are great friends, and often go on expeditions together. A few days ago they were at the Great Cornier, a rocky peak 13,022 feet high, to the left of the Dent Blanche. They also ascended the Aiguilles Rouges together, without knowing the way, and without even roping themselves together.

For a long time they have been studying and examining the Dent on all its sides, and over all its *arêtes ;* and they have in their head and in their eye the way we are to take up the side of the mountain.

Ah! at last! The Dent Blanche has pierced her canopy of clouds, the peak appearing above, while the middle part of the pyramid remains hidden; it looks like an enormous powdered hat of a clown, hanging in the air. The guides immediately stop, lie down on their backs, take out their glasses, and direct them towards the mountain. But no sooner have they everything nicely arranged, than down come the clouds, mixing with those below, and there is no longer anything to be seen.

"Ah! the wretch!" cries Gaspoz in a rage.

The guides rise, and we set off again more quickly, drawn on by the sight of the hotel of Ferpècle, which we can already distinguish in the midst of the stones and blocks that have rolled down from the Mourti. This hotel is a pretty, rustic, wooden building, surrounded by an open balcony. We are not long in reaching it; and, while I sit down on a bench near the door, my guides lay down their knapsacks and go to ask M. Crétaz, the landlord, to lend us a pan in which to make chocolate, at night, in the châlet. Master Crétaz, very obliging, brings a big pot with a long handle, which Bovier ties on his back, above his bottle. We set off, thanking the landlord, who wishes us good luck, without even asking where we are going.

We now follow the road to the Bricola Alp. It is a mule

path, climbing up a rocky wall overhanging the glacier of Ferpècle, which stretches out and diminishes far below. We pass among clumps of rhododendrons, then into vast cemeteries of stony ruins, where we stumble every moment, and need to look down constantly to see where to plant our feet. This wretched road is made up for by the view, which grows more and more extensive. Now it is the Bouquetin, whose curved horn appears on our right, beside the Zaillon peak, enormous, massive, and as if surmounted by a circumflex accent; now it is the needle of the Zâ beginning to peep out from behind. The Dent Perroc, a thin arrow, wrapped in a soft white drapery, stands proudly above all this confused labyrinth of peaks and summits. The Dent Blanche is resolved not to show herself, she is still hidden; it is most trying!

We approach the châlet by a very gradual ascent; and now we are going up more slowly, keeping step to the regular sound of the saucepan striking against the tin bottle, as Bovier moves along. We are beginning to be conscious of having eaten nothing since noon, and that we have been walking for four hours; so as soon as the ascent becomes a little easier, we quicken our pace. At last, after crossing several streams, we find ourselves on the terrace on which the châlet of Bricola has been set up.

It is a very low wooden cabin, leaning against a huge rock which forms its fourth wall; the roof is loaded with heavy stones. A few sheep with dirty grey wool are browsing on the scanty herbage that grows among the rocks. The shepherd stands leaning on his long staff, a goatskin over his shoulders, his legs hardly hidden by his old pantaloons patched with many colours, his feet out at the toes of his shoes; his face is sunburned so brown that he might be taken for a Red-skin; his beard, black and dirty, half covers his breast, and he has on his head an old battered felt hat, that must have seen very long service since it was black. This poor fellow receives twenty-five francs for taking care

20

of 300 sheep for a whole season ; in his spare time he carves out with his knife crucifixes and angels from pieces of fir-wood. These he paints and gilds, and sells to the peasants for a good price.

We enter the châlet, and while Bovier unpacks the provisions and Gaspoz goes for water to a stream near, I stand and look round.

The night is slowly falling; the valley is already lying in deep shadow, while the surrounding summits are still lighted up by the ruddy glow of the sun, which, as it sinks nearer and nearer to the horizon, leaves each peak in order of height. The Dent Perroc alone still shows a glittering point that grows less and less, and still less, then vanishes.

Since our arrival I have been hearing dull sounds, like distant reports of cannon, coming from the direction of La Zâ.

"What can that be?" I ask Bovier, going into the châlet.

"It is *séracs* rolling down from the top of Zaillon and breaking on the glacier. . . . Maurice and I once made a near escape of leaving our bones there. . . . One day, going to La Zâ, we had to cross the hollow track where those blocks come rumbling down, and if we had not stopped for a minute to nibble a morsel of bread, it would have been all up with us. A few yards from us a whole avalanche of *séracs* came rushing down with a horrible noise, so near that we felt the wind it made in passing. Mind you, it was no joke!"

But the chocolate is ready ; we attack it at once, and find it excellent; and Bovier is unanimously pronounced a very good cook. While we dine, Gaspoz tells me about his last expedition to the Grand Cornier, and shows me, lying in the châlet, an old door on which he had slept ; as for Bovier, his bed was a wormeaten plank, just wide enough to hold him!

While the guides are preparing a bed of hay for me, I go to look at the weather. It is cold ; no moon ; a few sparsely scattered stars are shining, and in the direction of the Dent

Blanche snow is falling. That is a pity; for when there is snow on the rocks the ascent is much more difficult and dangerous. I hope however that it will not be very bad; as the guides, in coming up, pointed out to me some transverse cracks in the glacier; these are called *windows*, and are a sign of fine weather.

I am to sleep in a little cabin, where I can hardly stand upright, a few yards from the châlet. I roll myself up in my plaid and creep into the hay; and then Gaspoz brings me a hot stone from the hearth; that is my warming-pan!

I really could not have been better in my own bed! The guides go back to the fireside, and I am left in darkness and silence. I feel as if I were underground, the air is so heavy in this narrow hut. Suddenly I start; there are more *séracs* coming thundering down over there at almost regular intervals, and shaking the mountain. At first this noise prevents me from closing my eyes; but I very soon get accustomed to it, and sink to sleep.

Suddenly I hear in my sleep some one calling me. I open my eyes; the guides are there; I must get up; it is midnight.

Still half asleep, I turn to the châlet without even thinking of looking at the sky. The fire is blazing merrily, lighting up every corner of the châlet; the guides have already prepared the breakfast; I drink with enjoyment a steaming cup of chocolate, and do abundant honour to the other provisions; for we must provide ourselves with legs; the climb is going to be very stiff. I inquire of the guides how they have passed the night. Bovier has had possession of his plank again, and Gaspoz of his door; but they have not had a moment's sleep, being too much excited at the thought of our ascent. So they have smoked all the time.

It is one o'clock; we set out. It is magnificent weather, the sky blue-black, and the stars,—what a size they are at this height!—glittering like electric jewels. And before us, enormous, overwhelming, its gigantic mass filling the horizon, stands the Dent Blanche, enveloped in a milky transparency, a changing gleam that plays over it like a luminous shiver and surrounds it as with a heavenly aureole; it seems as if the mountain itself were diffusing this pale light which gradually melts into the grey surrounding masses. To the left of the Dent, the moon, large and full, is shining like a ball at white heat discharged from some invisible cannon to make a breach in this icy citadel, inaccessible by man, protected by bottomless crevasses and threatening *séracs*. There is something exciting to the fancy in the sight of all those glaciers and snowfields and white summits in the moonlight. When you look steadily at them for some time they seem to be moving; you think you see phantoms stirring under their shrouds and coming towards you; and then, when you are least expecting it, the oppressive silence is suddenly rent by the thunder of an avalanche. The noise, repeated by numberless echoes, attains to formidable proportions, then gradually grows fainter and dies away, and all is silent again until the next avalanche comes to shake the earth anew. Such a scene is profoundly impressive; we feel so small in presence of those giant mountains; we wonder how we dare risk ourselves on those glaciers and snowfields, and what object we have in view in trying, at the peril of our life, to scale a most dangerous peak instead of staying quietly at home. What are we the better afterwards? Nothing whatever; unless for the pleasure of having gone along the edge of precipices, of having, with help of both hands and feet, scaled a perpendicular wall, and of having reached, at the cost of a thousand fatigues, a height to which everybody cannot attain.

For half an hour we follow the path leading to the Col d'Hérens, then we enter on the moraine. I know nothing more wearisome than the moraine; walking on lumps of rock so round that they roll under your feet and half crush them; slipping on a flat stone and coming down in a sitting position on a sharp one,—it is all simply intolerable. So it is with much growling at the moraine that we reach the glacier of the Dent Blanche, after crossing the innumerable streamlets of Bricola.

Here, on account of the crevasses, we rope ourselves together. Bovier goes foremost, I come next, then lastly Gaspoz. We all three hold the rope with our left hand, as high as our waist, for it must never be allowed to drag on the ice, lest our feet should get entangled in it, or it should catch on some jutting point. Just at first the glacier is pretty good, we have only to cross, on solid bridges of ice, some crevasses neither very wide nor very deep.

Suddenly we are brought to a dead stop by a vertical barrier of *séracs*, as big as houses. No opening anywhere. We turn to the right, to the left, we cross yawning crevasses on ice bridges no wider than our foot; we go round and round in a labyrinth of ice, from which we see no way of egress. At last we come to a place where the snow wall is somewhat lower. Bovier vigorously attacks a block with his ice axe. He cuts a dozen steps, and without very great difficulty gains the top of the *sérac*; there he unties himself from the rope and goes to take a survey, to ascertain if we can get any farther in that direction. He soon returns and calls to us that the way is open.

During his absence, Gaspoz and I were not in too comfortable a position, at the end of a bridge of ice, an immense crevasse at each side, with walls of deep blue ice as smooth as glass, and water perfectly black down in their depths.

Bovier ropes himself to us again, and begins to pull me up, while Gaspoz, on whose shoulders I have mounted, pushes me from below. I wish at least to make use of the cut steps, but I have no time; I am already on the top beside Antoine.

It is Gaspoz's turn to climb; but in mounting his shoulders I had knocked off his hat, which rolled away into the crevasse. "The plaguy thing!" he exclaims. He unties himself, and hanging on with his hands to the edge of the ice bridge, succeeds with the aid of his axe in recovering the hat, which had happily been stopped by a projection of the ice. With the exception of this incident we all three arrive successfully on the top of the first *sérac ;* and we surmount two more barriers in the same way. One crevasse, among other things, gives us great trouble. The bridges are not strong enough; the snow breaks away under Bovier's axe, with which he tries it before him. At last we find a bridge, which we cross, lying flat down, one by one.

It is nearly five o'clock; the moon is slowly waning, the darkness is beginning to yield, we see more clearly.

Before us rises almost vertically a beautiful declivity of snow, smooth, immaculate, which we attack with joy, for we are getting sensibly nearer the Dent, which has now the moon on the right. Bovier, who always goes first, plunges his strongly ironed shoes deep in the snow, and Gaspoz and I follow in his steps. It had seemed to me, looking from below, that the ascent would not take us more than an hour; and besides, the snow was so nice and soft under our feet! Ah, well! so it was; but it took three hours to reach the top of the snowfield, and I had soon more than enough of the snow, which pained my eyes horribly. I was exasperated, for the higher we got, the longer way there seemed to go.

At last, to get on more quickly, we take an oblique direction to the left, towards the Rocs-Rouges, a range of rocks beginning below an *arête* of the Dent, and stretching a good way into the snowfield.

It cost us—at least it cost Bovier—a great deal of toil to reach them, for he was obliged to cut I do not know how many steps in the ice, which was as smooth as a mirror. If one of us had slipped while the guide was working, we should all three have been hurled down to the glacier, nearly 1,000 feet below.

Arrived on the Rocs-Rouges, we quicken our pace, and suddenly find ourselves on the *arête*. On the other side, the ice stretches away to the very top.

What a striking scene lies before us! It is now full daylight, it is nine o'clock, and the sun is shining above our heads, and lighting up an immense panorama of snowy peaks and summits, of valleys and glaciers. It is as if the waves of a raging sea had been suddenly frozen when the tempest was at its height. White, white everywhere! My eyes are dazzled, and I close them for a moment.

It is hardly worth the trouble, do you say, to half kill one's self by persisting in getting to the top, if the view from the *arête* is so fine? I do not know what answer to make; but I am going to the top all the same.

The guides tell me the names of all the summits that are visible. In front of us there is Monte Rosa, a shapeless, hardly-defined mass, as compared with the proud needles that surround it; the Matterhorn, like a gigantic eagle's head, so near that we almost think we could touch it.

"There is the shoulder," said Bovier to me; "take the glass, and you will see the chains and cables that make the ascent of it easier than that of the Dent Blanche."

Then there are the Dent d'Hérens, the Mischabel, the Weisshorn, with its perpendicular cliffs, the Dom, the Lyskam, the Strahlhorn, the Breithorn, the Rothhorn, and I do not know how many other *horns*.

In Italy there is the Grand Paradis, the Grivola, the Cima di Jazi; to the right, the Vélan, the Grand Combin, the Mont Gelé, Mont Blanc, which one would certainly not take for the highest mountain in Europe; it looks so small, squeezed up among a confused crowd of rocky peaks that surround it, like waves beating on a reef. And there is the Dent de Morcles, the Aiguille Verte, the Dent du Midi. I take all those names on the wing, as it were, and I let many of them escape. To the left the whole panorama is hidden by the Dent Blanche. I take one more look at the ocean of frozen peaks that stretches from Monte Rosa to Mont Blanc, from the Apennines to the Jura, and then we set out along the *arête*, having on our right a frightful precipice. Bovier walks on as coolly as if it were the edge of a pavement; but I, for my part, find it the simplest way to go on all fours.

We arrive in this style at the first "*gendarme.*" This name is given to some pyramidal rocks, a few of which have a rough resemblance to a gendarme in a cocked hat; and the name has been attached to them all, whatever their shape. There we sit down side by side, with our legs dangling over the abyss, to refresh ourselves with a crust. Then Bovier perceives that the rocks of the Dent are covered with more than an inch depth of snow! That will make difficult work for us! So much the worse! Antoine and Gaspoz lighten themselves of their knapsacks, retaining only a little bread and chocolate, and the bottle of rum.

We are off again. Suddenly we hear on our left repeated sounds of "crôa! crôa!" I turn round astonished, and what do I see? Some crows standing in the snow a few yards from me, quietly looking at us as we pass. Their black plumage comes out sharply on the surrounding snow, and they go on uttering their doleful cry. I pick up some snow, make it into a ball and throw into the midst of them; but the birds hardly move. It is so rarely they see human beings that they have no fear of them.

After traversing a hollow track in the rock, full of snow, we are on the rocky precipice of the Dent; a wall of yellow rock rising perpendicularly above us, and behind us running down as far as the glacier. We are hanging between heaven and earth, holding on by our fingers and the points of our toes to the jutting points of rock; the snow, which partly covers them, melting under our hand and making it difficult to keep our hold. We had now little more than 1,600 feet to ascend, but at the rate at which we were going, it seemed to me we should never arrive. Bovier climbed

foremost, choosing the broadest projections and the in-
equalities of the surface most convenient to hold on by,
while Gaspoz and I remained stationary, leaning on our
sticks. When Bovier had got as high as the rope would
allow him, he set his back against the rock, and planted his
feet firmly in a fissure; then turning towards me, he held
the rope with both hands, and I climbed in my turn, slowly,
and trying each stone before trusting my weight to it; and
finally arrived beside Bovier at the same time as Gaspoz
who had followed me, and who walked up this aerial road
smoking his pipe, as much at ease as if he had been on the
high road.

For three hours we went on repeating the same performance! Sometimes Bovier could get no farther,—the rock
was entirely smooth; then we had to come down again, and
try to right or left till we found some practicable way. Often
the fissures were so shallow that Bovier was obliged to
embrace a rock to keep himself steady while waiting for
me; and if I had made a false step, he could not have kept
me up; he would have been dragged down with me, and
Gaspoz would have followed us, unless he could have
stopped us both, which was very unlikely.

As we rose higher, the air was becoming perceptibly
rarefied; we were obliged almost to shout in order to make
each other hear; and I felt an indefinable discomfort,—
my stomach oppressed, my head burning. I no longer
spoke; while Bovier was climbing I closed my eyes and
almost slept. Gaspoz had to tell me when to go on, or I
should have fallen asleep where I stood. I climbed without
enjoyment, without courage; I was so sleepy I hardly
looked where I was setting my feet, and I should have liked
to ask the guides to leave me there, lying on a rock, while
they went on alone to the top, and to take me with them on
their way down. This idea so took possession of me that I
did not think of the danger of such a step.

However, I go on, revived by a few drops of rum; and my

headache is a little relieved, thanks to some peppermint lozenges that I find in the bottom of a pocket. At last, drawing each other on, we reach the "*mauvais pas*," where the Lochmatters fell in 1882.

Here we must get round past a perpendicular edge by creeping out on an overhanging rock and then turning sharp round, with head and arms on one side of the rock, while the legs are still on the other; then we must at once cling to a hardly visible fissure, and draw round the rest of the body, gently, cautiously, little by little, and hang there by the points of our fingers until our toes find their way to a second fissure lower down. I made this passage like a bale of goods at the end of a rope, without being conscious of the danger, and I really do not know how I escaped in safety. If I am able to give all these details after my ascent, it is thanks to my notes, for to-day I have absolutely no remembrance of anything.

The "*mauvais pas*" cleared, we are on a snowy ridge, on the right of which a narrow ledge of ice curves gracefully above the chasm.

At this moment a fresh wind strikes my face, and my headache is gone as if by magic. I talk, I laugh, I sing. What a difference from the inert *bale* of a little while ago ! So I heartily congratulate myself on the change ; for I had not spoken for a long time.

And now, in a few moments, here we are on the summit of the Dent Blanche, 14,318 feet above the level of the sea, 1,413 feet lower than Mont Blanc !

On the bare rock, on the side looking towards Zermatt, we find a bottle containing the cards of four persons who have made the ascent. The latest of them is dated 17th September, 1886. Four days ago an Englishman had ascended the Dent, starting from Zermatt. The guides slip their cards into the bottle, and I write their names and my own on a bit of paper, which is also thrust in. Is that thin morsel of paper still up there ? Has some gust of wind

carried the bottle over into the abyss? Has some jealous
climber destroyed that frail witness of our presence? I
hope to find out ere long. We also find under the snow a
champagne bottle, ticketed Th. Roederer. What a pity it is
empty! The contents would have been a happy discovery!

The view is not much finer here than from the "*gendarme*" at the foot of the Dent; we see a few more summits
to the left; the Grand Cornier quite near us, and though
almost as high as the Dent Blanche, suggesting to us a
sugar-loaf; the Diablerets, the Oldenhorn, the Jungfrau, the
Mönch, the Finsteraarhorn barely distinguishable on the
edge of the horizon, and mingling with the whiteness of the
clouds.

Suddenly, on looking at Bovier and Gaspoz, I utter a cry
of astonishment: their faces and hands are deep blue, as if
they had been stained with mulberry juice. I look at my own
hands;—those of the guides have no cause to envy them.

But I have not time to inquire into the cause of this
curious fact. We must begin our descent, for great veils of
mist are coming nearer and covering the sides of the mountain. We linger a few moments more on this summit,
scarcely wide enough to hold the three of us; gained after
so many dangers, and rarely trodden by human feet;—and
then we start.

"Forward!" cries Bovier. And I feel as fresh and ready
as I was at one o'clock this morning. If only I had felt as
much at my ease in coming up!

Bovier finds a different way, by which we avoid the
Lochmatters' dangerous corner. The guides are crazy with
delight at having successfully carried through this perilous
enterprise. They sing and *jödel* loud enough to split one's
head. In three-quarters of an hour we come down where
we had taken three long hours to climb up. We have only
to let ourselves slide down the rock till we come to a fissure
in which we plant our iron-shod sticks and heels with a firm
grip, and so stop ourselves at once. I found, when we

reached the " *gendarme*," who, as Gaspoz said, was taking
care of our knapsacks, that the seat of my pantaloons was
by no means the better of this mode of descent.

At one of our halts Gaspoz kicks against something that
gives back a ringing sound.

" What in the world is that ? " he exclaims, and searching
under the snow he finds a bottle filled with a lump of ice.
He smells it—it is frozen tea.

The next minute I find a box of sardines, which I send
with a kick in the direction of Zermatt. We stop to eat a
second morsel, and while we are literally devouring our
provisions, Gaspoz sits down on the bottle to melt the ice.
Then he pours out the tea and puts the bottle in his knapsack.

" That is always one more bottle for me ! " says he, as we
set off again.

We again go along the *arête*; and we notice, in the snow,
footmarks that we had not observed in going up. These
are the tracks of the last party that made the ascent four
days ago, and who came down, like ourselves, by Ferpècle.
We see also some drops of blood, as if some bird of prey had
flown over the glacier with some unfortunate victim in his
grasp. In thus following the traces of the former party,
which Bovier thinks is the preferable way, we arrive at the
top of a beautiful snowy declivity, stretching away down
before us almost vertically. We all three link our arms
together, and—*houpp !* we are off ! Sliding down on our
heels and leaving a broad furrow behind us, we traverse in
a few minutes a slope that it would have taken us several
hours to ascend, and find ourselves on the glacier.

Then the *séracs* again give us plenty of work. My staff
has become quite blunted on the point, and hardly takes hold
of the ice. Suddenly I lose hold of it; it goes off like
an arrow, and sticks fast in the side of a crevasse. Bovier
unropes himself, heedless of my remonstrance, and climbs
down. Happily it is not very deep, and the guide reappears
almost immediately, proudly brandishing my alpenstock.

Farther on, in crossing a rather insecure bridge, my leg goes through the snow of which it consists, and I fall back. Bovier and Gaspoz, seeing me go down, at once pull the rope tight, each on his own side, with a sharp jerk that throws me upwards, and happily I come down on the firm surface of the glacier.

At last we can dispense with the rope. We leave the snow for the moraine, on which I twist each of my feet two or three times; and we reach the châlet of Bricola.

It is now seven o'clock, and we had said we should be back at three! I can now think of nothing but the terrible anxiety my parents must be feeling. And now I see my father running to meet me with open arms; he has been waiting for me since two o'clock, in a fearful state of uneasiness. We all go down together to Ferpècle, where we make an excellent dinner, during which the guides and I hardly speak a word,—we are too utterly exhausted. Bovier, especially, looks like quite an old man.

Then I go to bed. My head is heavy, my arms feel broken, my loins bruised, my nerves tense as cords, and my legs are so stiff that I can hardly lift them to walk upstairs. It was only now that I was conscious of the fatigue of my eighteen hours' walk.

In the night I had frightful dreams; I was falling from the top of the Dent Blanche, falling, and still falling, turning over and over, with my arms outstretched, striking against all the projecting rocks, and above me Bovier and Gaspoz were roaring with laughter at my giddy fall. I went on falling more quickly, the wind whistling round me; at last, with a terrible shock I reached the bottom of the abyss, —and awoke. I had fallen out of my bed!

If the rocks of the Dent Blanche had not been covered with snow, we should certainly have taken a much shorter time, and the difficulties would have been diminished by a half. I may therefore say with the curé of Evolena:

" With Gaspoz and Bovier you can go anywhere! "

CHAPTER XI.

WE spent a few days more at Evolena.
Before leaving, we made the beautiful excursion to
the glacier of Arolla, above which towers the enormous
snowy dome of Mont Collon. This glacier is another wonder!
But if I described them all, this volume would never come to
an end. Its grotto of recent formation, discovered by M.
Freudler, stretches out into vaults of an unknown style, and
crystal blue arches,—an ideal blue, like solid azure, in which
are dancing prismatic colours with the play of precious stones
and moonlight. A true fairy grotto, with its entrance like
that of an enchanted palace, its mysterious dim light sleeping
in the deep galleries, that seem built of green marble, and
where the gurgling of water is vaguely heard like the beating
wings of sylphs, the friends of the little white fairies.

On the way down to Sion we went up to Hérémence to see
the "doctoress," the wise woman of the valley of Hérens, to
consult whom people come from great distances: from Savoy,
from Canton Fribourg, and from every corner of the Valais.

A boy guides us through the bewildering confusion of
barns and storehouses and old châlets, that make the streets
and lanes of Hérémence an inextricable labyrinth. We

arrive in front of a wooden house, the door of which stands open ; we pass through an entirely dark kitchen into a square room, where we find the doctoress sitting on a bench writing at a large table. A soft air fills the room, for the windows, contrary to the usual peasant custom, are not hermetically closed. A man is looking on while she writes on a long strip of paper in large letters, like those of a child's copybook. The wise woman, already old, has the face of a polecat, with the dull, pale complexion of a person who is little out in the open air and sunshine. Her hands are clean, washed with soap, almost white. She wears the costume of the valley, in brown cloth with short waist ; round her neck the little red silk kerchief, and on her head the straw hat with broad brims, trimmed with a wide black ribbon.

By-and-by she lays down her pen, reads over what she has written, moving her thin lips ; then she looks at us. Her clear, shining grey eyes are like those of a cat. They glitter with cunning and intelligence, and examine us with a rather distrustful expression ; and when we try to pass ourselves off as real patients, she only laughs at us and says, jeeringly, "*Pouah!* nothing the matter ! Not sick ! Come to laugh ! *That* is sick," and she points to a poor woman with drawn, wasted face, and the look of a consumptive person, who has come in while she was giving her final instructions in *patois* to a man who was leaning with both hands on his umbrella while he listened.

When he had gone, the doctoress turned to the woman who had sunk down on the bench.

"Poor thing, you very sick, must put oiled blister on chest."

The woman, who belonged to the village, went out, saying nothing. When she had closed the door behind her, the doctoress added, as if speaking to herself, "Very ill . . . going to die."

Seeing that it was impossible to obtain from her a prescription for myself,—and we are assured that among her prescriptions are mixtures of serpents' blood, and frogs cut in two, and that a grave apothecary of Sion really prepares these witches' potions,—I next tried to make her talk; but the old woman was on her guard. One would have said she scented the journalist. She told me, however, that she had begun to practise medicine at the age of sixteen.

"How did you learn?" I asked her.

"In my grandfather's books."

"Oh! it would be exceedingly kind if you would allow me to see them."

In a short cold tone, and with a gesture of refusal, she replied,—

"That, no. Are there, locked up. Show to nobody." Then she added that the Sion doctors, who were jealous of her, and had a great ill-will against her because she cured all the people they could not cure, had tried to take her books from her, but had not been able; that they had had her sent to prison for practising medicine illegally; but that she only laughs at them, for she knows more about it than they do. Her grandfather, Stéphan, was "a great magician." He came from Germany. Was taken prisoner by the Turks, "who used to eat their prisoners;" but had contrived to escape from his prison, fled to the Valais and came to Hérémence, where he carried on the trade of a smith. When he escaped, he had been able to carry off a book with him, and it was by studying this book that he became "a great magician." Then she added, "My parents left property; I ask one franc a visit."

At last, in exchange for this moderate sum, she consented to give me two recipes.

"If bitten serpent, must apply quickly slices of hen's flesh. And if have cancer, slices of toasted bread steeped in vinegar."

We bit our lips that we might not laugh aloud. I had turned towards the door, and among a row of photographs I saw the portraits of MM. Koebel, father and son, apothecaries at Sion, who are the authorized dispensers of all the aged quack's extraordinary prescriptions.

She also related to us that one day a man came down the mountain to ask her for " a medicine that would kill his brother."

"Sent *him* to the doctor at Sion," said she, with a loud laugh.

As I was examining a painting that adorned the upper part of an old piece of furniture, she said,—

"Pretty! Painted by French deserter, once student of theology. . . . Did a stupid thing. . . . Killed his captain, and came here, to Hérémence. Was joiner. Is dead."

We asked ourselves, as we left, if this woman really had all her reason, or if all that she had said to us was just her way of saying nothing at all, and laughing at us.

In returning to the road we met a worthy priest riding ; his maid-servant, who was neither canonically old nor ugly, but fresh and rosy, walked behind, teasing the mule with a little sharp stick.

Suddenly we come in sight, on both sides of the dusty road, of pyramids of various sizes, shooting up, thin and light, and crowned with enormous flat stones. These are the famous pyramids of Hérémence ; formed by the slow sinking down of the sand under the action of rain and wind.

At nine in the evening we are at Sion, happy to meet, at the excellent table of the Hotel du Midi, the faces of Swiss artists who live in Paris, M. Pata, M. Bieler, and M. H. van Muyden, who have come to the Valais for the purpose of making water-colour drawings and studies for pictures.

M. Bieler has exhibited his pictures in London, where they had an enormous success. His great picture, "Leaving the Church at Savièze," which made a sensation in the Salon, has been bought by the museum of Lausanne.

M. Pata's "Dent Blanche,"—a master work, a mountain landscape worthy of Courbet—has gone I know not where.

Pata has wonderful talent; he is a charming artist, with

21

a sensitive soul, a mind teeming with fancy, and his heart
in his finger ends. At Sion everybody knew him, everybody
loved him. He was the popular man. From morning to
night people were calling him to come and drink, in the
open street, from the great tubs in which the grapes were
floating in the sweetened must. And Pata drank,—drank
like a joyous bee going from flower to flower.

In the vintage season, what a delightful town this little
white Sion is, lying in a voluptuous enjoyment that is truly
Italian, among its leafy bowers ! And what a place for kind
people !

We were obliged to tear ourselves forcibly away from the
delights of this gay little town, so amiable, so hospitable,
and so curious, both from a historical and an artistic point
of view. We were obliged to take leave of the venerable
and excellent bishop, the good Monsignor Jardinier, who is
so good a labourer in the vineyard, and who gave us to
taste of the joys of heaven while offering us the enjoyments
of earth, by passing in review before us the whole succession
of the noble growths in the vineyard of the Lord. We
were obliged to bid adieu to Savièze, smiling under its wal-
nut-trees, and to its graceful peasant girls, the prettiest in
the Valais, whom we went to visit with the painter Ritz and
other artist friends. We were obliged to come down from
the delicious hotel among the pasture-châlets, perched like
a nest among the larches, above the burning valley of the
Rhone. Setting out by the first train for Martigny, we went
up to the Forclaz and to the Trient Glacier ; then came down
by the Tête Noire and Finhaut to Salvan ; and from Salvan,
spread out in its magnificent green meadows, facing the
Dent du Midi, we went, on the second day, to rejoin the
railway at Vernayaz. Then from Glion we went on foot
towards Les Avants, and crossed the Col de Jaman to
finish our vacation journey with Canton Fribourg and the
Gruyère.

PART V.

IN THE GRUYÈRE.

CHAPTER I.

FROM the Col de Jaman, the view is superb; at your feet blue Leman, of a soft blue like a periwinkle, frames its great sheet of water in vineyards and mountains. The steamers go to and fro on it like great black and white flies.

To the south the Rochers de Naye, crumbling with age, dislocated, disintegrated, show their pointed ridges, worn and frayed by the winds; and further off is the Tour d'Ay, of the faded colour of a ruin, lodging the last of the fairies in its crevasses; and still farther away, the great mountains of Valais, calm as giants in eternal repose. Near them rises a pale white mountain, like a marble sarcophagus, Mount St. Bernard.

To the north the eye sweeps as far as the Moléson to the Dent de Broc, to Mortheys, to the Vanil Noir, which stands out like a reef in the midst of the sea of the Fribourg Alps; on the other side, one can see to Jura across an infinite expanse of blue and white; in the greyness of the sky which comes low, low down, a train of little humpbacked mountains makes one think of a caravan of camels, stopped on the edge of the forest, and half hidden by dust.

The frontier of the Canton of Vaud crossed, we arrive

soon at the little hamlet of Allières, on Fribourg territory. A gendarme and a curé, whom we see seated at table together, suggest to us that we are in the country of good gendarmes and of good curés, the country of big monks with florid cheeks and jolly expansive person, of sweet *religieuses* of every colour, of pretty nuns, fresh and rosy as wild strawberries. In this happy canton, the curés say, " *Our* land, *our* peasants, *our* excellent Government." Everything is theirs, everything belongs to them, both earth and heaven.

And this canton is not only a paradise for gendarmes and ecclesiastics, but it is a place of incomparable delight to the dreamer, the poet, the artist, whose eyes see nothing but the little paths bordered with nut trees, the clear sweet brooks, the meadows decked with flowers, the forests carpeted with moss, the smiling villages under the apple trees, the great mountains rising into the blue air, and at the top, white châlets, surrounded with the most beautiful herds in the world, great spotted cows with pink muzzles and kind deep eyes.

La Gruyère is the most picturesque part of the Canton of Fribourg, the mountainous part shut in by the Vaudois and Bernese Alps. It is the Oberland of French Switzerland. An Oberland without glaciers, but without railways ; [1] an Oberland with *diligences* and knapsacks, simple, gay, charming, *bon-enfant*, without pretentious hotels with gilded dining-rooms, waiters like apes, and bills higher than the Jungfrau. It is still the old hospitable Switzerland, idyllic and pastoral. Its hotels are inns ; but how comfortable one is there, how much at one's ease, and at what ludicrous prices ! You can have " *pension*,"—service, light, and bedroom, everything included, for four or five francs a day. [2] There

[1] The railway stops at Bulle ; it is joined to Romont (Lausanne-Berne line) by a branch.

[2] Wine alone is extra ; it is the native wine, and costs 80 centimes the litre.

was indeed, not long ago, a *pension* at 2 fr. 50! The price of a first breakfast in Paris. And to think that I know many people who live with the fixed idea that the Swiss innkeepers are the robbers of the *diligence!* They forget, as I cannot too often repeat, that there are two ways of travelling : to go as an artist, as a seeker after new impressions and sensations, or as a human package, a bale of flesh, packed in a top-coat. Artists alight at modest hotels, the old inns, where they are sure to meet with natives of the country, with types which interest and amuse them ; the others give themselves up, like the sheep of Panurge, to be shorn to the skin in those great stupid vulgar hotels, built for the English and Americans, and which disfigure every landscape in which they are found. Those hotels stick a flaming bill on your luggage,—the label of those who only travel for vanity, richly and stupidly,—and the hosier from London or the pork butcher from Chicago go on their way proud of this distinction.

We descend by a delicious road, shaded by the protecting branches of the great pines. A torrent, the Hongrin, roars at our feet. Near an old bridge the path divides ; crossing the water, you go towards Montbovon and Chateau d'Oex, the valley of Rougemont, and Zweisimmen ; continuing the first road and taking the hill on the slope, we arrive at the little village of Albeuve, on the way to Gruyère, to Charmey and Bulle.

Now it is pastures that we cross, rich, fat pastures, where we find a few rustic houses with pots of flowers in their windows ; and round them, like a double girdle, one variegated and one all green, lie a garden and a vineyard. Splendid cows browse among the succulent herbs swelled with the aromatic juices which perfume the milk of which the celebrated Gruyère cheeses are made. They are known and appreciated throughout the word, but by one of those whimsicalities which it is impossible to explain, the admirable little country which gives name to them, is still neglected and almost ignored by the foreigner. And yet where will you find more velvet lawns, more fresh and tranquil woods, paths so shady and sweet, mountains where you can have excursions to your wish, either restful walks or easy ascents not exceeding 8,200 feet ?

The triumph of Gruyère is in its wooded hills, with clearings opening on wide horizons of jagged peaks and profound gorges, clothed nevertheless in a unique verdure, where hundreds of herds graze. It is a land of vigour and health, rich in soil, rich in climate, and above all, rich in streams which water and fertilize it with their rocky deposits. It maintains an unequalled race of oxen, and its valleys have the fertility of the Norman plains, and the beauty of the food-producing countries. And, above all, it is the country of devoted hearts, of lofty souls, of open minds.

Gruyère has given birth to a crowd of eminent men who have made themselves illustrious in politics, in literature, in arts and sciences ; and it has been the cradle of the liberalism of Fribourg. It is from there that the signal has been given for all the noble revolts, and it was the mountaineers who, with their cudgels, drove the oligarchal Government of 1830 from Fribourg.

In 1798, the French were welcomed nowhere in the canton with more enthusiasm than in Gruyère. In every village they planted the tricolor. Bands of armed peasants marched singing to meet the French battalions.

One is specially struck in mountainous countries with the intimate relations which subsist between man and the soil on which he dwells. These mountaineers, full of the energy of this powerful nature, are of extraordinary strength, with the muscles of athletes; and they have the joy, the open robust cheerfulness, of their beautiful mountains, of their mild and smiling valleys; but in the goodnature of the peasant of Gruyère there is a charming vein of mischief, a touch of finely-pointed irony.

If it is true that the soul of a people is to be found in its songs,—the "*Ranz des Vaches,*" the national song of Gruyère, reveals their whole soul to us. It is not only the song of melancholy, of the homesickness in which the expatriated Swiss sees again as in a musical vision the châlet in which he was born, the mountains where the herds shake their bells as they graze; it is a satirical song as well,—a delightful picture of their manners, of their keen and quick wit.

It is only in the refrain that we hear the heart-rending, melancholy note, in this "*liauba, liauba pô-âriâ,*" thrown lingeringly to the winds, and going from echo to echo till it expires like a lament, and is lost like a sigh in the infinite depths of the valleys.

The contrast is striking between this refrain, of so poignant a sadness, and the couplets which precede it. The measure of the couplets is merry, full of gaiety and movement; their point, so satirical and so Gallic, makes of the "*Ranz des Vaches*" a delicious little comic poem.

It is the spring time; the mountain which a fortnight ago was quite white is now quite green; and the herd sets forth on its solemn march to the alpine pastures. But they have been in too great haste to set out; arriving at the edge of a torrent, they cannot pass; the water is still too high. What is to be done? What they do in the village whenever they are in a difficulty; go and knock at the door of the curé. But the sceptical Pierre replies to those who give this advice :—

> " Que voulez-vous que je lui dise,
> À notre brave curé?

Will a mass be sufficient perhaps?

Pierre goes down to the village. He goes to knock at the door of the parsonage, and it is a pretty servant who opens to him, her coquettish white apron showing against her dress.

Introduced to the curé, the shepherd explains to him the critical situation of the herd, and adds :—

> " Il faut que vous nous disiez une messe,
> Pour que nous puissions passer."

The good curé replies :—

> " Pauvre Pierre, si tu veux passer,
> *Il te faudrait me donner un petit fromage,*
> *Mais tu ne dois pas l'écrémer.*"

This is the first arrow ; those which follow are all vibrating with a fine satire and with irony. Pierre replies :—

> " Envoyez-nous votre servante ;
> Nous lui ferons un bon fromage gras."

> " *Ma servante est trop jolie,*
> *Vous pourriez bien me la garder,*"

responds the curé.

> " N'ayez pas peur, notre prêtre ;
> Nous n'en sommes pas si affamés.
> Et de trop embrasser votre servante
> Il faudrait peut-être nous confesser ;
> *De prendre le bien de l'Eglise,*
> *Nous ne serions pas pardonnés.*

This has an air of being nothing at all ; but what profound criticism, what biting satire in this dialogue between the mountaineer and the curé !

This literary side of the " *Ranz des Vaches* " has scarcely been remarked, but it is for us literary people the curious and interesting side of this charming comic poem in *patois.*

This population of so fine a humour has nevertheless endured for about ten years a depression which can only be attributed to the system of Government in the Canton of Fribourg,—a system of espionage, of shabby, base little tricks, of a policy mean and personal, striking without pity and tracking like dangerous animals every one who does not think like the syndics and prefects, every one who does not prostrate himself before the golden calf of the Government. The members of the old Conservative-Liberal party who succeeded to the Government sprung from the radical revolution of 1848 are now-a-days disgraced, insulted, put on the index, excluded from all the employments and councils of the Government; the venerable Bishop Marilley, an old prisoner of Chillon, fell into disgrace and was forced to give in his resignation and go into retirement; it is the young ultramontane and socialist school who have monopolised all the authority of the country. Its organs, *La Liberté* and *L'Ami du Peuple* (a sort of Père Duchesne), are directed and edited by an ex-professor of the college of Gimont, obliged to go abroad to hide his disaffection.

But this is enough of politics for a traveller, who does not make a business of them. How much more interesting at present is this road on which we are walking than these ferocious party quarrels, these rendings of one another, among men whom the Gospel calls brethren! Let us rather look at these flowery hedges, garlanded with blue blind-weed, whose blossoms filled with dew are open to all the birds of heaven, without distinction of plumage or song.

The sun has gone down behind the mountain; sheets of red, chased with gold, float on the horizon, and the trees stand out in black silhouettes. From the bottom of the valley rises a blue mist, which comes out of the forest, fills the hollows, blots out and effaces all the projections. The copper tints of the sky pass into pale rainbow hues, then to a faint pearl grey. Here and there spots still appear like great baskets of crimson roses. The pine woods blacken and take the appearance of big blots of ink. The dogs bark and answer each other from the different farms. The bells of the cows and the little goat-bells sound more distinct, more sonorous. A vague murmur rises from the villages. Birds pass rapidly, with the silent flight of bats. We hear the cries of the children at their play, the songs of young girls returning from their work. A stretch of the Sarine shows itself in its rapid course, shining in the distance among the pines. The windows of Lessoc and of

Albeuve twinkle with lights. An infinite sweetness, a deep and penetrating calmness and peace, fall on us from the sky and the mountains. And whilst in the sleeping fields the quails call to one another, and the crickets give themselves up to their nightly revels, the stars open their golden eyelids, and the moon noiselessly unfolds her great silver fan.

CHAPTER II.

ARRIVING at Albeuve at nightfall, we spent the whole of the next day there, resting from the fatigue of a journey of about ten hours without break. Albeuve, burnt down about ten years ago, is no longer the charming village it was formerly, with old houses, the wood reddened by the sun, the overhanging roofs covered with shingle and moss, with large chimneys by which the white smoke escapes, and the happy swallows enter, like messengers of heaven, the protecting spirits of the hearth. Albeuve, with its paltry stone houses, without distinction or originality, has the air of a suburb, the melancholy aspect of a manufacturing town. But what is not changed is the goodness of those excellent people, the amiability of the host and hostess of The Angel. No doubt they are bound over to this by their signboard : but the profession of angel is a terribly diffi-cult one in this world, even for an innkeeper who subscribes to *La Liberté* and to *L'Ami du Peuple*; and even although they give their readers the receipt for acquiring all per-fections, and all happiness in this world and the other— a receipt easy and not costly, which is summed up in

two words, "Be one of us." What a model of amenity,
urbanity and kindness, is this establishment of M. Musy!
You can hardly believe that it is at a hotel you have
alighted, so much do they surround you with attentions.
I should like to see one of those superb *maîtres d'hôtel* from
Lucerne or Interlaken come here, who imagine that Switzerland was created expressly for their use; what astonished
eyes he would open at the sight of all these kind attentions
without servility, at the innate cordiality of the mountaineers of Fribourg!

In the afternoon, after one of those plentiful and excellent
repasts which the cook of The Angel knows how to prepare,
M. Musy harnessed his *char-à-bancs* and conveyed us to
the foot of Gruyères, a picturesque little feudal town, forgotten by progress, which always takes the shortest cut,
and passes below on the high road.

Gruyère is planted on the summit of a lofty isolated knoll
overlooking the Sarine, the valley of Upper Gruyère, and the
long plain of Lower Gruyère. Its castle rises with a look
of royal magnificence into the blue sky, with its towers, its
pointed roofs, its sparkling tin weather-cocks, its red dormer
windows, its broad white façade, pierced with great bright
windows, and a little wood thrown like a velvet carpet at
its feet. Its founder must have been not only a warrior,
but an artist, for he could not have chosen a finer situation,
more conspicuous, more beautifully framed. When you see
a drawing or photograph of Gruyère, you would say it was
a vignette of the 15th century; the road, paved with great
pebbles, rises with the steepness of a scaling-ladder to a
double gate flanked with salient towers like pepper-boxes,
with a little round way for the sentry. The houses in
massive stone, constructed with very high dormers, and
hanging galleries, for observation and defence, are set close
together, and form a rampart; the belfry of the Maison de
Ville lifts its slender spire, which is seen from every quarter;
and higher up, at the extremity of the hill, surrounded by

strong walls, entrenched behind a second rampart, we see the red roofs of the castle and its towers.

Here we are climbing like goats the road which leads to the little town. The ascent is rough, the pavement uneven and angular. This cart track is called the "track of the dead," and after a few steps it is easy to see it has not been made for the living. We pass under an old gateway of romantic effect, and arrive in front of a great wooden cross, on which hangs a bleeding, expiring Christ; we find right before us a little stair, and ascending, we are in the principal street of the town—which has only two—in front of a curious house with its façade ornamented with heads of grinning clowns, rams' heads, armorial bearings, suns; its gargoyles are like the jaws of serpents; the windows of the first floor are framed in fine, lace-like sculptures, while those of the ground floor are curiously paired, married in assorted couples. The door, with its arch of a carmine red, is all ornamented with old iron work in strange arabesque designs. This house, of an architecture unique in Switzerland, and constructed by Italian masons in the middle of the 15th century, is the old house of the Count of Gruyère's fool, Gerard Chalamala. Inside, old frescoes are still to be found on the walls, and fragments of mottos, which could only have been thought out by a fool,—

"A spotted toad met on the way does not diminish the splendid majesty of the mountains, the beauty of the landscape, the freshness of the springs, the caressing sweetness of the meadows."

"Little souls alone have the secret of little souls."

"The resignation which is acquired with age, and which we take for the fruit of reflection and wisdom, is nothing but the first decay of the mind and of the strength of the soul."

We mount to the castle by a gentle slope, passing under the gate St. Germain and in front of an almshouse, its windows gay with delicious flowers, great bushes of china-asters, red geraniums, and pinks, which hang like draperies of old rose-coloured silk. Near the road a *religieuse* is weeding a garden in which are growing some very green lettuces, carrots, onions, and parsley. Some old men, already as dry as mummies, are leaning against the hedge, or sitting half asleep on the trunks of trees.

The castle is open at every hour of the day with a liberality of which only a proprietor as amiable as M. Balland is capable. We come first to a wide esplanade planted with trees, a terrace forming a rampart at the top of a steep escarpment. From the first step we see with what respect for both art and tradition, with what love, this castle has been preserved. None of those ridiculous additions which disclose a *bourgeois* spirit without taste and without pity. No glazed round towers, no Chinese kiosks on this vast fortified terrace, from which the eye can embrace all the magnificence of Lower Gruyère, that great basket of verdure in the midst of which the red roofs of Bulle look like a heap of apples. The eye reaches as far as the Gibloux Mountains, which stretch away in a diminishing perspective of woods and meadows. To the right the Sarine, cold daughter of the Sanetsch glacier, winds its silver links below the Chapel of Les Marches,—spoiled by a stupid addition,—and washes with its waves the little cliff on which still stands the empty steeple of the old church of Broc. A little higher is the village of the same name, its white and brown houses on a line with the top of the hills. And still farther in the depths of the blue valley are Charmey, Valsainte, the Black Lake, and the twisted peaks of the valley of Bellegarde, and of the Rio du Motélon: regions of rugged mountains with battlements of rocks, veritable fortresses in granite, like the Gastlosen, the Inhospitable.

Opposite the Dent de Broc, a harsh peak that seems to rend the sky rises on the left. It is the king of the Fribourg Alps, the Moléson. A whole people of inferior mountains appear as if bending before him; and at his base, on the first slopes of a little hill, we can see a new châlet with a sculptured balcony, and with tall poplars beside it, waving like plumes in the wind; it is the Baths of Montbarry, in the solitude and repose of an eclogue.

How sweet and calm is the whole landscape! In the midst of green meadows, with their abundant and tender herbage, the farmhouses smile behind their flowery gardens, under their great roofs of shingle, which cover them as if in a cowl. It is the beautiful situation which takes from this castle the melancholy and sadness of old manor-houses.

And how lovely the nights are on this high terrace which brings you near the stars! One walks as if in a dream, picturing to one's self the times when the castle was animated with its stirring feudal and warlike life. On the top of the towers the sentinels watched,—on the round way was heard the slow, measured tread of the men-at-arms. The drawbridge was raised, the portcullis let down, the gates were barred; all was tranquil and silent in the valley. In the hall, before the great monumental fireplace, where logs of oak were burning, cavaliers were seated in wide, carved arm-chairs; the count and the countess surrounded by their children; the chaplain, the notary; a brilliant suite of ladies, of cavaliers and pages; and Chalamala in his fool's costume, and shaking the bells of his cap, related stories and legends, improvised verses and songs. Chalamala presided also over the " Council of Fools." The Count Pierre had his place there, but he could only appear without his spurs; for when he married Catherine de Thurm, having asked his fool what he thought of the union, he replied : " If I were lord and master, I would send that ugly woman about her business and keep my beloved mistress." The count, in his anger, thanked him by sending his spurs into the fool's calves.

At this council of folly were discussed grave questions of carnival fêtes, of games and diversions ; they passed in

22

review all the good tricks of the pages and the love stories of the young ladies.

It was a court elegant and gay—a little French court—this court of Gruyère, which was the most charming and graceful in Switzerland. The counts were like the princes of romance, " the fathers of their subjects." They went among the mountains to bring justice to the threshold of the châlets; they adopted orphans; they gave dowries to poor girls; were first in the popular festivals and in combat; disputed the prize in strife with the shepherds, and themselves led the " coraules," the long sportive dances which stretched, accompanied with singing, to the length of two or three leagues. As it ascended the valley and unrolled its rings, the " coraule " was augmented by all the inhabitants, young and old, of the villages that it passed through. " Once," says the legend, " the dance began on Sunday with seven persons on the lawn of the castle, went up the valley increasing always, and finished on Tuesday morning at Gessnay with a chain of 700 dancers."

The last count, Michel, passed for the most accomplished cavalier of his time. Tall of stature, of sweet and noble features, he was a thorough prince, sumptuous and hospitable, a popular hero, generous, and full of bravery. But a bad management of his property, costly residences at foreign courts, a regiment of 2,000 men, which he equipped at his own cost and placed at the service of the King of France against the Imperialists and the Spaniards, ruined him. Declared bankrupt by the Diet of Baden, his lands and estates were put up for sale and bought by the Governments of Berne and Fribourg. In his financial distress, Michel gathered his subjects in the square of the town and said to them : " Charge yourselves with my debts, and I will enfranchise you for ever; you shall be as the bourgeois of the small cantons, and it will be my happiness to live among you." But the majority of the communes rejected this proposal, and, on the 9th November, 1555, the last Count of

Gruyère quitted his estates for ever, leaving an illegitimate daughter, to whom the Government of Fribourg allowed a pension of a few crowns.

We enter the castle, crossing a little court, the walls of which are fortified on the side of the esplanade. This double circumvallation made a surprise impossible. A spiral stair leads to the second storey—the most curious from a historical and archæological point of view. A roof in compartments with cranes (grues) of silver, a fireplace which bears engraved on its wide front the coats-of-arms of the counts, frescoes representing the principal deeds and the legendary episodes of the history of Gruyère, make this great hall quite a princely place. To begin with, here is Gruerius arriving first in the country and giving to it the name of the bird painted on his banner. Then there is the founding of a pious abbey, the departure of the Gruyèriens for the Crusade, with the cry: "It is for us to go; come back who can!" [1] Another painting shows a flock of goats, with horns on fire, putting the Bernese soldiers to flight. The women of Gruyère were alone in the town; seeing themselves attacked, they tied torches and lighted tapers to the horns of their goats, and, during the night, drove them towards the encampment of the enemy. The terrified Bernese, thinking they had to deal with a legion of demons, fled at the quickest. Further, we see a Count of Gruyère, with an enormous white plume, delivering a noble foreign lady, a prisoner in the castle of Rue. A very careful composition illustrates the legend of Jehan l'Escloppé, received at the table of the countess, and announcing to her the birth of a son. Last of all there are the two heroes, Clarimboz and Bras-de-Fer, who themselves, with their heavy double-edged swords, kept a whole crowd of Bernese at bay. These frescoes are the work of the former proprietor of the castle, a Genevese artist, M. Daniel Bovy.

The tower of torture has been transformed into a museum

[1] "S'agit d'aller, reviendra qu pourra ! '

of arms. The old tattered banners which hang on the walls have been dyed on glorious battle-fields. One of these flags was taken by the Gruyèriens from the Savoyards at the battle of Morat.

The corridors are encumbered with old carved chests, and other valuable old furniture, and in high glazed cupboards are piled collections of rare objects, precious pottery, curious trinkets, gathered from almost everywhere at great pains and cost. Looking at all this wealth of art and the truly marvellous state of preservation of this castle, we ask ourselves what would have become of it, if by chance it had fallen into other hands. The State was about to sell it to a contractor for building materials, for no one could be found, even among the Fribourg nobility, to save the historical monument from certain destruction, when two Genevese, MM. J. and Daniel Bovy offered the same sum as the mason, engaging to restore and preserve the castle. Daniel Bovy, a pupil of Ingres, then came and installed himself at Gruyères. The round tower was an abyss; the terrace a potato field; the roofs were in holes, as if they had sustained a rain of small shot; the rooms, which had served as prisons and guard-rooms for the gendarmerie, gave out suffocating odours, and their walls were adorned with sentences which had not been inspired by Monsieur the Curé; the wind howled at night, rushing in at the broken windows; everything was in a state of dilapidation and ruin. The gothic chests in the count's chamber had served as racks for guns! When once the great repairs were finished and the walls whitened, all Daniel's comrades, all the artists with whom he had studied in Paris, arrived, like a valiant army of decorators. And Corot, Français, Leleux, Baron, Menn, executed these admirable panels, and these beautiful medallions which make of one of the halls on the first floor a marvellous Louis XVth salon. Corot painted there a small view of an ideal Gruyère, all golden, with a superb tree in the foreground; he also painted a wood-cutter in a lofty forest; a spot of red among the green. Baron dressed beautiful ladies in toilets with furbelows and collarettes of aristocratic elegance; Français threw off an admirable landscape; Leleux painted flowers and garlands that seem to wave. This Watteau-like salon in the severe gothic castle, has the effect of a parterre of flowers in the midst of a pine wood.

And to think that there are people so devoid of sentiment of every kind as to deplore that the castle of Gruyères has become the property of a Genevese family! The restoration of this old manor has cost a fortune. It is not only the most beautiful old castle in Switzerland, but it is besides a historical and archæological museum which would be the pride of a great State.

CHAPTER III.

IN descending again to the town, we stopped at an ale-
house, the inn of the "Halle," which "gives lodging to
man and beast." There we saw a couple who interested us
greatly; seated on a wooden bench before a litre of wine
and a plate of bonbons, the man and woman were talking
in low voices, whispering tender things to one another. At
the end of the table was an older woman, who raised from
time to time the lid of a basket in which lay a new-born
child, crying. It was a baptism. The young man and
woman were godfather and godmother, and the woman with
the basket was the nurse. They have such a fear of
children dying without baptism, that they baptize them
some hours after their birth ; and when they come from a
little distance they are carried in a basket. A mother who
waits two days before having the stain of original sin
effaced, is considered to be a woman without religion. So
that of all Swiss children, it is the children of Fribourg that
are most numerous in Paradise. When St. Peter hears
himself summoned by the wailing of an infant of a day and

a half old, he never fails to say, smiling in his grey beard :
" I wager it is another little Fribourger !" and he opens
the wicket, and it is indeed a citizen of the Canton of
Fribourg who enters to augment the choir of angels and
to speak well of the Government.

In front of the inn of the " Halle " is a whole row of
singular stones, hollowed like vases with an opening at the
bottom. They are the old corn measures. Opposite, a little
higher up, is a stone in which the stake was fixed to which
they formerly tied thieves; the church is to the right, at
the foot of a little slope, but having suffered from fire about
thirty years ago, it offers absolutely nothing remarkable.
The statutes which the Curé Pierre de Gruyère gave in the
year 1550 to his clergy, throw a curious light on the manners
of the epoch ; he says: " He who having received a legacy,
does not call those who have the keys of the cash-box, that
he may pour it in there, shall be declared perjured." " Whoever cannot perform his service by reason of ignorance or for
want of voice, shall have a substitute and shall pay five sols,
every time that he does not present himself at the choir."
" He who arrives last shall carry the cross." " Whoever
absents himself for a year shall not be received unless he
gives a dinner to his brethren." " He who is not shaved on
solemn days, especially when the curé gives a dinner, shall
pay three sols." " The offerings which are made when wine
is brought to be blessed, belong only to the curé." " He who
dances *publicly* shall pay five sols ; nevertheless, on days of
a first mass, or on the marriage of relations, *he may dance
three dances.*"

Now-a-days, not only do the curés of Gruyères not dance,
but so far as they can they hinder every one else from
dancing.

The great street of Gruyères, with its houses of old date,
with great painted and half effaced cranes, its pavements
set in grass, its air of poverty and desolation, abuts on a
fountain where all the gossips of the town hold council,

then passes under the arch of a gate, and descends to the left, towards Pringy and Montbarry.

In the plain we find once more a delightful animation, and the hedges in flower, the trees, the gentle hills, make you forget the horrible old creatures grimacing above, round the fountain of the little town. The meadows widen, the road passes before a chapel and enters a little wood. The freshness is delicious. A blackbird whistles, while a bullfinch, with a black head and a red waistcoat, sings with all his might on the top of a pine tree. Now and then a squirrel, immovable on a branch, his tail raised like a plume, looks at you with his little black eyes; or a terrified hare, his ears erect and stiff, scampers away across the meadows. A little farther off the jays are calling, beautiful jays, with wings veined with azure, and whose cry is like a mocking note. Then it is a cuckoo, hidden and solitary, a cuckoo, uttering his cry of a sad and ugly bird, of a bird hypocritical and wicked, who is watching the propitious moment for taking possession of the nest of others. We cross a torrent fringed with lofty pines, arranged like the trees of an avenue. Briers throw over the bushes their ragged greenness, with red and white roses full of wild odours. And one feels wrapped in a great peace, plunged in a deep repose.

In a few minutes we arrive at Montbarry, the most primitive, simple, and modest of hôtel-châlets, but pretty in the white neatness of new pinewood, and situated like few of the Swiss hotels, on the edge of the wood, half-way up a green hill, having Bulle, with its red roofs, to the right, Gruyère, with its feudal castle and its old, embattled gate, to the left; at its feet emerald meadows, fields of golden grain, a whole graduated scale of pasture and cultivation; the freshness of great trees, of oaks and pines, shading lovely paths which run along by the happy brooks, and all around a magnificent horizon of summits with jagged sides, or covered with forests and pastures, in the midst of which a few châlets stand out clearly.

The balcony of the hotel opens like the box of a theatre on the admirable scenery of this vast amphitheatre. And it seems as if we were not staying at a hotel, but as if we had come to rest for some hours or days in a friendly little house, built there as a halting-place or a place of repose for passers-by; where those enervated by town, or fatigued with life, as well as tourists and climbers, find a beneficent repose, calmness of spirit and nerves, and the joy of health.

A sulphur spring which works miracles, and which has for fifty years cured all the rheumatic and gouty people of the country, attracts every summer to this privileged station as many people as can be contained in a hotel six times too small. All that is wanting is a doctor who can create, a Bonnefille, to transform this unknown and superb corner into a Mont-Oriol. Success would be certain and easy, for in all this delightful Gruyère there is not a single hotel for foreigners worthy of the name. But is this change to be desired? This land, almost untrodden as yet by English, what will become of it in the day when Cook leads there his long caravans? Montbarry will no longer be a sweet nest, a nest of peace and silence, hidden in a well-chosen retreat, almost in the wood, at the foot of the great, calm summit of Moléson. The happiness of its obscurity will be at an end, and yellow omnibuses with white horses will bring to it the noise and the mud of cities.

We passed the rest of the month of September here. And when it rained we improvised, in a shed, concerts and comedies, which brought all the peasants of the neighbourhood running to us. My son had established a theatre of marionettes, which amused them much more than our pieces. The peasant, let him be as cunning and crafty as he likes, has kept in a corner of his soul the *naiveté* of the child; and actions, facts, the blows of a stick given to the beadle, the policeman carried off by the devil, the bailiff thrashed, the wicked woman horsewhipped, the apothecary made game of—these things interest him much more than the

cooings of Clitander and Leander, scenes of love and sentiment which he does not understand, because he has never
experienced them as literature expresses them. On rainy
days we hunted—they hunt here the chamois, the hare, the
fox, the gelinotte or hazel-hen, the heath-cock, the quail,
the snipe, etc.,—for we made use of the days of sunshine to
take long walks in large companies, or in climbing. We
went to Grandvillars and its cascade, to the Lake of
Coudray, to the Dent de Broc, to Charmey to eat trout, to
Valsainte to drink Chartreuse, to Bellegarde, and to that
gem, the Black Lake, enclosed like a great bead of jet in a
stern setting of rocks, mountains, and forests. Three or
four times we climbed Moléson to see the sun rise over the
Bernese Alps, over Mont Blanc, over the Lakes of Geneva,
Neufchatel, and Morat. When we arrived at the top of the
mountain, the moon still shone, but quite small, gleaming
like a carbuncle. Long veils of mist floated over the plains
and the valleys. The red line which cut the horizon paled
as we looked, passed into a pale orange, and then gradually
died away. The sky became illuminated like a theatre
when the footlights are raised. To the right, in the direction of Valais, clouds more vividly lighted up resembled
sheets of burnished copper. The enormous mass of Mont
Blanc was bathed in a milky vapour which became transparent, its lofty walls of snow glittering with silvery reflections were more and more resplendent in proportion as
the sun, still invisible, rose behind the high cliffs, the rocky
chains on the horizon. From the depths of the valley
distinct sounds arose, the almost imperceptible ringing of
bells which was brought to us on the passing breeze.

Finally the sun appeared, at first like a great red blot.
One could quite well gaze at it; but almost immediately it
became of a vivid red, crimson, and ensanguined. A circle
of gold surrounded it, and suddenly it blazed and dazzled,
flooding the sky with its beams, filling it with tongues and
rockets of gold. It was no longer possible to look at it; its

light was blinding, and its beams seemed to run like trem-
blings of fire to the ends of the earth, which woke to sudden
life. Set on fire with dazzling reflections, Mont Blanc rose
like a fabulous monument of red marble, a palace of porphyry built for the gods.

The whole range of the Alps of the Oberland and the
Valais was sown with little flames, with vivid lights, which
scattered, and fell in streams of living embers down the sides
of their walls of snow; while the mountains of the Canton
de Vaud and of Savoy had a fainter radiance, a less burning
red. Between the rents in the cloud one saw shining the
blue waters of Leman, and on all the slopes of the hills,
farms and villages appeared, their little houses piled up
beside the long ribbon of road like heaps of sand.

From Moléson we have not, as from the Rigi, a simple
geographical map spread at our feet. The view, though
more restricted, is more familiar and full of pictures which
interest and amuse us. Here it is the Sarine which
meanders through dark forests, or at the foot of great grey
rocks; there, surrounded by a silver mist, the lakes of
Seedorf and of Morat glitter like precious stones or sparkle
like diamonds in a cloud of lace. Below is Gruyère, with its
streets in ramparts, its towers, its fortified castle. Black
forms are already moving about the fountain, like ants
round a drop of dew. And farther away in the green sheet
of plain, furrowed by silver streams, Bulle displays its red
roofs like poppies. Under the plume of smoke we see a
file of little carriages setting out: it is the train. One
would think it was a child's railway rolling on a footpath.
And quite near us, in the depths of a sky of turquoise-blue
hover beautiful mountain birds, with velvet plumage, and
wings that cut the air with the rapid flight of the swallow.

Patches of light spotted the plain, the pine woods
stretched like bands of black fur, while the fields of wheat
rolled their sheets of gold in the sun, and the meadows
spread their wide carpets of velvet.

We descended, running through the dew, in the midst of
the scents of the morning life, of the flowers opening freshly
under our feet. On these slopes spreading to the sun what
a superb flora! Bouquets hang everywhere, even on the
points of the rocks, great marriage bouquets for the peasants,
bouquets of hardy flowers which make the mountain smell
good! The names of these flowers!—oh, we care very little
about that. They were for us unknown beauties whom we
admired in passing, without asking whence they came or
what they were called. They charmed us with their beauty,
they pleased us with their perfume,—that sufficed us.

What variety and what attractions in these mountain
excursions! Every one finds his pleasure there in his own
way, with an enjoyment all his own. This one is interested
in the flora, that one in the minerals, that other in the
insects, the butterflies, the birds. And for the artist, he
finds here landscapes much more finished, more changing,
more picturesque and newer than on the sea-shore. Here
is a deep gorge, with uprooted pines bending over the foaming waters of a torrent. There a little chapel is hidden, its
spire like an extinguisher smoked with moss; under its
porch supported by huge beams, lies a mountaineer with
bare arms filling his pipe. Then there are in the forests,
that climb the slopes, mysterious sanctuaries with deep,
silent arches, and great trees lying bleeding with a red
resin, where the wood-cutter has struck them with his axe;
piles of fagots with leaves still green, extinct charcoal
kilns, clearings invaded by wild roses and long, bending,
palm-like ferns. In the pastures herds of cows wander at
will, with their white coats spotted with black, their great
bells, of an antique form, clanging like an old pot; and the
chálet rises on an esplanade, or cowers down in a hollow
under its broad, very low roof, which protects it from squalls
and tempests. And the rural scenes of the plain, so simple
and so grand! The field-work,—the peasant behind his
plough drawing his furrow; the harvest,—the swarthy mower

making his scythe fly, with its wing of steel, the beautiful
bare-armed girls binding golden sheaves, and the hay piled
on the enormous waggon, drawn by two great oxen.

On the road, too, and in the villages, what pictures!
Here are dragoons of the federal army escorting a procession of gypsies expelled from the Pays de Vaud; here are
pilgrims repairing joyously to the Chapel of Marches, their
chariot ornamented with young fir-trees with flying ribbons;
then it is a gendarme conducting a poor limping woman, or
a travelling musician who has played a little dance without
permission; there are carriages covered with dust and piled
with luggage bringing foreigners from Thun or the Château
d'Oex; or, it may be, the federal *diligence*. And then on
the fair-days and the market-days, there are long lines of
cattle for sale, cows turning their heads with an uneasy air
towards the alps they have quitted, great fat pigs, a string
round their foot, driven by women waving hazel branches;
chars-à-bancs pass with a clatter of old iron, with a calf or
a sheep lying under a net.

A great many people are going on foot along by the hedge,
the men in short, bulging blouses, a wide black felt on their
head, a wallet on their shoulder and a knotted stick in their
hand; the women in dresses of checked cotton, some of
them with a necklace and a gold cross round their neck, a
coloured apron and low shoes. The old costume is lost. It
was, however, very original, with the great lace cap which
stood out like a black aureole, the apron of light silk with a
bib, the stuff dress in classic folds. It is only the shepherds,
the "armaillis," who have kept their old mountain dress;
the waistcoat with puffed shoulders, the shirt with sleeves
in folds, and the hat, of straw a hand-breadth wide, cut out at
the back of the head like a gilded tonsure.

In the villages the stir becomes specially great at the
approach of the "bénichons," that is to say the annual fêtes,
when dancing is allowed. Then in every house they prepare
piles of fritters, they kill the fat sheep, they go to the town

to buy their little cask of white wine. And on Sunday, after vespers, the dance begins in front of the inn on a wooden platform surrounded with young fir-trees. They dance till Tuesday evening without rest, without break. And if by chance it snows, they continue to dance, under the falling flakes they turn slowly like them. The young girl makes a present, sends a handkerchief to the young man who has led her to the dance. She passes then for his "*bonne amie,*" and generally it is she whom he marries.

In summer vegetation is so exuberant, the foliage of the trees so dense, that the landscape has something harsh, energetic, wild, little fitted to please the eye of Parisian artists accustomed to the light colours of the banks of the Seine and the faint, pale trees of Corot. In Switzerland the colour is glaring, disorderly, violent in its abrupt alternations of tone.

The seasons, however, tone down and harmonize the crudities of the alpine landscapes in a charming way. The birth of spring, the slow departure of autumn, have shades of an infinite tenderness, of a moving poetry. At the end of September, the transformation of the woods is fairy-like. The oaks are surrounded with a golden aureole, the beeches are dyed in vivid red and yellow, which gradually melt away in pale and dying shades. In some places one would say that the forest is on fire, that it is full of burning bushes, and it seems as if we saw long saffron flames licking the flexible, waving branches of the pines.

In the midst of the crude greens, the blue greens, the dark greens of the meadows, the hedges make spots of crimson, of cinnabar, and of vermilion. And all the wooded hills, all the orchards, all the hedges, all the bushes along the sides of the streams, form, as it were, a marvellous symphony of colour, a concert of tones, a *pot-pourri* of varied tints and warmer shades, and replace by the gold of their leaves the sun which is absent for a while.

Some trees, young ash-trees, are like pomegranates in

flower. And solitary beeches stand like seven-branched candlesticks of copper. This warm colouring of the woods on the distant white of the mountains, already sleeping under their covering of snow, makes a striking contrast. In descending from Montbarry to Gruyères, at the bridge of Albeuve, I stopped often to admire one of these marvellous autumn landscapes. There the torrent runs with great waves, with a dull sound, among enormous white pebbles; beautiful hedges fringe its banks, nut-trees with bronzed leaves, wild cherries with crimson leaves, and barberries, like trees of coral, shed their small red fruit on the stones of the road. Near the water the osiers were purple, and on the hill-side the beeches and ashes, of the colour of old gold, mingled with the mournful black of the pines. Before me I saw the houses of the little village of Pringy, surrounded with apple-trees, and the chapel, the spire of which, covered with metal, shone like a long thimble. Everything was so calm, so tranquil; the light blue smoke which escaped from the chimneys alone indicated that the country was alive. To the left I saw Gruyère, with its heroic castle, placed like a superb *scene*, for the representation of a great opera in the open air. The old clock of the Hotel de Ville was slowly striking the hour, and crows were wheeling round its pointed spire like big black flies.

In the meadows the cows wandered, sounding their bells, goats clambered up to the hedges, a cat ran across the road, crows lighted on the meadows, or took their flight again one after the other; and a cart of manure passed, spreading abroad warm odours of the stable.

On the edge of the forest, on very high pines, you could hear the wood pigeons cooing, whilst farther away, on the oaks, jays were stuffing themselves with acorns, calling to one another, speaking loud and fast like chattering women.

Autumn is the delicious season, the voluptuous season, the season of crimson and gold. And it is not only the landscapes and the sunsets which take on incomparable and

inexpressible magnificence, but it seems that everywhere
life stirs and overflows : the fruit hangs in red bunches
from the trees, and the peasants gather it, perched on high
ladders ; along the hedges young girls, armed with long
hooked sticks, beat down the nuts into their aprons; in the
field the potatoes are piled in pyramids; the flocks browse
at the foot of the mountains; bending over the stream the
fisher catches the speckled trout that are making their way
up the stream ; and the hunter goes to track the chamois in
the defiles of the Dent de Broc, or below Moléson to surprise
the heath-cock making himself drunk on myrtle.

In autumn a sunrise in the plain is a strange spectacle.
Over the brooks and marshes long white vapours hang, and
climb to the foot of the hedges and trees; they cut the
houses in two, detach them from the soil, and make them
like little Noah's arks floating on a great lake of vapour ;
and while the valley is in mist, all the surrounding heights
shine, smitten with great strokes of light. As the sun
ascends, the veil of vapour stretched over the plain lightens,
becomes more transparent. Bushes take an outline like
submarine vegetation, half seen through the blue water of
an ocean. A crow with sombre flight crosses the line of
mist, his wings tapering like fins, giving him the appearance of a flying fish.

But in place of dispersing, the white vapours rise, mount
half-way up, hide the little mount of Gruyère, and the town
with its embattled gates, its towers, its smooth fortress
walls, its wooden galleries with watch-towers, and its bar-
bican windows. The Hotel de Ville with its belfry, and
the castle with its donjon, have the look of an aerial fortress hanging like a mirage between heaven and earth.

Surrounded by these mountains, so sweet and so hospitable,
which only evoke thoughts of an idyll, and recall no bloody
catastrophe, we have passed in this unknown corner never-to-
be-forgotten ravishing hours, with the exquisite sensation of
living hidden in a hermitage of verdure, far from the noise

of the towns and the cares of business, free from all constraint, and safe from all make-believe; like wise people
returning for a few weeks to a state of nature, and going
back to their paternal fields and forests. To strip off the
Parisian, the man of the world and of the boulevard, to become, in the midst of these scented pastures, a good, inoffensive, dreaming animal,—this is transformation enough
to cure the most pessimistic of men!

We lived in a châlet, for we had not come to Switzerland
to seek marble dining-halls and salons in velvet and gold;
our dining-room was a roomy arbour, the meadows and the
woods were our velvet salons, and the sun threw around us
enough of gold to make us very indifferent to mirrors and
console-tables.

Who would not return to this simplicity which was formerly the great attraction of Switzerland. Luxury has
become so exaggerated; the hotels have been made so large
that they have become immense wearisome barracks, where
the traveller is nothing but a number. In these long dining-
rooms with shining floors, everybody remains a stranger
to everybody else, and one always seems to be dining, between two trains, at the buffet of an international railway
station.

When nature is beautiful, the sky blue, the walks shaded
and easy, I laugh at all these luxurious *salles* and *salons*!
At Montbarry, during days of repose, we lived in a lovely
little gorge, a liliputian valley where there flowed in the
shade of the trees a brook, comically assuming the manners
of a torrent, and running into pretty little garden cascades.
There we had benches and tables, cool retreats hidden
among the foliage, and a footpath going up towards the
wood; a new landscape, an unexpected point of view opening between the branches of the trees at every step. Here
is Gruyère, set like a medallion; there is Bulle, two spots of
white and red; higher up is Charmey, with its ambitious
spire perched on a little mound, overlooking the village and

the valley. The little pathway is so narrow that only two can walk abreast, keeping close together like lovers.

> " Below, in the narrow ravine
> So mossy and flowery, there goes
> A footpath, two thickets between
> 　　Of wild rose.
>
> Shaded, for great boughs are meeting,
> With nests hid in arched leafy nooks,
> At even the murmurs repeating
> 　　Of the brooks.
>
> Narrow, for little girls tripping
> At morn, in their white garments drest,
> Cannot pass, under hazels dew-dripping,
> 　　Two abreast.
>
> Its gate a rock guards in repose,
> Moss-grown, in shade sombre and deep,
> Like a watch-dog, whose heavy eyes close,
> 　　Fast asleep.
>
> And there, too, the flocks of white goats
> Their way to the hill-pastures take,
> With bells tinkling silvery notes,
> 　　At daybreak.
>
> There lovers, on star-lighted nights,
> Go linked so that no footstep misses ;
> And cradle their love's veiled delights
> 　　In kisses.
>
> Like them, I thy solitude loved,
> Little footpath, thou knowest that yet ;
> In my study my fond heart is moved
> 　　With regret." [1]

And the silence is so profound, the air so pure, that the mere babbling of the little brook that runs among the mossy stones in the bushy embankment suffices to fill all the valley, as if a band of talkative little girls were chattering in the coppice.

[1] Translated from Albert Tinchant.

I think it is Jean-Jacques who says,—
" The only objects of which the eyes and the heart do not
tire are rural ones."

And in truth we never weary of admiring the view from
the plateau, where an arbour is placed as a belvedere. The
plain lies like an immense lake of grass, spotted with forests
as if with little black islands, on which the low houses with
their arched roofs look like heavy, immovable boats. The
slopes of the hills are of an intense green, a solid emerald
green, a substantial bushy green, a green, in fact, of Gruyère,
in which the eye plunges and bathes with exquisite sensations of dewy freshness. On these slopes, brown villages
and white churches with glittering spires are scattered in
rustic disorder; and whilst on the one hand the mountains
fall abruptly into green abysses, on the other soft valleys
open up, losing themselves in wavy undulations, in green
perspectives like those of ocean.

And in the evening when the sun was setting, the valley
was resplendent for a moment, powdered with gold-dust;
then from the folds of the ravines and from all the hollows
rose bluish diaphanous mist, which floated above the woods,
enveloping them and stretching far away, whilst the sky
decked itself with rosy spots, flights of little wandering
clouds like unknown birds. On the horizon also the clouds
took many forms and aspects. Sometimes they were islands
of fire, volcanoes, their sides running down with lava, fantastic kinds of vegetation, lofty palms, enormous crocodiles
crawling on a sand of rubies, or barks with crimson sails
which passed like luminous shadows, in the remoteness of a
dream.

Then the brilliant fairy scene died away; the sky and the
clouds paled, and took on subdued pearly tints,—the twilight was dying. In the neighbouring villages were heard
the sharp blows of the hammer making the scythes vibrate,
and the dogs answering each other. A distant symphony of
little bells, which only reached us at intervals in swells of

sound, came down from châlets perched on the surrounding
heights.   Then the crescent moon appeared between the
Dent de Broc and the Dent du Chamois, like a silver sickle,
all shining, freshly sharpened.

When in the evening the wind blew, and we heard the
dull creaking of the bending poplars, we gathered in front
of a great open fire, and heard the stories of passing hunters;
or some old peasant initiated us into the manners and customs of the country.

The idiom in use in Gruyère, besides French, which they
speak, read, and write freely, is a Romansch *patois*, derived
from the Latin.   This country was probably peopled by the
remains of the Roman colonies of Avenches and Nyon.
Other *savants*—we know that these gentlemen never agree
—hold that the idiom of Gruyère is a compound of Celtic
words.

Some proverbs will give an idea of this *patois* : " *Djamié
puéro na balla mia.*" (Jamais poltron n'a belle maitresse.)
" *Allâ de poué a caïon.*" (De porc se faire cochon ; that is
to say, to go from bad to worse.)   "*Pertot lé jouïé l'an le
bé.*" (Partout les oies ont un bec).

Picturesque in its words, energetic in its turns, this *patois*
is, like Italian, very musical and harmonious.   They have
couplets in the *patois* full of wit and point.   Besides these
songs and "coraules" native to the soil, there are numbers
of old French songs, songs of war and love, which the
young people repeat in the evenings.   These have been
brought to the country by the many Fribourg mountaineers
who have served in the armies of the French kings.   The
red coat had something fascinating for the youth of Gruyère ;
he sought it at the cost of a thousand dangers, that he might
return and marry his betrothed, conduct his "gracieuse" to
the altar, in a fine uniform with a sabre at his side.

Life is hard in these mountains, but nevertheless it
is happy.   In summer, mowers and reapers rise at three
o'clock in the morning ; in winter, too, work commences be-

fore daybreak. Whilst the townsman is still snugly tucked in his eider-down, the mountaineer is already up, has harnessed his sledge by the light of a lantern, and, his axe on his shoulder, sets out for the mountain, where, in the great forest sleeping under the snow, he will hew down the pines that have been marked for felling. He does not return till evening with his load of wood, and often he passes several days in the mountains. But when spring returns all is alive again ; the cows assemble in herds on the village green ; and to the sound of their bells, and of " *té, té !* and *oh ! oh ! oh !* " they begin their march, the handsomest cow at the head, whilst at the end marches the bull, with his compact body, his little pointed horns, his curly hair, and if he is of a wicked temper, a plate of iron over his eyes. The whole village is on foot, and the women are busy piling provisions, bedding, pots on a little cart drawn by a horse, which will go as high up as it can. All this paraphernalia will then be carried to the châlet on men's backs.

The herd stretches away in a long file on the road, and the *armaillis*, who conduct it, their pipe in their mouth, stop conscientiously at every inn.

They begin by browsing on the grass at the foot of the mountain, and then gradually, as the snow disappears and is replaced by a fresh carpet of verdure, they go higher, mounting insensibly, till in the month of August they reach the summit of the alp ; then in September they descend slowly and by degrees, as they went up. It is in these pastures, with their aromatic grasses, their vigorous alpine plants, which produce a rich and perfumed milk, that they manufacture the Gruyère cheeses, the renown of which is so well merited when they are genuine, and which they are even more fond of in Italy than in France.[1]

---

[1] The number of cheeses exported is over a million. It is the really productive commerce of this country—a country composed of mountains which are themselves meadows. M. Duvillard has been one of the great promoters of the dairy industry. By establishing model dairies, by

France contents itself with vulgar imitations. The true Gruyère cheeses are scarcely at all pierced with holes—the holes either indicate an inferior quality, or pieces wanting; they are of the colour of old ivory, firm, solid, compact, and melt in the mouth like a piece of butter.

When the white draperies of snow descend from the mountains to the valley, the herds return to their stalls, and the long, cold, gloomy winter begins.

The monotony of the long snowy winters is relieved by sledging parties and by social evenings, "veillées." Small light sledges, "luges," are carried to the top of a rapid slope, a "fin"; young men and girls crowd into them, and then they slide down the frozen surface amid shouts and laughter. Sometimes these parties are held by moonlight, and in intense cold; the white earth is, as it were, bathed with electric light, by which one sees almost as clearly as by day. It is like an autumn morning without sunshine, and with a sky covered with grey mist. At these gatherings there is singing and drinking; at times they dance,—whilst the old men play cards, silently, their pipe in the corner of their mouth, their cap on their head; or else—especially if there is an old soldier among them, a soldier from Rome or Naples—they relate coarse stories, causing bursts of laughter, traditions of the country, or tales and legends of the mountains. There is the story of the Green Cavalier, who appeared suddenly on his black courser with eyes of fire, in the midst of the round of dancers; or that of Jean-le-Vacher, who was so cruelly punished for mocking the spirits. They used to come down the chimney of the châlet of Tsuato every night to drink the cream which was prepared for them in a great wooden bowl. Jean cheated them one night; and was wakened at an early hour by a mocking voice which told him to go and see his herd. He

giving advice in numerous pamphlets to the mountaineers, by initiating them in new methods of manufacture, he has enabled Gruyère to keep the first rank in the markets of the world.

went out of his châlet, sick with fear and trembling in every limb. His beautiful cows, the whole herd, his only possession, had been precipitated over the rocks. And since that time the cows have never dared to go to Tsuato.

These watch evenings are almost always for the women and girls evenings of work : formerly they spun, and it was to the music of the familiar whirr of the wheels that the old stories were told, or that the whole party sang in chorus the old rounds of their *patois*. Now they plait. Gruyère furnishes an enormous quantity of straw, plaited for exportation. At six years old the children already know how to plait. In every household they cultivate a special kind of wheat for plaiting: it is sown in spring, and hung in bundles in the granaries, and then whitened with sulphur. They are paid thirty centimes for every twelve mètres of plaited straw. A good workwoman, plaiting from morning to night, can scarcely make more than a franc. It is the middle-men who are enriched, for in the hats that are sold to us in Paris for three or four francs, with a ribbon worth four sous, there is hardly fifty centimes-worth of straw.

Manners have remained gentle in this gentle country of Gruyère. Murders and thefts are extremely rare. In the village, the life is still the true pastoral life, that of the old times. The curé is the dictator, the master, the most important personage, with whom one had better not be at war ; for he often transforms the preacher's pulpit into a public tribunal, whence he hurls an easy anathema at independent spirits, or at families rebellious against a too severe clerical discipline.

A country curé's life is a happy one. Sprung from the people, he knows how, without showing too much the pride of an upstart peasant, to mould the soft mass of the rural populations, and so to fashion them as to make of them electors who will vote only for the deputies of his choice.

Let those who have still time to love the country perfumed with flowers, beautiful roads shaded by hedges, streams bordered with hazel copses, forests with carpets of moss,—mountains open and accessible,—corners of shade and solitude, of freshness and luxurious repose, let them seek this green and beautiful Gruyère, whose reputation has as yet been only a local one.

But one must bring to this simple country a corresponding simplicity; those who require great comfort, or delicate fare, will be very unhappy here. Hotels for tourists and strangers are entirely wanting. No one has thought of turning to profit this little unpublished Switzerland. As yet a remote almost unsuspected country, it has nothing of the vulgarity and servility of the Oberland; the people do not run to the railway stations to wait for travellers, quarrel over them, and snatch them from one another like a prey. They do not go to hunt for you: they stay at home; you must go and seek them out. And in doing so you have all the joy of a discovery! Speculation and money, which spoil everything they touch, have not put a turnstile at the cascades of Grand Villars or Bellegarde; there are no great idiotic shepherds posted along the roads to play the alpine horn, and hold out to you a wooden bowl like the blind man on the Pont des Arts; and there are no boys who run after you with pebbles, or with a pistol " to waken the sleeping echoes." It is primitive nature, the mountains such as God made them for the flocks and for good men, for artists and poets, the free mountains among the free Alps. One comes down from them a new, rejuvenated man, who has gone to drink at the fountain of Nature, at the source of life eternal.

Oh, beloved Gruyère, the railway stops at thy threshold, and those who come are forced to see thee in the sweet intimacy of thy flowery paths, paths which climb so gaily the sides of thy lovely mountains! Like Valais, the alpine Brittany, thou hast known how to preserve something of thine old legends and thine old manners. If ill-made laws, in contradiction to thy history and opposed to thy tempera-

ment, have somewhat altered thy character and softened the
independence of thy mocking and combative spirit; if thou
canst not without permission of the gendarme renew the
innocent dances of thine ancestors, nor make thy beautiful
daughters join in the immense " coraule " which winds its
chain from one end of Gruyère to the other; if thou hast
no longer the noble revolts of the past, and the blood of
Chenaux is appeased in thee ; and if thou hast forgotten
that the court of thy counts was a court of the gay science,
of folly, and of love,—thou art not for that the less beautiful;
and all who have visited thy superb mountains and hospitable châlets, all who have stretched their wearied limbs on
the softness of thy meadows, who have slept in the green
night of thy trees, drunk of thy fresh and limpid fountains,
eaten the fragrant strawberries of thy woods and the delicate trout of thy streams ; those who have felt the velvet
kisses of thy breezes,—*these* love thee and cannot forget thee,
and in quitting thee they never say Adieu, but *Au revoir!*

Butler & Tanner, The Selwood Printing Works, Frome, and London.

www.ingramcontent.com/pod-product-compliance
Lightning Source LLC
Chambersburg PA
CBHW032227010726
47494CB00002B/377